SON of miNe

MIKE FLORIO

ALSO BY MIKE FLORIO

Playmakers
(2022)

Father of Mine
(2023)

On Our Way Home
(2023)

Big Shield
(coming 2025)

30 America Avenue
(coming 2025)

Paperback: 979-8-9879440-4-2

Ebook: 979-8-9879440-5-9

To Alex

PART ONE

One

OCTOBER 23, 1973

J.J. MESAGNE

Abbondanza, Arizona.

I drove that Gremlin all the way here. Not exactly orange, not exactly yellow. I wasn't exactly sure it would make the trip from Wheeling without falling apart.

I brought Gnocchi. I liked the dog and the dog liked me. Why should he be stuck in a cage? If Bobby truly gave a shit about Gnocchi, he'd want him to be free.

I didn't think about it when I broke in and stole him. I just wanted him. I guess I also wanted to take something from Bobby.

Gnocchi refused to sit up front. I tried to put him there a few times. He'd scamper straight to the back seat and piss on the vinyl. Maybe he could tell the car had just carried two bodies from where they were shot to where they were buried.

My father cleaned the seat and the floor before I left town. There was no sign that Tony and Rico had been piled there, bullet holes and blood and brains.

They had me. Rico was about to shoot. My dad showed up at the last second and shot him. I still don't think Tony deserved it. We didn't get much of a chance to argue before the trigger was pulled, or after. When I got back to Wheeling, I packed and went.

I wanted to get rid of the front seat on that side. When I stopped for gas in Columbus, I tried to rip it out. Even if I had the right tools, I wouldn't have known how to do it.

Gas was harder to find the farther I got from home. I had to wait in line at a couple of stations. It made me nervous, sitting in one place with other people able to see me.

I had no idea how to take care of a dog. I shared some ham and cheese I took from home. When we got to St. Louis, I bought bologna at a grocery store close to the highway. I tore off pieces and tossed them over my shoulder. I could hear him gobble them down. He didn't throw them up. That was good enough for me.

I drove as much as I could, sleeping for an hour or two at a rest area after letting Gnocchi do his business in a place other than the back seat. I didn't spend the night until I hit Amarillo. I found a cheap Texas motel. I put Gnocchi in the tub and closed the door. I went next door to a cheap Texas bar. I tried to relax, but it felt like I was in a mushroom field of cowboy hats.

I got maybe six hours that night, with Gnocchi curled against my leg. I checked the map when I woke up. It looked like I had seven hundred miles to go. Even with that piece of shit car, I thought I could get there in twelve hours.

I made it in eleven, with two-and-a-half pieces of bologna to spare.

I had the address of the motel where they were staying. I parked near the entrance to a small office. Most of the paint had chipped away from the door. There was an air conditioner sitting lopsided in a window, roaring like a jet engine that needed a tuneup. Someone had rubbed *FUCK YOU* into the flimsy aluminum vents. Management hadn't tried very hard to rub the letters out.

I rolled down the windows on each side. I knew that much about keeping a dog from ending up dead.

It was cooler inside the office, but not by much. Two sets of roller blinds blocked the sun. Most light came from a black-and-white TV playing a game show I'd never heard of.

The clerk had small trails of sweat running toward a face filled with freckles. I wanted to ask if it was hot enough for him. It obviously was. I asked for the number of the room where Maria Jenkins and Leslie Fitzpatrick were staying.

He called first, which was good. I wouldn't have given the number to someone who looked like me. After he hung up, he said they were in room 226.

I left the office and headed for the stairs. After I made a wrong turn, I saw the numbers creeping toward 221, 222, and 223. When I passed 224 and 225, I noticed an open door along the hallway. I saw my mother standing just inside the room.

Her hair wasn't brushed. She didn't have eye shadow or lipstick or whatever else she always put on her cheeks and nose and chin, even when she wasn't leaving the house. It looked like she'd been crying. When she saw me, she started up again.

I reached out with my left hand that's missing a pinkie. "Is Leslie OK?"

She started sobbing. "She's fine. We're fine. The baby's fine. It's your father."

I pushed back from her. "What about him?"

She threw herself into my chest. She started to moan. Over her shoulder, I saw Leslie, standing next to one of the two beds in the room.

She was crying, too.

Two

OCTOBER 23, 1973

LESLIE FITZPATRICK

I STOOD THERE, watching. They were pressed together.

"He's gone," she said. "He's gone."

J.J. shook his head. "I saw him before I left."

Maria shook her head right back at him. "Son, he's gone."

"I saw him. He's in Wheeling. I saw him." His voice became less certain the more he said it. I walked over and put my hand on his back.

"I saw him," he said, melting from man to little boy in an instant. "I saw him."

He collapsed into Maria's arms. His shoulders heaved. He buried his face into her neck.

"It's all my fault," he said.

"It's not your fault," Maria said. She tried to stroke his face, but her hand trembled too much.

He stepped away from both of us. "I put this in motion. I got caught up in doing what he did. He told me not to do it."

He stared at me. I could tell what he was thinking.

"I didn't listen to him," he said. "Look what I did."

"He's dead because he spent his time with people who make people dead," Maria said. "It was just a matter of time before his number was up. I'm amazed it took this long."

"If I just stayed at school, none of it would have happened."

"If it wasn't that it would have been something else. That life was destined to take him at some point. Even though he got out, he was still in."

I listened to all of it. I didn't know what to say. I felt like I should say something. "It's my fault, too."

"Both of you stop it," Maria said. She didn't yell, but her voice was sharp and raw and almost a little mean. "It's nobody's fault except the guy who shot Johnny, and the guy who told him to do it. He knew what he was getting himself into."

"That won't work," J.J. said. "I did this. I made it happen. Now, I have to make it right."

We both pounced after he said that, telling him in loud voices the last thing he'd be doing was going back to Wheeling. Maria said he needed to let it go for the sake of the child growing inside me.

"I have to make it right," he said. "It's my duty."

"Duty my ass." Maria smacked a hand against her backside as she said it. "Your only duty is to take care of this family. If you don't come back, where does that leave us? You were mad at your father for leaving when you was ten. At least you got ten years." I flinched when Maria threw an open palm hard onto my stomach. "This kid won't get a single day of a father."

"What if I can take care of things and come back?"

"What if you can't?" Maria said. "Because that's all I'll be thinking about from the second you leave."

I saw his face soften a bit. Maria apparently noticed it, too, because that's when she went for the kill.

"You're dealing with professionals," she said. "To them, you're some punk they can squish like a bug. That's exactly what they'll do." She stomped her foot hard into the carpet and twisted it back and forth.

"You don't know that," J.J. said.

"I know what they're capable of. I know you well enough to know that's not you. It's one thing to steal a beer truck—yeah, I heard about that—or stand there when somebody gets beat up—I heard about that, too—but it's another thing to take somebody's life. That's not in you. For them, it's like breathing or eating or sleeping or shitting. You won't stand a chance."

J.J. looked at me. I turned my attention to the spot where my body will create an enormous bulge in the curves that helped make this mess in the first place.

"She's right," I said. "I've been around those guys a long time. They've got something you don't. Or I should say you've got something they don't."

He didn't say anything to that. He walked into the bathroom and closed the door. I heard him puke into the commode, twice. He came out after he was finished.

"By the way," he said, "we have a dog."

Three

OCTOBER 23, 1973

J.J. MESAGNE

I WENT TO the car to get my suitcase and Gnocchi. I carried them back to the room. I handed the dog to my mother. She held him away from her. He sniffed and licked her fingers.

I fell onto one of the beds. I wanted to sleep, but my eyes stayed open. There were water stains on the ceiling. I wondered how they got there. I could sense my mother and Leslie moving around me. I was too tired to be irritated.

"What are we gonna do with a goddamn dog?" my mother said.

"We feed it. We take it outside to use the bathroom. It's our pet."

"We don't need no pet."

"I like him."

"Then you take care of him. He stinks."

"I stink, too."

My mother handed the dog to Leslie. She held him the same way.

I laughed at them. "I sure hope that's not how you both will hold the baby."

"I sure hope the baby will be a little less ugly," Leslie said.

"Only if it looks like me."

Leslie didn't appreciate my joke. Saying it made me feel a little better. The feeling didn't last.

"It should have been me," I said.

My mother swooped in and yanked me from the mattress by the curls in my hair. "I don't wanna hear no more of that. You dragged us out here. We ain't going back. You're the man of the house, whenever we get one. Start acting like it. Not tomorrow or next week or next month but right now."

I glanced over at Leslie. Gnocchi's stubby tail was wagging. I pushed my mother's hand away and stood.

"You don't want me to do what the man of the house would do," I said.

"I thought we was past that," my mother said.

"I still need to figure it out. Fifteen minutes ago, I didn't even know it happened. How did you find out about it all the way out here?"

"I got people back there who know where I am."

"Hopefully not too many, or I won't have to go back there for them to take me out."

Leslie dropped the dog to the carpet and grabbed her own handful of my hair. She jerked my head toward her and nearly yelled in my ear.

"This is what you wanted. I left my life at the drop of a hat. I didn't even get to say goodbye to my mother. We knew what could happen back there. It did. Now we move on."

"That's easy for you to say. He won't try to kill you."

"What makes you think he won't?" She let go of my hair and shoved my head away with the tips of her fingers. "I dishonored him, or whatever bullshit he'll use to explain the blow to his ego. We came out here to get away from that. There's no going back. We make our way here. We stay here."

The dog barked. When we looked his way, he pissed on the rug.

"You better train that damn thing," my mother said.

"I thought he was."

"We can't have him pissing all over the place. I can't get used to that smell."

"It can't smell any worse than what the baby will do."

"The baby won't be pissing on the floor," Leslie said.

"She's right, son. Train him."

If I'd known they'd gang up on me, I wouldn't have let my mother come along.

I realized I was hungry. I'd seen a fast food chain down the road. I asked if they wanted anything. My mother asked for a plain hamburger. Leslie said two cheeseburgers, fries, and a strawberry milkshake. I wondered aloud whether her stomach was about to be sticking out because of the baby or the burgers. She flashed a middle finger my way, without my mother seeing it. I smiled.

When my mother saw my smile, she started crying again. I got up and left.

I went back to the Gremlin. I drove to the place called Jack in the Box. I searched for every coin I could find in the car. Before I walked inside, I moved toward a phone booth.

I went in and shut the door.

Four

OCTOBER 23, 1973

J.J. MESAGNE

THE RINGING CAME through the line. I could picture that black phone in the back room of Doggie Do-Rights, next to the Marsh Wheeling Stogies clock. I could imagine Tommy Two Plates waddling from the table. I could almost hear him complaining about having to get up.

After six rings, there was his voice.

"Yeah."

"Yeah yourself." I spoke before I knew what I'd be saying.

"Who the fuck is this?"

"Where's Bobby?"

"I ain't getting him until I know who wants him."

"It's J.J. Mesagne."

"I know a J.J. Jenkins, and he better never show his face around here again."

"I'm J.J. Jenkins. And J.J. Mesagne. And you'd better hope I never show my face around there again. If I do, it's the last face you'll ever see."

Tommy covered the phone with his hand. I heard him saying something. It was muffled, until it wasn't.

Next came Bobby. "Who the fuck is this?"

"It's me."

"Me who?"

"Me who's going to kill every one of you." I couldn't believe I was saying it.

Bobby laughed in a way that made me feel stupid. "Next time around, your old man won't be there to save your ass."

I wanted to hang up. I came up with something else to say.

"I've got a message for your boss."

"I ain't your fucking messenger."

"He's going down. If it's the last thing I do. He's going to die, and I'll be there to see it happen."

Bobby laughed at me again, the same way he did before. "Any time you wanna come back here, feel free. I figure you'd rather be buried right next to your old man, anyway. Not that you'll end up in a cemetery."

"Fuck you, Bobby." It was the best I could come up with.

"Fuck you, asshole. Everything was fine until you showed up. First I lose one of my best earners, and now Rico and Tony are gone. All because you thought it would be fun to try out what your old man does."

"Who killed him, you or Vinny?"

"I don't know what you're talking about."

"Who pulled the trigger?"

"That's for me to know and you to never find out."

"It doesn't matter. You're all going down."

He laughed at me again. "Just make sure you wear something you won't mind wearing for about a million years, because that's what you'll have on when we put you in the ground in Ohio."

He hung up. I looked at the receiver. I didn't know whether to feel good about what happened. I didn't know whether I'd go back. I wanted to. But my mother and Leslie were adamant. I'd have to bide my time and wait for an opening, if I ever got one.

It was a dumb idea. I knew it. Of course they'd kill me if I showed up alone. I'd need a tank. Or at least a bazooka. I was fresh out of both.

I still had the urge to do it. I didn't know when that feeling would go away. I didn't know if it ever would.

I knew it was something I could surrender to, at any time.

Five

OCTOBER 24, 1973

VINNY

PAUL SAT BEHIND that desk, like the one from *The Godfather*. The rest of the office was still a shithole. I looked around. There was junk all over. Not a lot. Random stuff that made no sense. An air pump for a bike. A tee for kicking footballs. A scuba mask. I mean, what the fuck?

Still, Paul looked like the genuine article, for a change. Dark gray suit, black tie. His white shirt had just enough starch to show he wasn't some jamoke who gets his good clothes washed at home.

Bobby was across from Paul, rumpled, lumpy, and sweaty. His jacket and pants fit like pajamas. Paul didn't mind how ridiculous Bobby looked. It made Paul look good.

I stood where I always do whenever Paul is at the desk. My suit fell somewhere between Paul's and Bobby's. I didn't wanna look better than Paul. I also didn't wanna look like a bunch of marshmallows stuffed inside an old sock, like Bobby.

We just buried Mesagne. We had to go through the motions. That's what happens when we don't put a guy in Ohio. Their funerals happen a long time after they disappear. When it goes that way, it's easier to not remember we did it.

Not many people was at the church. Mesagne's old man got killed fighting the Krauts in France or somewhere. It don't matter. Anybody who gives his life for his country is a sucker.

Mesagne's mother is dead now. His in-laws are gone, too. He didn't have no other family around. Which made it harder to pick up any clues about where that fucking kid went.

Paul stuck a new cigar in his mouth. "Did we find anything out?"

"Mesagne's only people is the people we're looking for," I said.

"Have we heard anything about where they went?"

I could tell Bobby was thinking about saying something. I also could tell he was trying not to say something stupid. "I got a little news," he said. "The kid called my place yesterday."

Paul pulled out the cigar and threw it at Bobby. A long trail of spit landed across the desk.

"Why the fuck am I just finding this out now?"

"He called late. After what happened with Rico and Tony the other night, I didn't wanna bother you at home again."

Paul looked up at the ceiling. "It ain't right they don't get a proper funeral."

"Lots of guys don't get one," Bobby said. I turned my head fast and made my eyes go wide so he'd shut the fuck up.

"Other guys are in Ohio for a reason," Paul said. "They wasn't supposed to be there. Rico's mother called the house last night worried sick about him."

"What did you say?" Bobby said it before he could think twice about saying it.

"I said I don't know and if I hear anything I'll call you," Paul said. "Does that meet with your approval?"

Bobby was getting more nervous. He needed to, the dumb shit.

"Wherever the kid is, it's far away," he said. "I could hear it in the phone."

"That really fucking narrows it down," Paul said.

"I'm just saying what I heard."

Paul leaned forward. I could see the initials stitched in the cuffs of his shirt. "So, tell me, what did he have to say?"

Bobby looked my way. I raised my eyebrows and tilted my head toward Paul.

"He said he's gonna come back here and kill us all."

Paul started laughing. A real laugh. Like he just heard a funny joke."The little shit said that? That's good. That's really fucking good."

"He sounded serious."

"Well," Paul said in a voice that mocked Bobby, "if he sounded serious, then by all means we should take him serious."

Bobby got confused, because that's exactly what a moron like him would do. "So you're taking him serious?"

Paul turned to me. "Vinny, should we take the teenager serious when he says he's gonna come kill us?"

"He's twenty," Bobby said.

Paul spun back to him. "I guess that changes everything."

"It does?"

"Vinny told me you got wobbly the other night when it was time to do the job with Mesagne. Maybe you need to strangle some of them puppies to get your edge back."

Bobby was getting scared. It was his own damn fault. I wasn't gonna help him feel any better.

"So what do we do about it?" Bobby said.

"We find him," Paul said. "We find him and we kill him. I thought that was a given."

"How are we gonna find him?"

"That's a great question," Paul said. "That might be the best question you ever asked. If only I had some guys working for me whose job it is to figure that shit out."

At least Bobby was smart enough not to ask Paul who he was talking about.

Six

NOVEMBER 11, 1973

JOHN MORRIS

I DIDN'T MEAN to make threats when I called. I felt like I had to say something. I didn't know what I would say. So I said what I said. I was worried someone would show up and kill me. I guess I wanted them to be worried about that, too.

It would be stupid to go back. It would be hard enough to avoid Paul on the other side of the country. If I went back, I'd make it a lot easier for him.

Having my mother and Leslie constantly pounding that into my ears let me accept the situation. Getting away from them would be harder than taking out Paul.

Besides, there was work to do. I had to connect with my father's people in Arizona. We started the process of changing our names. I wasn't thrilled with "John Morris." I'd just been getting used to having an Italian name again.

I took the job he lined up for me. I rented the apartment he arranged. Well, John Morris did.

The baby was getting bigger inside Leslie's stomach. I tried to get to know her better. Everything had happened so fast. It was chemical attraction. We assumed we'd get along. Mostly we did. Sometimes, we didn't.

My mother said it's normal for people who spend a lot of time together to argue. She didn't need to say it. I remembered it from when my dad lived with us. I kept telling myself it wouldn't be like that for my own kid.

I felt too young to be doing this. When I thought of the things I saw back in Wheeling, it made me feel a lot older. The baby was coming, and I'd need to be a good father. Being a good father meant among other things being a good man for the baby's mother.

It wasn't easy to spend time with Leslie, since my mother was always around. Finding ways and places to get better acquainted helped us get closer. We had a common goal. We had to be creative. We had to put some effort into it.

Of course, the fact that she'd be having our baby helped build a pretty solid bond, too.

Our apartment was too small. It made everything more difficult. There was one bedroom. Leslie and I shared it, even though we hadn't gotten married yet. My mother slept on a fold-out couch. She drank her Riunite and 7 Up and stood at an open window and chain-smoked cigarettes, keeping the cloud as far from Leslie as she could.

We had money. We'd need more. My mother told me she had eight thousand dollars under the bed at home. My father was supposed to give it to me. Leslie brought almost four thousand she'd saved. Most of it was bills she'd lifted from Paul's wallet whenever she could.

I told her to remind me never to leave my wallet around. She said there wasn't anything in mine worth taking.

My job at the hospital paid three dollars an hour, plus time-and-a-half when I went over forty. I always volunteered for more. I usually picked up an extra fifteen each week.

I didn't mind being at the hospital. Like I said, that apartment was too small.

The work was good and honest. We did things that needed to be done. It could get nasty, with all the sights and smells and stains and things that brought back memories of seeing Rico kill that woman in her own kitchen with his bare hands, and then seeing my father shoot Rico and Tony dead.

I became popular at the Scottsdale Community Hospital. It helped to be young and talkative, especially with so many women working there. Plenty of them made it clear they were interested in being more than co-workers. I was never tempted. I didn't drag Leslie thousands of miles from home to cheat on her.

I made some friends, too. I never really got along with other kids at college, and my friends in Wheeling were basically psychopaths. The men working at the hospital were a lot like me, doing what they had to do because they had mouths to feed and bills to pay.

I started spending time away from work with a couple of them. We'd hang out at a bar near the hospital. We watched football. Had a few drinks. Played some cards. I got pretty good at poker, the game that basically saved my life the night the shit hit the fan for the first time with Leslie, Paul, and me.

I won some money. I didn't tell Leslie or my mother about that. I probably should have. I just needed something that felt like my own.

Sometimes, I got asked about my past. I told them I worked at a grocery store for a few years after high school, and that I wanted to make a fresh start in a place that was warm and dry. It was an easy story to remember, even after a few drinks.

I decided not to let anyone know I came from West Virginia. I picked New Jersey instead. It's a pretty big state, and a whole lot of Italians ended up there.

Then again, I'd stopped using an Italian name. New Jersey still made more sense than West Virginia. Word could have gotten around fast that someone was looking for someone from a small state like West Virginia.

That plan worked pretty well. Right until it didn't.

Seven

OCTOBER 29, 1973

VINNY

BOBBY STARTED SEARCHING for the kid. He said it was like looking for a diamond in a haystack. I told him it's a needle. He asked me why a diamond would be in a needle. I ignored him.

That fucking kid could be anywhere. Bobby had no idea how hard it was gonna be to find him. Especially since Paul didn't want people knowing why he left.

It was time for a collection, so I went back to Bobby's place. I heard him cussing up a storm when I walked past the dogs to the back.

"I hope that don't mean you're short this week."

"It's the other thing. I don't know how to find him."

"Sounds like a problem."

"I hate to ask for your help on this."

"Well, I hate broccoli. So I don't eat it."

"What the fuck does that mean?"

"If there's something you hate to do, why do it?"

"I have to fucking do it. And if I ask you for help, I'm gonna owe you."

"You don't got many choices. Paul expects you to find the kid."

"How can I do that when I can't talk about him to anybody I know?"

"What about people you don't know?"

"How am I supposed to talk to them if I don't know them?"

"There's people you don't know who Paul knows."

"So you're saying I need to talk to people he knows even if I don't?"

I touched the end of my nose, the spot where they cut out that cancer.

Bobby smiled until he got confused. "If I don't know them, how do I talk to them?"

"You talk to Paul. He has contacts. You contact his contacts."

"How do I do that?"

"How do you think, Bobby?"

"What do I say?"

"You tell him you can't find the kid if you can't talk to people around town, so we need to get the word out to everybody Paul knows. We give them a description. We tell them to be looking for somebody from West Virginia. Somebody who's missing a finger."

Bobby got that confused look on his face again. "Why didn't Paul do that already?"

"He wants to see whether people can think of that stuff without him having to tell them. Sometimes, he just don't think of it, because he expects somebody to think of it for him."

"Now that we thought of it, what do we do?"

"Now that I thought of it, you go see him. You tell him we need to get the word out to every other place where Paul knows people."

"Then what?"

"Paul will smile."

"Then what?"

"Then you'll owe me."

"What'll I owe you?"

"It'll be whatever it is. Something I need, whenever I need it."

"What if I can't do it?"

"I'll only ask you for something I know you can do."

That dumb look was back on Bobby's face. "What if the thing you ask for is bigger than what you did for me?"

"We ain't weighing chipped ham here. But let's face it. Paul expects you to deliver. You couldn't do it without my help. Now, maybe you can. So, yeah, you'll owe me."

"Before I owe you something, we need to be sure Paul likes this idea."

"He will."

"How do you know that?"

"I'm around the guy every day. Besides, if he wants to find the kid, this is his only way to do it."

Bobby got quiet. I didn't think he was gonna say anything else. Then he did. "Do you think Paul should just let it go?"

"That ain't our concern."

"But do you think he should?"

"We've been through this before, remember? He makes orders, we follow them."

"If you was him, would you let it go?"

"I ain't him."

"I'd let it go," Bobby said.

"Paul's the boss. He gets to decide whether to waste his time and effort dicking around with that fucking kid if he don't wanna let it go."

"So you're saying you'd let it go."

"Here's what I'm saying. The sooner he finds that fucking kid, the sooner we all can focus on more important shit."

Eight

NOVEMBER 21, 1973

JOHN MORRIS

IT WAS THE night before Thanksgiving. I hadn't even been in Arizona a full month. Two guys from work wanted me to meet them for dinner and drinks. El Charro in Paradise Valley. They said we'd have lots of Mexican food and even more margaritas.

I didn't want to go. I only really knew one of them, and I didn't know him too well. Randy Wilson worked the same shift as me, on a different floor. We'd talk when our breaks lined up. I'd hung out with him a few times. We weren't exactly friends.

My mother and Leslie told me to go. They said it'd be good to get to know people from the hospital. I was surprised Leslie had no problem with me going out while she was stuck in our tiny apartment with a woman who would stand inside the curtains and blow cigarette smoke out the window all night.

I decided they were right. This was home, for now. Maybe for good. I needed to start acting that way.

I met the group at the restaurant. I was the last one to get there. Two came from the hospital, with three others I didn't know. We sat at a rectangular table. I took a corner, with Randy to my left, at one of the ends.

They pounded frozen margaritas. I tried to act like I was keeping up. Even though I wasn't, I was starting to feel the tequila.

I felt it enough to say more than I should have said.

"I've never had anything like this before." The words came through a mouthful of whatever they put in front of me.

"The closer you get to Mexico, the better the Mexican food gets," Randy said.

"I mean I've never had Mexican food before."

One of Randy's friends sat across from me. His blond hair with a hint of red hung along the sides of a face that looked like it'd taken a punch or two. They'd introduced me to him when I arrived. I'd already forgotten his name.

"How the hell have you never had Mexican food before?" Randy's friend said.

"I just haven't."

"Where are you from?"

I took another bite before answering. I glanced at Randy as I chewed. "New Jersey."

"Where in New Jersey?" Randy's friend said.

I swallowed what I was eating. "Trenton."

Randy's friend shot his attention to the other end of the table. "Hey, Timmy. This guy's from Trenton."

Timmy jumped out of his chair and hurried our way. His face was round and his black hair was cropped and he seemed to be taller sitting down than standing up.

He stood between Randy and me. "I can't believe this. How old are you?"

"Twenty," I said, although it came out more like a question.

"I'm twenty-two. Where'd you go to school?"

Needles rolled over my scalp, pricking and burning as I forced myself to think of something to say.

"I didn't go to school in Trenton."

That caught Randy's interest. "But you just said you was from there."

"I moved from there. I didn't grow up there."

"Where you're from is where you grew up," Randy said. He seemed more confused than suspicious. "You said you was from New Jersey."

"I said I came from New Jersey. I never said I grew up there."

Randy turned toward the friend who started this. "Billy, if I ask where you're from, what am I asking?"

"You're asking where I grew up."

I jumped in, trying not to seem rattled. "What if I ask you where you came from?"

"But that ain't what I asked you."

"You asked me where did I come from."

"I asked where you was from. I know what I said. I just said it two fucking minutes ago."

"Maybe he misunderstood you," Randy said. I couldn't tell whether he was trying to defuse things or whether he'd lost interest.

"So if you came from New Jersey, where are you actually from?" Billy said.

I took another mouthful of margarita. "Rhode Island." I waited. No one else said they were from there. I started to relax a little bit.

"Where in Rhode Island?" Billy said.

"C'mon, Billy," Randy said. "You're acting like this is the exquisition or something."

"The what?"

"You know, the exquisition."

"What the fuck is the exquisition?"

"It was something where they asked a bunch of questions."

"Did you just make it up?" Billy said.

"See? More exquisition out of you."

Randy laughed. He took another long drink of his margarita. I did the same.

I could feel Billy's eyes on me as I drank.

Nine

OCTOBER 31, 1973

BOBBY

I TOOK VINNY'S advice. There wasn't no other way. So what if I owed him something? I worked for the guy. He could already tell me to do whatever he wanted.

It was worth it. When I told Paul we should use people he knows to put the word out, he smiled. Just like Vinny said. I don't think I ever seen Paul smile before.

He opened one of the drawers in his desk. He threw me a pad of paper, then a pen. He pulled out an old notebook from another drawer. It had that metal spiral down one side. The wire was bent and twisted. He pushed the cover open. He told me to start listening and writing.

He was going fast. I was afraid to tell him to slow down.

Paul went through names and phone numbers. He said area codes I never heard of before. I looked them up later at the library. They was from Boston and Providence and New York and Philadelphia and Pittsburgh and Youngstown and Cleveland and Nashville and Tampa and Miami and New Orleans and Chicago and Detroit and Milwaukee and Omaha and Dallas and Houston and Albuquerque and Phoenix and Denver and Las Vegas and Los Angeles and San Francisco and Portland and Seattle.

I couldn't believe how many people Paul knew, in how many places. Why didn't he tell me from the start to call those people? Maybe he was testing me. If he was, I'm glad I passed. Even if I would've failed without Vinny.

Paul told me to never use the same payphone twice. He said not to leave messages. If the person I was looking for wasn't there, I was supposed to ask for a good time to try again.

He told me to say I got their names from him. He told me to make small talk only if it seemed like the person wanted to. He told me to tell them the kid might be going by J.J. Jenkins or J.J. Mesagne, and to give them a description, including the missing finger. Then I was supposed to tell them the reward for finding him was ten grand.

My knees shook every time I thought about that number. Ten fucking grand. It made me hope somebody from one of them other crews would hide in our town. It's the easiest ten grand anybody could ever make.

That was just the first part. I was supposed to tell them taking the kid out would pay another twenty dimes, once his hand with the missing pinkie was packed up in ice and personally delivered to Paul.

"I never dreamed that missing finger would come in handy," Paul told me after he gave me the instructions.

"How'd he lose that finger, anyway?" I said before I could stop myself.

He waved his hand through the cigar smoke. "Something from when he was a kid. His old man never talked much about it."

He ain't gonna be talking about it now, I thought. I was smart enough not to say that. It felt good to be smart, for a change.

"I got what I need to get started," I said. "I'll get the word out, and we'll find him."

"Do you think you'll find him?"

"We'll find him."

"I hope you find him," Paul said. "It's important that you find him."

I stood up from the desk. Paul got up, too. He opened his wallet. He gave me two twenties and a ten.

"You don't gotta pay me extra to do my job."

"You'll need money for all those calls. Take it to that bank where that guy we know works and get it changed to quarters."

I went from feeling a little smart to a whole lot stupid. At least Paul didn't give me a hard time for not realizing why he was giving me money. That didn't mean I wouldn't hear about it later from Vinny.

Those guys love having shit they can throw in your face. It's how they control people. I do it with the guys under me. I just ain't as good at it as Paul and Vinny.

I went back to my car and sat behind the wheel. I kept looking at the list of names and numbers. I hoped I could read my handwriting when it was time to start dialing.

"This really feels like a fucking shot in the dark," I said. "Hopefully I ain't the one who ends up getting shot."

Ten

NOVEMBER 22, 1973

JOHN MORRIS

I WORKED THANKSGIVING night. It paid double time. Easy money.

After I clocked in, I turned around. Randy Wilson stood right next to me. I flinched at the sight of him.

"You scared me," I said.

He reached for his own card and stuck it in the slot. That loud snap came fast. "You don't seem like the type to scare easy."

"I should say you startled me. You're right. I'm not scared of much."

"You seemed a little scared last night."

"Of what?"

"Maybe not scared. Definitely not startled. You seemed, I don't know, nervous."

He walked away from the time clock. I followed him. "Nervous about what?"

He stopped and turned. His long hair flopped around when he did. "That whole New Jersey thing. Billy don't believe you."

"Billy doesn't believe what?"

Randy started walking again. "He don't believe you're from Rhode Island, or wherever you said after you said you wasn't from New Jersey. Even though you said you was from New Jersey."

"Billy was drunk," I said as we got to the elevators. "We were all drunk."

"I've known Billy for a long time. He was drinking, but he wasn't drunk."

I pressed the button. "Why's it a big deal anyway? Is Billy jealous because he isn't your only friend?"

"You're saying we're friends?"

"I thought we were."

"Then tell me the truth. Where are you from?"

The elevator doors opened. Randy stood there, looking at me.

"It's a long story," I said.

"Unless you came from another planet, it's a pretty short story."

"Sometimes it feels like I did come from another planet."

"I need to get to my floor," he said, holding the elevator open with his wrist. "You need to get to yours. I don't really care where you're from. It's just not normal. It makes people wonder."

"Wonder what?"

"All sorts of things. I mean, if somebody ain't straight about where they're from, what will they ever be straight about? How can you trust somebody who's trying to hide where they came from?"

"I'm not trying to hide anything."

"You might not be trying. But you are. What are you scared of, especially if you say you ain't scared of much?"

"It's a long story."

"What makes you think I don't wanna hear it?"

He got onto the elevator. I followed him. "It's more complicated than long. You'd understand if I told you."

"Then tell me. How hard is that?"

The door slid shut. "If I told you, you'd understand."

"That's what you just said."

The elevator pulled us up. I felt my stomach drop. "I mean if I told you the whole story, you'd understand why it's hard to tell."

"We don't have to be friends. We just work in the same place. If you can't trust me enough to tell me where you're from, that tells me we ain't really friends. And that's fine. I got plenty of friends."

The door opened to his floor. He started to walk out. I stepped forward to keep it from closing.

"Look, I'm not from New Jersey or Rhode Island. I'm from West Virginia. I came out here because my girlfriend was dating a mob boss and now he wants to kill me. There. That's the truth. I don't need the truth getting around."

Randy raised his eyebrows and twisted his mouth. I couldn't tell whether he was amused or intrigued by what I said.

"That's it?" I said. "You've got nothing to say to that?"

"I thought you said it was a long and complicated story. It sounds short and simple to me. You don't want them to find you, so you're lying about where you're from. Not long. Not complicated."

"I'm trusting you with this. If we're going to be friends, I need to be able to trust you."

He walked away from the elevator. "I need to get to work. Have a good shift, West Virginia."

Eleven

NOVEMBER 1, 1973

BOBBY

I ENDED UP leaving a bunch of messages. Sometimes they told me when to try again, sometimes they didn't. The ones I reached was supposed to ring my place if they heard anything. I made Tommy watch the phone when I was out making more calls. Not that it ever rang.

Paul said to use a different phone for each call. That shit got old, fast. I started doing two at each place. Then three. Then I just said fuck it and stayed at the same one, outside a filling station.

The Cadillac rolled up as I was leaving. I was surprised it took so long for Vinny to be up my ass.

He rolled down the window. "How's it going?"

I went to the door and looked at the back seat. I was glad Paul wasn't there.

"There's gotta be a better way to do this shit. We all need to have walkie-talkies, or something."

"What?"

"It's just hard to track these people down. There's gotta be a better way."

"This is the only way. Get in."

"Where we going?"

"Nowhere. It's just easier to talk if you ain't leaning into the fucking window and breathing salami all over me."

I got nervous when he told me to get inside. There was a guy pumping gas, holding the nozzle in one hand and scratching his nuts with the other. I made sure I caught his eye so maybe he'd remember seeing me if I came up missing. I walked around the back of the car and got in, next to Vinny.

"Where's Paul?"

"At the office."

"You left him alone?"

"Who's gonna fuck with him?"

"Plenty of people probably want him gone."

"None of them will do it."

"All it takes is one."

"Who's got the balls for that? Look at what he did to Mesagne. Nobody fucks with Paul. That's the best thing about running the show in a town like this. In New York, they got five families. Here, there's one. Makes life easy."

"Life's easy," I said, "until it ain't."

"What the fuck does that mean?"

"It means the minute you let your guard down, you got a problem."

"Nobody's guard is down."

"Paul wouldn't be alone right now if nobody's guard was down."

"Don't get fresh. And don't forget who you work for."

I raised my hands. "I'm just saying Paul's alone right now."

"Paul can take care of himself."

"Then why does he have you around so much?"

"It's an extra level of protection. A show of force."

"But who's it for, if nobody's gonna do nothing?"

"It sure sounds like you spent plenty of time thinking about this."

"I'm just asking questions. I won't ask no more questions."

"Good," Vinny said.

"What happens when we find the kid?"

"What the fuck did you just say?"

"I said what happens when we find the kid?"

"You just said you won't ask no more questions, and you're already asking more questions."

"I meant questions about Paul."

"You didn't say that."

"I am now."

"Whatever."

"So what happens when we find the kid?"

"You know what happens. They find him, then they get twenty dimes to take him out."

"What if they don't wanna take him out?"

"Why wouldn't they?"

"Maybe they want more than twenty dimes. Maybe they got a thing against doing that."

"You think there's a crew somewhere that does everything but that?"

"It's a big world."

"If whoever finds him won't take care of it, we'll go do it," Vinny said.

"I'm still down two guys."

"We all got staffing problems."

"What's that mean?"

"I need to find somebody to take over Mesagne's operation. Cashews ain't cut out to make book. I got my hands full with that. So if whoever finds him don't wanna take care of him, you will."

"What if he's far away?"

"Then he's far away."

"It's almost Thanksgiving. I'm gonna have to drive to God knows where. And I ain't got snow tires. And then Christmas is coming."

"You worried about missing Santa Claus, Bobby? You know, them fucking dogs really did make you soft."

"It's just a bad time of year."

"Ain't no such thing as a bad time of year in this life. We been over that, remember? We do what we're told."

"Why don't you come with me?"

"I can't leave Paul. Not for that long."

"You just said nobody's gonna do nothing."

Vinny slammed his right fist hard against the steering wheel. The thud made the whole frame shake.

"What is it with you? I don't need to hold Paul's hand every minute of every day, but that don't mean I'm gonna leave for two or three or however many days it'll take."

"None of it matters until we find him."

"Until you find him."

"It still feels like a wild goose chase."

"Maybe you'll be surprised."

"So it's not?"

"People who end up in places they don't belong stand out. It's too hard to blend when you're trying to hide. People notice that shit. That's what we're counting on. Especially with guys like us all over the country. You think the kid is gonna steer clear of every bar or club or wherever else somebody might notice him? Guys like us are always looking for people who don't fit in."

"We are?"

"Ain't you?"

"I never really noticed."

"When it happens, you will."

I didn't understand none of it. I just hoped he was right. I hoped the kid would stand out. I hoped it would help us find him.

I hoped it would help me find him.

Twelve

NOVEMBER 25, 1973

RANDY WILSON

I WAS OFF Sunday night, so I picked up a day shift. Billy wanted me to meet him at a place near his house after I finished. It wasn't too far from the hospital. I said I'd meet him there.

There was just a few people inside, by the bar. I saw Billy at a table in the back. He nodded and waved. I walked over and sat across from him.

He had a pitcher of beer. About half was gone. He poured me one and filled his own back to the top.

I raised my glass and waited for Billy to do the same. We clinked them, and we each took a drink.

"Glad you could make it," Billy said. "I was starting to wonder."

"Have I ever stood you up before?"

"There's a first time for everything." He took another drink. Some foam was still on his lip. "Especially since you work at that hospital with all them hotshot doctors and nurses."

"Them hotshot doctors don't know I exist. And them nurses is too busy trying to exist with the doctors."

He put the glass down and looked at me. "What's the story with that fucking guy?"

"What fucking guy?"

"The one who said he's from New Jersey until Timmy started talking to him and it changed."

"He's a guy I work with."

"Something ain't right. I know it. You do, too."

"What do I know?" I said. I took another drink. I watched Billy the whole time.

"You know what's up."

"What do I know? I work with the guy. That's it."

"Who lies about where they're from?"

I put my glass next to Billy's. "It don't matter to me. Why's it matter to you?"

"I get the sense he's running from something."

I picked up my glass and took another drink. I put it down harder this time, hard enough for some of the beer to splash over the top and onto the table.

"We ate. We drank. We had a good time. You're probably never gonna see him again. Why do you care?"

"How long have you known me?"

"Not long enough, apparently."

"You know who I know, what I do. You know how that world works."

"You collect on loans. That's a whole world of its own now?"

"Those worlds is connected. All over the place. I got a feeling somebody else in that world would like to know where your friend is hiding."

I finished my beer. I needed to play this right, or I was gonna have a problem I didn't need. "So just because you don't believe a guy is from where he says he's from, you think people are looking for him?"

"Why else would he lie about something so simple?"

"He's just some guy I work with."

"Then why do you care if somebody is looking for him? Maybe he did something bad."

"Maybe somebody is just mad at him for something they shouldn't be mad about."

Billy smiled. He picked up his own glass and drank real slow. "Randy, you probably should never play poker."

I filled my glass until the pitcher was empty. I thought about what he said. I thought about the look on my face. "What the fuck does that even mean?"

"Why are you protecting him?"

"He's a good kid. Who cares if he said he was from New Jersey but he's from Rhode Island? Who cares if he's not from Rhode Island? You think that automatically makes him into a guy who's on the lam or something?"

"Yeah. I do."

"I think he's a guy who's trying to get by. Like me and you."

"I am trying to get by. One way to get by is to help make people who did something they shouldn't have done face the music."

I stood up. I didn't know what else to do. "You need to let this go. Whatever you think he did, whoever you think he is. He's my friend, just like you. I want you to leave him alone. I don't wanna hear nothing more about this."

Billy just looked at me. I waited for him to say something else. He didn't. I thanked him for the beer and left.

Thirteen

NOVEMBER 25, 1973

BILLY

I WATCHED RANDY leave. After he went through the door, I flipped my chin toward the bar. Marco had been sitting there with his bourbon on the rocks. He carried the drink over to the table.

"Did you hear any of that?" I said.

"Your friend seemed a little upset."

"He knows more about that kid than he's letting on."

"What are you gonna do about it?"

"What can I do? The guy's a friend of mine. I got everything from him I'm ever gonna get. I got enough to know this guy who said he was from New Jersey is into something. I don't know what. Eventually, it's gonna catch up to him."

"What good does that do for me?"

"If you hear somebody is looking for a guy who's about twenty years old with curly brown hair, we might be able to make a little money."

"Sounds like a stretch."

"We wouldn't want in on it?"

"If it turns into something, we'll handle it. And I'll make sure the right people know you found him."

"Maybe we should move on him now and, you know, preserve the evidence," I said.

"What? Snatch him and keep him locked up in a basement until we find out whether somebody's looking for him?"

I shrugged. "I guess that would be a bit much. I'm still new at this. Plus, he ain't going nowhere. I know where he works. We'll watch and wait and maybe at some point we'll get a chance to do something."

"It still sounds like a stretch."

"If it ain't, maybe there's an easy score in it."

"Billy, there ain't no such thing as an easy score."

Fourteen

NOVEMBER 26, 1973

JOHN MORRIS

I CLOCKED IN again. I turned around again. Randy Wilson was standing there again.

There was a weird look on his face. He seemed serious. Almost scared.

"Meet me outside the stockroom at your meal break."

I nodded. I kept looking at him.

"You know where it is?" Randy said.

I nodded some more. He looked around.

"Is everything OK?" I said.

He looked back at me. "Everything's fine."

The way he said it didn't convince me anything was fine.

Time went fast. Time went slow. At break time, I went to the stockroom. It was basically a warehouse inside the hospital, a giant place where they kept all the stuff that would go wherever it was needed.

When I got close to the entrance, Randy was coming from the other direction. He still seemed almost scared to me.

"Inside," he said, pulling the door open.

We walked through the racks of hospital supplies toward the back of the room. I saw an old man sitting at an older desk.

"What's up, Pop?" Randy said.

"Who's there?" he said.

"It's Randy."

"How's your mother?"

"She sends her love."

"I'd send mine back if I could find it."

I laughed at the line. Randy's smile and nod told me it's one of Pop's greatest hits. "Can we go back to the playpen for a little bit?" Randy said.

"Have at it."

He pulled out a five-dollar bill and put it on Pop's desk. "Fifteen minutes," Randy said.

"Five bucks gets you half an hour."

"We only need fifteen minutes."

Pop looked at me and raised his eyebrows. "Enjoy your fifteen minutes."

Randy motioned for me to follow him deeper into the room.

"What's the playpen?" I whispered.

"Don't worry. Pop can't hear nothing."

"So what is it?"

"Here it is," he said. It wasn't much. A corner with a small table and two chairs, the kind that would end up in a hospital room. Against the walls there were four stacks of mattresses piled nearly to the ceiling.

"What is this?" I said.

"It's a place where business gets done." Randy titled his head toward the mattresses. "All sorts."

"I assume we're not here for that kind of business."

"I like you," he said, "but not like that."

He dropped into one of the chairs. I sat across from him.

"Wherever you're from, why you're here, whoever you are, I don't care," he said. "You said something to me the other night, and I still don't know whether it was some kind of joke."

"I told you the truth."

"Then you need to be careful."

"I'm trying to be."

"Billy is onto you."

"What did you tell him?"

"I covered for you. But he's tied in with something here in town—the mob or whatever—and he's got some kind of feeling. He thinks you're hiding."

"Do you swear you didn't tell him anything?"

"Why would I be telling you anything now if I already told him something?"

I thought about what he said. It made sense.

"Just be more careful," he said.

"What can I do? If he's already suspicious, how can I make him less suspicious? Especially when his suspicions are right?"

"Maybe you need to think about taking off."

"Taking off?"

"Leaving town. Going somewhere else. Same as when you came here."

"We're just getting settled in. I've got a kid coming soon."

Randy stood up. "Do whatever you want. If I was you, I'd leave."

I rubbed the stump where my pinkie used to be. "I don't want to leave."

"That's your decision."

"What do you think Billy will do?"

"If he starts asking around and pieces everything together, you're gonna have a problem."

"It sounds like I already have a problem."

"It sounds like you're starting to pay attention to what I'm trying to tell you," Randy said before he walked away.

I sat there for the rest of the thirty minutes.

Fifteen

NOVEMBER 29, 1973

BILLY

I'D KNOWN RANDY since second grade, maybe third. I got held back at some point. I can't remember when.

We'd always been friends. I'd go to his house. He'd come to mine. We'd run around and do shit. We got in a little trouble. Not as much as we should have.

We was in the second class to ever graduate from Saguaro High School. Randy thought that was kind of cool. I didn't give a shit. Especially since I didn't exactly graduate. I never told him that.

Neither of us went to college, not that I could have. His mom made him get a job. My mom didn't care enough to tell me what to do. I found ways to make money when I needed it. I didn't want regular work. Didn't want nobody telling me where to be and when to be and what to do.

Randy ended up at that hospital. I didn't tell him what I thought of it. I figured he knew. He didn't tell me what he thought about what I'm doing. I definitely know.

It's weird we stayed friends. I never thought whether it would last when we started getting older. Probably because I never really thought much about the future at all.

I met Marco at a bar where I'll spend some of the money I made whenever I felt like making it. We got to talking, drinking beer and shooting pool. I tried to hustle him. He ended up hustling me instead.

Marco told me about a way to make my money back. Some guy from New York bought a mansion. He was gonna remodel it. We got paid to rip out all the bathrooms.

Me and Marco got to be pretty good friends. I figured out he does some stuff that maybe ain't quite legal. He said he works for his dad, that his dad is one of the bosses. Marco said he'll be a boss one of these days, too. It was good to be friends with a future boss.

One night, he offered me five hundred bucks to help start a fire at some liquor store. I didn't ask no questions about why the place needed to burn.

I got nervous when I saw something in the newspaper about it. I can't read too good, but I knew it was a big deal from the size of the headline. I kept my mouth shut. Waited to see what happened. When we never got in trouble for it, I liked how that felt.

Marco had me help him get money from people who made bets and didn't pay. At first, I was just going along. It wasn't hard. We'd show up, he'd say what he needed to say, and we'd get the money. One time, we didn't. The guy promised to pay within a week. When we went back to see him a week later, Marco got rough. I felt my eyes go wide at first. I got myself under control fast.

Before long, he had me make them visits by myself. I usually got the money. Every once in a while, I had to do what Marco did. I wrestled some in school, mainly because it felt like permission to beat somebody up. That made it simple to get rough whenever I needed to.

I liked making money this way. Especially since the money was good. It was no big deal. I'd get in a guy's face and yell a little and twist his arm a lot and tell him this was just the start and that if he don't pay it'll get worse. It never got to the point where it got worse. Sometimes I wished it would.

Marco took me around some of the other guys in his outfit, like

Frankie C and Ronnie the Schnoz. They looked like badasses. I hoped I looked like one, too. I tried to act that way, without getting into fights. I could handle myself with gamblers who didn't pay. I didn't know if I could handle myself with those other guys. I wasn't ready to try.

I started to hear some of the names of the people Marco worked for, like Marco's dad, Angelo. Also, Sally Balls. Otto was at the top. It was a whole organization, even if it didn't feel too organized. They never told me I was part of it. I just sort of was.

I knew we was doing stuff we shouldn't be doing, but according to who? Nobody was keeping us from doing what we did. I also felt safe being part of a group that got so many badasses in it. I kept trying to act like the rest.

Randy and me stayed friends through it all. I kind of liked having two different worlds. The one I always knew and this new one I didn't expect. I still lived at home with my mom. She never asked about my job. She seemed happy to get some money for food and other shit, electric bill or whatever.

Things had been going good in my new world. I didn't know where I ranked. I just knew Marco kept giving me stuff to do, and I kept making good money doing it.

Maybe it was from hanging around Marco that I started thinking about ideas for making more money. He never told me to do it. It just happened. I started keeping my eyes and ears open for ways I could help them make a score. I knew I couldn't do it on my own. Having Marco and the rest of his guys made me realize there's always people who can get things done.

I went from collecting money to helping them steal shit, mainly from trucks. Sometimes, we'd rob a store at night. There was always somebody on the inside who helped. That made it even easier than roughing up a guy who didn't pay what he owed.

I did plenty to prove myself to Marco. I still wanted him to think of me as somebody who could come up with ways to make money. That's why I got curious about Randy's friend from the hospital, after that bullshit about where he came from. I'd been around enough of Marco's guys to get the feeling the kid knows this world. When his story had holes, that's when I thought maybe he owed too much money to somebody and took off. Or maybe it was something else. Either way, I had a feeling the guy was running.

That's why I had Marco come to the bar on Sunday, when I met Randy. It's why I had him sit close enough to hear some of what we talked about. I thought I had something. I wanted Marco to think I was right. Even if I was wrong, I wanted Marco to think I was trying. I also didn't wanna waste his time. I didn't want him thinking I'm some bozo with piss-poor instincts.

I ended up not wasting his time. A couple days after I saw Randy, Marco said he got word from his dad to be on the lookout for a guy from West Virginia. That his people got a call about it a month or so before. I wanted to ask why it took so fucking long for them to tell him. I was just happy to hear I might be onto something.

We were looking for a guy named J.J. Last name was Jenkins or some Italian thing I could never pronounce. The description matched Randy's friend. There was one extra thing that would help nail it all down.

The kid was missing a finger.

Marco told me what it would pay to find him. I liked the sound of that. Then he told me what it would pay to take care of him. I liked the sound of that more.

I wasn't no killer. I never wanted to be. But this world has rules. I was learning them, bit by bit. I knew from the first time I seen Marco rough a guy up that, at some point, it would be more than that. It was too late for me to worry about labels.

This was my chance to bump up a little higher. To really prove to the other badasses that I'm as bad as the rest. Maybe even badder, in a good way.

I couldn't sweat the details. If the guy had to go, he had to go. If getting the money they was offering meant taking off a hand and taking it all the way to West Virginia in a cooler full of ice, so be it. It was the chance I'd been waiting for.

Marco got pissed when I said I don't know whether the guy's missing a finger. I said I was only around him one night, that we was drinking and eating and talking and I just didn't notice. Marco told me to pay more attention to little shit like that in the future.

Marco didn't need to tell me the next step was finding out whether the kid was missing a finger. As soon as we finished talking about it, I left the bar and went to my car.

I headed straight for Randy's place.

Sixteen

NOVEMBER 29, 1973

JOHN MORRIS

I TALKED LESLIE into going to that Mexican restaurant in Paradise Valley, the place I went with Randy and the others. I wanted more of the food. I wanted Leslie to try it, too. My mother said she didn't feel like going out. That didn't upset me.

It was nice to spend time with Leslie. We were still getting to know each other. Everything had happened so fast in Wheeling. It moved even faster after we got to Arizona. I had no doubts about being with her. I didn't want her to have doubts about being with me. The baby continued to help my case.

We ate too much. I drank too much. She saw something somewhere, in a newspaper or a magazine, that maybe she shouldn't drink while she was pregnant. She wanted to be safe.

That word hit me hard. *Safe.* I wondered how safe we really were. I wanted to talk about it with her. I didn't want to make her nervous. She had enough to worry about. I wanted her to be happy. I wanted her to be in a good mood.

As best as I could tell, she was in a pretty good mood.

Her good mood wouldn't last much longer.

MARIA SAT AT the small table in the small kitchen of the small apartment. Everything about the place was cramped. Confined. After years of complaining about being stuck in a small house, it was the Taj Mahal in comparison to the nine hundred square feet with three adults and just as many bedrooms and bathrooms as dogs.

The kitchen table had become her sanctuary. It was the closest thing to what she had in the house she'd abandoned without giving it a second thought. Whenever she began to regret leaving, she reminded herself why she had.

At least she still had a place where she could sit and read and do crossword puzzles and play solitaire. When Leslie was gone, she didn't need to stand at the window. She could sit at that table and fill an ashtray while drinking her usual Riunite and 7 Up.

She hummed a Sinatra song while flipping cards and creating more butts. She'd been pestering J.J. to get a record player. She reminded herself to remind him again.

She was feeling good, rolling her neck to the music in her head and doing the things that always gave her comfort in whatever chaos she was dealing with.

It was a nice feeling. She thought about the baby. Her grandchild. Someone she could take care of until the child would be old enough to give her a new set of worries. She already had enough to worry about.

She heard knocking on the door, loud and fast. Gnocchi sprang up from the floor and started barking. She told him to shut up while wondering whether to answer.

The knocking stopped for a few seconds. She waited. It started again.

JOHN MORRIS

YES, LESLIE WAS in a pretty good mood. I was too stupid to realize I was about to ruin it.

"There's something we need to talk about," I said.

"There's plenty of things we need to talk about," she said. "I still can't believe we did what we did. It's hard to have many meaningful discussions when my future mother-in-law is always close enough to hear."

"We'll make time to have as many conversations as we need. I know this was a big deal, for both of us. We have to figure out how this is going to work."

She rubbed a hand on her stomach. "We've got six months or so to do it."

"I have no doubts about any of this. Do you?"

"I'm here. I didn't have to be."

"That's what we need to talk about," I said. "Being here. I thought it would be fine, especially since we changed our names. There might be a little problem."

Her green eyes had gone from shiny and bright to dull and focused. "Why do I have a feeling what you're about to tell me isn't little?"

Maria moved toward the sound. A cigarette dangled from her mouth. She opened the door without removing the chain lock.

"Can I help you?"

"I'm looking for John," the man on the other side said. "John Morris. Does he live here?"

"He's out. Can I take a message?"

"Do you know when he'll be back?"

"That's all I know. I can tell him you stopped by."

"Thank you very much."

"Who should I say it was?"

"Just tell him a friend."

She started to push the door shut without saying another word.

"One more thing," he said.

"It's fine if you don't want to give your name. I'll tell him what you looked like."

"I know this might sound silly, but a friend and I have a bet we need to settle."

"A bet?"

"A bet."

"What kind of bet could I ever help you settle?"

"Is John missing one of his fingers?"

JOHN MORRIS

"When I was here last week, one of the other guys was from New Jersey."

"A lot of people are from New Jersey."

"He's from Trenton. I've been saying I'm from Trenton."

"I thought you weren't giving a city."

"They asked me. What am I supposed to say when someone asks me? They never named the place?"

"So you're from Trenton, he's from Trenton. A lot of people are from Trenton."

"He's about my age. He asked where I went to school. I froze."

"That's not good."

"That's why I'm telling you. I said I grew up in Rhode Island, and then we got into this whole thing about when you ask someone where they're from, are you asking where they grew up?"

"Of course you are."

"I had to say the opposite."

"Sounds like it didn't work."

"I thought it did. But then Randy, the guy I work with, tells me this friend of his is suspicious."

"What did you tell Randy?"

I took another drink from my fourth or fifth margarita.

"What did you tell Randy?"

"I told him the truth," I said.

"That's just fucking great."

"HE'S NOT MISSING a finger," Maria said, "but you're gonna be missing one of your balls if you don't get out of here."

The man held up his palms and smiled. "I meant no offense. John's my friend."

"That's a pretty weird question to ask about a friend. If you're his friend, you'd know the answer."

"Sometimes you don't notice things like that," the man said. He turned to go. "I'm sorry if I upset you."

"I've got a deal for you," Maria said.

He stopped and turned back around.

"I won't tell my son you were a rude prick who made a pass at me if you promise to pretend you never knew him."

"I didn't make a pass at you."

"And I won't tell him you did. Are we clear?"

"We're clear," Billy said, smiling and nodding at Maria before walking away.

Seventeen

NOVEMBER 29, 1973

JOHN MORRIS

I THOUGHT MY mom would be asleep by the time we got home. She was sitting on the couch, smoking a cigarette.

"A friend of yours was here." She said it before I could even close the door.

"A friend of mine?"

"I don't know how much of a friend. He comes off as connected. He was looking for information."

"What information?"

She took another drag and blew out the smoke. "He wanted to know if you were missing one of your fingers."

"What did he look like?"

"Young. Blond hair. Almost red."

"That's all he wanted to know? Whether I'm missing a finger?"

"He asked for you at first. He only asked about the finger once I said you weren't here. Do you know this person?"

"I have an idea."

Leslie grabbed my elbow, "Is this the guy you were telling me about?"

"I think it is."

"Who is it?" my mother said.

"A friend of someone I work with. Remember when you both told me I should go have dinner with those guys and I didn't want to go? Remember how my story is I came from New Jersey? Well, it turned into a big mess. This other guy has been suspicious of me ever since."

"Why's he suspicious?" my mother said.

"You thought he was connected. I think he might be. And he might be hoping he can make some money by turning me in."

"So that's it. They found us. Already."

"This guy wouldn't be asking about me missing a finger if he already knows I am. My friend didn't sell me out."

"Unless you plan on growing that finger back, he's gonna figure it out," my mother said. She looked at Leslie. "We need to go to Oregon or somewhere like that. Maybe Alaska."

"We'll be fine," I said. "I can deal with the situation."

"I don't like the sound of that," my mother said.

"I don't like the sound of it either," Leslie added. "Maybe we should leave."

"If we run now, we'll always be running. This is one guy. I can deal with him."

"There will be more," my mother said.

"You don't know that. One guy got lucky because he heard me say where I was from and another guy at the table happened to be from the same town. It was a fluke. No one else knows."

"I thought you weren't giving a town."

"It had to be done."

"What if this guy tells someone?" my mother said.

"I need to make sure he doesn't."

"How are you going to do that?" Leslie said.

"I work with his friend. I can find a way to get him to be reasonable."

"Here we go with the Don Corleone talk," my mother said.

"I'll do whatever I have to do to protect this family."

"If that's the truth, the family is protected if we leave," my mother said. "We can go anywhere."

"Except back to Wheeling," I said.

"You know what I mean."

"I don't want to leave. Give me a chance to fix this."

Leslie put her hands on each side of my face. "Are you sure we shouldn't just leave?"

"If we leave here, we'll leave the next place. And then the next. If I can find a way to get this guy to back off, no one will know who we are or where we're from. Especially since my days of talking to anyone about who I am and where I'm from are over, for good."

"I still don't like it," my mother said.

"I don't like it either," Leslie said, dropping her palms from my cheeks. "But I guess I'd rather not move if we can avoid it. I like my doctor. I'd like to have the baby here." This time she took my hands in hers. "I know we talked about this at the restaurant, and I know I wasn't sure what to do. I think I am. Do whatever you have to do to keep us from having to leave."

"Whatever he has to do?" my mother said. She made the sign of the cross and rattled off the names of five or six saints.

"I mean it," Leslie said, green eyes boring into mine. "When I packed my suitcase and walked out of my house, I knew there could be moments like this. In moments like this, I want to know someone is ready to do what needs to be done."

I broke away from Leslie's gaze. I looked toward my mother. She didn't say anything. That was everything I needed to hear.

Eighteen

NOVEMBER 16, 1973

VINNY

PAUL SAT BEHIND his desk, giving Bobby the eye. Bobby just sat there. I stood where I always do.

Paul had a fresh newspaper ready to read. I could tell he hadn't opened it yet. There was something on the front page about Nixon and banning gas sales on Sundays and something else about that Watergate shit. I seen something else about Gerald Ford getting closer to being the new Vice President. I didn't know who would name their kid Gerald. It was still better than Spiro.

"What do we know about the runaway?" Paul said to Bobby.

"I talked to everybody you told me to talk to."

"All of them?"

"All but maybe two or three."

"So, not all of them."

"Almost all of them."

"What about the others?"

"I'm trying."

"Try more."

"The rest of them know what he looks like. They know his name."

"He won't be using that name for long. He ain't stupid."

"They know he's short a finger, too."

Paul turned to me. "Which one is it again?"

I shrugged. I figured Paul knew.

"It's his pinkie," Bobby said. "On his left hand. Most of it's gone. There's still a little bump to it. They all know twenty dimes goes to whoever sends the rest of the hand."

"They're sending his hand?" Paul said.

Now, Paul already told Bobby to have them send the hand. I could tell Bobby wanted to say that. I figured Paul was just messing with him.

"They could chop off some dead guy's hand and then cut off the finger and send it," Paul said.

"It's all scarred over," Bobby said. "I seen it. It almost looks normal, like he was born that way. We'd know it's not his hand."

"They could find a guy with a hand like that and cut it off and send it," Paul said.

I didn't really wanna help Bobby, but this was getting ridiculous. "There ain't a bunch of guys walking around with a stump for a pinkie on their left hand," I said. "And nobody would pull a stunt like that."

"For that kind of cash, people pull all kinds of stunts," Paul said. "If we got a call like the ones Bobby's been making, I'd send you guys door to door looking for somebody with a hand like that."

"Do we want them to send his head instead?" Bobby said.

"God, no," Paul said. "We ain't animals."

"We can tell them to hold the body so we can make sure it's him," I said. "Or once somebody finds him alive, we can go handle it ourselves."

"Who would I send?" Paul said.

"Whoever you wanna send," I said.

Paul sat there and thought about it. "What if we get the word out that if they find him, they should keep him?"

"I already told them about sending the hand," Bobby said.

"You can tell them plans changed."

"I'd have to call them again."

"Unless you plan on sending postcards, you're right."

"You want I should send postcards?"

"I just want this done," Paul said. His voice was getting louder. "I want the people I pay to get it done. Is that too much to ask?"

"So you want him alive?" Bobby said.

"Just tell them to get him and hold him. Once they have him, I'll send someone to take care of him."

"Who?" Bobby said.

"Don't you listen? I'll send whoever I wanna send. Probably you and somebody else. I don't know yet. I know you're light right now."

"He ain't the only one," I said.

"What are you gonna do with that place?" Paul said. "Cashews ain't cut out for that work."

"I'm going over there in a little bit to talk to him," I said. "He says he's got an idea. I'll see if his idea is any better than his paperwork."

"Then it sounds like we got a plan," Paul said. "Let's get moving before a frozen hand shows up in the mailbox."

Paul sat forward and picked up the newspaper. It was the signal to leave. Bobby got up and walked out. I started to follow.

"Hang around a minute," Paul said. "We need to figure out how much to put in the envelopes for the guys at the Christmas party. I don't want all this bullshit with Mesagne and his kid to make anybody forget we had a pretty good year."

"We did have a pretty good year," I said, "even with all that bullshit."

Paul looked at me. "You know, we both just said 'bullshit,' but you said it different."

I started talking before I could change my mind. "Can I say something?"

"You can say anything you want. Unless your mouth ain't working."

"I'll never question what you decide. But sending Bobby and somebody else to go get Mesagne's kid and bring him back here? I don't know. If it was me, the hand would be enough. Or maybe it would be enough to get a picture or something. At some point, we need to trust that people did what we paid them to do."

"I need to know the kid is gone. I don't need to worry about him looking to get revenge for his old man."

"He's just a kid. He wasn't suited for this life. He ain't ever coming back."

"If we know he's dead, he definitely won't."

"Ain't there a point where this can get in the way of what we're trying to do?"

He stared at me. I couldn't tell if he was getting mad. "Do you think it is?"

"I think it could."

"Until it does, this is what we do. I don't need to worry about that kid. And I still have a point to make."

"Didn't we make it?"

"That's why we need to finish the job. The kid will want to get even. We need to handle him before he has the balls to try something."

"Nobody around here has the balls to try something."

"That's easy for you to say. You're not the one he'd be coming after."

"You don't think he'd try for me, too? I'm the one that took out his old man."

"He don't know that."

"He knows to get to you he has to go through me."

"Then you should want this, too. You don't need to worry about him coming back, either."

"I ain't worried about that fucking kid."

"If he's got any of his dad in him, you should be."

"His dad was a good soldier."

"*Was* is the key word. We made *was* happen to his dad. We need to make *was* happen to the kid."

Nineteen

NOVEMBER 30, 1973

JOHN MORRIS

I SAT BEHIND the wheel of the Gremlin. I kept my eyes on the tiny foreign car Randy bought just before I met him. After I finished my shift, I went straight out and waited for him to come to the parking lot.

The sun was rising behind me. My teeth rattled. I was more nervous than cold.

I saw him heading for his car. He was walking with someone else. I recognized the other guy. They stopped and talked for a few seconds. They laughed about something and went their separate ways. When they did, I stepped out of the Gremlin and started for Randy.

BILLY

THE KID GOT in his car and sat there. I wanted to follow him home or wherever he was gonna go. I parked the Fiat outside a doctor's office across from the hospital. I was hoping to get moving before people started showing up for work.

I'd been there almost an hour. I nearly slept through the alarm. If normal people get out of bed at six, I was fine not being normal.

I had a gym bag with me. I was gonna go to the Y and hit the weights, since I was already up. I didn't bring my piece. I figured I wouldn't need it, not yet at least.

I got binoculars at the sporting goods store where my cousin works. Even with his discount, they cost me five bucks. When would I ever use binoculars again? I still needed them for this.

I wanted to know if John Morris had nine fingers. Once I knew for sure, Marco and me could figure out our next move.

I tried to get a good look when he came out. It wasn't easy. I never used binoculars before. The kid moved too fast for me to focus. I should have practiced. All I could do was try to get a good look whenever he stopped.

I waited for him to drive away. I didn't expect him to leave the car. When he did, I picked up the binoculars and tried to see his hands.

JOHN MORRIS

RANDY FLINCHED WHEN he saw me. "I was starting to think you called off last night."

I kept walking until I got close enough to whisper. "Let's go get breakfast. Someplace we can talk."

He looked at my face. I tried to make it clear I was serious. He shrugged and opened the door to his car. I walked to the other side and waited for him to reach over and unlock it.

BILLY

I LEANED FORWARD against the steering wheel. I tried to hold still while I looked through the binoculars. I pulled them down when I saw the kid get in Randy's car.

It jerked backward out of the parking spot and pulled off. I threw the binoculars on the passenger seat and started following them. Something was going on. I hoped like hell Randy was smart enough to not do something stupid.

JOHN MORRIS

"I DIDN'T KNOW you was a breakfast person," Randy said.

"I made an exception today."

He kept glancing my way as he drove. "Is there something I should know?"

"I have a feeling you do."

He drove to a diner a couple of miles from the hospital.

"Is this a good place for us to talk?" I said.

"No one from the hospital comes here. The breakfast sucks."

"I'm not worried about the food."

"I figured."

He cut the engine and got out. He led the way inside.

BILLY

I PARKED ACROSS the street, up against a building. It looked like a spot where I could see the door without nobody inside the place spotting me. I watched them go in.

Randy seemed like he was out of sorts. Not really nervous, but fidgety. I kept hoping he wasn't helping the kid, for his own good.

JOHN MORRIS

WE WENT TO a table in the back of the room, near the kitchen. I ordered a cup of coffee, a cheese omelette, and a side of bacon. I looked at Randy. He just sat there.

"You're up," I said.

"I'm not really hungry."

"I'm not either."

The waitress looked confused.

"What's good here?" he said to her.

She shrugged. "It's breakfast."

"I'll have pancakes."

"The cook usually likes it when we give a number."

"He'll have three," I said. I stared at Randy as she walked away.

"So we're here," he said. "What do you need to talk about that we couldn't have talked about at work?"

"Your friend showed up at my house."

His eyes bulged. "He did?"

"What did you tell him?"

"He came to my house and started asking me a bunch of questions. I didn't tell him nothing."

"He knows something."

"He said your name is J.J. I think he said J.J. Johnson."

"Jenkins. But I stopped using that last name."

"I told him your name is John Morris. He asked if you're missing a finger. I told him as far as I know you're not."

"As far as you know? That must have really thrown him off the scent."

The waitress brought two coffees. I didn't move my eyes from Randy. He waited for her to go.

"What was I supposed to say?" he said. "You told me plenty of stuff. I didn't make you do that. I didn't tell him shit."

"I need to be sure."

"I tried to buy you time. And I could have told you that without coming out here. You didn't have to make me think you're gonna do something."

"Do something? What do you think I am?"

"I know you're not who you say you are. I know you're on the run.

I know Billy thinks he knows it, too. He knows people who are looking for you. I know the kind of people Billy runs with. You apparently run with those kind of people, too. So, yeah, the possibility of you doing something crossed my mind."

"Are you involved with them?"

"I've known Billy forever. I know what he does now. I usually try to keep my distance from him."

"You don't try hard enough."

"What does that mean?"

"It means if he hadn't been out to dinner with us, none of this would have happened."

"I didn't have any reason to think I shouldn't invite him. It was the night before Thanksgiving. He wanted to get together. He's my friend. Maybe you're the one who shouldn't have shown up that night."

He was right. I didn't say it. I didn't know what to say.

"I know it's not your fault," I said. "I guess I believe you. He wouldn't be trying to figure out whether I'm missing a finger if you told him. He would have just done whatever he's going to try to do."

Randy took a drink of coffee. The cup shook as he moved it to his mouth and as he put it back on the table. "This ain't my problem. I don't wanna be involved."

"I don't want you to be involved, either."

"As far as I can tell, I am."

"You won't be after this. You'll take me back to my car, drop me off, and forget all about it."

"How can I forget what I know?"

"That's all I want you to do, no matter what happens next."

Randy forced himself to take another drink. "Do I wanna know what happens next?"

"It'll probably be one of two things."

Randy sat there. My words hovered over the table. They hung there until the waitress brought two plates, dropped them onto the table a little too hard, and left again.

BILLY

I FELT LIKE a half-assed spy or some kind of pervert while I held the binoculars. I didn't know what I was looking for, other than whether the kid was missing a finger.

I saw them come out and get back in Randy's car. I still couldn't get a clean look at the kid's hands.

The car left. I waited a little bit this time, since I knew where they was going.

I got back to the lot across from the hospital. When I pulled in, the kid was getting into his own car. Randy's car rolled away. The kid left after him.

I followed him back to his place.

Twenty

NOVEMBER 30, 1973

BILLY

I PULLED THE binoculars up again. I wasn't getting any better with them. The more I tried to focus, the more I was sweating. I wanted to drop the top of the Fiat, but I didn't want it to stand out any more than it already did.

I'd stopped at a filling station across the street from where the kid parked. I found a spot away from the pumps. There was a bush and a cactus sort of in the way. I tried to look around them. I kept sweating while I made the binoculars work right.

I waited for the kid to get out. The door opened. He stood up. I saw him close the door. He picked out the key that would lock it from the outside. I tried to see his hands. Once I felt like I maybe had a chance, he turned away and started walking.

He had the keys in his right hand. I tried to focus on the other one. I couldn't make out the fingers. I was sweating more and more. I was getting frustrated. I wanted to take the binoculars back to my cousin's store and shove them straight up his ass.

I pulled the binoculars down and tried to see if I could make his fingers with my bare eyes. He was too far away. I tried again with the glasses. There was a wheel on top that was supposed to help. I spun it back and forth. It didn't.

He was getting close to the building. I had maybe a few seconds before he was inside. I wasn't gonna knock on his door again. I didn't want him to worry about me any more than he already was, not until Marco and me was ready to move.

I saw him stop by the door. He stood there. It looked like he was messing with his keys. I remembered there was mailboxes.

I tried to get a look at his hands. I started too high. I could see his face. He turned my way. It felt like he was looking right at me. I ducked behind the dashboard and waited a few seconds.

When I came up again, he was still there. I saw him move a key toward the mailboxes.

He pulled the small door back with his right hand. He lifted his left hand and stuck it inside. I kept twisting the wheel. I aimed for where his left hand would be after he got the mail.

I thought I had the right spot. I lost it. Then I had it again. I kept sweating. I focused on his left arm, waiting for the hand to come out. I held my breath. I didn't blink. I felt two or three different lines of sweat on my forehead.

I twisted that wheel, back and forth and back and forth until the image was as clear as it was ever gonna be. I pushed the end of the binoculars up against the windshield.

I held them as steady as I could. I saw his left arm move. I saw his hand holding a stack of mail. I saw three fingers up against a bright white envelope. I saw the spot where a fourth finger should have been.

"I got you."

After he went inside, I started the car and left. I rolled the window down to get a breeze while I drove. When I pulled out of the filling station, I saw a phone booth up the block, outside a grocery store. I parked next to it. I got out and went inside. I fed the coin in the slot. I dialed Marco's number.

It woke him up. I didn't care. This was too big. I said I needed to come see him. He told me it better be worth his time. I told him it was. I didn't wanna say no more than that. Marco told me to always assume somebody was listening to every call I ever made.

Marco said he was gonna sleep until I got to his place. He told me to knock hard when I got there. He also said to take my time.

I didn't. I couldn't. We was right. I was right. We was gonna score, twice. Once for finding him, and once for taking care of him. I got so excited I didn't even think maybe Marco might expect me to do it myself. Maybe I got so excited because deep down I was hoping he would.

I pulled into the driveway at Marco's house. His Buick was parked there. I pulled up right against the bumper before I killed the engine.

When I stopped the car, I noticed all the sweat. Big stains under my armpits. The front of my T-shirt was wet, too. I pulled it off and used it like a towel. I reached behind me for the gym bag. I took out the shirt I was gonna wear when I went to the Y. I didn't want Marco to see me looking like a mess. I put the clean shirt over my head and stuck my arms through it. I stuck the sweaty shirt in the bag.

I was feeling good again. I checked my hair in the mirror. I kept a comb in the glovebox. I pulled it out and got everything in place. I was still sweating some, but I looked a hell of a lot better than I had. I winked at the guy in the mirror, because that guy was about to make more money than he'd ever made in his whole life.

I turned to get out of the car. Before I could open the door, I felt something hard hit the spot right between my eyebrows. I looked up and saw the barrel of a gun.

Twenty-one

NOVEMBER 30, 1973

JOHN MORRIS

I PRESSED THE end of the gun into Billy's forehead.

"What the fuck are you doing here?" he said.

"What the fuck are you doing following me?"

"I wasn't."

"Bullshit. This car stands out like a sore thumb. Or should I say like a missing finger." I pulled my left hand up and put the stump in front of his eyes.

"I don't know nothing about that."

I pressed the gun deeper. It broke the skin and forced a small trickle of blood onto the end of the barrel and down toward his nose. "That makes no sense."

"It's hard to make sense with your gun in me."

I pointed with my free hand at the house. "Who lives there?"

"Nobody."

"Nobody has a pretty nice car. Whose is it?"

"Randy never told me you was fucking nuts. You didn't seem fucking nuts the other night. But you're fucking nuts. Look at you, standing here in broad daylight, acting like a goddamn cowboy."

I looked around to see if anyone was watching. "Don't move," I said.

"Don't worry."

I walked around the front of the car, pointing the gun at him the whole time. I climbed in the passenger side. There were binoculars on the seat. I threw them in the back.

"Drive," I said.

"Where?"

"The desert."

"I know you're new here and all. But everywhere is desert."

"Just drive out of town."

"Any specific direction?"

"East."

"East it is." He backed out of the driveway and headed in the direction of the sun. "You're just gonna leave your car parked on the street back there?"

"It was either that or leave yours parked in the driveway behind the car that belongs to nobody."

"I don't think you've thought this through."

"I don't think you've thought it through. I know what you're up to."

"What am I up to?"

"You were at my place. You asked my mother about me. You asked her if I'm missing a finger."

"Like I told her, I was trying to settle a bet."

"How stupid do you think I am?"

"How stupid do you think I am? New Jersey, my ass. You ain't from Jersey, or Rhode Island. You're on the lam. People are looking for you. No matter what you do with me, they're gonna find you."

"Does your pal know about this?"

"Who?"

"The guy who lives in that house. You drove right there after you stopped and made a phone call."

"He don't know nothing."

"Sure he doesn't. That's why you were driving so fast. To tell him about something he doesn't know anything about."

"He's part of the local crew. He's a made guy. You shouldn't fuck with him."

"You shouldn't worry about him," I said.

Billy started laughing. "What are you gonna do? Kill me? You think that ends this? Your best play is to buy a little time and then get the fuck out of town."

"What if I don't want to leave? What if I knew when I came here I'd have to deal with someone who thought they could make a little money by selling me out?"

"It's not a little money."

"How much?"

"Ten grand for finding you, and twenty grand for taking your hand that's missing a finger back to Virginia."

"West Virginia."

"Wherever. The money's the same. Taking care of me ain't changing nothing. People know about this. They put the word out. Everywhere."

"For now, you're the only one who knows it's me, because you never had a chance to tell your friend."

"What if I told him when I called?"

"You wouldn't have driven over there so fast right after you did."

"Think what you want. Even if you kill me, you'll be looking over your shoulder for the rest of your life, however long or short that might be."

I crammed the gun into his ribs, as hard as I'd jammed it into his forehead. "You need to be looking right here for the rest of your life, however long or short that might be. I've got other people out here. I'll do whatever I have to do to protect them."

Billy scoffed. "You never killed nobody. And you ain't gonna kill me while I'm driving. So I'll take you wherever you wanna go. Whenever we get there, I know one thing. You ain't pulling that trigger, no matter how much you think you will. Maybe you'll leave me out in the middle of nowhere, but you ain't pulling that trigger."

I raised the gun up and shot a hole through the cloth top.

"Hey! That shit's expensive!"

"Do you believe I'll pull the trigger now?"

"I believe you'll shoot the roof of a car. I guess we'll find out whether you'll do anything more than that."

Twenty-two

NOVEMBER 30, 1973

JOHN MORRIS

THE CAR PASSED through Apache Junction. We ended up on Route 88. Every few minutes, I told him to keep driving.

We went through Tortilla Flat. The road ran close to the river. We followed it until we came to a dam with a lake above it. At Government Hill, Route 88 turned into Route 188.

"Any idea how far you want me to go?" Billy said.

"Are you low on gas?"

"Half a tank."

"Then keep going."

Route 188 went inland, deeper into the desert. The car came to a sign that said J Bar Road. I told him to turn right. We were heading south.

"Where to now?"

"Just keep driving."

After a couple of miles, I told him to pull into a flat area of desert that ran down to the brush.

"This car wasn't built to drive on anything but roads," he said.

"Just keep driving."

"There's gotta be a way we can forget any of this happened."

"Just keep driving."

He ran the Fiat over rocks and divots. I felt the bottom scrape two or three times. The ride was getting rougher. I turned around. There was no sign of the road behind us.

When he noticed I wasn't looking straight ahead, he slammed on the brakes. The car skidded and spun. The two wheels on the left side lifted off the ground before slamming down to the dirt.

"What was that?" I yelled. "I told you to keep going."

"I'm done. Whatever you're gonna do, just fucking do it."

Twenty-three

NOVEMBER 30, 1973

VINNY

I STOOD IN the back room of the dog shop. I went before picking up Paul. I told Bobby to meet me. He complained how early it was.

It wasn't too early for him to sit at his table, rolling a joint.

"I don't know how you can smoke that shit," I said.

"It calms me down."

"We ain't supposed to be sampling the merchandise."

"I pay for it."

"Retail?"

"I ain't stupid. Have I ever been a penny short?"

He was right, so I let it go. "What have you heard about our little friend?"

"Most of them know we don't want the hand no more."

"Most ain't all."

"What the fuck am I supposed to do? Send a telegram? I pumped enough coins into the phones to keep Ma Bell fat and happy for five years. I can't help if the people I need to talk to ain't there."

"What happens if somebody finds him?"

"I gave them all my number. They call here, and they say that they found that lost poodle I've been looking for."

"Not that. What if somebody finds him before they know we don't want the hand no more?"

"Then I guess we'll get a hand."

"That ain't what the boss wants."

"The boss just wants him dead. So do I. That fucker took my dog. I love that dog."

"There's plenty of dogs out there. Love one of them."

"You don't know what it's like to care about a dog. Best I can tell, you don't care about nothing."

"That's where you're wrong." I moved up against the table so he'd know he was about to cross the line. "I care about plenty of things. I care about doing my job, the way my boss tells me to. That's the only thing you should be worried about. The sooner we get this problem solved, the sooner I get Paul focused on what's important."

"So you're saying this ain't important."

I recovered fast. "This is important to him, so it's important to me. It needs to be important to you. It needs to be way more important than some fucking dog."

"I'm doing everything I can to find the guy. And I know I'm the one that's gonna be told to go get him."

"Unless his hand shows up first," I said.

"Paul will still tell me to go dig him up and make sure it was him. You know that."

"What I know is I need that fucking phone to ring. I need to get this chapter of my life over, like it should've been when you sent those guys to Ohio."

"That wasn't my idea."

"I ain't saying it was. I'm saying you sent them. And that's when it should have been over."

"I want it over, too. None of this shit is helping my bottom line. I figure it ain't helping nobody's bottom line."

"Bottom line is we both need this done," I said. "As much of a pain in the ass as it is for you to find him, it's even more of a pain in the ass to keep the boss focused on everything else. I'm dealing with it. You're dealing with it. Hopefully, we'll be able to deal with that fucking kid and get everything back to normal."

"I feel like nothing will ever be back to normal."

"What's that supposed to mean?"

"Everything's different. Everything's off. I don't know how finding the asshole that stole my dog is gonna make things right again."

"Once it's right for Paul, it'll be right for the rest of us."

"What if they don't find the kid?"

"We can't afford to think like that. We have to think they'll find him. I have to keep things together while they keep looking."

Bobby lit his joint. I made a face at the smell.

"I thought finding the kid was the hard part," he said. "Seems like holding things together is even harder."

I slammed my fist on the table. The joint went flying from his mouth and landed on the floor. "Do you know something I don't?"

Bobby stood up. "All I know is this is fucked. I can feel it. I figure everybody can feel it. If you can't, I don't know what else to say."

"I don't want you to say nothing else. I just want you to find that fucking kid."

He stared at me. "Can I just ask one more question?"

"It better be a good one," I said.

"Can I smoke my joint now? I need it more than I thought."

Twenty-four

NOVEMBER 30, 1973

JOHN MORRIS

BILLY GRIPPED THE steering wheel with both hands.

"Get out of the car," I said.

"If you're gonna shoot me, do it here. Nice and close. So you can watch me die. So you can hear how it sounds." He pointed to his temple. "Put one right here. Show me you're man enough."

I pushed the gun deep into his rib cage. "How about I just blow a hole in your stomach?"

"It'll take longer that way. That'll be worse for you."

"It'll be even worse for you."

"Eventually, I'll be dead. You'll still be living with it."

"Weren't you going to kill me?"

"Somebody would have. Maybe me. Maybe the guy who lives back at that house. Maybe somebody else. I was just the one who found you."

"If you would've just minded your own fucking business, none of this would have happened," I said. It was hot in the car. We both were sweating. A small beam of sunlight came through the hole I'd made in the top.

"This is my business. I work with people who are connected. Everybody who's connected is connected. It don't matter where they live. When somebody goes on the lam, they have ways of working together. You became my business when you ran away and came out here and they put out word to find you."

"Your business isn't going to end well for you."

"I'll believe it when you do it. Worst you'll do is make me drive ten miles deep into this shit, tell me to get out, and hope I die out here."

"What makes you think you know that?"

Billy grinned. He wiped some of the sweat from his forehead and flicked it into my face.

"I know that because if you was gonna do it you already would've."

MARCO

I ROLLED OVER on the mattress. The heat pounded against the roof and the walls. It was almost more than the air conditioner in the window could take. I opened my eyes and looked for the clock. It was blocked by my wallet and my gun.

I cleared a path with the back of my hand. It was eleven-thirty.

I guess he decided it wasn't that important, after all. I adjusted my crotch and turned the pillow over.

JOHN MORRIS

I GOT OUT of the car and walked to the other side, keeping the gun on Billy the whole time. He kept smiling, mocking me for not pulling the trigger.

"Get out," I said.

"If you're gonna shoot me, you're gonna have to do it while I sit right here."

I stepped toward the door. The window was still down. I stuck the gun inside and aimed the barrel at the left side of his head.

"That's right. Be a man and make it quick. But first you gotta figure out how close to get. Closer the better. You want the bullet to go straight in and end things fast. If you're off by even a little, you got a real mess on your hands."

I moved the barrel until it was pressed against his head. I didn't say anything else. I could feel my breathing start to slow down.

"Of course," he said, "if you shoot me in here, you won't be able to take the car back. Unless you plan to sit with a bunch of blood and brains and shit. But you probably thought about all that."

He was right. My face probably showed it.

"You need me to get out of this car. As long as I'm sitting here, you can't shoot me." He closed his eyes and rested his head against the back of the seat. "Not that you'd ever shoot me anyway."

I looked at the gun. I was holding it with both hands. I kept pushing the end of it into his head, in the spot between his forehead and temple.

"Not there," he said, eyes still shut. "You need to put it through the temple if you wanna make it quick. Maybe you should have practiced on a few hobos to make sure you was ready to do this for real."

I slid the barrel to his temple. I held it there. I cocked the hammer.

"How about that? Looks like your nuts is gonna drop today. But before you shoot me, you're gonna have to put your finger on the trigger. You haven't had it on there yet, except when you shot my roof."

Sweat covered both of my hands. I slid my right index finger into the steel loop. "You mean like this?" I said.

Billy opened his eyes and shifted them to the gun. "That's the way to do it. Guns don't work too good unless somebody got a finger on the trigger."

I stood there, with just a bit of pressure on the curved sliver of steel. "Tell me you were going to kill me."

"I already told you it might not have been me."

"Tell me you were going to kill me!"

Billy laughed. "That's what it's gonna take for you to do it? You need to think I was gonna kill you? Fine. I was gonna kill you. I was gonna shoot you ten times, maybe twenty. Then I was gonna cut your body up and feed it to some stray dogs."

"Shut up! Just shut up!"

"You told me to say I was gonna kill you. Should I tell you something else instead?"

"Just shut up." My hands were shaking. My voice was getting weak. My throat was dry. I realized how thirsty I was.

I loosened my grip on the gun. The barrel slid down the side of his face. I stopped on his collarbone. I put my head down. I started crying. I started breathing faster.

It was time.

As I tightened my grip on the gun again and started to pull it back toward his temple, it was too late.

Twenty-five

NOVEMBER 30, 1973

JOHN MORRIS

THE FIAT 124 Spider has a latch under the arm rest. I'd just used the one on the other side of the car. That made it easier for Billy to throw his left arm against the door and, in one motion, pop the thing open and shove it into my thigh.

I pulled the trigger when the door hit me. He ducked below the barrel. The bullet ripped another hole in the top.

Before I could aim again, he jumped out of the seat and lunged. He landed on top of me.

I felt a rib crack under his weight. The sound I made was part gasp, part scream.

I still had the gun, but my right arm was pinned under Billy's side. I didn't think to twist my wrist toward his stomach and start firing.

He turned and saw the gun. He grabbed my wrist and lifted it. He slammed it down onto a rock that was mostly buried in the dirt. I heard another bone break. I let go of the gun on impact. I watched it skitter across a layer of sand.

He moved for the gun. I grabbed him around the waist. Fighting through fresh pain in my ribs and wrist, I held tight and tried to drag him back down. It hurt like hell, but it was working.

We rolled around on the ground, each trying to get on top of the other. At one point, I was flat on my back. He butted his forehead against mine. That was bad. The back of my head hitting the hard land was worse.

I fought to think straight. I realized my right hand was free. I crawled with my fingers for a loose rock. I grabbed one that felt like it might have a point on one end. When I tried to grip it, the pain from my broken wrist made me cry out. I forced my way through the misery and jammed the rock into his side, twice.

He shouted and rolled away. He put a hand on the spot where the rock had stabbed him. There was blood all over it.

I made my way up. I kicked him hard in the spot where I'd stuck the rock. I kicked him there again. I wanted to do it a third time. Before I could, he threw himself at my legs, knocking me down.

He rolled his body up and over my torso. I hit him with my left forearm as he moved. It wasn't nearly enough to stop him.

When he made it to my head, he dropped his right fist onto the side of my face. The momentum of the punch carried him off of me. I scrambled back to my feet and kicked him two more times, in the same spot as before.

He was doubled over, coughing pink spray. As I started into another kick, he headed for the gun.

I bounded over to it and scooped it up, just as he dove in the dirt for it. I turned and tried to aim at him again. It made my wrist hurt even more to hold it, so I switched hands.

A laugh gurgled from the back of his throat. He looked up at me with blood on his lips.

"You ain't gonna shoot."

I fired a bullet into the ground to the left of his head. He flinched. When he realized he hadn't been shot, he went back to laughing.

"Congratulations. First, you shot the roof of my car. Now you shot the ground. You still ain't shot me."

I pointed the gun at his head again.

"Can I roll over first? I need to get this blood out of my mouth."

I nodded. He flipped onto his stomach. He pulled up his head and spat, twice.

"Just do it," he said. "Base of the skull. You don't even have to look at me. Just put the gun there, pull the trigger, and that's it. It don't get much easier than that. Especially since you got me out of the car."

I stood there. My side and wrist hurt. His arms stuck out straight from his body, elbows at ninety degrees. His hands were flat on the surface, one on each side of his head.

"Well?" he said. "We ain't getting no younger."

I stepped closer. He was still except for the breathing. I wondered whether he would die if I didn't shoot him.

"I guess this is the way it has to be," I said. I stood directly over him, one foot on each side of his head.

"You're gonna get brains all over your shoes."

I looked down at my feet. There was already blood covered in sand on the shoe I'd kicked him with. I didn't notice he'd worked his palms closer to his head. When I started to step back, he shoved himself up. The rear of his head jammed into my crotch.

I squeezed off another haphazard shot as the impact lifted me off the ground and made me groan. He clamped his arms around my legs and tried to push even higher. He was too weak to pull it off. He fell backward, taking me with him and dropping us both onto the desert floor.

It felt like I broke more ribs. He got up while I writhed. I saw him move toward a gathering of rocks. He stuck his hand into the pile and picked one up. It looked big enough to do real damage.

He came back toward me, holding the small boulder with both hands. I pointed the gun at him again.

"How many bullets you got left?"

"I only shot four times."

"How many was in it to start?"

I looked at the gun. I didn't have time to check. He came at me with the rock. I aimed at him again. Just before he was close enough to hit me, he screamed and fell.

I pushed away from him. He was still alive, still screaming.

"Did I shoot you?"

He kept screaming.

"Did I shoot you?"

He didn't answer me. I popped out the cylinder.

There were two bullets inside.

Twenty-six

NOVEMBER 30, 1973

JOHN MORRIS

I FLIPPED THE cylinder shut. I looked over at Billy. He was grabbing his leg, down by his foot. He was making a sound that was almost crying, but wasn't.

I tried to push myself up. I felt the pain in my wrist and fell again. I rolled over and used my left hand.

Billy was still making a lot of noise. When he finally quieted down, I heard something else. I stopped and listened.

I figured out what it was. The tail of a rattlesnake, shaking hard. The snake was near Billy's feet. It seemed like the thing was looking at me.

I backed away, hoping I wouldn't trip and fall but unwilling to turn my head away from the snake.

"I got a feeling you ain't taking me to the hospital," Billy said.

I kept staring at the snake. The rattling stopped. It slithered away. I turned around and walked to the car.

"Thanks for nothing." Billy was trying to yell his words, but he couldn't.

He cursed through his moaning. I got inside the car. He tried to beg me not to steal his car. The words didn't come out in the right order.

I decided not to take it. I didn't tell him that. I was doing my best to pretend he wasn't there. It was the only way to do what I had to do.

I climbed into the driver's side of the Fiat and left the door open. There was a bag in the back seat. I found a T-shirt that stunk of sweat and body odor inside. Under it was a pair of mostly clean gym shorts.

I rubbed the shorts over any spot where my fingers or palms might have touched something. After that, I wiped my prints off the gun. I started to look for a place to leave it. I thought twice about doing that.

I got out, holding the gun in my left hand. The gym shorts were draped over my broken wrist. I stuck the gun in my back pocket. I used my left hand to cram part of the shorts into the pocket on the other side. I started walking toward the road. I didn't turn back.

Billy kept moaning and crying and cursing. I couldn't make out much of what he was saying. I heard the last thing before he gave up.

"Fuck you, whoever you are!"

I kept going.

Twenty-seven

NOVEMBER 30, 1973

MARCO

I WOKE UP just before five. The air conditioner managed to keep the room almost bearable. I looked up at the ceiling. Once I came out of it, I made a face.

I rolled to the edge of the bed and reached for the phone. I dialed Billy's number. After ten rings, I hung up.

The fucking guy never showed.

I walked to the bathroom and pissed like a priest after Easter Vigil. I took a cold shower and got dressed. I went outside and slipped into the Buick.

There was a car next to the driveway. It was sort of yellow and orange, mixed. An ugly little piece of shit.

I drove to the parking lot outside of the Dry Dock. I asked if Billy had been around. Nobody had seen him.

One of the guys asked if there was any word on the guy from Virginia with the nine fingers. I said there must have been a false alarm.

Twenty-eight

NOVEMBER 30, 1973

JOHN MORRIS

I MADE MY way back to J Bar Road, one step at a time. I walked over the yellow dashes in the middle of the two lanes toward Route 188. I looked and listened for other cars, coming either way. I saw nothing but waves of heat shimmering from the asphalt.

My chest and back ached. My wrist throbbed. My head hurt, in the front and back. The only thing that didn't bother me very much was the spot where he'd punched me in the face.

My shirt was soaked. My jeans, waterlogged. It felt like I'd jumped into a hot bathtub fully clothed. I must have lost at least ten pounds. I prayed I would see someone heading back to town, someone who would be willing to give a filthy mess like me a ride.

I had no idea what time it was. Based on the sun, I guessed it was the middle of the afternoon. I would walk all the way back to Scottsdale, if I had to. I didn't bother to wonder whether I could make it.

I didn't have to. A cowboy in a blue pickup truck rolled my way. I tried to wave my left arm. The daggers of agony in my ribs made me double over.

He stopped in the road, opening his window and sticking his head through. "What the fuck happened to you?"

"My car broke down. I climbed under to check it out. I thought I could fix it."

"Where's it at?"

"Back there somewhere."

"You a mechanic or something?"

I tried to shake my throbbing head. "That's probably why I wasn't able to fix it."

"Maybe you need a jump. I got cables."

"It's not the battery. I need to get back to town and get a tow truck."

"Which town?"

"Scottsdale."

"I'm only going to Apache Junction."

"Could you take me the rest of the way? I'll give you money for gas."

A shadow of mild suspicion crossed his face. "You look hurt."

"I did it when I tried to crawl under the car."

"What kind of car is it?"

"Gremlin."

"Sounds like it's full of gremlins." He laughed at what he said. I did, too, only because I needed him.

"So you'll take me?"

"Five bucks for my gas and my time, and I'll drop you off on the outskirts of Scottsdale. No curb service."

I used my left hand to dig inside my right front pocket for wet, crumpled bills. I found a five. I smoothed it out and handed it to him through the window.

He took it with his fingertips and threw it on the dashboard. "You just bought yourself a ride to Scottsdale."

Twenty-nine

NOVEMBER 30, 1973

JOHN MORRIS

HE DROPPED ME not far from the *Welcome To Scottsdale* sign. I was still wet and grimy. Still hurting in some places more than others. It still felt like I'd climbed out of a vat full of simmering sweat.

I thought about hitching the rest of the way. I decided to walk back to the apartment. I'd worry about finding the Gremlin later.

My legs were the only things that weren't aching. Everything else did. Even though I was thirty and hungry and sore and spent, I kept thinking about the questions I might get when I walk through the door.

I put the key in the lock and spun the knob without making a sound. I tiptoed to the bathroom. If the apartment was bigger, I might have made it.

My mother spotted me. At first, she made noises, not words. Then came Leslie. She started crying when she saw me.

"I'm fine," I said to them.

"You look like shit," my mother said, more than once.

"It looks like you've been wrestling raccoons," Leslie said.

"How'd you know?"

"Stop it," she said, eyes blazing. "You tell me what happened right now."

"Nothing happened."

"Do you think we're stupid?" my mother said. She turned to Leslie. "He thinks we're stupid."

"You're hurt," Leslie said. "Your arm. And you're not breathing right."

"We need to get you to the doctor. Leslie, get the car."

"I got a little banged up, OK? I had to take care of something."

My mother made the sign of the cross again. "Dear Lord, please send me to hell instead of him."

"What are you doing?" I said.

"Thou shalt not kill."

"I haven't killed anyone."

"You still need to get looked at," Leslie said. "It looks like you've got a broken arm and broken ribs."

"For someone who still doesn't know me very well, you sure know me pretty well."

My mother dusted off the voice she'd use to get me to eat vegetables. "John Joseph, you have to get looked at now."

"Let me get rid of these clothes and take a shower. We can go to the hospital when I'm done."

"What are you going to tell them?"

"I'll say I fell in the shower. For all I know, I will."

My mother moved toward me. "I see that gun in the back of your jeans. Did you shoot somebody? Tell the truth."

"I shot a hole in the roof of a car. I shot some dirt. But I haven't shot anyone. At least not yet."

"Not yet means maybe you will."

"Not yet means maybe I'll have to."

After I said it, I thought about the house where my car was still parked.

Thirty

DECEMBER 1, 1973

JOHN MORRIS

WHEN I TOLD them I didn't have the Gremlin, they didn't push for an explanation. Leslie and I took the city bus to the hospital. We talked my mother into staying behind. I really didn't need to hear her, and she really needed to sit at the kitchen table and smoke.

I also needed a cast for my right arm. They gave me a wrap for my stomach to hold the broken ribs in place. We didn't get home until after ten.

That's when they finally asked about the Gremlin. I said it'd be fine. Truth was I didn't know how to find it. My only choice was to go out and try.

Before sunrise, I got dressed and snuck out of the apartment. Gnocchi's yapping almost blew my cover. I gave him some food to keep him occupied while I put four fresh bullets in the gun and crammed it back in the pocket of my other pair of jeans.

Every step made my ribs ache. They hurt worse than they did on my way home.

I looked for anything that seemed familiar. After about thirty minutes, I started to think I was getting somewhere.

I forced myself to walk fast enough to get to where I was going but not so fast that I'd stand out. A few cars rolled past. I knew there would be more once it got brighter.

It felt like I was getting closer. I found a neighborhood that could have been the right one. I trusted my instincts, since that was all I had to work with.

I went down one of the main roads. I checked each side street for any sign of the Gremlin. After passing five or six intersections, I started to think I'd guessed wrong. I decided to check a few more.

At the very next one, there it was. I started to do a victory dance, but it felt like someone was sticking knives in my side and wiggling them.

As I got closer, I saw the Buick in the same driveway. I had no idea how many people were in the house. There was at least one. I had to assume he knew about me.

I wondered if anyone knew about Billy. Probably not yet. Someone would find him, at some point. It would be a big deal. Young guy, car off the road in the desert, bit by a snake but also banged up from fighting with something, or someone. Not to mention a couple of bullet holes through the cloth top of his car.

If the guy in the house knew Billy was following me, he might think I had something to do with it. It might make them even more determined to find me.

I felt more nervous, the closer I got to the car. I thought for a second I forgot the keys. I checked my pockets. I put them in my left hand and got ready to unlock the door.

"Morning."

I turned my head both ways. An old man stood at his front door, not far from where the Gremlin was parked.

"Morning," I said.

"That your car?"

I held the keys up. "Yep," I said, just loud enough for the old man to hear. "All mine."

"It was sitting right there, all day and all night."

"Sorry for any inconvenience."

"It ain't much to look at, that's for sure. You live around here?"

I motioned with the cast behind me. "Couple of streets over."

"Then why did you leave it here?"

"Again, I'm sorry for any trouble."

"What happened to your arm?"

"Fell in the shower."

"What street do you live on?"

I pulled the door open. "A couple of streets over," I said.

"You already said that."

"Again, I'm sorry for any trouble. Thanks for keeping an eye on her."

I got inside and started the engine. As the car moved away, I watched the mirror. He was still standing there. It looked like he was writing something down. Probably the numbers on my license plate.

At that point, I didn't care. I probably should have.

Thirty-one

DECEMBER 3, 1973

JOHN MORRIS

LOCAL MAN FOUND DEAD OF SNAKEBITE.

The headline to the Monday edition of the *Arizona Republic* blared through the front of the newspaper machine on the corner outside the apartment building. I dropped a dime into the slot and took the top copy from the stack. I held it with both hands. Above the fold, Billy Potenza's eyes stared back at me. He had an ornery smirk and damp hair neatly parted and pressed against his head.

The body of Scottsdale resident William J. Potenza, 23, was found near J Bar Road in Gila County, south of Cholla Tank. According to the Gila County Sheriff's Department, Potenza died of an apparent snakebite to the lower leg. He had other injuries that were believed to be the product of a struggle with the snake, or the result of his attempt to return to his vehicle, parked nearby, after he had been bitten. Potenza, who attended Saguaro High School, was self-employed.

Potenza's car was several hundred yards from J Bar Road. Gila County Sheriff Lyman Lee Peace said it wasn't clear why Potenza had driven so far off the road.

"It's a tragedy," Sheriff Peace said, "but it's one of the realities of living here in Arizona. We all need to remember that wherever we go,

poisonous snakes and insects inhabit the area. The farther you get from cities, towns, and roads, the greater the chance you'll run into something like that. Whenever you enter the desert, keep your eyes and ears open at all times."

Various species of rattlesnakes are found in Arizona. The Mohave rattlesnake is the most toxic. Peace declined to speculate on the type of rattlesnake that bit Potenza. While deaths from rattlesnake bites are rare, immediate medical attention remains critical to survival.

I tucked the newspaper under my arm. I looked around to see if anyone was watching. I pulled it out and checked the article again. Nothing pointed to the possibility of someone else being there. It was a simple and straightforward situation. A guy got too close to a rattler. He got bit. He died. Life goes on. Except for him, that is.

My shift had just ended. I went into the apartment. I put the newspaper on the kitchen table. Leslie was leaving soon for her new job as a cashier at one of the local grocery stores. After she went, I took a shower. I had to keep my cast out of the water, which was pretty much impossible. I started to climb over the tub. I almost tripped on the side when I heard my mom yelling.

"It's him! It's him!"

I wrapped a towel around my waist and shuffled through the bedroom and out the door. I yelped with every step from the pain in my sides.

"It's him," she said, shaking a lit cigarette at the front page of the paper. "The guy who came here asking about your finger. It's him. He's dead." She looked at the picture and turned back to me, stabbing the air with the orange tip. "That's where you were the other day. You were out there with him."

"Didn't you see the headline? It was a rattlesnake."

"He was out in the desert. It looked like you were out in the desert, and it looked like you were fighting someone. Those other injuries he had, he didn't get them from no snake."

"I didn't kill him."

"It looks like you didn't have to. It looks like maybe you were going to."

"Like I told you, I'm going to do whatever I have to do to protect us."

She looked down at the picture of the dead boy. She made a sign of the cross with the hand that still held a cigarette. "Does that end this?"

"I don't think so."

"Who else is there to worry about?"

"Whoever he was working with. Some guy who lives in town."

"Who is he?"

"I don't know. I don't even know what he looks like. I just know where he lives."

"What are you gonna do?"

"Whatever I have to do to protect you, Leslie, and the baby."

She took a drag and blew a thick white cloud of smoke from her nose and mouth. "Good luck finding another rattlesnake to do your dirty work."

Thirty-two

DECEMBER 10, 1973

MARCO

MY DAYS AIN'T too complicated. Home by sunrise. Sleep 'til sundown. Get up. Do it all again. I don't take days off, except for big holidays. I like working. I like making money.

We're doing pretty good. There's always steady cash in the usual stuff, gambling and whores. We're getting more and more drugs from Mexico. We steal whatever ain't nailed down, and some shit that is. We're always looking to make a score.

I didn't think nothing of it when Billy started talking about somebody he met who seemed like he was on the lam. Then I heard about getting ten dimes to find some guy who ran off from his crew. When I found out it was another twenty to get rid of him, it made sense to see if Billy was on the right track.

I didn't really like the part about cutting off his hand. Then again, for that kind of money, I'd drive it back there myself. Make it the hood ornament on my car.

When he called that morning, Billy had me thinking he found him. I don't know what the hell happened after that. Dead from a fucking rattlesnake. I don't know what he was doing all the way out there. I'm not sure I wanna know.

They don't think anybody else was with him. I ain't so sure about that. I wonder if he was messing around with somebody he shouldn't have been messing around with. Maybe a woman. Maybe a man.

All I know is Billy was trying to find out if the one who works with his friend has nine fingers. He called me that morning and never showed up. Sometimes I wonder whether I dreamed the whole thing.

Would the bosses have ever accepted Billy? He was doing good work. He had a long way to go. He knew it. That's why he wanted to be the one who found the guy. He needed a big notch in his belt.

After Billy turned up dead, I wanted to let it go. It all felt cursed. I ain't usually superstitious. On that one, I sort of was.

Then I heard they changed things up. They don't want the hand no more. They just wanted someone to find the guy and keep him until they can come make sure it's him. That made me think it was different enough to get back in.

I still wanted to think about it. I didn't tell nobody Billy thought he found the guy.

It all died down pretty fast, but it wasn't like the guy was hiding in a cave. There was a chance somebody else was gonna spot him and that hand missing a finger. There was a chance somebody else would have got the credit.

So I went from thinking I should leave it alone because of Billy to thinking maybe I should keep going because of Billy. To prove Billy had been right. Getting a piece of the money would have been nice, too.

Right then, I didn't need to make no final decisions. So I didn't.

JOHN MORRIS

FOR A FULL week, I drove through that same neighborhood after my shifts ended. I always saw that Buick sitting in that driveway. I never saw the old man next door. I don't know if he ever saw me.

I had the gun on the seat to my right. I thought about using it on whoever lived in that house. I didn't know if he knew about me. I didn't want to find out the hard way he did.

Every time I saw the house, I thought about going in and ending it. Would that really do it? The gun would be loud. I'd run out and drive away. The old man would see the Gremlin.

I wished I had the Oldsmobile. I thought about renting a car. I didn't want to waste the money. I didn't know whether having something different would have gotten me to go in that house, anyway.

I never stopped. I just went around the block and then home. It became part of my routine. I didn't know why I kept driving by. I wasn't going to do anything. Maybe one day I'd change my mind and do it before I could change it back.

My mother kept watching me. She didn't ask questions. Either she didn't know what to ask, or she didn't want to know the answers.

Leslie could tell something was off. She hadn't mentioned it. Getting deeper into pregnancy gives someone other things to think about.

My mother knew what I was thinking about doing, I could tell. I didn't know if she thought I could actually do it. Maybe she did. After all, my father could.

I didn't know whether to be ashamed or proud of not being able to do what I thought I needed to do. I got lucky with Billy. I didn't know if I could pull the trigger with whoever lives in that house.

The only good thing about any of it was that I spent less time worrying about Paul. Then my mother told me out of the blue I don't have to worry about Paul anymore.

She told me why. When she finished, I asked whether that meant the rest of them would stop looking for me. She said she wasn't sure, that maybe she'd know more later. That was enough to get me to keep thinking I had to take care of the guy who might know who I was.

Thirty-three

DECEMBER 17, 1973

MARCO

I KEPT GOING back and forth about whether to go after the guy. Yeah, the money would be nice. I still didn't know what happened to Billy. I couldn't say the guy had nothing to do with it. I didn't know if I was a little scared of him or what. He was mobbed up. He knew Billy was onto him. Maybe he killed Billy. I didn't wanna get myself killed. As long as I didn't tell nobody what Billy said on the phone that morning, I didn't have to feel ashamed to nobody but myself.

I never really made a decision to let it all go. It just happened. There's other ways to make money. After they buried Billy and everybody else got bored with trying to figure out why he was in the desert and how he ended up getting bit by a snake, we moved on.

I guess life has a way of making us forget shit like that. There's always new shit that comes along to worry about.

Thirty-four

DECEMBER 18, 1973

MARCO

CHESTER FROM NEXT door kept rambling about the ugly car that was in front of his house the day Billy died. He said it came by a few times a week. When I was leaving last night, he said he saw it again that morning.

He told me he got the license plate. I told him to keep the number in case I needed it. He mentioned it again last night.

I had a feeling it could be the guy. I never wondered why he'd be on my street. He told Chester he lives close by. I'd never gone looking for that car. Maybe I should have.

Chester said the guy had curly hair, that he was walking funny and had a cast on his arm when he picked up the car. I tried not to connect dots back to Billy. It's something I just didn't wanna mess with. I made my decision. Once I do that, I don't go back.

Chester said the car usually rolls by not long after seven. I got home that morning at six and couldn't fall asleep. I decided to get up and have a look for myself. I didn't know why I did it. I guess I was curious.

I went down to the first floor and walked over to the front door. I stood in a dark spot, where I could look out without anybody seeing me.

I got bored pretty fast. There was a clock in the main room. It was fifteen after seven. I told myself I'd give it another minute or so before trying to take a crap and going back to bed.

JOHN MORRIS

I FINISHED ANOTHER shift. My arm still hurt like hell, every day. My ribs were sore, too. I wondered if they'd ever not hurt again.

I went through the usual questions at work about my broken wrist. I stuck to my story that I fell in the shower. Everyone wanted to sign the cast. Leslie asked questions about the girls whose names were on it. I told her she shouldn't be worried about someone who I'd let put her name on my cast. So then she got curious about whoever didn't sign it. I asked her if she really thought I wanted her to run away with me so I could find someone else.

That wasn't the only reason. It was dangerous to get close to me. I already worried all the time about something happening to Leslie and my mother. I didn't need to pull anyone else into quicksand with me.

There had been talk in the hospital about the poor kid who died of a rattlesnake bite. Everyone knew he was a friend of Randy's. I didn't say a word to him about it, and he didn't say anything to me. Once we settled into not talking, it stayed that way. I wasn't mad. He was just someone I didn't want to put in any more danger than I already had.

I got in the Gremlin and drove home. Which meant swinging by the house with the Buick outside and the guy inside. The one who possibly knew too much. The one I kept wondering whether I'd ever go inside and shoot.

My father did it. I wondered whether he struggled at first like me, or whether it was easy. If it was something genetic, maybe it skipped a generation. When I'd think about that, I worried about what it would mean if Leslie had a boy. I wished on those mornings she'd have a girl.

I never asked Leslie if she felt the same way. Sometimes, you know things without asking.

My mother knew I was thinking about doing it. I told her the time had to be right. She said there's never a right time for that. Which confused me, because most of the time I felt like she didn't want me to do it. She wanted it to be done, and she knew there was no one except me to do it. Maybe that was why she never flat out told me not to do it.

I took the Gremlin on the same path back from work. Into that neighborhood and down that street and past that Buick. Like every time before, I slowed down. I thought about stopping and going in. I never had a chance to go in because I never stopped.

I still didn't know whether anyone else lived in the house. I had a feeling he was alone. I wished I'd asked Billy more questions about him. It would have been easy to get answers when I had a gun pressed into his gut.

I wanted to know my family was safe. I didn't want to do what would make them safe.

It's not that I didn't want to do it. I didn't think I could.

MARCO

I STARTED YAWNING while I stood there. I checked the time again. The sun wasn't all the way up, but it was getting brighter. I took another step back so I wouldn't be seen by whoever was driving by.

I yawned again. I stepped over to a bare spot on the wall and leaned. I rested my face against the paint. It felt nice and cool on my cheek. I kept looking out the window. I yawned some more.

I saw a kid on a bike, delivering newspapers. I saw a pickup truck. I saw a car that wasn't the car I was waiting for. I felt my eyelids droop. I decided to give it another five minutes before going back upstairs. If I stayed any longer, I'd end up falling asleep standing up like a horse.

JOHN MORRIS

I GOT CLOSER to the house. I saw the Buick, in the same spot where it always was. Again, no other cars were parked in the driveway. Again, I noticed nothing happening inside the house.

I did something I hadn't done before. I hit the brakes and stopped, right in the middle of the street. I tried to look for anything I could see.

Just as my eyes were starting to focus, I heard someone yelling.

Thirty-five

DECEMBER 18, 1973

JOHN MORRIS

I LOOKED IN the rearview mirror. The old man who lived in the house next door was in the street. He moved as fast as his bowlegs could churn. He hollered the whole way.

"I know who you are! I have your license number! Why do you keep coming around here?"

I hit the gas. I checked the mirror. He was still in the middle of the street, hands and elbows flailing and rickety knees wobbling. It looked like he was a puppet and the guy pulling the strings had a seizure.

He was still yelling, even if I couldn't hear him.

"Well," I said, "that's the end of that."

MARCO

THE SOUND MADE my eyes fly open. I saw a car driving away to my left. To the right, I saw Chester. Out in the road. Flapping his arms like he was hoping to fly. I went to the door and pulled it open.

"What's going on?"

"That car," he said, pointing down the street and breathing hard. "I told you I got his license plate. I got half a mind to call the cops."

"Has he done anything other than drive by?"

Chester started walking my way. "Not really. He just drives by in the morning. Slow, like he's looking for something. He stopped today."

"There's no law against driving slow, Chester. Or against looking. Or stopping."

"I still got his license number. Do you want it?"

I thought about it for a few seconds. "Sure. I'll take it."

JOHN MORRIS

I CURSED THE whole way home. I went inside and handed the keys to Leslie. She was getting ready to leave for her shift. She asked why I'd been getting home later than usual. I told her she didn't have to punch in until eight, she still had plenty of time. She gave me a dirty look and left.

After she was gone, my mother stood there, staring at me.

"What are you up to?"

"I'm doing what I have to do."

"So you haven't done it yet?"

"I know where I have to go to do it. I know when I have to go there."

"When will that be?"

"I'm off Thursday night. I'm going in the middle of the night. I think he lives alone. I figure he has guns. I need to get in while he's asleep."

"I can't believe we're talking like this."

"I'm either going to protect this family or I'm not. He's a threat."

"How are you going to get inside?"

"Maybe he doesn't lock his doors."

"Maybe he does. How do you get inside a door that's locked?"

"Maybe I'll pick the lock."

She laughed at that. "What do you know about picking locks?"

"How hard can it be?"

"Pretty damn hard if you don't know how to do it. Do you even know anyone who could teach you?"

"I could find someone at the hospital."

"That'll look great. You start asking around for someone who knows how to pick locks. That won't raise suspicions."

"I'll say I lost my keys to whatever it is I need to open."

"You can say whatever you want. If enough people hear you're looking for somebody to teach you how to pick locks, somebody will get ideas."

"What if I just go over there and find an open door? Maybe an open window? Then I won't need to worry about finding anyone to show me how to pick a lock."

"You're pinning your plan on that? If this guy really is in a crew, do you think he leaves any doors or windows unlocked?"

"Maybe being in a crew makes him less careful. Maybe he thinks no one will mess with him, other than the people he works with. And they won't do it at his house."

"You mean like they didn't do it to your father at his house?"

"He wasn't living there when they did it."

She lit a cigarette. "I don't like it." She inhaled hard and held it in before blowing it out.

"Do I have your blessing on this?"

"Why do you need my blessing?"

"I need someone to tell me I'm doing the right thing. Because I sure as hell don't know if I am. I only know I need to protect this family. And I know I don't want to pack up and keep running."

"When you put it like that, it sounds like you don't really need my blessing. Or anybody else's."

Thirty-six

DECEMBER 18, 1973

MARCO

I CALLED THE police station and asked for Phil.

"Who's calling?"

"Fred Tackleberry."

I heard voices as whoever answered called for Phil to pick up.

"Hello, Fred. This is a surprise."

"It usually is."

"What can I do for you?"

"I need you to run a plate."

I heard him get more quiet, like he'd cupped his hand over the phone. "There's a procedure for this."

"I had to do it this way. This one's for me, not them."

"What's in it for me?"

"You tell me."

"I found out my alternator's shot. How about a hundred?"

"To run a plate?"

"You can always do it through the normal procedure," Phil said.

"One hundred."

"You're not gonna haggle this time?"

"I hope you remember that next time."

I gave Phil the information. He said he'd call back. I paced around the house. I looked out the window a few times, even though I figured that same car wasn't coming back soon, if ever. After about twenty minutes, the phone rang.

"It's registered to Mary Elizabeth Clark."

"Not a guy?"

"Not unless somebody named a guy Mary."

"What's the address?"

"It's a place in Scottsdale. You ready?"

I found a scrap of paper and a pen. I told him to tell me.

"You're sure about this? There's no John Morris?"

"I'm sure there's a John Morris somewhere. But he ain't the owner of the car that goes with that plate. You sure you gave me the right number?"

"I'm sure," I hung up the phone without saying goodbye. I held the sheet with the address in front of my face.

"A hundred bucks for this?"

I folded the page in half and threw it toward the kitchen table.

Thirty-seven

DECEMBER 20, 1973

JOHN MORRIS

AFTER I FINISHED my Thursday morning shift, I went home. Leslie had the day off. She wanted me to stay up for a little bit. I went to sleep around ten, got up after four. My mother cooked a large pot of pasta. I ate it with some of her cheap wine from the refrigerator.

I kept drinking wine and watching TV. Leslie went to bed around eleven. I said I wanted to stay up and watch Johnny Carson. I couldn't tell whether Leslie was upset she'd sleep alone or happy to have the mattress to herself for a while.

I looked at my mother and my mother looked at me after Leslie went to bed. We didn't say anything until after Johnny told his jokes to start the show.

"When are you going?" she said once the commercials started playing.

"When this is over."

"You're not driving?"

"His neighbor knows the car. I have to walk. I've done it before."

"Not in the middle of the night."

"Who's going to bother me? I have a gun."

"I don't like any of this."

"I don't have a lot of options. This guy knows too much. We won't be safe."

"What if he's not the only one?"

"I'll deal with that when it happens."

"If you have the chance."

I said nothing to that.

"This can't keep going," she said.

"It'll keep going until it stops. Have you heard whether it's stopping?"

"Not yet."

"Then we have to assume it'll keep going."

She lit another cigarette. The end seemed to glow hotter than usual. "Don't close your eyes when you do it."

"Excuse me?"

"Don't close your eyes. You need to be sure you don't miss."

I shook my head. "For someone who doesn't want me to do this—"

"If you're gonna do it, you need to do it right. You have to keep your eyes open. You have to be sure."

It felt like my stomach was starting to look for a way to empty itself.

"What will you do after?" she said.

"I don't plan on raiding the refrigerator."

"You'll need to get out of there. You'll need to run. At some point, you'll need to stop. If somebody sees you running, you'll look suspicious."

"So run like hell and then don't?"

"You know what I mean. When you're clear of the neighborhood, you need to seem innocent."

"How many people walking around in the middle of the night look innocent?"

"The smart ones. And you need to be smart about this before, during, and especially after. None of this helps us if you get caught and end up in prison for the rest of your life."

Carson was back. Joan Rivers was the first guest. She said she wasn't sending out Christmas cards this year. I hadn't even thought about Christmas, and it was only five days away.

I sat there until the next commercial. I got up and started to get myself ready to do what I had to do. Before I left, I turned to my mother. She was working on another cigarette.

"What are you going to tell Leslie if she wakes up?"

"I'll tell her the truth. You went for a walk."

Thirty-eight

DECEMBER 21, 1973

JOHN MORRIS

IT WASN'T AS dark as I expected it to be. The streetlights and traffic lights helped. Some of the stores along the way had left a bulb or two on. It made me feel less conspicuous, even if it also made it easier to see me. That didn't make sense to me, but it did.

I left the rib wrap at home. The pain was going to be there either way. Without that thing, at least I could breathe. The hunk of plaster was still on my wrist. I'd use it like a club, if I had to. Then again, never take a cast to a gunfight.

Of course, I had a cast and a gun. The gun was loaded. A few squeezes, and my problem would be solved.

Until the next one. But there would always be a next one. All I could do was keep them from piling up.

MARCO

THURSDAY NIGHT IS craps night. They've been teaching me how to deal.

The guy who does it is old. Jimmy Rigatoni. When he's not dealing craps, he's in charge of the lot where we keep the hot cars we use for whatever jobs we do. It's not a bad gig. He works one night a week and the rest of the time he don't do shit unless the phone rings to go give somebody a car.

He shuffles around that lot like a crippled penguin. When he's working the dice table, look out. It's like Clark Kent turning into Superman. He goes from being all bent and slow into a guy half his age when those bones come out. He works the stick just right. Watches every inch of the felt. He whispers and motions to me in a way that don't screw up the flow.

He's teaching me because they told him to, and because my dad's one of the bosses. I can tell he don't like me, mainly because he thinks they're gonna force him out. He don't realize as long as he keeps dealing the way he does, he ain't going nowhere.

He gave me a break after a couple hours and told me to make it quick. While I was taking a piss, one of the others asked me about the guy with nine fingers. I told him it was a dead end. Which was true, sort of.

I went back to the table. The game broke up right after three. Some of them was going to a diner that stayed open all night. I said I was tired. I also didn't feel like getting any more questions about the guy with nine fingers.

JOHN MORRIS

THE FARTHER I got from the main road, the darker it was. I made it to the right street. As I got closer to the house, there was just enough light to notice something fairly important.

The Buick wasn't there.

I cursed as I walked. I thought about going home.

I walked past the house where the Buick should have been, where it always had been every time I'd been there. I kept going for a couple of blocks and started back that way.

When I got to the house again, I slowed down. I tried to see if there was a garage or some other place where I could wait without the old man next door noticing me. I spotted something that looked like a shed.

I turned to the neighbor's house. No light came from inside. I moved for the shed. I found a place where I could peek around it without being seen.

I sat down and waited. The ground was hard. I hoped like hell there weren't any rattlesnakes around.

MARCO

I PULLED IN at half past three. I shut off the car. I went up to the front door. I hadn't locked it. I never do. Nobody in this neighborhood is gonna fuck with me. Part of me wishes somebody would try.

I noticed some mail sticking out of the box. I grabbed it and took it inside.

I pushed the door shut, tossed the envelopes on the table in the dining room, and went up the steps. I turned on the air conditioner, took off my shirt and jeans, and landed on the bed. I fell asleep fast.

JOHN MORRIS

I SAW LIGHTS shining back toward the shed. I felt my heart beat faster. I reached back with my left hand and took out the gun. The door of the Buick opened and closed. Four thumps up to the porch. A short pause. A door shoved open and slammed shut. It didn't sound like he unlocked it. I wondered whether he locked it after he went inside.

The fake Rolex caught just enough moonlight to show me it was thirty-five after three. I decided to wait.

The minute hand moved slow. I just sat there, trying to go over my plan. Not that it was much of one. Try to get inside. Try to sneak up to his bedroom. Try to shoot him. And then get the hell out of there. Unless he shoots me before I shoot him.

At twenty after four, I stood up. My hand was sweating on the gun. I moved it to my right hand and wiped my left hand on my jeans. I put the gun back in my left hand. I held it down by my hip and started for the house. I couldn't tell whether my feet were making any noise. All I could hear was my heart thumping, faster and faster.

Thirty-nine

DECEMBER 21, 1973

JOHN MORRIS

I CREPT TOWARD the house. My heart kept racing. I climbed a low porch to a back door with no screen. I twisted the knob. Locked.

I went back down. I looked at the house where the old man lived. I had to get to the front porch, and the steps to it were across from his house. I walked on a concrete path that led to the driveway. I came to a door along the side. The screen was locked. I kept going for the front door.

When I got to the Buick, I bent over and tried to hide behind it. I felt the pain in my broken ribs. At least that made my heart slow down.

I got to the stairs. I looked at the old man's house again. I turned back and walked up the steps. At the top, I put my right hand on the knob. I spun my wrist. It felt like a screwdriver was digging into it. I pressed my lips together and swallowed the sound that came from the back of my throat.

The door popped open. That made my pulse speed up again. I stuck my head inside. I thought for a second about an ambush. It was too late to worry about that, since my face would have been an easy target.

I held my breath and stepped inside. I left the door open behind me.

I couldn't believe I was actually doing it.

MARCO

I WOKE UP. I wasn't sure whether I heard something other than the air conditioner in the window. I decided it was nothing. I checked to make sure my gun was on the nightstand.

I had to piss. I didn't feel like getting up. I decided if I didn't fall back to sleep right away, I would.

JOHN MORRIS

I HELD THE gun in front of me and walked through the first floor. If anyone was waiting, I didn't see them. If someone with their own gun had seen me first, I never would have known the difference.

I saw a table. Envelopes were on it. There was just enough light from the kitchen to let me make out a name. Marco Morelli.

I found the stairs. I started climbing, one at a time. I'd step with my left, and then I'd bring my right foot to the same level.

I listened for anything. I could hear an air conditioner coming from upstairs. There was a light on in a bathroom. That made it easier for me to see. It also made it easier for me to be seen.

One of my shoes got caught in a rug that ran down the middle of the wooden stairs. I stumbled against the wall. I stopped and listened for anything other than that air conditioner.

MARCO

I WOKE UP again. Still had to piss. I checked the clock. I turned the pillow over and put my cheek into it. I tried to fall back to sleep again.

I told myself the next time I wake up I'll go to the bathroom.

JOHN MORRIS

I GOT TO the top. I walked heel to toe toward the sound of the air conditioner. There were two rooms with open doors. The sound was coming from behind the one that was closed. I thought about leaving. I wanted to leave.

I kept going.

I stood at the door. It was painted white. I held the gun up and tried the knob with my right hand. I felt the pain again in my wrist. It opened without making a sound.

I pushed just enough to fit through the opening. I turned my body. My broken ribs didn't like that. I slipped inside and raised the gun.

The air conditioner was loud. It sounded like it was on its last legs. I hoped I wasn't.

The light from the bathroom showed me the outline of a mattress. I saw the large lump on top of it.

I pointed the gun. I held it out from my body. I wanted to be sure I didn't miss.

I took another step forward. The lump moved, just a little bit. I flinched and almost pulled the trigger. I took another step forward.

It was time. Him or me. Him or my family. It seemed like this was going to be too easy. It almost didn't seem fair.

I didn't trust my aim with my left hand. I moved the gun over. It didn't fit perfectly into the spot where the cast covered my thumb. It would have to do. I wrapped my thumb around the handle and put my index finger on the trigger.

A squeeze or two, maybe three. That's all it would take. I didn't even have to look him in the eyes. I wouldn't have to see the life leave his body. It was too late to not know his name.

I stood there. A squeeze or two, maybe three. My arms trembled. My heart pounded. Sweat was starting to run over my eyebrows. I watched and waited.

A squeeze or two or maybe three. I'd run down the steps and

through the front door and out of the neighborhood before anyone else realized what happened. That's all it would take.

A squeeze or two. Maybe three.

I GOT BACK to the apartment not long before daybreak. I unlocked the door and eased myself inside. My mother shot up from the couch. She locked her eyes onto mine.

"Well?" she said.

"Well what?"

"Did you do it?"

I looked toward the bedroom. "Did she wake up?"

My mother repeated the question.

The dog ran over to me. I bent down to pet him. He licked the salt from my hand.

She repeated her question.

I stood up. I didn't realize I was crying.

"I'm sorry," I said.

She bolted up from the couch. "Sorry about what?"

"I didn't. I couldn't. I can't."

"So what does that mean?"

"I guess we'll just have to wait and see."

"That's not good enough."

I started crying harder. "That's as good as I can do. I couldn't pull the trigger."

Leslie came out of the bedroom, rubbing her eyes and asking what was going on. I looked at her stomach and thought about the baby inside it.

I repeated my daily prayer that she's carrying a girl.

Forty

JULY 4, 1974

JOHN MORRIS

I WALKED INTO the room at the hospital. Leslie was asleep. My mother sat in a chair holding a thick white blanket. I went over to her. She extended her arms and gave the baby to me. I pulled the bundle close against my body.

I looked at the baby. The eyelids were closed. The lips quivered.

"It's a boy," my mother said.

I kept looking at the face. "John Joseph Morris, Junior?" I said.

"How long will that be his name?"

"I don't know. As long as it needs to be. I do know this. He won't get caught up in the things me or my father did."

"You can't guarantee that."

I looked at the baby again.

"All I can do is try."

PART TWO

One

NOVEMBER 16, 1973

JIMMY DACEY

I RETIRED FROM my job. My wife died. My best friend was killed.

I didn't know what to do with myself. Seventy-two years old and nowhere to go. No reason to go. No reason to live.

I was waiting for something while waiting for nothing. The only thing that kept me going was my lifelong goal to make it to eighty. What's the point?

Family, sure. But we haven't been close. There's been a wall. The harder I try to break it down, the stronger it seems.

My routines have become simple. Sit in my house. Watch TV. Read, more and more poems. I've always preferred them flowery and mysterious, with verses that waft in my mind well after I wedge the book into its spot on the shelf.

The other day at the grocery store, I ran into another regular from John Mesagne's bar. Ronald. They call him Dickhead. That nickname isn't very flowery or mysterious.

He told me John's place is still open. He said a man named Cashews Ciccone is running it. I'd heard that name from John. Cashews works for Paul Verbania. Ronald said it's a short-term thing, that it'll last only until they find someone to take over the bookmaking operation John had managed.

I told Ronald I might go back soon. Even with my friend gone, it's still the same place. It still has the same people. The only difference is John was shot and killed on the sidewalk near the house where he used to live. And the new man in charge works for the man who ordered the hit. My first thought was to see that as a negative. I came to regard it as a positive.

I went back the next day. I got there at my usual time, went to my usual spot at the bar. I started to feel a little emotional about the situation until I saw Cashews Ciccone.

His black hair was greasy and unkempt. It looked like he towels it off for a second or two and lets it do its own thing until the next time he washes it. Weekly, at most.

His face was narrow, thin. Angles, but no symmetry. The bridge of his nose zig-zagged. It curved down near the tip, making it look like a broken beak. His eyes were too close together. One was a little smaller and sat a little lower than the other.

His chin was weak. His neck, loose and fleshy. He wore a tight yellow polo shirt over a physique far more floppy than firm. Thick hairs sprouted from the V-shaped neck and hung like weeds from the bottom of his sleeves.

I managed a smile. I told him my name. I said I used to come to the bar every day, before that unfortunate thing happened. I explained I hadn't come back because I assumed the place had closed down.

Cashews told me they opened up and put him in charge, after only a couple of days. He said he wished they hadn't. That he's not too good with numbers.

I nodded as he spoke. I instantly disliked him. I also liked the situation and the opportunity it might present.

I started going there every day. Like before. I sat where I always did. I watched. I listened. I placed some bets. I won some, I lost some. Like before.

I'd gotten more comfortable, and I'd gotten Cashews to talk. He complained more and more about running the operation. He kept saying he doesn't really know what he's doing. He kept saying he doesn't really want to do it. He kept saying he's accepted he'll do it until the boss finds someone else.

"How hard can it be?" I asked him, six days from Thanksgiving.

"Harder than I figured." His voice came out raspy and uneven, like he just sprinted up three flights of stairs. "I'm gonna be stuck here until after the Super Bowl."

"Have they talked to anyone else?"

"They don't tell me nothing but to keep going."

"I've been coming here a long time. I know how John did business. And I used to be an accountant."

He regarded me with those mismatched eyes. I didn't know which one to look at. "Accountant, huh? That's numbers right? A-counting?"

"I spent many a year a-counting."

I waited for the gears in his brain to grind. He didn't seem particularly suited either to a-counting, or a-thinking.

"How old are you?"

"Seventy-three next month."

He made a face even uglier than usual. "Seventy-three?"

"Is there an age limit?"

"If I tell them I found an old guy who hangs around the place and he's good with numbers, they'll ask me how old he is."

"If I may ask, who's them?"

Cashews glanced both ways to make sure no one was listening. "Paul runs the show. But it's mainly Vinny."

"I'm familiar. Large fellow. Stern. Dark. Hole in the nose."

"He needs a hole or two someplace else."

"It's not for me to say this, but it seems as if the boss and his right-hand man spent a lot of time worrying about things involving the man who used to have this job. Along with his son."

"His son." Cashews crinkled the crinkly skin around his nose as he spoke. "Don't get me started."

"What happened with his son?"

"That ain't for me to say."

I just nodded, locking eye with Cashews. "The last thing I would ever do is pry."

And then I waited to see whether I'd said enough to get him to keep talking.

Two

NOVEMBER 16, 1973

JIMMY DACEY

CASHEWS KEPT TALKING. I kept listening. When he paused and waited for me to say something, I didn't. That made him keep going.

Before long, Cashews told me about a colleague named Jerry Pasquale. They're both a step under Vinny. They both believe Paul Verbania has been wasting too much time on John Mesagne and his son.

They thought Paul worried too much about whether some kid was sleeping with his mistress. They didn't understand why a married man who was fooling around with another woman would get so bent out of shape if the other woman was fooling around with someone else.

"Is it really cheating if he's already cheating?" Cashews said. I raised my eyebrows, shrugged my shoulders, held out my palms. And Cashews kept going.

Cashews and Jerry had become disgruntled. That part became clear. They felt business was being neglected. They've considered making a move to replace the boss and his right-hand man. They didn't know which one would run the show and which one would become the new right-hand man. They decided to figure it out later. They saw that as a good problem to have.

I kept listening. My facial expressions and body language persuaded Cashews to keep spilling his guts in a way I never dreamed he would. He seemed to be close to deciding to do something about it. I enjoyed what I was hearing.

I've never been one to stir up trouble. I never really had a reason to do it.

"I like you," Cashews said at one point. "You make good conversation."

I nodded. I thanked Cashews. I reminded him of my interest in becoming the new bookmaker in residence. Cashews said he liked the title, even if he didn't know what it means. He said he'd talk to Vinny. Who would hopefully talk to Paul. Who would hopefully make the decision I wanted him to make.

I felt optimistic as I started to leave. Cashews hates the work. No one else in the operation seems to be inclined or able to do it. Cashews said I have as good a chance as anyone. Other than me, I don't think there is anyone.

"Thank you," I said again. "And think about what we discussed."

Of course, I hadn't done much discussing. It was all Cashews, sounding out ideas for a potential takeover.

"If you're unhappy with the current situation, you should evaluate your options," I added. "That's probably how the current structure ended up in place. I assume that's how businesses like these undergo changes in management. If you and Jerry think the boss has lost his focus, it's fair to address it. If you deem it necessary to take action to alter the situation, so be it."

Cashews gave me a look, squinting one of his already squinty eyes. "You sure you ain't never been in this life?"

"All I've ever done is come to this bar, sit in this seat, and keep my ears, eyes, and wallet open."

"Why would you wanna get involved in something like this now?"

"What else will I do? Wait around to die?"

"If we end up making a move, you might not have to wait around very long for that."

He was involving me in the plan. I liked it, even if I wasn't thrilled with that specific implication. "You also could end up at the top of the mountain," I said. "It's easier to stay on top than it is to get there."

Cashews looked away from me. I could sense it was working.

"Top of the mountain," he said, sounding out the words. He said them again, this time with more confidence.

I nodded and raised my glass. "Here's to the top of the mountain."

Three

NOVEMBER 19, 1973

JIMMY DACEY

I SHOWED UP at the bar every day. I hadn't asked Cashews for an update about the job they might be giving me. Yes, I was curious. I didn't want to seem anxious or pushy.

It happened three days before Thanksgiving. Cashews said in a very casual way that Vinny would be stopping by, that he wanted to talk to me.

"So it's an interview?" I said.

"He just wants to talk to you about the job."

I didn't explain that's what an interview is. "When will he be here?"

"With that guy, you never know."

"Should I wait?"

"Wouldn't you be here anyway?"

"You're right. He won't have to look far."

I stayed on my usual stool. I nursed a beer or two. I went to the toilet once. I still have that limp. I don't know how I got it or whether it will ever go away.

Four hours later, Vinny pushed the door open. He moved in a prowl, like an oversized jungle cat that hadn't fed in a week. He came to the end of the bar where I sat. Cashews stiffened up at the sight of him.

I nodded at Vinny. He nodded back. I couldn't tell if he remembered me from the times he'd show up and hassle John. Before I could say anything, Cashews got started.

"This is the guy I was telling you about."

I introduced myself, extending a palm. The liver spots and swollen knuckles highlighted my vintage.

Vinny kept his hands in his pockets, ignoring my gesture. "Wasn't you always here when Mesagne was in charge? You two seemed thick as thieves."

I curled my fingers away. "John Mesagne was a good man. I miss him."

"I miss him, too," Vinny said, "because now I gotta find somebody who can run this place. The guy currently doing it ain't doing too good."

"That's what we've been talking about," Cashews said, ignoring the insult or not noticing.

"So Cashews thinks he's found his man. A retired accountant who was in cahoots with the last guy in charge. Somebody who never even had a parking ticket. Now he wants to make the shift from buyer to seller. Do I got that right?"

"You've put a lot more thought into this than I have. I know your associate is doing the job temporarily. Temporarily has lasted longer than expected, because you're having trouble finding someone who can fill the job permanently."

Vinny sneered. "I'm not sure calling it permanent helps your case. For someone like you, permanent and temporary might be the same."

Cashews laughed. I could tell he felt like he had to. I mustered another polite smile. "My father told me a long time ago growing old is far better than the alternative. As I see it, you might not have any alternatives to this old man."

Vinny dipped his head and furrowed his brow. I tried not to stare at the hole in his nose. "What's your angle?"

"What do you mean?"

"You don't need this headache. You don't need the money. Why do you want this?"

I shrugged. "I'm here anyway. I might as well make myself useful."

"He is here," Cashews said. "I mean, every single day."

"It's one thing to be here," Vinny said. "You show up when you want, you leave when you want. Relax. Talk. Bet a little money. Drink a little beer. Once you make it into a job, it all changes."

"I've had jobs. For a long time I had a very good job. I know how having a job works."

"I don't know why you want this job," Vinny said. "It don't make no sense to me."

"If you have someone else in mind, by all means you should hire him."

Vinny kept eyeing me. He didn't say anything else. After a little while, he shifted to Cashews and motioned with his chin to the back room.

After they walked away, I felt a smile pop and spread. I made a fist with my right hand. I held it close to my chest and pumped it three times.

"It's happening," I whispered to myself, and maybe to whatever part of John Mesagne still floated in the room. "It is happening."

Four

NOVEMBER 19, 1973

JIMMY DACEY

VINNY EMERGED FROM the back. He clomped toward me in those big shoes John used to make fun of.

I twisted my body to face him. He walked out without saying a word. I spun back to the bar.

"Charming guy," I said once Cashews returned.

"That's when he's in a good mood."

I took a drink of beer that was getting a little too warm and a little too flat. "Looks like I won't be coming out of retirement," I said.

"Actually, they're going to let you give it a try."

I couldn't believe what I was hearing. My facial expression gave it away.

"Don't celebrate too quick. You start Thursday."

"That's Thanksgiving. I'm going to my daughter's house in Pennsylvania."

"Not if you want this job. Washington and Detroit get started around one. Miami and Dallas play at four. Then it's Alabama and Louisiana State. You're spoken for, all day."

I didn't say anything to that. I took another drink of the tepid beer.

"Don't tell me you plan to quit before you even start," Cashews said.

"I hadn't expected to get the job, especially not so quickly. Will you be here, too?"

"Most of the bets will come through the phone."

I shook my head. "You deserve a day to yourself. Spend time with your family."

"I'll go to my aunt's. I'll eat some food and fall asleep on the couch, and then I'll go home."

"That's it?"

"What else is there?"

"Based on what we've been talking about, that could be a perfect time for you and Jerry to talk about the future."

A thin clot of greasy hair dangled over Cashew's left eye. He pushed it away. It fell right back. "Maybe we've already been talking about it."

"Maybe Thursday night would be a good time to talk about it some more," I said.

Cashews freshened my beer from the tap behind the bar. "Why are you so interested in what me and Jerry talk about?"

"I want what's best for the business, now that I'm part of it."

"I guess you are." He grabbed an empty glass and poured one for himself. He held his beer near my face. "Here's to the top of the mountain."

I raised my own and tapped it against his.

"Here's to the future."

Cashews laughed at me.

"What's so funny about that?"

"If I make it your age, the last thing I'll be thinking about is the future, because I won't have much of one."

"You might not have much of one now, depending on how things go."

"I guess you're right about that."

"Here's the difference. I can't control my future. You can control yours."

"I like how you think," Cashews said. He took a long drink. "I like how you think a lot."

"I've been around. I've got some ideas."

"What kind of ideas?"

"Ideas on how to get things done. Ideas on how I can control my future, and more importantly on how you can control yours."

Cashews stared back at me. I could tell he was thinking about what I said. His face twisted a bit, probably when he realized that, yes, this could end badly for him.

"So you'll be here Thursday?" he said. "I can count on you?"

"I'll be here. And I'll stay here until they kick the ball between Alabama and LSU."

"What then?"

"Go home. Get something to eat. Go to bed."

"I was already thinking maybe Thursday night I might talk to Jerry. Now I'm thinking maybe you can join us."

I took another drink and waited for Cashews to say some more. I knew he would.

Five

NOVEMBER 22, 1973

JIMMY DACEY

MY FIRST DAY on the job had gone well. There was no reason it shouldn't. I spent most of my life doing tax returns and preparing balance sheets and tracking accounts receivable and compiling depreciation schedules. Writing down on a piece of paper that some guy from Glendale had put twenty dollars on the Cowboys to cover was a breeze.

Cashews was right. Most of the bets came over the phone. Only a couple of the regulars showed up at the bar. I felt bad they didn't have family to spend the day with.

I felt bad for myself, too. I would have been in Kittanning, watching football and eating turkey and mashed potatoes and stuffing and pecan pie. Even with that wall between us, I missed not being able to see my daughter and her family. I would have slept in the bed of the oldest boy, Mark. He would have been happy to give it up, if it meant having me spend the night. I might have even stayed over until Saturday.

I told my daughter I wasn't feeling well. She offered to come down and check on me. I told her it's just a cold, maybe a touch of the flu. Not that she would have actually made the trip. She still wanted me to drive up for a visit on Friday if I was feeling better. I told her I would.

I couldn't. The job would keep me busy. College games on Friday and Saturday. Pro games on Sunday. I wouldn't be going anywhere on any weekend, any time soon. Unless they fired me or I quit. I had a feeling neither would be an option, at least not until football season ended.

After the night game started, I went over the checklist. I put the slips in a manila envelope that went under a trick floorboard in the office, just in case the place got robbed or burned down. I told Cashews the hiding place probably wouldn't help the paperwork survive a fire. Cashews said as long as the envelope gets put where it's supposed to go, he can't be blamed for whatever happens to it.

There wasn't much to clean. The beer glasses had long been washed. I hadn't charged for any of them. I doubted anyone would care, especially since the cash register was just part of the flimsy cover. I'd always told John he should give it away. Let it flow. It'll loosen the pocketbooks, just like it does at the casinos.

It was time to lock up. I removed the keys from the pocket of my pants. I tried not to think I'd done the same thing a little over a month before, the night they killed John. It came back to me all at once. How could it not? Same keys. Same door. Same lock. I couldn't stop thinking about him. I couldn't stop thinking about what they did to him.

I've never been a violent man. I've always been slow to anger, often too slow for my own good. Thinking about what happened to my friend kept my blood at a constant boil.

I fumbled with the keys. I didn't want to hold them the same way I had the night they killed John. There was no other way to do it.

I stood outside the door after the keys were back in my pocket. The air was cold. I breathed it in. I felt the anger slide to the background.

Someone was on the other side of the street from the bar. The figure started moving my way, crossing a street with no traffic. I was too old to make a run for it. I waited to see who it was and what he wanted.

I should have figured it would be him.

"How'd it go today?" Vinny said.

"It went."

"No problems?"

"It went just like I thought it would."

"How much came in?" He was making a slow circle around me as he spoke. I tried not to react.

"The handle was sixteen hundred, give or take. Most of it was on the Dallas game. And most of that was on the Cowboys."

Vinny stayed silent. I looked at him. He glared at me.

"Miami covered," I said. "We made money."

"You put everything where it's supposed to go?"

"I did everything Cashews told me to do."

"I still don't get why you wanna do this."

"I still don't understand why it's such a mystery."

"I've seen a lot in my time. I ain't never seen nothing like this."

"I'm not sure what else I can tell you."

"If you was about twenty years younger, I'd have other ways to be sure you're telling me the truth."

His comment made my left knee weaken. I fought it off and stood firm. "As I've said, to you and to Cashews, if you have someone else who can do this job, that's fine with me. I'm happy to go back to being a customer."

"It might be too late for that."

"It might be too late for a lot of things."

"What does that mean?"

I felt the boil return. I tried to keep my face under control. "It means what it means."

"Where are you going now?"

"To my car. Then to my house. Then to bed. If I was about twenty years younger, I'd have other ways to blow off steam after giving my Thanksgiving day to a job my new boss doesn't seem to want me doing."

Six

NOVEMBER 22, 1973

JIMMY DACEY

I'VE HAD THE Buick for seven years. I kept the other one in the garage, for fun. I haven't had much fun lately. Sometimes I wondered if I ever would again.

I drove away from the parking lot near the bar. I checked the mirror now and again to see if anyone was following. Tailing, as they would say in my new world. I wasn't sure how to spot a tail. I also didn't know what to do if I saw one.

I thought about changing cars. I decided not to. The other one would stand out.

Cashews told me the address of his aunt's house. I knew the neighborhood. I remembered the number. I hoped it would be easy to find. I continued to ensure I wasn't being tailed.

Vinny was already suspicious. He'd be a problem at some point. It made me determined to get them to move, before whatever mobster sixth sense Vinny might have let him piece everything together.

I had faith in my own ability to give nothing away. I didn't trust Cashews. I had to assume Jerry was as shaky as Cashews when it comes to mental acuity and verbal ability.

The house was on a street connected to the main road. It would have been nice if the place had been tucked more out of the way, but as they say that's the hand I'd been dealt.

I made the turn and started down Locust Avenue. I checked the houses. It was dark and not easy to see the porches. I saw one with a light on, and then another. I was heading the right way. The farther I could get from the intersection, the better I would feel about leaving the Buick in plain view.

I spotted the house. I kept going until I found a place to park. I backed up as close as I could to the car behind me, so that the plate couldn't be seen by anyone driving by. Did Vinny know the numbers? I was about to bet my life he didn't.

I got out of the car. It was as quiet as any Thanksgiving night ever is. I limped toward the house with determination, like I belonged there. At least I told myself I did.

I stopped on the sidewalk in front. A single bulb in square casing over the door threw a soft glow onto the stoop. It was all stucco and bricks. It felt like the entrance beckoned for me. At least I told myself it did.

I started up the concrete walkway. Two steps would take me to the destination. Where that destination would take me was still to be seen.

I removed my fedora and held it in my right hand. I knocked on the frame with the other.

Almost instantly, a woman opened the door. She seemed to gasp a bit at the sight of me. I hoped it was the good kind.

Why shouldn't it have been? I'm elderly. She's elderly. I have a full head of hair, even if it's all white. I dress well. I still have my original teeth. That makes me a catch, given the demographic.

"Well, hello," she said. She smiled a friendly smile. I might have sensed a little more than that. "I was told to expect a much older man."

"I wasn't told to expect such an attractive young lady."

The smile broadened. I noticed a blush. She pulled the door open and invited me inside.

Her hair was golden. Short and wavy with the ends flipped up near her ears. She also had a wide curl hanging down toward brown eyebrows. If this woman was Cashews's aunt, it had to be by marriage.

She removed her eyeglasses and grasped them in her palms. She motioned for me to come in.

"It smells heavenly," I said. "I fear I've missed quite a meal."

"There's plenty of food. I'll fix you a plate."

"I shall not impose on you."

"Don't be silly," she said, pulling out a chair from her kitchen table. "Sit here. Charles and that friend of his are downstairs. They can wait a little while longer. You look like you haven't eaten. And of all days to not eat."

I started to place my hat on the table. She snatched it. She motioned for my overcoat and deposited it on a hanger in the hall closet.

I relented to everything. I was too tired to reject her hospitality. Plus, I was too hungry to pass up an unanticipated Thanksgiving meal.

I sat at the table. She produced a clean plate, filling it with turkey, mashed potatoes, gravy, and corn from pots on her stove. She slid it in front of me. She handed me a knife, a fork, and a napkin.

"Thank you," I said, receiving the utensils. "I feel guilty accepting this food given that we haven't properly met."

"I'm Aunt Carol."

"First name Aunt, last name Carol?"

She covered her mouth and laughed. "Caroline," she said after she pulled her fingers away. "Technically, Carolina. Carolina Ciccone."

I stood and offered my right hand. She extended her own. I grasped it with gentleness and lifted my wrist up and down twice. "It's a pleasure to meet you, Mrs. Ciccone. I'm James. James Dacey. Friends call me Jimmy."

"The pleasure is mine, Mr. Dacey,"

I lowered myself back into the chair. She took a seat and waited for me to start.

"My word," I said after the first bite had been properly chewed. "I'm not sure I've had anything this delicious in years."

She smiled again. "Thank you, Mr. Dacey."

"Call me Jimmy."

She nodded. I wanted to hear her say my name. She didn't. I told myself maybe it would happen the next time I visited.

Seven

NOVEMBER 22, 1973

JIMMY DACEY

I FINISHED THE plate. I thanked her. I laid it on a little too thick. Regardless, Aunt Carol deserved it.

Aunt Carol. Caroline. *Carolina.* I liked the sound of that.

She showed me to the narrow door that led to the basement. There was no railing. I steadied myself by pressing a hand against the wall and took the stairs with great care.

"If you need anything at all," she said as I dropped lower and lower from view, "just let me know."

I paused, I turned. I met her eyes with mine. "We will," I said. "And thank you again, Carolina."

Saying her name made my stomach rumble. Hearing it made her lip quiver. I saw it. Subtle, but it was there.

I also think I heard a soft laugh of delight as she closed the door. The sound made me smile. I forced the expression away as I got closer to the basement.

The concrete floor was smooth. It had been painted brown, roughly the same shade as sewage. *Fitting for the current occupants,* I thought.

I saw light from a bare bulb over a card table, the top of it slanted on thin metal legs. Haphazardly placed beer cans were on the surface, at least ten. An ashtray overflowed with cigarette butts. I could see on the floor a collection of rings and tabs.

Slumped in lawn chairs on either side of the table were Cashews and Jerry. I nodded at them without speaking or smiling.

"You're late," Cashews said.

"I've been here for twenty minutes. Your aunt fed me."

"You're still late," Jerry said.

"Would you prefer I be rude? She insisted I eat. I'd wager she did the same thing to the both of you."

"She don't like Jerry," Cashews said. "She thinks he looks like a creep."

"She told you that?" Jerry said.

"It was Italian. I think it means creep."

"What was the word she used?" I said.

"*Finnochi*," Cashews said. That made me chuckle.

"So what does that mean?" Jerry said.

"Not creep," I said.

I saw another lawn chair propped against the wall. I opened it and sat down.

"Dacey ain't no Italian name," Cashews said. "How come you know Italian?"

"Dacey used to be D'Agostina," I said. "My parents changed it when we moved here from Italy. I was three."

"How old are you now?" Jerry said.

"A lot older than three," Cashews said.

"I'm seventy-two. None of us can control when we're born. Most of us can't control when we die. I try to make the most of each day I have."

Cashews added to the mountain of butts and lit another cigarette. "What's the most you can make of this day?"

"You tell me."

Jerry took a drink before lighting a fresh one of his own. "Cashews trusts you. I'd maybe trust you more if you wasn't so late, and if you wasn't so old. I'll give you the benefit of the doubt on both. He told me you've been talking about our problem."

"We've been talking about it. More importantly, he said you and he have been talking about it."

Cashews took two fresh beers from a Styrofoam cooler that was missing a large chunk from its lid. They dripped water from the melting ice.

"It's a big move," he said, handing me one of them, "with plenty of risk."

The can was cold and wet. I forced a finger under the ring and pulled the tab away from the opening. I placed the curved piece of metal on the table and poured some over my lips. It tasted bitter and cheap.

"Every business has risk," I said. "Every risk has reward."

"It ain't about risk," Jerry said. "It's about what's right. Paul is letting things go to shit because he's too worried about finding the kid who ran off with his girlfriend. He's obsessed with that shit."

"There's still risk," I said. "Let's not kid ourselves. You're contemplating a *coup d'etat*."

"Coo the what?" Jerry said.

"A mutiny. An uprising. All or nothing. It's a pass-fail test. And if you fail—"

"It's we," Cashews said. "If we fail, that's it for all of us."

I put the can on the table and lifted my palms. "Gentlemen, I'm just a consultant. This isn't my concern."

"Bullshit it ain't your concern," Cashews said. "Do you think I'm stupid? You've been working on me to try to take out Paul because Paul took out your friend."

I picked up the pack of cigarettes and removed one. I couldn't remember the last time I'd smoked. When neither of them offered me a light, I grabbed matches that were in front of Jerry and used them.

"It's too late in the day and I'm too tired and I have too much of your aunt's turkey in me to play games. I won't lie to you, not now and not ever. Paul had John Mesagne killed. So, yes, I would very much like to see that mutherfucker dead."

Jerry started laughing. He kept laughing. Tears spilled from the corners of his eyes. "All of a sudden I like this old man," he said.

"If I'm putting my own neck on the line, I want a piece of the upside," I said.

"Upside?" Cashews said.

"If you guys take over the business, I want to be part of it."

Jerry started laughing again. Cashews joined him. I wondered if they were being loud enough to make Carolina think Henny Youngman had paid us a visit.

"Most gangsters are retired or dead by the time they're his age," Jerry said to Cashews, as if I wasn't sitting right there. "This son of a bitch is thinking about taking over at seventy-two."

"I don't want to run anything. Like I said, every risk has reward. If you expect me to assume the risk, I want to share in the reward."

Jerry looked at Cashews. Cashews looked at Jerry. They both looked at me.

"You help us pull this off," Cashews said, "and you'll be part of what comes next."

"How much?"

"We'll figure it out when we get there," Jerry said.

"I want a clear commitment now. If the three of us will be taking over, it's only right for the three of us to split the profits equally. My role will be to keep track of the money and make sure it's all divided fairly. Thirty-three percent each."

"That's too much," Jerry said.

I pushed myself out of the chair. "I'm sure you two can figure this out without me."

I started back to the stairs. I couldn't tell if I was disappointed or relieved.

"Twenty percent," Jerry said. I acted like I didn't hear him.

"Twenty-five," Cashews said. I kept walking.

"Thirty," Jerry said. I put my foot on the first step and wished them luck with Paul and Vinny.

"Fine," Jerry said. "Thirty-three percent."

I stepped back down to the brown concrete and went to the table. Could I trust them to honor their promise? It wouldn't matter if I was the one counting the money.

I could tell Cashews was trying to do the math. "Don't that leave one percent?" he said.

I looked up toward the first floor. "We can give it to your Aunt Carol."

Eight

NOVEMBER 22, 1973

JIMMY DACEY

WITH AN AGREEMENT in place, we started brainstorming. Cashews wanted to put a bomb in Paul's car. I liked that idea. I suggested doing it during the holidays. That's when his guard would be down, if ever.

They had a problem with doing it before Christmas. I suggested the day after Christmas. They looked at each other. Neither said no. I took that as yes.

Cashews had experience planting car bombs. The fact that he lived to tell about it implied a minimum degree of competence. He said he'd place seven sticks of dynamite at the back of the engine block, near the firewall. He'd use something called a tilt fuse. When the mercury in the fuse shifted, that would be that.

That was the easy part, relative to the rest of the plan. Sure, placing and wiring the bomb would be a challenge. The bigger one would be getting Paul inside the car.

He never drove. Vinny did. And Vinny always started the car before Paul got inside. We'd need to create a situation that made Paul have to drive on his own.

I said they'd need to take care of Vinny first, and they'd need to make Paul think there's an emergency of some kind. Something that would get him to drive to wherever he thought the emergency was.

They knew they'd have to take care of Vinny, even if the mere talk of it made them clam up and shake a little. If they hit Paul and not Vinny, he'd come after them immediately.

I had to stop myself at one point; I couldn't believe what I was saying. It made me feel woozy. It went away when I remembered what they did to my friend.

Cashews said Vinny goes back to Paul's place every Wednesday night to do a final count for the week, after dropping Paul off at his house. I told them the day after Christmas this year happens to be on a Wednesday. They asked me how I knew that. I didn't tell them the twenty-sixth of December was my late wife's birthday.

Jerry spitballed the idea of recruiting Vinny to join us. He thought Vinny might be tired of Paul worrying about John's son, too. Cashews sneered at that. He said Vinny would kill us all for even mentioning it. I knew Vinny well enough to have no reason to argue the point.

I was glad they were talking these things through. I needed them to decide on their own that killing Paul couldn't happen without first killing Vinny, especially if there was no way Vinny would ever join the *coo-the-what.*

We had the beginning of a plan. On the night after Christmas, Cashews and Jerry would kill Vinny. They'd make Paul think Vinny needs help. They'd get Paul to start his car and drive it far enough for the mercury in the tilt fuse to move and the bomb to explode and Paul to be transformed into a couple hundred pounds of ground chuck.

I couldn't believe I was part of this. For my friend's sake, I was glad to be involved.

Nine

NOVEMBER 23, 1973

JIMMY DACEY

THE HOUSE STILL feels like a replica of the home it once was. The beer didn't change that. The clock, as best I could tell, told me it was well after midnight.

I drank too much. I smoked too much. I'm at least two decades too old for this.

I'd need to get up and go to the bar. I'd need to be sharp. I wasn't interested in losing this new job so soon. Especially not with other plans taking shape.

I lobbed my overcoat toward a chair. I loosened my tie and slipped out of my jacket. It landed on the carpet my wife had picked from eleven different options, thirteen months before the diagnosis.

I whistled random notes. I felt happy, in a way. Happy to have a plan. Happy my friend might be avenged.

The bed made for two welcomed me with its usual reluctance. Sleep remained hard to find. I gave up after nearly an hour. I found an unopened bottle of Canadian Club in the dining room. I couldn't remember when I'd bought it.

I sipped the whisky for a while. I gulped the rest of the first glass and poured another. I took it to the couch and rested it on a table. I stretched out. I closed my eyes. I don't know if I slept.

Sunlight crept onto my face. My neck was stiff. My head throbbed. I could feel the heartbeat in the space behind my eyes.

I got myself ready for Day Two of this new life. I had a pep in my step, as they say. The air was crisp and invigorating. I started whistling again. I kept whistling as I got in the car and drove to the bar. I whistled until the moment I saw the Cadillac parked on the street next to the front door.

Vinny climbed out and glared at me. "You," he said, pointing behind him, "get in."

I nodded. I looked at the car. There was a head in the back seat, right behind the spot where the driver sat. I walked around and opened the door. I didn't need to guess who was sitting there.

"Hello," I said.

"He told you to get in."

I complied without another word, removing my fedora and dropping it in the space between us.

Paul turned to me. An unlit cigar drooped from his lips. I could smell the wet tobacco.

"Where'd you go last night?"

"I'm sorry?"

"After you left. Where'd you go?"

"I had Thanksgiving dinner."

Vinny got back inside. His eyes taunted me through the mirror.

"Where did you have Thanksgiving dinner?" Paul said.

"I went to the house of my dead wife's sister."

"Where does she live?"

"Martins Ferry. In Ohio."

"I know where Martins Ferry is."

"I don't understand this."

"Vinny drove by your house last night around eleven. Your car wasn't there. You told him you was going home and staying there."

"She called and invited me right after I got home. So I went. Time got away from me. Am I late?"

"You're right on time. Do you feel fine?"

"Should I not?"

"What's your sister-in-law's name?"

"I have a feeling you already know."

"You understand what you've agreed to do here?"

"I've agreed to show up every day. I've agreed to take the bets. I've agreed to record them properly and ensure the money is accurately counted. I've agreed to tell your friend in the front if anyone who owes money hasn't paid it within seventy-two hours. I assume I've also agreed that, when my work here is done, I'm free to come and go as I please."

"Does your sister-in-law know what you're doing?"

"Excuse me?"

"Does she know about your new line of work?"

"I can understand why you'd have some misgivings. As I understand it, however, there weren't many options. I can assure you I will handle this job as well as anyone who has ever done it for you. I also understand the importance of discretion."

"Discretion. I like that word. So you understand discretion?"

"I understand a lot more than that."

"You got any children?"

"I have a daughter in Pennsylvania. I was supposed to spend Thanksgiving with her family. I didn't, because I made a commitment here."

"What did you tell her?"

"I told her I wasn't feeling well."

"Are you feeling well?"

"I feel fine."

"Do you wanna keep it that way?"

"I'm sorry," I said, "but this is all very confusing. Have I done something wrong?"

"You tell me."

"I don't have to do this. I'm retired. I was a customer here. I've been a customer here. A loyal customer. Your man who had been filling in wanted someone to take over. He offered it to me. Your man in the front seat approved, as far as I know. If there's a problem with that, I can go back to being a loyal customer."

A laugh came from deep within Paul Verbania's esophagus. "That's a good one."

"Excuse me?"

"You're in this life now. You act accordingly. That means doing your job. It means doing your job with no surprises."

"How does visiting a family member on Thanksgiving night constitute a surprise?"

"It don't. As long as you can be trusted to use discretion."

I smoothed my slacks with both hands. "I assume you've been in this business a long time. I suspect you've seen the full gamut of smart and stupid, discreet and indiscreet. I'll promise you that of all the employees you've had who have caused you problems, I will cause the fewest."

"Fewest ain't good enough. I want none."

"I don't plan on causing any."

"Good, because I got enough problems. I also got a feeling you know how I deal with problems."

"I don't plan on finding out."

"In the end, that's up to you."

"I've been around long enough to know how not to cause problems."

"Then we have an understanding," Paul said. "Just so we're clear, some problems can affect other people, too."

"Other people?"

"I don't know how else to say the words."

I picked up my hat. I held it with both hands. I looked at it. I glanced at the reflection of Vinny's dark eyes and hollowed-out nose. I nodded at both of them.

"I know what I've signed up for."

Ten

NOVEMBER 25, 1973

JIMMY DACEY

I TRIED NOT to think about the things Paul had said. At one point on Friday, my right hand started trembling. That hadn't happened in a long time.

"It's too late to turn back now," I said to my fingers.

The weekend unfolded one hour at a time. I checked the clock more often than I should have. Each passing second carried me closer to the day after Christmas. When not looking at the time, I eyed the door, waiting for Vinny to burst inside. He didn't.

I did my job. Tracking bets and collecting money and paying the winners and raising my eyebrows just a bit to those who said they needed a day or two to come up with what they owed because I knew and they knew what could happen if they took any longer than that.

Thoughts of Cashews and Jerry peppered my mind. I had instigated them. I wanted what they wanted, for different reasons. Still, Paul needed to go.

If we succeeded, he'd be gone. If we failed, we'd be gone. I wanted to make it to eighty. They might not make it to forty. Or maybe to thirty. I can't tell how old anyone under fifty is.

Paul had made a vague threat against my family. I didn't buy it. I'd be stupid to dismiss it. I'd be ready to take precautions, if it came to that.

The Steelers lost to the Browns on Sunday. It ended up being a very good day for the operation, since pretty much everyone in town had bet on Pittsburgh to cover. I knew Vinny would be pleased with the profits, if pleasure is something he's capable of feeling.

After the late games ended on Sunday, the bar cleared out. I drove the Buick home. I parked it in the usual spot. I went inside through the usual door to the usual room and considered the usual options for a usual dinner.

The phone rang before I could get started. I wouldn't be eating in my house that night, after all. I went upstairs to shave my face and brush my teeth. I changed into a fresh suit, the one I'd been planning to wear the next morning.

I opened the cabinet in the kitchen, right above the sink. I found the metal ring with two keys on it. I tried to remember how long it had been. I hoped the battery wasn't dead.

I walked out the back door, the one in the kitchen. I pulled it shut behind me. I strode through a blanket of darkness to the garage. The streetlight by a neighbor's house guided me.

I never locked the garage. I grabbed the handle on the door and pulled it up. It made me feel strong. It helped that I kept the rollers heavily greased.

The grassy smell from the lawnmower greeted me. There was comfort in it. There was even more comfort in seeing the car.

Corvette. 1963 model. The only item on which I had ever splurged.

It was dusty but clean. I got in, turned the key. I held my breath before the starter engaged. I smiled when that beautiful noise filled my ears. The rumbles coming through the seat made me feel like I was the machine and the machine was me.

I backed out. I pulled the garage door down. I checked the house. Enough lights were on to make Vinny think I was there, if he decided to conduct another surveillance operation that night. Having the Buick parked out front wouldn't hurt.

I then made my way to the alley and to the road. Toward Carolina's house.

Eleven

NOVEMBER 25, 1973

JIMMY DACEY

I'D ALMOST FORGOTTEN the feeling of driving it. I bought it for Sunday drives with my wife. I glanced over to the place where she used to sit. I wondered what she'd say right now.

Maybe she'd be happy. After all, the things I was doing could hasten a reunion.

I hadn't been tailed. I parked near the spot where I'd left the Buick on Thanksgiving night. I followed the same path back to Carolina's stoop. I approached the door with the same demeanor. I knocked the same way I had before.

It opened quickly. She looked different. She wore makeup. She was dressed like she was ready to go somewhere. Her hair was more immaculate than it had been before.

I fumbled to remove my hat. "Hello," I said.

She pulled the handle toward her and stepped aside. "Welcome back."

I inhaled the aroma, pulling it toward my nose with my hand. "That's not turkey I smell."

"Roast beef. I have some ready for you. They can wait."

"An excellent cook and a mind reader."

She laughed. "What a sweet talker you are." Her hand covered her mouth as the smile under it expanded. She asked for my coat and my hat. I went to the table and waited for the plate. It barely made a sound as she slid it before me. A long, thin candle glowed in the middle of the table.

"Bon appétit," she said from the chair next to mine.

"I didn't know you were French."

"It sounds better than *mangia*."

I wasn't as hungry as I'd been the other night. I still ate it all. We chatted about the weather, the weekend, the common relatives and acquaintances that bind a small town together. When she mentioned the holiday season, I thought about the day after Christmas. I coughed hard through the food.

She jumped up. "Do you need some water?"

I waved her off. "This meal is magnificent. You really have outdone yourself. If I keep coming here, I'll need to visit the tailor so he can alter my trousers."

She smiled again. As her hand went back to cover her mouth, I grabbed it.

"That smile is far too beautiful to hide."

She looked at her hand, covered by mine. Our eyes met. I pulled my hand away. She reached for it as I did. She held it. Our eyes met a second time. She pulled away.

"I don't know what's gotten into me."

"Whatever it is," I said, "I like it."

She inched her hand back toward mine. I stood and kissed her. I felt her flinch, but she let me continue. I leaned against the table. My fork tumbled to the floor with a clang.

She pulled away after several seconds. "I really don't know what's gotten into me."

"Don't apologize, Carolina. You're human. I'm human. The fact that we've been human a little longer than everyone else doesn't change that."

I kissed her again. She didn't resist. She drew her head away and whispered into my ear. "How I wish they weren't downstairs."

"They won't be here all night. Once we're finished, we'll all leave. Maybe I'll come back?"

Her eyes danced in the silence. "I do believe I'd like that. I'd like that very much."

"Then it's settled. Wait for me. But if you fall asleep, I'll understand."

Her eyes narrowed. "How old do you think I am, Mr. Dacey?"

"I'm just being courteous."

"We're far too seasoned for courtesies." She kissed me again. She led me to the basement door. I opened it and began shuffling through the steps to the brown concrete below.

I looked back at her and smiled again as I moved down the stairs.

Twelve

NOVEMBER 25, 1973

JIMMY DACEY

I GOT TO the basement and turned toward them, slouching in their lawn chairs and drinking the same crappy beer while force-feeding the white cloud above them.

"Look," Jerry said. "The old man got a shit-eating grin."

I kept the smile alive. "Who, me?" I said.

"I don't see no other old men down here."

"C'mon," Cashews said, "show a little respect."

"I'm in a good mood," I said. "I won't apologize for that, especially not at my age."

"None of us should be in a good mood until this thing is done," Jerry said. "We should be worried about what happens if it goes sideways. Being in a good mood don't make no sense right now, for none of us."

A can of beer waited for me on the table. I opened it. I swallowed and belched. "Like I said, I won't apologize for being in a good mood."

Jerry watched me as I sat there smiling. "Why are you so happy?" he said. "You get lucky with the old broad?"

Cashews reached over and slapped Jerry. Jerry grabbed Cashews by the wrist and bent it backward. Cashews cried out.

Without thinking, I threw my beer at Jerry's head. The steel can hit him in the cheek and bounced away, splashing foam on his face and hair.

The good news was it made Jerry let go of Cashews. The bad news was Jerry stood up and pulled a revolver from the back of his waistband. He pointed it at my forehead.

"What the fuck is wrong with you, old man?"

"Quiet, Jerry," Cashews said, springing to his feet. "You'll wake up Aunt Carol."

I looked at Jerry. I needed him to know I wasn't scared of him. "If the yelling didn't wake her up, a gunshot might do the trick."

"The old man got a death wish," Jerry said. "We don't need to be working with somebody who got a death wish."

"I don't have a death wish, but I'm not afraid to die."

"There ain't no difference," Jerry said.

"Sure there is. I don't wish to die, but I don't fear death. And here I thought you were the smart one."

Cashews and Jerry looked at each other. It looked like they didn't know which one should be offended.

"Just put the gun down," Cashews said. "We got enough shit to deal with. We don't need to be driving to Ohio and digging tonight."

Jerry turned back toward me. "I will if he apologizes."

"For what?" I said.

"You just threw a fucking beer can in my face." He put his finger on the lump that was already growing below his eye.

"You just put a fucking gun in my face. How's about we call it even?"

"Let's call it a night instead," Cashews said. "Everybody's a little on edge."

"I was fine. I was in a good mood."

"Sit down," Jerry said to Cashews. "I started it. I was out of line."

"I'll accept your apology," I said.

"I ain't never apologized. All I said is I was out of line. That ain't no apology."

"I'll accept you saying you were out of line."

"That ain't how it works," Jerry said.

Cashews sat down and pointed an index finger at each of us. "Let's just forget about it. We don't need this shit. What we're planning to do is hard enough. If we start fighting, it'll never work. Then we'll all be stacked in the same hole."

The basement went silent after that. I waited a couple of beats before speaking.

"I call the top."

That made Jerry laugh. Which made Cashews laugh. Which made me laugh.

I laughed until I realized how close I'd come to never laughing again.

"So," I said, "where are we on this thing of ours?"

"I'll be getting the dynamite from a guy in Pennsylvania," Cashews said. "Up in Erie. That part'll be easy."

"Getting the dynamite and setting the bomb were always going to be the easy part," I said. "We all know what the hard part will be."

"Fucking Vinny," Jerry said.

"Yes," I said. "Fucking Vinny."

"What are we gonna do about fucking Vinny?" Cashews said.

"I think I have an idea," I said. "Cashews, can your man in Erie get some canisters of tear gas, and maybe a few gas masks?"

"If he can get dynamite, I figure he can swing those."

"Good," I said. And then I explained my idea.

After I finished, Jerry nodded and smiled. "Maybe I was wrong about you."

"Why, if I didn't know better," I said, "I'd say you're now in a good mood, too."

Jerry shook his head, but he kept smiling. He pointed at me and looked at Cashews.

"I don't know where you found this guy, but I think he missed his calling. He could have been the boss. Maybe the boss of all the bosses."

Thirteen

NOVEMBER 26, 1973

JIMMY DACEY

I DROVE THE Corvette through the alley. I could hear gravel crunching under the tires.

It was early. The edges of darkness carried vague hints of the dawn to come. After my time with Carolina, I dozed off. I still would have been asleep if she hadn't accidentally jabbed an elbow into my ribs.

I stopped near the garage. I went through the paces of putting the Corvette away. I kept looking around, looking mainly for Vinny.

I took slow, careful steps to the back of the house. If Vinny was lurking, it wouldn't matter if I ran, walked, or crawled. That didn't stop me from acting as if the concrete was a high wire and my last name was Wallenda.

The Flying Wallendas. Sometimes they fly, sometimes they die. I hoped to emulate the flying kind, as long as I could.

I unlocked the door to the kitchen. I searched for anything that was out of place. Not that I took a clear mental picture before I left.

It all seemed normal. I had a weird feeling, nevertheless. I assumed I was being paranoid. It's not like I didn't have reason to be.

Was it too early to drink? Or was it too late? I was too rattled to care.

What happened with Carolina was unexpected. After my wife died, I hadn't even considered the possibility of anyone else.

Did I feel guilty? Not really. Did I feel shame? Why should I? Still, constantly worrying about Vinny made me feel like I needed some whisky.

I poured something close to a double shot of Canadian Club into a juice glass. I took off my coat and put it over one of the chairs at the kitchen table. I sat in the seat next to it.

I sipped, waiting for gray daylight to peek through the windows. Before it did, I got up and flipped the light switch. I opened the drawers by the sink until I found a notebook.

It was new. It felt thick and sturdy. I had no idea how long it had been in there. There was a small orange sticker with the price stamped on it. Twenty-nine cents.

I removed the notebook and a pen and went back to the chair. I took another drink. I opened the cover.

The horizontal blue lines began to hypnotize me. Or maybe it was the Canadian Club. I took another drink. I stared at the page.

I took the cap from the tip of the pen. I stared at the page some more. I drank the rest of the whisky.

I fetched the bottle. I poured. I drank. I stared at the page. I poured some more. I stared at the page.

I gripped the pen in my left hand. I pressed through its goopy tip on the top line. I wrote in capital letters.

LAST

I sat back and looked at the word. I kept going.

WILL AND TESTAMENT

On the second blue line, I wrote *and other stuff*.

I put the pen down. I drank more whisky. I stared at the page. I picked up the pen. I started writing some more.

It took me at least an hour, maybe two. I counted the pages. Eighteen. Double-sided and single-spaced.

When I finished, I didn't read it. I closed the notebook and put it back in the drawer. I pushed the chair tight against the kitchen table.

I checked the clock over the oven. It was just after eight. I went upstairs. I removed my suit. I sat on the edge of the bed in boxers, undershirt, and socks. I decided to lay back and rest my eyes before showering and going to work.

The phone started ringing at noon.

Fourteen

NOVEMBER 26, 1973

JIMMY DACEY

I HURRIED TO answer without thinking who it might be. I should have known.

"Where the fuck you at?"

"I must have dozed off."

"Didn't you sleep last night?"

"I guess I overslept."

"I thought you was dead," Vinny said.

"I'm alive and well."

"If you wanna stay that way, get your ass in there. You got customers waiting."

"I'll be there in ten minutes."

"The last guy I thought I'd need to tell the hours to is the guy who was there all the time."

"It won't happen again."

"I knew something wasn't right about you."

"I'm sorry." I was a little sharp with him, which was easier to do without him glaring at me from behind that nose with an empty sand trap at the end of it. "It was an accident. As I've told you, if you have someone else who's available to do the job, feel free to hire him."

"You keep saying that because you know I ain't got nobody else. As of right now, I'm gonna start looking."

"Paul made it clear the other day it's too late for me to be replaced."

"It's too late for you to get out. It ain't too late for you to be replaced."

"What are you implying, sir?"

"You know, all that fancy talk won't mean a damn thing when it's time."

"Time for what?"

"For now, it's time to get your ass down there. But don't act like you don't know what you got yourself into. That proper gentleman bullshit won't matter. You got your only verbal message the other day. The next one won't be. I don't give a fuck how old you are."

The line went dead. I stared at the receiver before fumbling to put it back on the square base. I missed. The plastic handle bounced on the floor. I could hear the faint sound of the dial tone. I left it there and moved as fast as I could to get myself ready.

It took more than ten minutes. I should have known it would. When I parked the Buick, it was just after twelve-thirty. Three of the regulars stood by the door. I pushed through my limp and forced a smile.

"Glad to see you didn't end up like the last one," one of them said.

That made me drop the keys.

THE DOOR FLEW open just after three. In came Cashews, more sweaty and fidgety than usual. His eyes moved like he was looking for something but not seeing anything. He eventually focused on me. He pointed toward the back with a skinny finger. I saw a scab near the tip of it.

I tried to walk without attracting any more attention than Cashews had with his entrance. I didn't check to see if he was following.

The office wasn't much to look at. No desk, lots of clutter. Holes in the wall. Cracked and peeling paint. Water stains on the ceiling. Long, twisted strips with dead and dying flies stuck to them. I went in and waited for Cashews.

"What the hell happened today?"

"I overslept."

"By two fucking hours? For your sixth day on the job?"

"It's my fifth."

"That don't make it no better. I got my ass reamed by Vinny. He said he went by your house last night and your car was out front, but for some reason he thinks you wasn't there."

"That's because he saw that my car wasn't there on Thanksgiving night."

"That would've been nice to know."

"I should have told you. I handled it. I said I was at my wife's sister's house."

"If your car was there last night, how did you get to the meeting?"

"It's not my only car."

"Well, Vinny's suspicious. I can't blame him. You've been here like clockwork every day as a customer, and now you're a no-show on your sixth day on the job?"

"Fifth."

"Again, that don't make it no better."

"So what do we do now?"

"We need to be more careful. We can't afford no more fuckups. Vinny's smarter than you think. He can sniff out bullshit."

I trained my eyes on his misshapen face. I wanted to see his reaction to what I said next. "Do you think he's trying to sniff you out?"

"I know how to deal with him. He didn't ask nothing about me. He's focused on you. And that ain't good for you."

"He told me he's looking for a replacement."

"He told me the same thing."

"What happens when he finds one?"

"That ain't a conversation for right now."

"Should we accelerate our timetable?"

"I need to talk to Jerry. Maybe we got no choice."

"Today's the twenty-sixth. We have exactly one month. How much sooner could we do it?"

"A week. Maybe two."

"How about Wednesday the twelfth?"

"I think Paul's having some kind of Christmas party the next night."

"Maybe we could be having a party of our own the next morning instead."

"This ain't time to get cute."

"Would we not celebrate our success?"

"I'm trying to let you know how serious this shit is. I can't afford to have Vinny lean on you. He has ways to make people talk."

"You don't have to worry about me."

"I already am."

"You can stop. It'll be fine. He'd never get a thing out of me."

"It ain't fine. I'll talk to Jerry. Just me this time. It's too hot right now for us to be seen together."

"You realize we were just seen together a few minutes ago?"

I could tell Cashews realized he'd made a mistake by coming to the bar. "I didn't have no choice. And that's your fault, not mine."

"What am I supposed to do?"

"Lay low. No more mistakes. And when you go to sleep tonight, make sure you set an alarm."

"Should I do anything else?"

"Yeah, get on your knees next to your bed and pray he don't find somebody else to do this job in the next two weeks."

Fifteen

NOVEMBER 27, 1973

VINNY

I SHOWED UP on Tuesday to make the collection. The old man did a good job with the paperwork, I'll give him that much.

I stood at the bar and spread everything out. I counted the money, nice and slow. I did it twice. I wanted him to be nervous.

I wasn't really looking for somebody else to do the job. I just had to keep him in line. I had to make him sweat. I had to make him think he could end up in Ohio. I knew there was no way Paul would sanction it, at least not yet. Not that I wanted to kill an old man. It wouldn't have been the first old man I killed. Or the second, now that I think about it. Still, he'll need to do worse than show up two hours late to get Paul to give me the nod.

I decided to count it again. I don't know how long I stood there. Maybe half an hour, maybe more.

"Everything looks OK," I said. "I'm gonna check this one more time at Paul's."

"I don't know how this business has performed in the past, but as best I can tell we had a good week."

"There's more than one way to judge a week. Like I said, it looks good. But that don't change things."

I gave him my best evil eye to see just how nervous he was. If he was, the old bastard wasn't showing it.

"I understand," he said.

"I still ain't sure you do. I still ain't sure I do. The best thing you can do is keep doing what you're doing, just like you've been doing it. With no more accidents."

"You have my word."

"I had your word before. I ain't so sure about your word. Then again, I never was."

JIMMY DACEY

I STAYED AT the bar until the basketball games tipped off. I kept thinking about Vinny's vow to find someone else. I hoped he saw from my work that he wouldn't find anyone who could do the job as well as I can. That had to count for something. The goal of any business is to make as much money as possible, with minimal headaches. Yes, I had foolishly fallen asleep on Monday morning. I'm determined not to let that happen again.

I drove the Buick back to my house. I went through all the rooms, looking for any sign that someone had been there while I was gone. If so, they'd left no traces.

I opened a tin of soup with the electric device that had given my wife a real thrill the first time she used it, as if it was so difficult to use a manual can opener. That memory used to make my cry. It was finally starting to make me smile.

I ate slowly. I dipped buttered bread into the broth with noodles and small chunks of what was supposed to be chicken. I read the evening newspaper. After the food was gone, I went back to the bottle of Canadian Club. It was going fast. Pretty soon, I'd need to go to the liquor store and buy another one.

I took the whisky back to the table. I sat there, trying to enjoy the simple reality of existing. It was hard to do, now that my existence had an expiration date that could arrive sooner than expected.

The phone on the wall started to ring. I stared at it. I didn't want to get up. I wasn't interested in talking to anyone. It stopped.

A few minutes later, it started again. I decided I should answer, in case it was my daughter.

"Dacey residence," I said, as if anyone resided there other than me.

"James? Is that you?"

"Carolina?"

"I'm sorry to call. This isn't like me."

"I'm very glad to hear from you."

"I was a little confused after the other night."

"There's nothing to be confused about."

"I still don't know what's gotten into me. It's been a very long time since I behaved that way. I hope you won't think less of me."

"Heavens, no. I had a wonderful time."

I heard her exhale through the line. "I hope we'll have a chance to spend more time together. I'm not quite sure how this works. It's been so long."

"I'm not either. But I'll need you to be patient with me, at least for a little while."

"Patient?"

"I'll explain the next time we're together."

"Do you know when that will be? I'm not ashamed to admit my dance card is fairly open."

"Soon, I hope. For now, though, I have some things to take care of. I hope you understand."

"I know that if you're involved in something with Charles, there could be complications. My husband died a long time ago. He was in that same line of work."

"This line of work is a little new to me. As with anything else, there are some adjustments I need to make."

"I understand. And I'll be patient. I waited this long to have another man in my life. I can wait a little longer."

She wished me a good night. I waited for the line to click before hanging up.

I stopped and wondered whether anyone else might have been listening to what had been said. I told myself I'm being paranoid.

I reminded myself, in my current situation, it's probably good to be paranoid.

Sixteen

NOVEMBER 28, 1973

VINNY

CASHEWS RUNS A hardware store on Market Street, up by the tunnel. Last month he hired a guy who came back from Vietnam. That damn kid never shuts up.

Cashews makes decent money selling wrenches and screws and plungers and shit like that. It's a lot more than Bobby gets for shaving dogs' asses, or whatever he does there. Plus, we can sometimes sell some of the stuff we stole at Cashews's place.

I walked in and went straight for the back. The kid started flapping his trap. I ignored him and kept going, like I always did.

Cashews has a pool table in the storage room. He won it playing poker. He never plays pool, but he loves that stupid table. He keeps the felt covered and uses it like a desk. It always has papers all over it. He was messing with some of them when I pushed the door open hard enough to get his attention.

"I didn't know you was coming today," he said.

"I didn't either."

"That don't make sense."

I kept going until I was standing over him. "You know what else don't make sense? The new guy fucking your aunt."

Cashews pushed his chair back and stood up. "That kid ain't more than twenty-one. I know he's a little shell-shocked, but not enough to mess around with my aunt."

"I ain't talking about that new guy."

I watched his eyes. They didn't get too wide. He wasn't as surprised as he should have been. "Jimmy and Aunt Carol?"

"Tell me, how did Jimmy meet Aunt Carol?"

I kept watching him for anything. His eyes shifted a little bit, but not much.

"That old bastard. I invited him over for dinner the other night and he—"

"Which night?"

"Saturday."

"Bullshit. His car never left his house after he got home from the bar."

"I picked him up. She had a bunch of leftovers."

"Leftovers?"

"From Thanksgiving. Look, I know you probably ate tuna fish from a can last Thursday. Normal people get together around a table with way too much fucking food and then they spend the next week eating the rest."

"So you're saying you brought the old man to your aunt's house after his third day on the job to eat leftover turkey and stuffing?"

"It ain't what I'm saying. It's what happened."

"When did they have a chance to be more than dinner partners?"

"It must have happened when I had to run out for a few minutes."

"To where?"

"I got those rental units up on Edgington Lane. The power went out and I had to go fuck around with the fuse boxes."

"So you left?"

"The fuse boxes wasn't gonna fix themselves. They was just sitting there, drinking coffee. They're both adults. They're both single. They're old, but still they're human."

I kept watching him for something that would show he was feeding me a line of bullshit. As much as I didn't wanna think it, his story held up.

"How does any of that even matter?" he said.

"I've been keeping eyes and ears on the old man. Something ain't right about him. I already told you that. I got reason to think him and your aunt are an item, and I didn't know how something like that could've happened. Now, I guess I do."

"I guess you do."

"I hate to say it, but the old man does a pretty good job. I never seen paperwork as clean as what he puts together. It's way better than the shit you used to give me."

"I told you from the start I wasn't good at that. Taking bets is different than counting hammers and nails."

"It ain't really all that different."

"It is for me. That's why I vouched for him. I knew he could do it. I don't understand why you think a guy like that would be up to something. I don't think he's ever been up to anything his whole life."

"Maybe that's why I think he is. Seventy years of not being up to something is pretty good cover."

"He's just a guy who knows he's only got a few good years left. His wife died. He's lonely. That's probably why he started coming to the bar. That's probably why he wanted the job. It's probably why he was interested in Aunt Carol."

"I guess I can close the book on it and move on."

"I don't know why you ever opened it."

"Don't pretend to know what I do and why I do it. My job ain't like yours. You help make the money. I protect the thing that allows us to do it."

"If the biggest thing you have to worry about is some old man who probably never jaywalked, your job must not be as hard as I thought it was."

"My job is to spot any and all threats and take care of them."

"There must not be many threats, if worrying about who some old man is sleeping with is taking up your time. Unless you get off on that shit."

I leaned closer to Cashews. "Remember who you work for."

"You'd never ever let me forget it."

I wanted to punch him in the face. Maybe it would be an improvement. I also wanted to knock him down and stomp his head until it busted like a red grape. I knew it wasn't time for that. Not yet.

I turned around and left. I wasn't entirely done with this. If something was up, he'd go find a payphone and call the old man as soon as I left. Cashews was dumb, but he was smart enough to think I had his phone tapped, even if I hadn't gotten around to it. I also hadn't set up a tap at the bar, which was dumb of me.

At least I had the phone at the old man's house tapped, and that was what I would keep working with.

Seventeen

NOVEMBER 28, 1973

JIMMY DACEY

I STOOD BEHIND the bar, rinsing out glasses. Four of the regulars were in the room. Two played dominoes. Another sat at the table where I'd take a break from time to time. The other one sat at the bar, reading a newspaper and drinking beer.

I've started smoking again. I'm no longer worried about the tobacco shortening my life, not with other possibilities lurking.

It was almost noon. The bar never had much of a lunch crowd, for a very good reason; it doesn't serve lunch. Usually, there would be a spike in traffic after folks ate somewhere else and swung by to make a bet or two before going back to wherever they worked.

The phone rang. I walked over and answered.

"Has Vinny been there?"

"Who's this?

"The guy who used to work there."

"The guy who used to work here isn't capable of making phone calls."

"This ain't the time to fuck around," Cashews said.

"He hasn't been here today."

"He's coming. He tried to make me think he ain't. But he is."

"Well, I'll be here."

"He knows about you and Aunt Carol doing whatever you did."

"I don't know what you're talking about."

"I ain't the one you need to lie to, and you need a better story than that. I told him I picked you up at your house on Saturday night and that you ate Thanksgiving leftovers with us."

"How did that become the other thing?"

"I told him I had to leave, that there was an issue at rental units I got up the road. I told him something must have happened between you and Aunt Carol while I was gone."

"I'm very confused by this."

"You need to get unconfused, fast. Because I guarantee he's gonna be walking through that door soon, and he's gonna make sure our versions match."

"Is there anything else I need to know?"

"That's it. Saturday night. Leftovers. I drove you. I had to leave. I was gone maybe thirty minutes. You can fill in the gaps with Aunt Carol. I don't care what you say, but he knows something happened."

I turned away and cupped my palm over the mouthpiece. "Does he have the phone tapped at my house?"

"I wouldn't put it past him."

"So wouldn't he have this one tapped, too?"

"I think I got the wrong number," he said as he hung up.

CASHEWS

HOW FUCKING STUPID could I be? I used a payphone because I figured he had my line tapped, and I don't think he can listen to the line at the bar? That's what happens when you get nervous. You do stupid shit.

I pulled more coins out of my pants. I called the guy in Erie. I wrote his number down once. I went over it fifty times until I knew it by heart. Then I burned up the paper. Not too bad for somebody who does stupid shit.

I told him I need the stuff as soon as I can get it. I told him I'll pay extra. He said I could get it Saturday. That made me smile.

I stopped smiling when it hit me I couldn't drop everything and drive to Erie on a Saturday afternoon. I asked if I could pick it up in the middle of the night. That made him act weird, like he was gonna call it off. When I told him how much extra I'd pay for picking it up at night, he changed his tune about staying up really late, or getting up really early.

I went back to the store to get my keys. I told the kid I'd be back in maybe an hour. The kid started talking about his usual dumb shit. I told him it was fine and I left. I could hear him still going after I walked out.

I figured Vinny was going straight to Jimmy. That gave me a chance to go see Jerry at his five and dime in South Wheeling. I drove down there and parked a couple of streets away, just in case.

Jerry was in the back room with Pisspants Pete. I couldn't say what I needed to say with Pete hanging around. I told Jerry I needed to talk to him about a Christmas present. He got my meaning. He told Pisspants to take a hike. Once he was gone, I told Jerry that Paul needs to get his gift even sooner than we planned.

Eighteen

NOVEMBER 28, 1973

JIMMY DACEY

THE DOOR FLEW open with a crash that sounded like a cherry bomb going off in a broom closet. First, I saw the daylight. Then I saw the shoe. A big, flat contraption hanging in the air at the end of some sort of cockeyed karate kick.

Vinny lowered his foot and walked inside. He was the lion. I was the gazelle with a bad leg.

He stopped to inspect for damage. He seemed disappointed to find none.

"Good door," he said to anyone and no one. "Durable."

He turned to the room. It was me and four others.

"I got a question for everybody in here," he said while pointing a stubby finger at my forehead. "Has this one gotten a phone call in the last ten minutes?"

I tried to watch the others from my peripheral vision. I didn't want to turn my head their way. I couldn't afford to let Vinny think I was worried. I made a decision before anyone could speak.

"There was a call," I said. "My doctor's office."

Vinny focused on the others. "Is this true?" he said, scanning through each of them. None responded.

“Is it true?!” I could see the saliva spray against the light from the open doorway behind him.

“I don’t know who it was,” Pinky McGill replied from his seat at the bar. “I couldn’t hear the other end. Sounded like he was getting some kind of news.”

“News about what?” Vinny said. “News about someone showing up somewhere?”

“Didn’t notice nothing other than it sounded like he was getting some kind of news,” Pinky said.

I eased toward Vinny. I extended my hands and flickered my face into a smile. “Why don’t we go in the back and talk about this?” I said.

He looked at me, looked through me. He searched for any crack or glimpse or hint. He spun back to the others to see if anyone had anything to add. His attention returned to me. “Lead the way.”

I fought through my limp. He clomped behind me. His breath landed on the back of my neck, coating the spot where the barber had shaved away a collection of white fuzz that morning. I could hear others making for the exit. They were smart for getting while the getting was good.

“We’ve scared off the customers,” I said as Vinny closed the door.

“That’s the least of your worries.”

“Why are you concerned that my doctor’s office called?”

“I’m concerned that Cashews called.”

“Cashews doesn’t work for my doctor.”

“Don’t get cute, old man. I went to see Cashews before I came here. I figure he called you.”

“I haven’t heard from him in days.”

“Not since Sunday night, right? When you went to his house for dinner?”

“Actually,” I said, “that was Saturday night. He and his aunt had food from Thanksgiving. Since I didn’t have a proper meal that day, I decided to go.”

“So you drove there?”

"Cashews insisted on picking me up. I didn't mind. I don't see too well anymore when I drive at night."

"So you went there, you ate dinner with Cashews and his aunt, and then Cashews brung you home?"

"Yes and no. He had to step out for a bit. Something about rental property he owns. Once he finished with that, he brought me to my house."

Vinny eased closer to me. "So then it was you and his aunt, all alone? I'm sure a gentleman like you wouldn't be trying anything with Cashews's aunt."

"They have a wide assortment of magazines at the shop around the corner if you have a prurient interest that needs to be satiated."

"What the hell did you just say?"

"What I'm saying is it would be impolite for me to talk about anything that might have happened between Cashews's aunt and me. Surely that's not why you're here."

"I'm here because something's going on."

"I wish I could help you. From my perspective, all that's going on is I'm doing my job to the best of my ability when I'm here, and I'm living my life when I'm not. Given that I don't really have much life left to live, I hope you won't begrudge me that. And, please, spare me the subtle threats that I might have even less life left to live. It's tiresome."

Vinny's eyes flared at that. "Are you fucking with me, old man? You're the one who decided to walk into this world. You get treated like anybody else. And when anybody else gives me reason to think something's going on, this is what I do."

"Maybe you only think something's going on because you're used to dealing with—how should I best put this?—a bunch of fucking morons."

A sound emerged from deep within Vinny. It was visceral, guttural. It was a chuckle that became a laugh that exploded from his mouth and evaporated.

"You're smart," he said. "Don't never think you're smarter than me. Out there, maybe you are. In this life, you don't know jack shit."

I nodded at him, trying to seem overwhelmed by his intellect.

"I'll try to remember that," I said.

Nineteen

NOVEMBER 28, 1973

JIMMY DACEY

I STAYED AT the bar until closing time. The regulars who ran out didn't return. No one else came, either. Word apparently got around.

As soon as I got home, I started searching for bugs. They would have been easier to find if I had any idea what I was looking for. I checked inside lamps and light fixtures and under furniture and behind picture frames. I drank Canadian Club until I no longer cared about finding them.

Maybe they didn't bother to put them there. It's not as if anyone ever comes to my house. I assumed the phone was tapped. I have no idea how it works. I checked them both, in the kitchen and the bedroom, for anything that seemed out of place.

I know they're listening to the calls. It's the only way they could have known about me and Carolina.

I went to the drawer in the kitchen. I took out the notebook with my will in it. I read it again. I put it back in the drawer and pushed it shut.

I saw the keys to the Corvette, still on the rack where I'd left them. "Do they know about you, too?" I whispered.

I put on my shoes, my hat, and my jacket. I tightened my tie. I slid my arms through the sleeves of my overcoat. I went out the back door. I probably shouldn't have been driving, but I told myself I hadn't had enough Canadian Club to be intoxicated. Even if I was wrong, it wasn't nearly as stupid as the other things I'd been doing.

The air cleared my mind, just enough to find the garage without staggering or stumbling. I got in the car and drove back to the house on Locust Avenue.

CASHEWS

JERRY DIDN'T LET me go too far at his store before saying we shouldn't talk about it there, just in case. We decided to meet that night at Aunt Carol's.

Did they bug her place? She don't go out much. Jerry said there was a chance they snuck in while she was asleep. I didn't buy it. Vinny had just found out about Aunt Carol and Jimmy the night before.

Could we have met someplace else? I didn't wanna get too cute. We got a decent head start. If somebody saw Jerry and me out someplace, it would have been goodnight, Irene.

I told Jerry he should walk to Aunt Carol's, through the side streets. He said it was too far. I told him he needed the exercise. He told me to go fuck myself. He grumbled some more before saying he'd do it. When Jerry showed up, he still bitched about the hike. I told him walking five miles is better than riding to the cemetery in the back of a hearse.

Aunt Carol was good about giving me room to do what I needed to do. It helped she was married to somebody who used to be in this life. She knows when to ask questions, and she knows when not to. I could tell she wanted to ask questions when I showed up all nervous and jumpy. She didn't.

After Jerry and me went downstairs, we talked through things. The bomb would be easy. We still needed a plan to deal with Vinny. We had to figure out how to get Paul to drive. Jerry wanted to let Vinny pick up Paul like usual. He said maybe the bomb wouldn't go off until after Paul was inside. I wasn't willing to risk my life on maybes. Tilt fuses can blow even if the car hasn't rolled. Just a jerk of the chassis from shifting the gears could do it.

We skipped the beers that night. We smoked two or three packs of cigarettes to calm our nerves as we kept talking.

"I wish the old man was here," Jerry said. "He's smart."

"The old man can't come around for a while. He told us what we need to do. Now we just have to do it."

"I still don't get how this is gonna work."

"Vinny makes his rounds on Tuesdays and Wednesdays," I said. "He does the count on Wednesday night, after he drives Paul home."

"How do you know that?"

"How do you not know it?"

"I don't pay attention."

"He'll be sitting at that table out front after he takes Paul home, counting all the money and filling the envelopes."

"He fills the envelopes?"

"Who do you think does it, the tooth fairy?"

"I just said I don't pay attention."

"Pay attention now. When he's in there doing the count, we bust a window and throw tear gas into the room. We let it do its thing. We go in with the gas masks on and shoot him."

"How do you know tear gas will work on that mutherfucker?"

"Tear gas works on every mutherfucker. This is military grade shit I'm getting from my guy in Erie."

"He has at least two guns on him. All the time."

"He can have a nuclear bomb strapped to his ass for all I care. Once that gas kicks in, he ain't doing shit."

"Killing that bastard ain't gonna be as easy as you think. But let's say we do. Then we set the place on fire?"

"We get Vinny's body to the back room. You know, the place where

Paul has that desk he's so proud of? We come out front, we call Paul and say his place is on fire. Then we turn it into a Christmas tree and get the hell out."

"That won't be enough to get Paul to show up."

"When we tell him Vinny is tied up in the back room, he will. Even Paul ain't so big of a prick that he'll let his top guy burn to death. If he is, well, maybe he'll show up to save his desk."

Jerry tried to light his next cigarette with what was left from the one he was smoking. His hands was shaking.

"How are you gonna do this later if you're that nervous now?" I said.

"I'll figure it out."

"I ain't doing it alone."

"Why can't you? You make it sound like it's a breeze."

"I'm already driving to Erie in the middle of the night to get the dynamite and the tear gas and the gas masks, and I'm setting the bomb."

"You're doing the easy stuff. Killing Vinny is the hard part."

"We're in this together," I said. "We both need to take out Vinny. That's the plan. I don't care if you need booze or pills or whatever to get yourself ready. You just better be ready."

"What if I go to Erie? That part don't make me nervous."

"He almost backed out when I said I wanted to get it in the middle of the night. If I tell him somebody else is coming, he'll call the whole thing off."

"Fine. I don't have to like it, but I'll do it."

"I'm going to Erie to get the shit and I'm putting the bomb under the car. I don't have to like that, but I'm doing it."

"And now you wanna do this next Wednesday night? That's three weeks before we said."

"You really don't pay attention."

"I just wanna be sure."

"I'm sure. You're sure. And I'm sure as shit not sleeping on Saturday night when I drive back and forth to Erie, on top of all the other stuff we have to do to make it look like nothing is going on."

"I won't be sleeping on Saturday night either," Jerry said.

"You're not coming with me."

"That ain't the point. I can tell you right now I ain't sleeping any night at all until this fucking thing is done."

"Then I guess it's good we're doing it earlier than we said."

Twenty

NOVEMBER 28, 1973

JIMMY DACEY

I STOOD ON the porch, hat in my hands. She opened the front door, just a bit. I heard her say my name.

She threw a hand up, showing me her palm. "I don't have my face on. And my hair's not done."

"I'm sorry to just show up. I wanted to see you. This was the only way."

"This is unexpected," she said.

"I wanted to call. I couldn't."

"Is your phone out of order?"

"Yes and no."

"Just give me a few minutes. Come in and sit down."

"Are you sure?"

"I wouldn't have it any other way."

I could see both ends of a smile sneaking out from behind her hand.

VINNY

I DROVE TO the old man's house, after taking Paul home. I saw the car parked out front. I still had a feeling he wasn't there.

I pulled up the street and turned onto an alley. My Ford was almost too big to fit. I saw the back of his house. There was a garage. The door was up.

I shut off the engine. I grabbed a flashlight from the glove compartment. I got out slow. When I stood up, I could feel little rocks on the bottoms of my shoes. I tried to make no sound. It wasn't easy.

I didn't need the flashlight until I got in the garage. I flipped it on. I tried not to shine the beam out the windows on either side.

There was a wooden rack running across the back wall with old coffee cans and boxes. More stuff than I would have thought from someone who pushed paper his whole life.

He had tools. Lots of them. Claw hammer. Ball peen hammer. Mallet. A whole bunch of screwdrivers. Vise grips. Wrenches.

I scanned the wall with the flashlight. There was a sign to the left of the rack.

Corvette Garage. Life's Too Short To Drive Slow Cars.

I turned around and looked at the spot behind me in the garage. I looked back at the sign and then again at the empty floor.

"The son of a bitch got two cars."

JIMMY DACEY

I SAT AT her kitchen table, sipping from the glass of ginger ale and ice she poured before going upstairs. I tried to relax. We exchanged smiles when she returned.

"Have you eaten?" she said.

"It's too late for dinner."

"My kitchen never closes."

"That makes it a very good kitchen indeed."

She sat next to me. "What's wrong? I always know when something's wrong."

"Do you know what your nephew does for a living?"

She shrugged. “He does plenty of things. I know some of those things aren’t conventional.”

“They’re also not legal.”

“He and that other one were here earlier.”

“How closely did I miss them?”

“They left an hour ago. They were down in the basement, like always.”

“Did they use the phone?”

“They never do.”

“I doubt it’s happening yet, but there’s a chance someone is listening to the line.”

“In my house? Why would they care about me?”

“Because you called me. And they’re listening to my line.”

“Why on earth do they care about you?”

I told her.

VINNY

I TURNED OFF the flashlight and walked to the back of the house. I went up the steps to the porch. I tried the knob. It turned easy. I should’ve figured he wasn’t somebody who felt like he should lock his doors.

I went into the kitchen. There was a glass on the table with ice that hadn’t melted all the way. I picked it up and sniffed. The old man had been boozing.

I put the glass on the ring of water. I walked around and opened some of the cabinet doors. The stuff inside—plates, bowls, glasses—looked dusty.

I went to the refrigerator and popped the door. It looked like he kept a lot of the same stuff I did, which was not much stuff at all.

I kept looking around. There was drawers. I pulled them all. One had all his forks and knives and spoons. Another had spatulas and shit. Another one had envelopes with bills and papers.

I saw a notebook in there. I pulled it out and flipped the cover. I saw the words on the top of the front page.

I sat down at the table and read the whole thing.

Twenty-one

NOVEMBER 29, 1973

JIMMY DACEY

I SPILLED MY guts to Carolina. I hadn't planned to be so candid. I knew I could trust her. I told her if we didn't talk now, I wasn't sure when we could. I told her we had to assume both of our houses would be bugged, soon.

She listened to what I said, without saying much back. She said when she opened the door for me on Thanksgiving night she assumed I was involved with whatever her nephew and his friend were doing. Once she saw me, she didn't care.

Her husband had lived that life, and he'd been gone a long time. She had no qualms about knowing someone else who was in that same line of work.

I told her I was new to this world. She knew. She'd heard of me during my time as an accountant. She wasn't sure how I'd gotten caught up with her nephew. Again, she didn't care. She said she'd been lonely for too long.

I couldn't tell if she was surprised when I told her we planned to make a move on the boss. She said she'd never liked Paul Verbania. I got the impression he might have had something to do with the death of her husband. She didn't say that. She didn't even imply it. It was just a feeling I got. I know that doesn't make much sense. As she was talking, it did.

After I told her my story, we talked some more. About little things. The weather. The holidays. The poor job her nephew had done putting a tilted tree in her front room.

We laughed about that. Before I finished, she stood up. She took my hand. She led me to the stairs. We climbed in a slow, even pace. We entered the bedroom with a sense of reverence to the fact that she had shared it with her husband, long ago. That element definitely had been missing the last time, when it was sudden and fresh passion.

The passion eventually returned, without the awkwardness of the first time. I tried to be gentle. I could tell she appreciated it, until her own desires overpowered mine. I liked it. How could I not? I'm old, not dead. Well, not dead yet.

After it was done, I told her I should leave. I said my house was possibly being watched. I explained I'd brought my second car. I told her it was just a matter of time before they figure out that I have it, and that I'm using it.

She didn't protest, even though I could tell she wanted me to stay. After I dressed, she gave me a gentle kiss. I felt eighteen again. I loved that feeling. I still had to go.

I drove the Corvette home. I followed the same steps from the garage. I walked to the back porch. I twisted the knob on the door. I pushed it open into the kitchen.

Twenty-two

NOVEMBER 29, 1973

VINNY

"We got a problem."

I said those words to Paul as soon he got in the Cadillac the morning after I went to the old man's house.

"We got plenty of problems," he said.

"This is a new problem." I turned the rearview mirror so I could lock eyes with him.

"You drive and talk. I'll sit and listen."

I backed the Cadillac out the driveway and headed for town.

"The new guy who's making book at Mesagne's place. The old man. He's up to something."

"Him again?"

"You told me to be looking for things that ain't right."

"I've known my share of old men. There ain't something right about most of them, mainly because they're old."

"I went to his house last night. He wasn't there. He's got another car. I think it's a Corvette."

"How's that a problem?"

"I went inside his house."

"You broke in?"

"The door was unlocked. I checked the place out."

"And?"

"And what?"

"I figure there's something. Why else would you be acting like this?"

"I looked through his drawers. I found a notebook."

"Well, now you got my interest."

"It was his will. I read the whole thing, twice. He leaves it all to one person."

"That's what some wills do."

"This one leaves every penny to Mesagne's kid."

Twenty-three

NOVEMBER 29, 1973

JIMMY DACEY

I LOOKED TO see if anything seemed out of sorts. I smelled the air, breathed it deep into my lungs. I could feel beads of sweat forming on my forehead. My heart began to thump, in a very different way than it had at Carolina's house.

I studied the kitchen table. I focused on the chair. I always push it all the way in. It was sticking out, a bit. My eyes circled the room, left and right and up and down.

"Hello?" I said. My voice sounded weak. Weak and scared. "Is anyone here?"

I listened for anything that would suggest I should run. Not that I could. Not that I could even walk very fast.

I focused on trying to speak with more volume and authority.

"I have a gun," I lied. "I'm not afraid to use it."

I stopped and waited and listened.

I moved past the kitchen and into the dining room, listening for anything that would let me know whether whoever had been in the house was still there.

"Hello?" I said. "This is your last chance. I shoot first and ask questions never."

I listened some more. I cocked my head in the darkness beyond the kitchen. I leaned with an ear, deep into the unknown. I decided the house was empty. I looked back at the chair that wasn't where it had been when I left. I walked back to the kitchen door and locked it.

Twenty-four

NOVEMBER 29, 1973

JIMMY DACEY

I TRIED TO sleep. Every creak and crack made my eyes fly open. I walked down to the couch. If anyone would be breaking in, at least I'd know it was coming. Not that I could do anything about it.

I kept waking up, shifting my gaze in the two-thirds darkness for real or imagined sounds. Once daylight began to show itself through the front windows that faced the main road, I finally fell into a sustained slumber. Right up until the alarm clock I'd brought from the bedroom started to rattle two hours later.

I thought about turning it off. I couldn't. I forced my way upstairs to get ready for work. I went to the kitchen for a cup of instant coffee before heading back to the bathroom to brush my teeth. That's when I stopped cold.

The drawer. It wasn't completely closed. The notebook was in there. The one with the message I had so carefully written. The message that made clear to the world my affinity and affection for the son of the man who had been killed by Paul Verbania barely a month earlier.

I walked to the drawer. I pulled it out to see the notebook was still inside. I pressed the drawer closed. I went back upstairs without making coffee.

VINNY

I PARKED THE Cadillac around the corner from the bar, in a spot where I could see the top of the front door when it opened or closed. Paul sat behind me, like always.

"The old man is late again," I said.

"What time does he usually show up?" Paul said.

"Ten. He overslept on Monday. Or so he said."

"Maybe this time he died in his sleep."

"That would make things a lot easier."

"Maybe that's what you should do."

"What?"

"Make him die in his sleep. All it takes is a pillow. It would be simple."

"I'd need to talk to him first."

"So talk to him, then do the pillow thing."

I turned around and looked right at Paul. "I don't think it would be so simple if he knows it's coming. Sure, he's old. But he'd fight back. It wouldn't look like he just died."

Paul waved his hand. "You're probably right."

I turned back around. "I'll just take him to the warehouse on the island. I'll figure out what he's been up to, whether anybody else is involved."

"What could the old man be up to? Didn't you say he was an accountant?"

"People can change. Not many accountants retire to become bookies."

"He's an old man. He don't know enough to be up to anything."

"He was with Cashews on Saturday night."

"They went to his aunt's house for dinner, right? And then the old bastard had himself some dessert. Unless you think the aunt's in on it, too."

"Maybe she knows something," I said.

"We don't fuck with civilians."

"How do we know she ain't more than that? Maybe she knows what you did to her husband."

"That prick had it coming."

"She might not see it that way. Maybe she holds a grudge."

"It was twenty-five years ago. She would've done something about it by now."

"If you don't want me to talk to her, I won't. I wouldn't rule it out, at least not until after I talk to the old man."

"I'm not sure when your talk with the old man is gonna happen. Here's hoping he only overslept."

"What else would it be?"

"If he's tight with Mesagne's kid, maybe he did the same thing Mesagne's kid did. Packed his shit and scrammed."

Twenty-five

NOVEMBER 29, 1973

CHESTER MALONEY HUSTLED back to his office in the far corner of the third floor at the First National Bank of Kittanning. Four closings so far that afternoon, one to go. He held a fresh cup of stale coffee in one hand and a thin black attaché case in the other. He spotted the new messages on his desk.

Pink sheets made a pile that looked like a short deck of unshuffled cards, *While You Were Out* printed on each one. They showed the names of the people who had called or stopped by. His secretary had filled in the usual information, checking *Please Call* or *Will Call Again*. Or *Wants to See You*.

He sat in the wooden chair with three squeaky wheels and the one that often got stuck in place. He pulled himself toward the metal desk. He began to flip through the messages, seven in all. When he got to the fifth, the phone to his right began ringing, long and piercing and sustained.

He ignored it. He lifted the pink square closer to his face. He studied it while the phone rang.

"Marcia!" he said. "Marcia! Come here!"

She stood in the doorway while the phone continued to ring. "Are you going to answer it or should I?"

He held up the slip. "This one," he said. "When did he call?"

"Whenever it says on the sheet," she said.

He looked at it again. He hadn't noticed it said thirty-five minutes after two. "Sorry," Maloney said. "You're right." He held it up again. "You took this message?"

"I'm pretty sure I took all of them."

"And these are all for me?"

Marcia smiled through her confusion. "I don't know who else they'd be for. I said, 'Chester Maloney's office' when I answered each one. Nobody said they had the wrong number."

He stood and walked toward her, showing her the sheet. "This one," he said. "He wants me to meet him at the Downtown Bar and Grille at four thirty?"

"He sounded like a nice man," she said. "Do you know him? I asked what it was regarding and he said that wouldn't be necessary. I know you said I'm supposed to be more thorough than that but he was so friendly I just didn't think to be."

Maloney looked once again at the message from James Dacey.

"Did you tell him I have a closing at four?"

"He said he'll wait," Marcia replied. "He really did seem like a very nice man."

VINNY

I WALKED BACK to the Cadillac. I'd parked it across the street from the old man's house, right behind his Buick.

"He's gone," I said. "He took that Corvette from the garage. Packed in a hurry. That will I told you about is gone."

"Just like I thought, the old man is on the lam," Paul said. Then he sat up and slapped his hand against the top of his bald head. "He probably knows where the kid is."

"The will didn't say nothing about where the kid is."

"Why would it? It don't need to. But if anyone knows where that kid is, it's the old man."

"Now if we only knew where the old man is."

"We'll find him."

"We ain't found the kid, and it's been more than a month."

"We didn't have no good leads," Paul said.

"I know that well."

"That ain't my point. On this one, we got a possible lead."

"Who? Cashews's aunt?"

"He's too smart to tell her something. But he's got a daughter in Pennsylvania. I bet she knows where he is."

"You said we don't fuck with civilians. I know you made it sound to the old man like you'd go after his family, but I've heard you say shit like that before to scare a guy who don't know better."

"There's a way to get the information without fucking with his family. Or maybe this is the one time we make an exception."

"To kill somebody that ain't in this life? His daughter? Who else? Her husband? Her kids? We'd be crossing way too many lines. The heat would be on us big time."

"You're probably right. And I'll probably listen to you. Because you were right about the old man. He's up to something. The sooner we find him, the sooner we know what it is."

"So are we leaving the family in Pennsylvania alone?"

"I don't wanna take no options off the table," Paul said. "Maybe we start with the people we have here."

"So you want me to talk to Cashews's aunt?"

"First, I want you to talk to Cashews."

"I gotta be clear on this," I said. "Do you want me to talk to him, or do you want me to just talk to him?"

"For now, just talk to him. Beyond that, like I said, I don't wanna take no options off the table."

Twenty-six

NOVEMBER 29, 1973

CHESTER MALONEY WALKED inside the Downtown Bar and Grille right after four thirty. He waved to Lenny, the day-shift bartender. Lenny motioned Maloney to the edge of the bar.

"Some guy's been waiting for you," Lenny said. "Old guy. Looks rich."

"He's not as rich as he looks."

"Seems nice," Lenny said. "Little strange, though."

"That sounds like him."

"He asked me whether I spell my name the normal way, or like the guy from something that belongs to mice and men, whatever the hell that means. So I told him how I spell it. And then he said maybe I should spell it the other way. How the hell else would anybody spell Lenny?"

Maloney shrugged. Lenny offered a beer. Maloney said he'd take his at the table. Lenny told Maloney the man was in the corner of the inner room, up against the wall that was covered with mirrors.

Maloney worked his way past tables that were mostly empty. Workers prepared for the dinner crowd. In the other room, a smattering of early birds ate while Jimmy Dacey sat alone, drinking a beer and smoking a cigarette.

Jimmy brightened at the approach of his son-in-law.

"I thought you quit smoking," Maloney said.

"I started again."

Maloney smiled at the man he hadn't seen since the Fourth of July.

"May I sit?" Maloney said.

"By all means," Jimmy said, taking a drink of the beer. "Nice place. Bartender seems friendly."

"It's new," Maloney said. "I've been here a few times. Lenny used to work across the river."

"I had a good friend who was a bartender," Jimmy said. "Well, he wasn't really a bartender. He was, but he wasn't."

Maloney pushed round spectacles against his face with an index finger. "I'm curious, and I'll be blunt. Why are you here? I mean, I can understand why you'd come to the town where you daughter lives. Why are you here to see me?"

"Don't take this the wrong way," Jimmy said, "but your generation seems a little impatient. Surely you realized that, at some point during the conversation, I'd address why I asked you to meet me here."

Maloney smiled. "I'm sorry. I've had a busy day. I'm just concerned something is wrong. Why else would you come all the way here?"

The waitress who had been keeping Jimmy occupied with frosted mugs came back carrying a fresh one for him, and one for Maloney. "Thanks, Louise," Maloney said as she placed both on the table.

"You still working on the other one, Hon?" she said to Jimmy. He picked it up, drank the rest in one gulp and handed it to her. He thanked her by name.

"Alice will get nervous if I'm not home by five thirty," Maloney said after Louise left the table.

"Alice might be getting nervous either way," Jimmy said. He took a drink from the new mug. That prompted Maloney to lift his own and take a much longer drink than his father-in-law had.

CASHEWS

I WAS IN the back room of the hardware store, counting out the money for the week and sticking it in an envelope. The door flew open hard and Vinny came through. I heard the kid asking Vinny a question.

"Christ, don't he ever shut up?" Vinny said.

"I guess he likes you."

"That's a small fucking club." He walked over to where I was sitting.

I held the envelope up. "I was just getting the nut together. Not a bad week so far."

He slapped my hand. The envelope went flying. Money spilled out all over the place.

"What did you do that for?"

"Your employee is on the lam."

"You just seen him."

"Not that one."

"The old man took off?"

"He left this morning. Maybe last night."

"Why would he do that?"

"That's what I'm trying to find out."

Vinny hovered over me. I started to say something else. Before I could, he jammed his hand against my throat.

"You got one chance to get this right," he said. He squeezed tight and let go.

I coughed and rubbed my neck. "How would I know why the old man went on the lam? I barely know him."

"You know him well enough to invite him to your aunt's house for Thanksgiving leftovers."

"What was I supposed to do? We give him a job, we put him to work on Thanksgiving. He canceled his plans to go see his family without batting an eye. I'm sorry I don't treat the guy like shit. If you didn't realize it, he helped us out of a jam. And the guy does pretty good work."

"A monkey with no arms would've done good work compared to you."

"That was all the more reason for me to be nice to him. Just because I'm nice to him don't mean I know what he's up to."

"Where's Mesagne's kid?"

"How the fuck would I know? And what does that have to do with the old man?"

"Mesagne and the old man was pretty tight."

"We knew that when we hired him," I said.

"Maybe he knows where the kid is."

"You think he left town because he knows where Mesagne's kid is?"

"Have you seen anything—and I mean anything—that would make you think the old man knows where Mesagne's kid is?"

"The old man never talks about Mesagne. He's never mentioned Mesagne's kid. Not once. I don't think the old man even knows Mesagne's kid."

Vinny stood there, looking at me. I kept my eyes on his hands. Not that I could stop him from doing something. I just wanted to know when it was coming.

"You got any idea where the old man went?" he said.

"He has a daughter in Pennsylvania. But he ain't dumb. If he's gonna disappear, that's the last place he'd go, since that's the first place we'd think he went."

"Maybe I should go talk to your aunt."

That made me stand up without thinking whether I should. "Aunt Carol ain't got nothing to do with this."

"She's got something to do with this. We already know that, don't we?"

"Do you really think the old man would tell her anything?"

"I don't know what he would do. I didn't think he'd disappear. I can't put nothing past him at this point."

I stepped back from that hole in Vinny's nose. I bumped into the table and almost fell over. "Why don't you let me talk to her?"

"I got a better idea. Why don't we talk to her together?"

"That'll only scare her."

"Fine. You talk to her. But on one condition."

"What's that?"

"I'm putting a wire on you. As much as I wanna hear what she'll say, I wanna know what you'll say, too."

"Wire me up right now and I'll go ask her whatever you want."

Vinny stood there, watching to see if I was really willing to do it. "You stay here. I'll go get the stuff. When I get back, we can take a ride to Aunt Carol's and you can go in and find out what she knows."

Vinny walked back to the door. He turned after he opened it. "Don't bother trying to call her, because we got her phone tapped."

I still didn't know whether he was telling the truth. I wasn't gonna take the chance of finding out.

Vinny left. I heard the kid say something to him about Christmas decorations. I listened until I heard the bell at the front ring. Then I went to the bathroom and threw up in the toilet.

Twenty-seven

NOVEMBER 29, 1973

JIMMY DACEY

I HAD TO explain the situation three different ways to my son-in-law. I think it finally registered. I could tell he didn't want to regard as plausible my story of gambling and bookmaking and a plot against a mob boss. He would have had a hard time accepting it from anyone. He had a very hard time accepting it from me.

"I'm sharing this only because I'm not sure what these people are capable of," I said. "I'm embarrassed by my involvement. I let myself get caught up in my emotions after they killed my friend."

He was stunned by my nonchalance. I couldn't blame him. I would have felt the same way, if I'd been the one hearing it.

"Why do you think they'd come all the way here?"

"It's not that far. They have cars, you know."

"Why do you think they'd even know to come here?"

"I made the mistake of telling them I have a daughter in Pennsylvania. I said it when they told me I need to work on Thanksgiving."

"I thought you were sick on Thanksgiving."

"It was my first day on the job."

"So you've had this job for a week, and you're already involved in a plot—" He looked around before continuing. "A plot to assassinate your boss? Do you realize how that sounds?"

"When you put it that way."

"What am I supposed to tell Alice?"

"I'd prefer you didn't. I'll trust you to tell her only what she needs to hear. I don't want her to think less of me."

He took another drink. "You should have thought of that before you went to work for the mafia."

"I'll admit I made my bed. My main concern right now is the safety of your family. Tell her whatever you have to. And be on the look-out for anything out of the ordinary. They don't know where you live. They don't know your names. At least, they don't know those things yet."

He leaned forward. "What if they catch you and, you know, force you to tell them?"

"I don't care what they do to me. I won't tell them anything."

"So why are you telling any of this to me?"

"I want you to be aware of the possibility they might try something. And I want you to know the truth. Whether I make it out of this or not, I won't be coming around. Not for Christmas. Not for Easter. Not for anything. Alice will call the house, no one will answer. She'll become concerned. You'll need to help her deal with this. More than anything else, I need you to keep her and the children safe. Can I count on you?"

I looked through his glasses and straight into his pupils.

"You can," he said.

"Do you have a gun?"

"God, no."

"I know I can rely on you to always provide for my girl and my grandchildren. But I can't completely count on you with this unless you have a gun. As soon as you leave here, go get one."

CASHEWS

THE BROWN BAG was all wrinkled and smeared. It looked like it was about to fall apart. There was a grease stain on it, maybe more than one. I didn't count them. I was too worried about the guy carrying it. Vinny dumped out everything onto the pool table.

"Take off your shirt," he said.

I pulled it over my head and held it in my hand. He looked at the hair on my chest. He told me to turn around. I did what he said.

"What a forest you got," he said. "Front and back. You look like George 'The Animal' Steele. I should've brung a razor. Or maybe hedge clippers."

"If I shave it, it grows back worse."

He held up a roll of electrical tape. "This is gonna hurt like hell when you rip it off."

Vinny taped a transmitter to the bottom of my back. The wire came around to my stomach. He used more tape than he needed.

"You ain't being very stingy with that stuff."

"It might as well hurt like hell in as many spots as possible."

I put my shirt back on when he was done.

"Careful," he said. "Don't knock it loose."

"This is humiliating."

"Call it whatever you want. I call it necessary. So does Paul."

"What do you want me to do?"

He picked up a gray receiver with a white cord and a plug on the end. He stuck it in his ear. He spun a dial on the box.

"Go out front and talk to your boy. But don't stay long. Them batteries might die before he shuts up."

"Are you taping this?"

"Do you see a tape?"

"I don't know how this shit works," I said. I walked out front and asked the kid how it's going.

"It's been a pretty busy day I'm not sure why it's so busy today maybe it's the weather I don't know then again when the weather is bad people might be more likely to go shopping and when it's nice they'll work outside so I don't really understand it maybe it's just one of those things that you can't really figure out well OK I'll just keep things under control out—"

I walked back through the door. "Now do you see why I stay back here?"

Vinny pulled the plug from his ear. "It works. Let's go see your aunt."

Twenty-eight

NOVEMBER 29, 1973

JIMMY DACEY

I SHOOK MY son-in-law's hand. I told him goodbye, possibly for good. I walked to the lot where I parked the Corvette. For the first time in my life, I looked over both shoulders to see if anyone was following me.

"Where to now?" I said as the low rumble serenaded me. "Yep. That's where."

I pulled away from Kittanning. I made the drive back toward Wheeling, toward Carolina. Toward whatever destiny I had crafted for myself, accidentally or on purpose or some of both. I didn't know whether I'd be bidding her farewell or taking her with me. I wouldn't know what she wanted to do until I asked.

If I asked. If I was willing to put her at risk. I wasn't sure if I was. I'd have some time to figure it out.

"What do they have in store for me?" I said to the Corvette as it rolled toward Wheeling. "Whatever it is, I'm ready."

CASHEWS

I HAVE A key to Aunt Carol's house. I use it all the time. She don't mind. She wants me to come and go as I please. She never had kids. I'm the closest thing.

I still knocked this time, hard like a stranger would. It was my way of letting her know something wasn't right.

I could tell by her face she got the message. Standing there, I realized I love her. She might be the only person I feel that way about, me included. It made me even more determined to keep her out of hot water. To give myself up before they'd ever consider doing anything to her.

"Hello, Charles. This is quite a nice surprise." She said it like she hadn't seen me the night before.

"Hello, Aunt Carol." I tried to talk the same way she was. "How have you been?"

"Well, just fine. Please, come in and visit."

I knew she'd take me to the kitchen.

"Are you hungry? I can fix you a plate. There's plenty of food."

"Maybe some coffee, if it's not too much trouble."

"It's never any trouble at all," she said, starting right away on getting the pot ready. "Do you mind decaf? I try not to have caffeine after noon."

"Decaf is great. Thanks."

"I'm glad you stopped by," she said. "We so rarely get a chance to visit."

VINNY

I TOOK THE Cadillac to Paul's house and took my Ford to the aunt's house. Cashews drove himself. I parked down the block. Everything sounded scratchy and distant, but I could hear them. I kept my eyes closed to focus on what they was saying. I had to remember as much as I could.

On the seat next to me was the same gun I used on Mesagne. This time, it had a silencer on the end. And more than enough bullets to handle both of them, if I had to.

CASHEWS

SHE CARRIED OVER two mugs. She asked me how I take mine, even though she knew.

"So what's new in your world?" she said. "We didn't get much of a chance to talk the other night, what with your friend here. Mr. Dacey, that is."

"He's a nice man."

"A very nice man."

"I have a question for you, Aunt Carol. Don't take it the wrong way."

"I'd never take anything you ask me the wrong way."

"What do you know about him?"

"I know we fed him on Saturday night. I know he was well groomed and very polite. I know that, for someone my age, maybe he's someone I could envision as a companion."

"What happened between the two of you when I went to the apartments?"

"There are certain things a lady should not discuss. Especially not with family."

I tried to laugh. It didn't come out all the way. "I have a different question, then. Do you know where he is?"

"Have you lost him?"

"He's not at his house. We don't know where he is."

"Why would you think I'd know?"

"You seemed to like him."

"I do," she said. "It's a shame you've lost him. I do hope you find him."

Twenty-nine

NOVEMBER 30, 1973

CASHEWS

I WALKED PAST my car to the spot where Vinny parked his big ugly Ford. I opened the door on the passenger side and fell into the seat. I pulled the handle hard. It made a loud slam.

"All due respect," I said, "but fuck you for making me do that to my aunt."

He didn't react. Maybe because he could tell I really wanted him to.

"She's clean," he said. "You done your job."

I considered what he said. Aunt Carol and me spoke in something like a code. I led her on the right path. She knew what to say and what not to say. Vinny didn't get the idea anything was off. That was the best news I was gonna get.

I still acted pissed, just to make it look like I didn't have nothing to be nervous about. "So who do I have to talk to next?"

"Nobody, unless you hear from him. I'll stake out his place. I'll see if Paul wants me to go to Pennsylvania to talk to his family. Hopefully he just runs and never comes back. Hopefully Paul lets him go. Unlike that fucking kid."

"I thought you wanted to see if the old man knows where he is. I thought that's why you made me talk to my aunt with this fucking wire."

"I'm making the decision that I don't think he knows."

"What if he turns rat?"

"He wouldn't even know how to do it. And why would he? He's got no heat on him. He seems like a smart guy. I hope he's smart enough to live out his years anywhere but here. He probably has the money. He had enough to buy a Corvette."

"I didn't think we let guys off that easy."

"We don't, *Charles*. This is a special case. And you should thank me for making sure Paul don't hold none of this against you."

"I ain't the one who hired him."

"I'm the one that spends ten hours every single day with Paul. If I want him to put the blame on you, I can say whatever I need to say in order to get him to."

"That don't seem fair."

Vinny started chuckling. "When in the fuck did fair have anything to do with anything we do?"

"I should go. May I please go, sir?"

"If I didn't know better, I'd think you was being fresh. It might be a good idea to get the fuck out of here before I decide you are."

I got out and went to my car. I drove home. I knew he followed me. I didn't care. It was better for him to be on my tail than sitting outside my aunt's house, wondering whether to go in and talk to her himself.

I acted like I didn't see him down the street from my place. I had a spot close to one of the windows where I could see if he was still there. He stayed for at least five hours. He probably wanted to be sure the old man wasn't coming to see me, or that I wouldn't be going to see him. He finally left after one.

I figured he was heading for the old man's house. That old man sure is smart. I hope he's smart enough to not be there.

Thirty

NOVEMBER 30, 1973

JIMMY DACEY

I PULLED THE Corvette down Locust Avenue just after eleven. I parked in front of her house. I sat there, staring at the windows and the curtains and anything I could see for any sign that she noticed my car and would wave me inside without me having to knock so late, again.

It didn't happen. I got out and walked to the door. I rapped on the frame. It was soft at first and then a little louder. When she didn't come, I opened the screen door and used my knuckles against the wood.

I saw a light come on upstairs. I heard the creaking of the steps. I expected her to seem both surprised by my presence and mortified at her appearance, like the last time. Instead, she swung the door open. She grabbed the lapels of my overcoat and pulled me toward her.

"Get in. It's not safe."

I stepped inside, nearly stumbling. "Your nephew has been here, I assume?"

She walked into the kitchen and started brewing a pot of coffee. I sat at the table, in my usual spot.

"Right after dark. He was acting strange. I think they had a listening device on him. He wasn't himself. He was tentative. And scared. I could tell. They're looking for you."

"I know."

"It's not safe for you here."

"I know."

"So why are you here?"

I stood. I held my hat in my hands. "I couldn't leave without telling you goodbye."

"I would have settled for a postcard."

I tried to muster a smile. "I also wanted to ask you a question."

"Should I sit down for this?"

"You can stand." I walked over and ran my hand through the yellow strands that were hanging loose over the left side of her face. "I have a feeling you already know what it is."

"Yes," she said, "I color my hair."

I smiled for real this time, naturally and earnestly. "Come with me."

"Come with you where?"

"Wherever you'd like to live out the rest of our golden years."

"Won't they come looking for us?"

"Surely the Wheeling mob has more to worry about than a guy in his seventies who worked for them for a week and then took off."

"Do I have to give you an answer right now?"

"For something like this, any answer other than yes is no."

"I just need to get a few things in order. I think I want to do it. I'd like to have a plan. Right now, we don't really have one."

"So the answer is yes?"

"I just need a little time."

"How much?"

"Monday?"

"That's four days away."

"Is that too long?"

I smiled again. "That's perfect. I'll pick you up Monday night at ten."

"Why so late?"

"The Steelers play on Monday night. The game starts at nine. They'll all be watching, rooting for the Steelers not to cover the point spread."

"How much should I pack? I doubt very much will fit inside the trunk of that sports car you parked outside."

"How do you know that?"

"I looked out the window before I came down here."

"I've got a bigger car. Assuming the coast is clear, and I'm fairly certain it will be, I'll leave the Corvette at my house and we'll take the other one."

"That's quite a sacrifice," she said. "Giving up that car."

"You're making a much bigger sacrifice. And taking a much bigger risk."

"Well," she said, "life's too short to not take risks."

My eyes danced at her reply. Sure, I wanted to leave then and there. It would be more than worth the wait, if it meant she was coming with me.

Thirty-one

DECEMBER 2, 1973

CASHEWS

JERRY BORROWED A pickup truck with a camper top from a friend who trusts Jerry more than he should. Jerry said he wanted to use it for a fishing trip to Seneca Lake in Ohio and he planned to sleep in the back so that he could get an early start.

As he drove it to the oversized parking lot at a restaurant not far from my house, I walked there, head on a swivel the whole way. I asked how far it was to Seneca Lake. He didn't know. I almost told him I hope it's as far away as Erie, or his friend is gonna wonder why there's so many miles on it.

That was Jerry's problem. I drove him to his place and then I made the trip to get the dynamite and the tear gas and the gas masks.

I checked the mirrors over and over to make sure nobody was following. The truck rode like it needed to spend a few days in the shop. I hoped it would make it up and back.

Jerry heard out about the old man disappearing. He wanted to know the whole story. I didn't say much. Not that it was a secret. I didn't need him any more freaked out than he was gonna be when it was time to do the thing. The truth was, if Vinny found the old man and if the old man talked, we'd never get the chance.

We had four days to Wednesday night. Four days don't seem like much, until your life is riding on getting through them without everything going any more haywire than it already has.

Jerry was way more nervous than he should have been. He kept talking about no loose ends. He said something about maybe taking out the guy in Erie after I got the stuff. I asked him if I should be sleeping with one eye open.

I laughed a little bit after I said it. He didn't.

I told Jerry if he wants to take out the guy in Erie he should come with me and do the honors. He could also handle getting rid of the body. He said he wasn't going to Erie in the middle of the night.

He still kept working on me to do it. He reminded me I'd killed plenty of guys for no good reason. This one at least had a reason.

I told him I'd think about it, just to get him to shut up. The more I thought about it, the more sense he made.

I was taking two guns with me anyway. I'd decide whether to use one of them when I got there.

I had the directions on the back of the envelope that had my phone bill in it. There was a trail that connected Port Access Road and Ore Dock Road. It was close to the Erie wastewater treatment plant. He picked the place. He would have gone with something not so far out of the way if he knew what I was thinking. Of course, if he knew what I was thinking, he wouldn't have shown up.

As soon as I made the last turn, the headlights of the truck reflected off the taillights of a green station wagon. I pulled alongside and parked. I grabbed a pistol and stuck it in the front of my jeans before I climbed out.

"You're late," he said before I could even tell him hello.

"It wasn't too easy to find."

"You got the money?"

"You think I'd drive all this way without it?"

He walked to the back of the station wagon. "I just wanna get this over with. I still don't get why we had to do it in the middle of the night."

I felt the gun pressing against my stomach while I followed him. "I'm paying good money for the privilege of keeping you from your beauty rest."

He pulled the door open. "That's just another reason for me to ask if you got the money."

I moved toward him. I didn't wanna get too close. "Does anyone know about this meeting tonight?"

He gave me a look. "Who would I tell? I said to my wife I got business. She don't care. Saturday nights, she's passed out drunk on the couch before Mary Tyler Moore ends."

I could see brown boxes in the back of the station wagon. I put my hand on the pistol.

"Are you gonna help carry these?" he said. "Or does the extra money mean I have to move it myself?"

I let go of the gun and picked up the box that had tear gas canisters and two gas masks. He followed me with the dynamite. I held the box against my waist with one arm and pulled the gate on the truck down with the other.

"It's all here," he said. "Eight cans of tear gas. Two masks. Eight sticks of dynamite."

"I said I only need seven."

"I sell it in pairs. The price I gave you is the price, whether it's seven or eight."

I reached in my pocket with my left hand to get the wad of cash. I put my right hand on the pistol again.

"Here it is," I said. "It's all there. You can count it."

He walked back to the station wagon. "I'm going to. I need the dome light to see better."

He pulled the driver's door open and bent over. He started thumbing through the bills. He had no idea what I was thinking about doing. It would be quick and painless, at least for me. I could even keep my money. As long as I didn't get his blood all over it.

The money don't matter. This was about making sure word didn't get back to Wheeling. No loose ends. I kept my hand on the gun. I squeezed it tighter.

He turned back to me, holding the cash.

"It's all here," he said. "Counted it twice."

Thirty-two

DECEMBER 2, 1973

CASHEWS

I DROVE BACK from Erie. I tried not to go too fast. I knew enough about probable cause to know a cop couldn't just open the gate and start looking. I also knew enough about probable cause to think a cop could put it together pretty quick if he pulled over a guy who looks like me driving a truck that ain't mine in the middle of the night.

I got back to Wheeling before the sun came up. If the sun was even gonna shine. It felt like it was gonna be another dreary day. I parked a block away from my place and walked. I should've paid more attention to whether somebody was watching. I was way too tired to give a shit.

I didn't even make it to bed. I landed on the couch with my jacket and shoes still on. I slept until the phone rang. I didn't know what time it was, but enough light was coming through the windows to tell me it was close to the middle of the day.

"Meet me at the place."

"What place?" I said. I was still more than half asleep.

"Your place."

"When?"

"Now."

I had that haze that kept me from remembering right away what

I done. I took a shower. I shaved fast enough to miss a few spots. I drove behind the hardware store. Jerry was standing there, next to a car I didn't recognize.

"Did you get the stuff?" he said.

"You look like shit."

"I told you I wasn't gonna sleep until this is over."

"You need to take a pill or something. You'll be a zombie by Wednesday night."

"That's what I'm trying to avoid."

"Well, then you should sleep some."

"That ain't what I mean," he said. "Ain't zombies dead? I'm trying not to end up dead like some fucking zombie."

"You really need to calm down, Jerry."

"Don't tell me to calm down. That only makes me more nervous."

"Don't be nervous about the stuff. I got it all."

"What did you do about the guy?"

"What do you think I did?"

"I don't like guessing games. Just tell me whether we need to worry about him."

"You don't need to worry about him."

"Good," he said, "now I can keep worrying about everything else."

"It'll be over in three days."

"Sooner the better. I can't live like this. Something's gonna go wrong. It already has."

"Something always goes wrong. We need to be ready to adjust."

"You never told me that when we planned this."

"You never planned nothing before? There's always changes."

"I never planned nothing like this."

"We done plenty of jobs before. They ain't perfect. They still get done."

"This one needs to be perfect," he said.

"Why do you think it won't work? It's bad luck to assume it ain't gonna work."

"It's worse luck to do something we know ain't gonna work. If they find the old man—"

"That don't have nothing to do with the plan. The plan will work. It won't work if you can't think straight because you ain't slept in a week."

"Maybe we should move sooner," he said. "You know, before they find him."

"How are we gonna do that? Wednesday is the night to get Vinny alone at Paul's. There ain't no other way to do it."

"I keep telling you we can wire the car and maybe get them both."

"Or we can wire the car and only get Vinny."

"What's Paul gonna do without Vinny?"

"You seem to forget Paul was Vinny before Vinny was Vinny."

"Fuck it," he said. "We'll do it Wednesday. We just have to hope they don't catch the old man before then."

"Have you heard from him?" I said.

"Why would I hear from the old man? He don't work for me. Have you heard from him?"

"You think I wouldn't tell you if I did?"

"What about your aunt?"

"What about her?"

"Maybe she heard from him. Maybe she knows where he is."

"I already scared the shit out of her the other day, when Vinny made me go in there wired up. I don't wanna test her heart no more than I have."

"Maybe you should. Maybe she knows enough to help us get a little—what do they call it?—peace of mind."

I told him I'd think about it. I said it to get him to shut up. The more I thought about it, the more I figured maybe there was a way to talk to her without making things worse. I didn't like it. I was running out of choices.

I sat in my office behind the hardware store, waiting. I didn't know what I was waiting for. Part of me was waiting for Vinny to show up and start banging on the outside door, since the place was technically closed on Sundays. Part of me was waiting for the cops to show up if somebody saw me drive away from the station wagon. That was stupid, but I was still waiting for it. Part of me was waiting for Jerry to come back and tell me he couldn't take it no more and was off to the looney bin. Part of me was waiting for the old man to call.

More than anything, part of me was waiting to figure out whether I should go talk to Aunt Carol. I didn't want to. She's been through enough. And what if Vinny followed me there or saw my car? Then I'd have to answer a bunch of questions about why I went. He might make me go in with a wire again. Or maybe he'd talk to Aunt Carol himself.

I sat there all day, just waiting. I didn't even turn on the radio to listen to football. I didn't care about nothing except staying alive until it was time to make Vinny and Paul dead.

I didn't even realize it got dark until I opened the back door to leave. It surprised me at first. I wondered if I fell asleep in there. Maybe I had. Maybe I'd sleep a little extra to make up for Jerry not sleeping at all.

I decided to go see her. I drove extra before heading to her house to make sure I wasn't being tailed. I didn't want to get all paranoid like Jerry.

I let myself in with the key. I heard her upstairs. I called her name. She didn't hear me at first. She was walking around, going from one room to another. I called again.

She came downstairs. She didn't look right. It was like she was almost sweating.

"Is it smart for you to be here after that stunt they made you pull?"

"Nobody knows I'm here. What was you doing up there, calisthenics?"

"I was just moving a few things around."

"You ain't moved nothing around since Uncle Al died."

"Maybe it's time to move things around. Do you want some coffee?"

"I ain't gonna stay long. They didn't follow me here, but I don't know that somebody won't check to see if my car's outside."

"You could have called."

"I don't know if that's safe. We gotta assume the lines are tapped."

"You give them too much credit."

I waited for her to sit down. I looked in her eyes. "Do you know where he is?"

"I don't."

"What was you really doing up there?"

"Just straightening up."

"You can talk to me," I said. "It ain't like the other day."

"I have nothing more to say. I told you everything."

"I really need to know where he is."

"I told you I don't know. I don't know why it's so important."

"I need them to not find him, not for a few days at least."

"Why would you think I know where he is? I barely know him."

"I think you know him good enough."

"Charles, I can't help you with this one. I don't know where he is, and you'll just have to accept that."

"I never would've brought him here if I knew it would come to this."

"Come to what?"

"You're choosing between me and him."

She didn't get mad about that. I was sort of hoping she would. She just stayed calm and kept talking.

"I don't know where you're getting these ideas. I'm telling you I barely know him. If that's not good enough, I don't know what else to say."

I took out a cigarette and lit it. "I don't need to pretend no more. Some wheels are in motion here. I have a feeling you know what they are."

"I know no such thing."

"I got a feeling you do. And I got a feeling you know where he is."

She still wasn't getting mad. It was like she expected every question and she already went over what she was gonna say.

"Have I ever lied to you, Charles?"

"It don't matter. What matters is if they find him, that's gonna be bad for him and for me. Do you realize that?"

She stood up and straightened her hair. "If they find him, bad things will happen to him and to you and maybe to me."

"Nothing's gonna happen to you."

"How do you know that?"

"I guess I don't know nothing no more. I figure that's the way it's gonna be until Wednesday night."

"Why Wednesday night?"

"Aunt Carol, I got a feeling you already know."

Thirty-three

DECEMBER 3, 1973

JIMMY DACEY

I CARRIED THE suitcase from the room. The air tingled my freshly shaved face as I walked to the spot behind the building where I'd hidden the car. I wedged it into the trunk. I had to slam the lid twice to get it to latch.

It was time to bid adieu to the Grandview Motel. Two miles west of Lorain, Ohio. I registered in my mother's maiden name. I paid for a full week, in case I decided to bring Carolina back there as we planned our next move.

I pulled around to the front. I looked at the building. Three of the other twenty-six units were occupied. There was a gutter on the edge of the building with no downspout. When it rained two nights earlier, it sounded like a waterfall. It helped me sleep.

"I think we'll find slightly nicer accommodations," I said.

I started the drive back to Wheeling. It was four in the afternoon.

CAROLINA

I FINISHED PACKING my bags after eating a bowl of soup for lunch. I had a little wine. It would help settle my nerves.

I opened the refrigerator. I hated the thought of the food going to waste. I thought about bringing some of it with me. I decided that would be foolish. I hoped Charles would eat some of it.

I went upstairs to take a nap. I knew it would be a long night. I cranked up the clock. I set the alarm for four.

I woke up feeling excited and scared. I had more wine with dinner. I wished we weren't getting started so late. Better late than never, I thought. I smiled at that.

After I ate, I went upstairs to get ready. I turned on the light above the medicine cabinet. I looked at what time had done.

"Why does he want some old woman?" I said.

I poked with my pinkie at the bags under my eyes. I grabbed the skin that hung from my jaw. It reminded me of wet clothes hanging on the line in the backyard.

I considered the creams and pastes and powders. They would roll back a few of the years.

On the inside, it seemed like more than that. I felt young again. I lived here my whole life. I'd never really gone anywhere. I didn't regret any of it. It made me decide to be more excited than scared about whatever is coming next.

JIMMY DACEY

I LEFT EARLY so that I could take my time. I stopped for a light meal and some coffee. The waitress said it was fresh. It didn't taste that way. I didn't mind.

I never did. I've never been one to complain. I'm not about to start now. I've lived a quiet and careful life. This turn came more easily for me than it should have.

It all started because I couldn't sit in that empty house. I had to do something. I found a place to go. I had the money to gamble. I found a friend. I made no decisions to do any of the things I had done. They just happened.

I hadn't been back to church since the funeral. I gave up trying to figure out what I believe. There are forces that take us wherever they choose. We're all just along for the ride, aren't we?

It's been quite a ride since they killed my friend. I don't want revenge as much as I want justice. Justice won't happen, not the way it's supposed to. I knew justice would have to come in a different way. I couldn't think twice about it. I didn't feel guilty, at all.

For all I knew, the plan was still on. What would they do if it works? I had a deal with Cashews and Jerry. I could only assume they'd honor it.

I hadn't told her about that part. She thinks we're leaving for good. I'd let her decide whether to come back. If it's safe to be in Wheeling, maybe she'll want to. If not, I'll revisit the deal with Cashews. Being with his aunt couldn't hurt my chances.

If something happens to me, she'll be taken care of. I brought my notebook. I changed my will. John's son and Carolina will share my estate, if it comes to that. I stopped at a post office and mailed it to my son-in-law's office.

I got back to Wheeling at fifteen minutes until nine. The Steelers game would start then. And my window would open to make one last visit to the house Betty and I had bought forty-five years ago.

What would she think about all of this? That's something I've pondered from time to time. She'd want me to be happy. I felt like I was finally on my way to making that happen.

CAROLINA

I DRAGGED THE suitcase down the steps. It thumped on each one. I fought to keep it from sliding to the bottom. It would have taken me with it.

I went back up and packed a smaller bag with the things I'd use to make myself presentable each day. I was able to fit everything I'd need. I carried it down and rested it on the floor next to the bigger one.

The perfume and the hairspray made it seem like I was going to church. It surely didn't feel that way. I stared at the door that would soon open to something very new.

I had time to drink a little more wine. It was nearly nine.

JIMMY DACEY

I DROVE PAST my house. Nothing seemed out of the ordinary. My Buick hadn't been confiscated or set on fire. I parked on the street, close as I could to my other car. I sat for a few minutes, listening and looking for anything that would prompt me to start the Corvette and take off. A small part of me wanted to see how fast she could go.

I opened the door. I stood. I breathed, in and out. I opened the trunk. I looked around some more, took another deep breath. I pulled out the suitcase.

A car rolled past, toward the hill that leads to town. It didn't slow down. As I walked, I found in my pocket the key that would open the Buick's trunk. I stopped again to listen. I pulled out the ring of keys. I opened the trunk and lifted the suitcase into it. I pushed the lid down.

It was time to put my hypothesis to the test. Gone four days. Monday night football. The Steelers and the Dolphins. Pittsburgh, getting eight points. Every bookie in town will be loaded up with bets on the local team. Everyone in the operation will be watching the game and praying the Dolphins can build a lead and hold it.

I crossed the street. I watched the house as I moved. I kept my right hand on the key ring in the pocket of my overcoat. I was confident I could make it back to the car if I needed to get away. After ten steps or so, I knew I'd have no chance to outrun whoever might be waiting.

I tried to exude confidence. Not that it mattered. They were either there or they weren't. My theory about the football game was either right or it wasn't. It was my own personal Manhattan Project. The bomb would not go off, or it would.

I got close to the steps leading to the front door. I slowed down. Again, not that it mattered.

I had three to climb. The wood made a loud crackling noise under the weight of my shoe. I paused. I remembered my new mantra.

I took another step, then another. A similar crack came each time. There was a sound more like a thud when my foot fell on the porch.

I tried to peer through the curtains into the window of the front room. It was dark inside. I should have left a light on. I wondered whether I did.

It was time. I could stand and wait or I could go in. *Not that it mattered.* I took the key ring out. I unlocked the door.

I put the key ring back in the pocket of my overcoat. I placed my hand on the wood and shoved.

Thirty-four

DECEMBER 3, 1973

JIMMY DACEY

"HELLO, OLD MAN."

My bowels strained to release. My bladder did, at least a little bit. I had guessed wrong.

"I knew you'd come back at some point," Vinny said. He was in the chair where I used to sit and read. "I figured you thought during the game would be a good time to try."

"Why wouldn't I come back?" I said in the calmest voice I could muster. "I live here."

"Now isn't the time to act like I'm stupid. You went on the lam. Now all I need to figure out is why." He turned on the lamp next to the chair. My brain tried to count the number of hours I'd spent in that spot over the years.

I made my body stiff, my face blank, my voice clear and confident. "I decided I no longer want the job. I didn't realize I was required to give two weeks' notice."

He let out a long sigh. "Why do you have to get cute? You don't seem like the type who likes to get cute."

I could feel the wetness in my pants. I hoped he wouldn't see it.

"I'm not getting cute. I just didn't want to work there anymore. So I stopped."

"You knew from the get go this ain't like no job you ever had. You knew the stakes. You knew there wasn't no exceptions for old age."

"How has any of it harmed you?"

"Excuse me?"

"How has it harmed you? I assume you put Cashews back in the job."

"Cashews can't count his toes. We got someone from Jerry's crew to handle it."

"So it didn't affect you. The bar stayed open. The bets are being made. No harm done."

"No harm done yet," he said, pushing himself up from my chair.

I dug my right hand deep in the pocket of my overcoat. "Sir, I'll caution you that I'm armed."

"Sure you are," he said. He started grinning as he got closer.

CAROLINA

I SAT AT the kitchen table. I sipped more wine. I tried not to watch the clock. I failed. It was getting closer and closer to ten.

I looked through the kitchen into the hallway near the front door. My bags were ready. I was ready. Ready to go wherever he would take me, for however long we would stay.

I took another sip. I fought to keep my eyes away from the clock.

JIMMY DACEY

"I'M GIVING YOU fair warning," I said.

The grinning yielded to laughing. "Why are you warning me? I thought you said you was armed. If you are, use it."

He kept getting closer. I could see the hole in his nose. I could smell something on his breath. Cheap meat. I felt a surge of anger or adrenaline or desperation.

"I will," I said. I held one of the keys between my fingers. I jammed it into his left eye.

He screamed and fell. He propped himself up with one hand. He put the other over his eye.

I turned around and ran out.

"Get back here!" he yelled. "Get back here, you old bastard!"

I hurried off the porch and down to the street. I went for the Corvette. Yes, it was time to find out how fast she can go.

He wasn't following me. I didn't know what to think of that. Surely I hadn't killed him with a key to the eye socket. Maybe I should have tried to slash his throat with it.

I heard an engine revving. I couldn't see a car. He had parked behind my house.

I got inside. I wiped his blood off the key and put it in the ignition.

CAROLINA

I STOPPED AVOIDING the clock once I realized he was late.

I poured more wine and sat there. I drank it, taking more than sips. When the glass was empty, I picked up the bottle. Nothing was left.

I got up. I walked toward the front door. There were no headlights or taillights or any other lights from any car that wasn't already parked on the street.

I walked upstairs to make one last check for anything I might have forgotten to pack. I wished I had another bottle of wine.

JIMMY DACEY

I COULD HEAR the other car roaring through the alley. I put the Corvette in gear and jammed on the gas. It started toward the hill that led to town.

"Well, this night just got slightly more interesting," I said.

The car zoomed up the steep stretch of asphalt. The road curved gently to the left as it climbed. I accelerated while checking the mirrors for any sign of Vinny. I saw two white lights behind me, drawing closer.

I pushed the pedal to the floor.

Thirty-five

SEPTEMBER 1, 1777

Major Samuel McColloch addressed the group of roughly forty men and boys.

"We're going down to Fort Henry."

Most grumbled through faces so caked in dirt it had become part of their own personal topography.

"I said we're going to Fort Henry," McColloch repeated. "The British have been working with natives, and now they're attacking any village they can find. They're coming for Wheeling next. We must fight off the savages."

Some members of the company sat side-saddle on their horses. Others slumped forward onto the long, thick necks of the beasts. Still others stood or squatted on the ground that had cracked in the late summer. They all fell silent after the Major's reproach.

"Well?" he said. "Mount up! We are needed as soon as possible."

The attack had already begun when they arrived from Short Creek, with British soldiers and roughly two hundred members of the Mingo, Shawnee, and Wyandot tribes plundering the village and then targeting Fort Henry, where the residents of Wheeling had arrived safely.

The enemies turned to McColloch and his men. Some escaped into the fort, others fought their assailants. McColloch waited for any who had survived the onslaught to get inside before the gates slammed shut. When they did, McColloch found himself on the wrong side of the barrier.

McColloch fled, away from the fort and the village and up a steep hill. Natives and British chased him, spraying lead balls through leaves and branches on either side of the Major but never coming close to connecting.

The pursuit continued. McColloch reached the crest and rode along the edge of a steep and drastic cliff. Up ahead, more natives closed in.

Major Samuel McColloch had gotten himself trapped.

DECEMBER 3, 1973

JIMMY DACEY

THE REFLECTION OF the headlights in the rearview mirror made me jerk the steering wheel. The car kept racing up the hill. I'd pressed the pedal on the floor. I fought to keep the Corvette in the right lane.

The car went faster, even though it was hardly staying straight and true. Vinny was still back there. I think I heard shots being fired.

When I got to the top of the hill, I saw headlights from another car, coming at me in the other direction. The other car turned, blocking both lanes. Two men got out. It looked like they had guns.

I had gotten myself trapped.

VINNY

AFTER I SAW the old man park the Corvette in front of the house, I went to the phone and called Bobby's place. The fat man answered after six rings. I told him to get Bobby right now.

Bobby came to the phone and asked what was wrong. I told him to go to the old man's house. I told him we'd have some work to do in Ohio tonight. He started to ask another question. He stopped. Maybe he ain't as dumb as he acts. I told him to be watching for a Corvette coming the other way, in case the old man decides to take off without coming inside.

SEPTEMBER 1, 1777

McColloch pulled back hard on the reins. The horse whinnied. It lifted its front legs into the air.

He turned the steed toward the edge of the cliff. With certain death to his left and his right, McColloch looked straight ahead at the plunge of nearly three hundred feet to the creek bed below.

He had no other option.

McColloch pressed his lower legs into the horse and shouted "Hyahhh!" The horse refused to move. They kept getting closer, from each side.

He threw his feet out and pulled them back, digging each of his spurs into the animal's underside. "Hyahhh! Hyahhh! Let's go! Hyahhh!"

They kept getting closer.

The horse held firm until the moment it bolted forward, taking McColloch over the steep incline to a demise every bit as certain as it would have been if he'd stayed where he was.

DECEMBER 3, 1973

BOBBY

I told Tommy he shouldn't have answered the phone. We could have said we was watching the game and didn't hear it ring.

When we got to the top of the hill, we saw headlights coming the other way. They was jerking all over the place.

"He's out of control," I said. "I think it's our guy. I think he's running."

I slammed the brakes and pulled the steering wheel to the left. The car spun sideways in the street.

"What are you doing?" Tommy said.

"Get out," I said. "Get out and start shooting. That's our guy."

JIMMY DACEY

THE CORVETTE ROARED toward the car that blocked the road. The other car was coming up the hill fast behind me. My foot was still on the gas. I kept fighting to straighten it out.

I heard gunshots. I saw flashes in front of me, coming like lightning. I cranked the wheel from the left to the right and the car shot forward with a burst.

SEPTEMBER 1, 1777

THE HORSE LEAPED.

McColloch pressed his legs hard against it as they soared together.

Instead of plunging to the bottom, they landed on the face of the cliff and skidded and slid and somehow maneuvered all the way down to the bottom of the hill, as the natives and the British looked on in amazement. McColloch had survived.

McColloch had escaped.

DECEMBER 3, 1973

JIMMY DACEY

THE CORVETTE WENT over the edge, not far from the monument commemorating McColloch's Leap. The car soared down the side of the hill. It felt like I was riding on a meteor of headlights and spinning wheels.

The hood of the Corvette gleamed. I looked not down but out into the sky.

A fingernail moon drew my gaze, to whatever is out there. Wherever my wife is. Wherever my friend is. Wherever I would soon be.

I closed my eyes and smiled. I had not one regret.

CAROLINA

AT MIDNIGHT, I decided to go to bed. Before climbing the steps, I looked at the bags that sat there, ready to be taken wherever they might have gone.

I went back to the bathroom, back to the mirror. I removed the makeup. I studied my face once again. I let out a deep sigh.

"Oh, James," I said. "My poor James."

I heard the gentle sound of someone knocking on the front door.

Thirty-six

DECEMBER 3, 1973

CAROLINA

I HURRIED DOWN the steps. The rapping continued. The smile forced its way back onto my face, widening with each step. My eyes brightened. They might have been sparkling.

I passed the bags that remained ready to go. I felt foolish for even considering the possibility of taking them back upstairs.

I got to the door. I grabbed the handle and pressed the lever with my thumb. I held my breath. I was ready for this new life to begin.

I pulled the door open.

I was confused. "What are you doing here?"

VINNY

I STOPPED THE Ford at the spot where Bobby turned his car. Him and Tommy stood there on the edge of the sidewalk. They stared down the hill. Their faces was lit up from the fire. I climbed out and walked over, with my hand pressing a hankie against my fucked-up eye.

"What happened?"

"He spun out," Bobby said. "Then he floored it. Right over the edge. What happened to you?"

"Don't ask." I looked toward the creek. "I assume that ain't somebody's campfire."

"It blew up as soon as it hit," Tommy said. "I heard it."

"Poor bastard," Bobby said.

I sneered at them. "He got out easy. I was taking him to the warehouse."

Bobby turned toward me. "You was gonna work on that old man?"

"That old man knew what he got himself into. And now I got questions that ain't ever gonna be answered."

Bobby turned back to look down at the fire. "Not unless you wanna pull out the body and see if you can make it talk."

CAROLINA

I SAT AT the kitchen table for a long time after Charles saw himself out. He told me I'm safe. He told me I don't have to worry. He didn't ask about the luggage near the front door. I suppose he didn't need to.

I cried softly when he told me what had happened. After he left, I sobbed. It came in waves, starting and stopping and starting again.

There was comfort in knowing it was over. That only made me feel guilty. My life would go back to what it had been before the hours after Thanksgiving dinner, before the man with the white hair and the coat and tie and hat and the unintentional charm had turned everything upside down.

I'll spend the rest of my years thinking about that night, trying to put everything inside me back to what it was before he showed up at my door for the first time. I know it will be impossible to do that, especially after what was soon to come.

CASHEWS

I WENT STRAIGHT from Aunt Carol's house to Jerry's. He hadn't heard about the old man. It made him more nervous.

I told him it was good news. We didn't have to worry about Vinny getting anything out of him. We could do what we planned. If it worked, we wouldn't even have to give the old man a cut.

Jerry was still confused. He thought they followed me. I told him that part was over. The old man died. I told Jerry the window was wide open, we needed to finish the job.

He was shaky. Shit, so was I. We talked through the plan. He kept asking whether we should just forget about it. If I wasn't so focused on keeping him focused, maybe I would have agreed.

Jerry would have quit trying to get me to pull the plug if he knew what I was really thinking. I couldn't trust him to not say something at some point. If we didn't go through with it, I'd have to handle Jerry.

I keep telling myself it'd be over in two nights. Two nights until Vinny and Paul retire from the business. Two nights until we're in charge.

VINNY

I ONLY GO to Paul's house after hours when it's really important. Between that and my eye, his wife didn't seem too upset when she saw me at the front door. She went upstairs to get Paul. He came down in a robe. He seemed pissed off. I figured it was mainly because the Dolphins had a huge lead and then figured out a way to blow the number.

He told me to follow him to the living room. He asked me what the fuck happened to my eye. I told him the whole story. When I got done, he told me to tell it again. Then he asked a bunch of questions.

We didn't know what the old man knew or why he ran. We decided that, whatever the old man was up to, it was over. I apologized for all of it.

Paul waved it off. "What matters is how we dealt with it," he said. "You dealt with it."

Was it perfect? No. It was good enough. It had to be. Why worry about some old man who walked into a maze and didn't know how to get himself out? He didn't understand the life before he got into it. Now he was out of it, for good. It was a fucking mess, but it was still cleaner than it would have been if I'd gotten him to the warehouse.

Paul thanked me for coming over. That meant it was time to go. He said we'd act like none of it ever happened.

I still wondered what I would have gotten from the old man. I made myself quit thinking about it, because there was no way to know.

Thirty-seven

DECEMBER 5, 1973

VINNY

I DROVE PAUL home just after seven, before I went back to finish the count. We talked about going to the old man's funeral on Friday morning. Paul thought it wouldn't look right if a couple of wiseguys showed up.

Cashews asked if he could take his aunt. Paul said there wouldn't be no harm in that, as long as he dropped her off and didn't go in. I told him some of the customers from the bar might be there. Paul wasn't worried about that, either. He said the old man's family would just think he used to do their taxes.

Paul seemed more relaxed. He still wanted to find Mesagne's kid. He talked about it every day. But he started saying things like, *It's a big country and we're doing all we can.* Maybe he was figuring out we ain't gonna find him soon, if ever.

I hoped he was getting there. The operation needed more of Paul's attention. We lost two guys from that mess in Ohio with Mesagne and his kid. We had to find more guys we could trust. Maybe after the holidays Paul would be ready to move on. I'd do my best to nudge him that way.

I pulled the Cadillac into the driveway and walked the boss to the door. My Ford was parked in front of his house.

"What time tomorrow?" I said.

"Make it nine. I wanna get a little sleep tonight."

I got in the Ford and drove back to Paul's place.

CASHEWS

AFTER VINNY PULLED away, I sat up in the front seat of the Chevy I'd hot-wired in Steubenville. I put a West Virginia plate on it. I didn't wanna take no chances. I mean, no more chances than I was already taking.

I stole a mechanic's uniform for a job we did a couple years ago. I still had it. It still fit, mostly. It came with a baseball cap that matched the shirt and pants. I pulled it down tight. It said *Pittsburgh Truck Sales* on the front. The shirt had the name *Ralph* stitched on it in thick black thread.

I brought a brown leather briefcase. It didn't look right, a grease monkey carrying that thing. It was like a lawyer taking a toolbox into court. I wanted to carry all that dynamite in something softer than steel.

I walked up the driveway to the front of the Cadillac. I couldn't believe I was doing it. I popped the buttons on the front of the case. I held the metal flaps down with my fingers. I let them up real slow.

A window on the side of Paul's house was right above me. Light came out from in between the blinds. I heard noises like forks and knives hitting plates. Paul and his wife was talking. I couldn't make out none of the words.

Sweat was starting right under the hat, across my forehead. I opened the bag. The dynamite was inside, one stick in the middle with six around it. They was all taped together in a bundle.

I had a thing of metal wire for hooking the dynamite to the engine block. The mercury fuse was in there, too, with electrical cords that would make the fuse set off the bomb.

I sat down in front of the Cadillac. I picked up the dynamite and the spool with the metal wire on it. I laid down flat and pushed myself under the car. Sweat was running down each side of my face.

I found the right spot. I held the dynamite in place with one hand. I put the spool of metal wire between my legs and pulled on it with the other. I really needed to wipe my face. I looped the wire under the front end of an exhaust pipe and ran it back under the bomb. I tied the end of the wire around a wingnut near the dynamite.

I reached in my pocket for a set of tin snips. I cut the wire at the spool. I ran the end of it over the wire that was by the wingnut, pulled it tight, twisted it in place, and cut off the extra. I was sweating more than ever.

I did it all over again from a different angle. It made a basket that would hold the dynamite. It looked shitty, but it wasn't like it had to stay there for long, once the car got going.

I shimmied out to get the fuse and the electrical cord. I sat up and wiped my face. Before I went back under the car, I heard them again, eating and talking inside.

I felt sweat on my shirt now, and in my pants. I cut a piece of the electrical cord and used it to tie the fuse around one of the metal wires that held the bomb in place. When the fuse was in the right spot, I put one end of the electrical cord into the dynamite and the other end into the fuse.

The bomb was live. If I hit that fuse, I sure as hell wouldn't have been.

I slid my way out. I sat up and listened again. They were done eating. I closed the briefcase real slow. I held the buttons open and pushed the latches in without making any sound. I got up. I pulled off that hat and wiped the sweat from my forehead. I wanted to get out of the uniform and throw it away. It didn't stink before I put the bomb in place. It smelled like shit after.

I went back to the car and checked my watch. I got the bomb in place in less than fifteen minutes.

That was the easy part, compared to what we had to do next.

Thirty-eight

DECEMBER 5, 1973

CASHEWS

JERRY HAD A gas mask strapped to his face. It looked like he came from outer space. I had one on, too. I figured I looked just as weird.

We ran up to the front of Paul's place. I was carrying a baseball bat and a canister of tear gas. I had two more in the pockets of my coat. I gave Jerry the other five.

It was supposed to be Jerry busting the window. He was too nervous to be trusted with the hard parts of the job. So I went right up there and smashed the glass with the bat. I moved it back and forth to make sure the hole was big enough. I pulled the pin on the first canister and chucked it inside.

I was starting to throw the other one when the gunshots started. I still got it through the window.

I can't say the same for Jerry. When he heard the gun go off, he threw a canister and missed the hole. It hit the building and landed on the sidewalk. I kicked it down the street, but that white cloud came out right away. Jerry just watched it. I yelled at him to throw another one. He stood there like a fucking moron. More shots was coming. The flashes lit up the gas that already filled the place up.

I wanted to set off more than two canisters. I thought Vinny might make it outside before it would matter. I pulled a gun from my belt and busted through the door. I started shooting into the fog as more shots came out of it.

I was too scared to tell myself how stupid it was.

VINNY

I EMPTIED THE clip before running down the hall to Paul's office. I slammed the door to keep some of the gas out. My right eye was burning. The other one was still covered with a patch.

I wish Paul would have put a fucking phone in that office.

CASHEWS

I KEPT FIRING into the cloud. Jerry was right behind me, like I was his shield.

"There's gas all over the place," he said. "Someone's gonna call the cops."

"Call Paul!" I yelled through the mask. "Call Paul and tell him the place is on fire and Vinny is trapped in the back!"

"Is Vinny dead?"

"If he ain't, he will be soon enough."

The fog was thick. The shooting stopped. I figured Vinny went back to the office, unless his body was already on the floor.

Jerry picked up the phone. "I can't see the numbers."

"Is it buttons or dial?"

Jerry pressed his fingers against the face of the phone.

"I feel buttons."

"Well, then it's easy," I said. "One, two, three at the top. Then four, five, six. You don't need to see it."

I hoped Jerry was smart enough to figure out how the ten numbers on a phone was laid out. I didn't have time to worry about that. I had to find Vinny.

VINNY

I PUT A fresh clip in my gun. I had forgotten about the backup I kept strapped to my leg. I pulled it out and carried it in my other hand.

It was getting smokier in the office. I looked around.

I saw that stupid scuba mask. I smiled.

CASHEWS

I COULD HEAR Jerry yelling into the phone as I walked down the hall to Paul's office.

"Your place is on fire and Vinny is trapped in your office! . . . I'll tell you who the fuck this is. It's the guy who tied up Vinny in your office and set your place on fire!"

Jerry had delivered. I smiled inside the mask.

Then the white smoke got bright with flashes from two different guns. I think I heard the phone ringing through the sound of the shots.

PAUL PULLED THE phone off the wall and threw it.

"You're fixing that," Sally said.

"Sure I am."

"What the hell is wrong with you?"

"Somebody's fucking with me. They said they have Vinny tied up at the place and they set it on fire."

"Oh my God. Did you call him?"

"I just tried. No answer."

"You need to go there."

"Where are the extra keys?"

"You never drive."

"Well, the bus line don't run by the house."

"I'll drive you," Sally said.

"You stay here. Where are the keys?"

"In the drawer by the stove."

He yanked it open and pulled them out.

"Should you have someone meet you?"

"Call Cashews, Jerry, and Bobby," Paul said. "Tell them to get to my place right fucking now."

He walked through the front door and down the steps. He climbed into the Cadillac.

CASHEWS

I THREW MYSELF against the wall. The bullets missed me.

Jerry wasn't as lucky. I heard him scream. Then I heard him fall. Then I heard him gurgling.

I turned to look through the gas. I thought I should help him. That wasn't the time for it.

I turned back to the door. I saw Vinny standing there. He had something on his face. It wasn't a gas mask, but it covered his eyes. He had two guns pointed at my head.

"Take off your mask!" he yelled. "Take off your fucking mask!"

I realized he didn't know it was me.

VINNY

AFTER I OPENED the door, I didn't know what I was looking at. A guy in a gas mask, like an army man from a movie or something. I wanted to know who it was before I shot him. When he turned away, I pulled up the guns and got ready for him to turn back.

I told him to take off the mask. I thought maybe he'd just shoot. I guess I yelled loud enough to get his attention.

I stepped closer to see the face. It was Cashews. That ugly little mutherfucker.

I held the guns up to his face and pulled both triggers. After he dropped, I filled his chest with the rest of the bullets until both guns was empty. I went to the phone and called Paul.

A recording said the line was out of service.

Thirty-nine

DECEMBER 7, 1973

CAROLINA

I SAT IN the pew. The wood always makes my back ache. I wore the same black dress I'll wear to my nephew's funeral.

I rode the bus to the church. I saw the woman who was his daughter, the man who is her husband. Their children. One of the boys looks just like his grandfather.

The mass ended. After they brought the casket out to the hearse, I went up to his daughter. I expressed my condolences. I said her father and I had become friends. She asked for my name.

Her husband's head twisted my way when he heard me say it. He introduced himself. He said we'd need to talk, in a week or so. I gave him my phone number.

I had no idea what it could be about.

Forty

JULY 4, 1975

VINNY

SALLY TOLD ME the bomb went off after Paul backed the Cadillac into the street and started driving. Pieces of the car flew everywhere. The hood went right over a house and landed in the backyard. One house on the other side of the street caught on fire.

Paul survived, somehow. Something about the firewall by the engine block. The dynamite still fucked him up. It fucked him up pretty bad.

I guarded Paul while he recuperated. It took a long time, more than a year.

At first, he sounded like somebody who was done doing what he did. As he got better, that changed.

He still wanted to be the king of the mountain. He said they took their best shot, and they failed to take him out. He was determined to stay on top. He swore that nobody would knock him off, ever.

That was good. And it was bad.

PART THREE

One

OCTOBER 17, 1975

VINNY

I LET MYSELF think Paul forgot about that fucking kid. I should've known better.

With all the shit that happened after he took off with the girl, after everything I had to clean up, I figured it was over.

With Paul, nothing's ever over. Maybe I knew that all along. I fooled myself into thinking he changed. He never will.

I can't do much about it. I mean, I can. But that ain't my way. Even if the boss ain't the same as he used to be, he's still the boss. That's how it works. I took the oath.

Sure, others made moves before me. I never knew how they came to terms with it. I don't wanna know. It ain't nothing I'm ever gonna do. Even if it would be easy to do it.

How easy it would be. I try not to think about that. The more I try not to think about it, the more these ideas pop into my head. I treat them like tests. Testing my honor. Testing my will. Testing my loyalty.

The boss is still the boss. He's the boss until he decides not to be the boss, or until he's dead. Yeah, it would be easy to make him dead. I've had chances. I've still got chances. I can do it whenever I want.

That's the thing about being tested all the time. You can pass every one. Then you don't. I need to keep passing those tests. Sure, I wanna be in charge. But I don't want it to come to me that way.

I realized for the first time how easy it would be earlier this year. Paul finally healed up. He started going out of his house again. He bought every ticket at the Vic one night so the two of us and nobody else could see the sequel to his favorite movie. *The Godfather, Part II.* Couldn't they come up with a better name? *Part II.* Seems lazy.

Sitting in that theater while he kept bitching about how the movie kept jumping around, it hit me. I could take him out whenever I wanted. And then take over. Maybe I would have, if I knew he was gonna swing back to worrying about that fucking kid.

The whole time we watched Pacino and then DeNiro and then Pacino and then DeNiro again, Paul said he didn't wanna know about the dead father's past. He wanted to know about the alive son's future. I didn't make the connection to whatever Paul was still carrying around about that fucking kid. Maybe Paul didn't, either. Here, the father was dead. Ain't that enough? Paul was almost dead, too. That definitely should have been enough. Why not let that fucking kid go?

Besides, nobody but me knows the kid knocked up Paul's girlfriend. That ain't something Paul ever told me. I could tell from how he was acting back then. None of the other guys knew nothing, I made sure of that.

At first, Bobby was trying to find the kid. I should've taken over. Of course, that might've made me even more distracted than I was. I was almost too distracted.

That's probably one of the main reasons I've never done nothing to Paul. I still feel guilty for not paying more attention to what was happening. I let that old man get involved. He must have stirred up the other two, just enough to make a huge mess.

Now, Paul's doing good. He's back to his old self, or at least as close to his old self as he'll ever be. He looks like his old self, if you only look at part of him. He's definitely acting like his old self.

He's thinking like his old self, too. Which ain't great. Instead of just letting it go, he wants to finish the job. What's that saying? Revenge is a dish best served cold? Well, this dish has turned into moldy fucking icicles. He needs to forget about all of it.

I've tried to get him to. I acted at first like he was just joking. Like he wasn't gonna reach back two years and start messing with things that almost got him killed. I had a feeling in my gut that something stupid like this would bring him down. It almost did. I'm still worried it will.

Or am I? Maybe I just don't feel like wasting time and money finding the kid and taking him out. If I don't care about him, why should Paul? I guess that's why I dragged my feet when Paul told me to find out the new name he's using. It wasn't cheap, but they found him. What he calls himself. Where he works. Where he lives.

I couldn't hide that from Paul. I kept trying to slow play it. In the end, I didn't have no choice. I can't kill Paul, and I can't lie to him.

He was sitting behind that desk from the first movie when I told him what I found out. He perked up. He had a little bounce in his shoulders. He lit a cigar he'd been chewing on for like two hours. He started going on and on about how to do it. I let him keep talking while I stood there, trying to pay attention.

His office was the same shithole it had always been, except for that desk. As if one nice piece of furniture makes any difference. After all that time he was home in bed, it seems even more run down and empty in there.

The things in there don't make no sense. He has an old adding machine we ain't used in years, just sitting on a table. A cassette player is turned upside down, with the back open and the batteries long gone. That fucking scuba mask is still on the floor. Of course, that thing came in handy.

Paul's still in charge of Wheeling and the other towns we run. Ain't that enough? I guess this other thing is like a smudge on the hood of his car. It's gonna bug him until he cleans it off.

It's been almost two years since we took out Mesagne. That's three days away. Then comes the two-year anniversary of Paul almost getting taken out. He wants the other thing done, soon. He's got this idea it should happen exactly two years from when we killed the dad. What can I do? Well, I know what I can do.

I won't. It would be wrong. The fact that it would be so easy makes it seem even more wrong. What's the other saying? Shooting fish in a barrel? It would be even easier than that.

I wouldn't even have to shoot him. I could walk up from behind and cut his throat. Or from the front. What's he gonna do? I could strangle him. I could snap his neck. That makes it harder for me to not think about doing it, knowing how easy it would be.

Them thoughts came back in my head while I stood there, pretending to listen as he got all wound up about finally taking that fucking kid out. He decided to go take a piss to celebrate having a plan.

I knew what that meant. I stood up and pushed my chair out of his path. He made it clear from the start he don't want no help moving his chair, not even from me. So I put my hands in my pockets as he pushed himself back and swung them big wheels past me.

As he went by, I saw the two stumps where his legs used to be.

I didn't make a move.

I passed the test, again.

Two

OCTOBER 17, 1975

JOHN MORRIS

I CAN'T BELIEVE it's been almost two years.

At times, it feels a lot longer than that. At other times, it seems like yesterday.

Nothing tells the truth like a calendar, though. In three days, it'll be exactly two years since they killed my dad—and since we made our escape to Arizona.

It took the rest of the year for things to settle down. After I couldn't shoot Billy Potenza and wouldn't shoot the guy in the bed at that house, Marco Morelli was his name, I worried non-stop about someone coming after me.

I knew what happened to Paul. I couldn't believe he survived. Once it looked like he'd live, they thought he'd retire. Regardless, it was enough to get them to call off the nationwide search for the son of John Mesagne; my mother confirmed that a few weeks before Leslie went into labor.

Once the baby was born, everything changed. We found a bigger apartment. We had no choice. My mother got a job at the same store where Leslie was working. She went back a few months after the baby. They had different shifts, so the other one could take care of him.

I got promoted to manager, but it was still on the night shift. I want to work normal hours at some point. Unfortunately, hospitals aren't normal businesses.

We had gotten married. We'd been talking about maybe having another kid. I eventually wanted a whole house full of them. First, we needed the house.

I needed to make more money for that to happen. I looked into getting a degree. I could go to school by day and work at night. I got the brochures. Business, or something like that. Maybe it would be enough to get an office job at the hospital. They changed the personnel department to what I thought was "human racehorses" when I first heard it. I learned a little more about what they do. It would be a good way to work in the hospital without having to keep doing hospital work.

It felt good to have a plan. To think about something more than just surviving. I was still young, even if I didn't feel like it. I didn't look it, either. Worrying every day for six or seven months about getting shot will do that.

More than a year after not having to worry, it was in the background. Part of it had to do with the vague possibility of Paul coming back. Part of it would probably always be there.

It was a hell of a feeling. On one hand, I couldn't bring myself to kill someone else. On the other hand, I couldn't stop thinking about someone else killing me.

The constant feeling that it was coming for me started to go away. Having a real family helped. Having real goals helped, too. I was starting to think that background noise of anxiety will get quieter.

I miss that feeling.

Three

OCTOBER 17, 1975

VINNY

THEY'RE ALREADY CALLING him No Legs. Nobody will say it in front of me on purpose. I've heard them do it once or twice by accident.

I didn't say nothing about it. It ain't complicated. When is it ever? The more obvious something is, the easier it is to come up with a nickname that fits.

Paul has bigger worries than that, because he truly has no legs. He wants me around more than ever. It helps me avoid things, like going to Arizona myself to take care of that fucking kid.

That's the good news. The bad news is he still expects me to get it done.

Paul told me over and over how easy it'll be. It's two years later, he said, the kid's guard will be down. He figures word made it to Arizona about the bomb. He said the kid will be comfortable if he thinks Paul is out of commission.

We know they're in Scottsdale. The kid's going by the name John Morris. His mother changed her name from Maria Jenkins to Mary Clark. The girl went from Leslie to Liz.

Liz. I ain't surprised she gave herself a fancy name. She always thought who she was.

She married that fucking kid. They had a boy. The kid's boy, even if Paul wants me to think it's his.

Paul's pride saved the girl from having a hit of her own. If the baby is his, which it ain't, that means he can't kill the mother.

I don't give a shit either way. It's cheaper to take out one instead of two. I got no attachment to the girl. I always knew she'd be trouble. I'm glad I don't have to worry about her no more.

I wish I didn't have to worry about that fucking kid. What's he gonna do, come back and settle the score? If he was gonna do that, he would've by now.

Still, Paul wants the kid gone. Unless I'm gonna make a move, it's on me to make it happen.

First, I needed to hire somebody to do it. The crew in Phoenix tracked him down. I figured I should give them a chance to finish the job. My only other choice was to get people in Vegas to drive down there. They'd charge too much. And, yeah, I was looking to keep costs low.

I didn't ask Paul who to use. If something goes wrong, what's he gonna do? He needs me now more than ever, unless them legs are gonna grow back.

That would make things easier. If he could go back to being who he was, I could stop thinking about how easy it would be to take over.

I wonder sometimes if he can tell I'm thinking it. What would he do? He could shoot me when I don't expect it. Then what? He needs protection. I'm the only one he trusts.

One time when I was like five years old I came across a turtle flipped on its shell. That's what Paul is. All I gotta do is step, like I did back then. All I gotta do is want it.

I don't. I don't know if I'll change my mind. It'll be a lot easier to not change my mind if Paul would change his own mind about that fucking kid.

I know he won't.

Four

OCTOBER 19, 1975

VINNY

I MADE CALLS to Phoenix from a bunch of different payphones. It'll happen in Scottsdale. They'll wait for him to come out of his apartment. They'll shoot him in the parking lot. They'll take his wallet and his car. It'll look like a robbery, something random and unlucky and not connected to what happened to his old man. He'll be an easy target.

Of course, I thought he would be an easy target when we sent Rico and Tony to take him out in Ohio. He should've been. This time, his old man won't be around.

Paul keeps telling me it needs to happen two years to the day after the old man went down. It's stupid. But if we're gonna do it anyway, who cares when? If Paul wants it to happen on that day, that's when.

I don't know the guys who are doing it. I got no reason to think they'll fuck it up. They're pros. The kid won't see it coming. Even if he's got a gun, he'll be outnumbered. If he clips one of them, not my problem.

What choice do I have? If Paul still had legs, I'd have to go do it myself. It would've been a major pain in my ass, but I would've done it.

I wanna know all the details, in case Paul asks a bunch of questions. They probably think I'm being paranoid. I don't care what they think.

They promised it'll happen on Monday. Three are going over. I wrote down their names. They'll use a blue Chevy Bel Air, 1974 model. California plates and California registration. The guy I talked to asked if I need to know the color of the steering wheel. I told him the money they'll be getting is green, so shut the fuck up.

I made the guy read back the address back to me, three times. I told him what he looks like, all the way down to the missing finger. I don't figure he changed much in two years. He was twenty when he took off. He's twenty-two. He ain't gonna make it to twenty-three.

If I had kids of my own, maybe I'd think that's too young to die. But I don't. I just want Paul to get himself focused again.

After everything was set, I drove by the house where Bobby and me took out the old man. Not that Bobby did very much that night. If anything, he almost fucked it all up.

I don't know why I went back. It was almost dark. There was two kids playing in the front yard, just a few feet from where I shot Mesagne. Maybe I wondered if I would feel something. I didn't. I was doing my job. If my job right then had been to kill those kids, I guess I would have done it without a second thought.

Five

OCTOBER 20, 1975

THE CHEVY REACHED the complex on East Garfield Street. It had nearly three hundred apartments. Their target lived in one of them.

"Do we know the license number?" Joey Turtle said from the back seat. He was too low on the ladder to be talking much, but he was feeling too nervous to keep quiet.

"I know what he looks like," Frankie C said from behind the steering wheel. "I spotted him, remember?"

"Besides, fuck the plate," Ronnie the Schnoz said. "It's a '63 Olds. It's red. If somebody else is driving a piece of shit like that, he deserves to get whacked."

"What about that?" Joey Turtle said, pushing his luck. "What if we shoot the wrong guy?"

"We ain't shooting the wrong guy," Frankie C said.

Ronnie the Schnoz laughed. "That's what you said the last time we shot the wrong guy."

"I mean it. We fucked up twice now. Do those guys back east know about that?"

"We're getting twenty grand," Ronnie the Schnoz said. "Even if we get the wrong guy, they ain't gonna know."

The Chevy eased into the lot. The three men started searching for the red Oldsmobile.

"Do we even know if this guy's home?" Frankie C said.

"He works nights at the hospital," Ronnie the Schnoz said. "Eleven to seven. It ain't far from here. We find a spot close to the car and wait. When he shows up, that's that."

"Remember," Frankie C said, "this one's a robbery. We take his wallet and car. Which one of you is gonna drive it?"

"Not me," Ronnie the Schnoz said. "You wouldn't catch me dead in that fucking thing."

Frankie C looked in the rearview mirror. "I guess that leaves you."

"I wish I had some of that seniority you guys keep talking about," Joey Turtle said.

"You wanna shoot him instead?" Frankie C said.

"I figured we all was gonna shoot him," Joey Turtle said. "We all got guns."

"That's for backup," Ronnie the Schnoz said. "You should know that by now. We don't need the cops finding bullets from three different guns."

"What if there's witnesses?" Joey Turtle said.

"We'll kill them," Frankie C said, laughing as he did.

Then he stopped.

"We'll kill them."

Six

OCTOBER 20, 1975

LIZ MORRIS

THE BABY HAD been throwing up all day. When we managed to hold him still long enough to put a thermometer in his rear end, it looked like his temperature was close to a hundred and three.

We kept cold compresses on him. He kept fighting. He kept throwing up. He kept filling up one diaper after the next.

"Are we taking him to the hospital or not?" J.J. said, just after half past ten. "I need to be there in twenty minutes."

"It's just a fever," Maria said. "You had plenty. It'll break."

"His temperature's getting pretty high," I said.

"That's what a fever does," Maria said. "It gets high, then it breaks."

"It can't hurt to take him," I said. "We need to be sure it's nothing serious."

"It's nothing serious," Maria said, as one of his feet jabbed her stomach.

"It can't hurt," J.J. said. "And I work there. They'll be extra careful with him."

"I'm being extra careful with him," Maria said. "I know how to deal with a fever. He'll be normal by the time you get home."

J.J. looked at me. I rolled my eyes. I hoped Maria didn't notice.

"We should take him," J.J. said. "He's our kid."

"You're doing that again?" Maria said. "You tell me he's yours when you don't wanna listen to me. But when she's at work or you're at work or the both of you are out gallivanting, he ends up being mine."

The baby screamed even louder. I took him and tried to rock him. He was hot and sweaty. It made me hot and sweaty, too. I shot another glance at J.J.

"We appreciate everything you do," he said. "Sometimes, we need to make the decision. This is a decision we're making. No, it's a decision I'm making. Remember when I got here and you told me I need to be the man of the house? As man of the house, I'm saying we need to get him checked out."

Maria fired a dirty look at J.J. She flashed some of what was left at me.

"Let me change," she said in a huff.

"We don't have a lot of time," J.J. said. "I'm going to be late."

"You can go without us," Maria said.

"It'll be better if I'm there," J.J. said. "I know all the nurses in the emergency room. You don't."

"How well do you know the nurses in the emergency room?" I said.

"Is this really the time for that?" he said.

"Just wait," Maria said. "I'll be quick."

Maria walked to the bedroom she shared with the baby. He kept screaming. I kept trying to get him to stop.

"We need to get some clothes on him," I said.

"Can't we just wrap him in a blanket or something?" J.J. said.

"First of all, he's burning up. Second of all, we live in Arizona."

"Just put a shirt on him. Does he need a clean diaper?"

"You know, that's the first time you've ever asked that question. Are you volunteering to change him?"

"We can just bring a clean diaper."

"That's what I thought you'd say," I said.

J.J. moved close to me so that Maria couldn't hear. "Why are you making this so hard?"

"I'm not making anything hard."

"Well, that's for damn sure."

"You made a crack like that now?"

"I know this isn't easy," he said. "That's what happens when a kid gets sick. I supported you. Otherwise, it would have been you and her dealing with him."

"You're a regular Prince Charming," I said while I fought to get a shirt over the baby's arms and chest.

Maria was back. "Let's go."

"We should take both cars," J.J. said. "You and Leslie take him in the Oldsmobile. I'll drive the Gremlin."

"You're letting us drive your precious car?" I said.

"The other one's too small for two adults and one Tasmanian devil," he said.

He picked up the keys to the Gremlin. He gave me the keys to the Oldsmobile.

"Where's the other car parked?" he said.

"It's where I left it. Out there in the lot. Near the Oldsmobile, I think."

"This isn't the best time for an Easter egg hunt," he said.

"I parked it pretty much where I always park it. It's hard to miss. All this time you spend asking me about it is time you could spend finding it."

J.J. sighed. I kept trying to get the baby ready. He walked to the door.

"Remember to lock up," he said.

I tried to soften my attitude. He did get Maria to agree to take the baby to get checked out. "J.J.," I said. "Thank you."

"Yeah," Maria said, "thanks to both of you for not trusting me to take care of him the way I know how to."

Seven

OCTOBER 20, 1975

JOHN MORRIS

I WORKED MY way through the hallway and down the stairs from the second floor. It was faster to take the steps. Besides, that elevator always has a weird smell.

When I got to the bottom, I took a quick left and a quick right and pushed open the door to the parking lot. I started moving in the general direction of where I'd left the Oldsmobile. Leslie said the Gremlin was close to it. I looked around as I walked toward the spot where I'd parked.

THE BEL AIR sat one row away from the Oldsmobile, facing the red car. They could see anyone who was coming toward it. They'd been waiting for more than an hour.

"I need to piss," Joey Turtle said.

"Join the club," Ronnie the Schnoz said.

"There's a club for guys who gotta piss?"

"It's an expression. It means I've got to piss, too."

"Hey Frankie, are you in the club?" Joey Turtle said.

"No, I'm already in the shut the fuck up and do my job club."

"He should be coming soon," Ronnie the Schnoz said. "He clocks in at eleven."

"We'll make sure he clocks out before then," Joey Turtle said.

Frankie C shot him a look in the rear-view mirror. "Quit fucking around. This ain't no game we're playing."

Ronnie the Schnoz raised his eyebrows. "All due respect, we are kind of playing a game. It's called let's make sure we get the right guy this time."

Joey Turtle put his hand over his mouth. Frankie C raised a fist. Before he could decide whether to use it, he noticed something.

"Is that him?" Frankie C said.

"I think it is," Ronnie the Schnoz said.

Joey Turtle moved his hand and pointed a finger. "I don't think he's alone."

JOHN MORRIS

I TOOK A few steps, stopped, and looked some more. I did it again. I saw the Oldsmobile. I couldn't spot the Gremlin, even with that horrible paint job. I was getting a little sweaty. I had a decent excuse for being late. I still didn't want to be.

I turned back to the building. I decided to wait for them. Unless Leslie couldn't remember where the Gremlin was, either.

I moved toward the Oldsmobile. I went back and forth between looking for the Gremlin and checking to see whether they were coming. I looked at my watch. I had ten minutes.

I heard someone call my name. Leslie was holding the baby and walking toward me, fast. My mother was two steps behind them.

"I think he's getting hotter," Leslie said. "We should hurry."

I reached for the baby while she got ready to get inside the Oldsmobile. "I can't find the Gremlin," I said.

She pointed a finger away from the Oldsmobile. "It's right over there," she said.

I looked at her index finger. The tip of it disintegrated in a red cloud.

FRANKIE C OPENED the door and started to get out. "Let's go," he said.

"He ain't alone," Ronnie the Schnoz said. "There's two others."

"Too bad for them."

He raised a gun with the silencer on the end and fired a round. A scream made him flinch just as he squeezed the trigger again. The second bullet whizzed by J.J.'s head. Frankie C saw him duck behind a car.

"He's got a baby with him," Ronnie the Schnoz yelled from the passenger seat.

Frankie C looked back inside the Chevy. "Get the fuck out here and help."

Then came a loud bang.

JOHN MORRIS

I DIDN'T KNOW what had happened. Leslie didn't either. She looked confused for a second. She turned her head. I did, too.

A guy with black hair combed back straight and wet held a gun that looked like a small cannon. He was pointing it at my head. Leslie screamed, louder than I'd ever heard anyone scream in my entire life.

I heard a zing. I covered the baby with my arms and hit the asphalt, landing on my knees and elbows and rolling in front of the closest car.

I'd stopped carrying my gun after I realized I'd never use it. I knew right then how stupid I'd been.

I didn't know what to do next. My chest was soaking in the heat from the baby. I ran through my options. I could tuck him under the car that was in front of us and charge them. I doubted I would survive. But they had come for me. If they got who they were looking for, maybe they'd leave the rest of them alone.

I had no other choice. I'd forgotten it was the anniversary of the night they killed my dad. The memory came back to me, out of nowhere. It clinched things for me. I'd give myself up to save my son, the same way my father had for me.

Just as I started to put the baby under the car, the shot came. It was loud. It definitely wasn't the gun from before.

I jumped up. The man who shot Leslie fell.

The door on the other side flew out. Another one stood up. He was shorter and skinnier than the other one. It looked like he had the same gun. He raised his arm and pointed it at me.

There was another loud bang. He dropped out of sight, too.

I heard something from inside that same car. It was almost like a dog crying. After a few seconds, the engine started and it jerked backward, both doors still open. The car rolled up and over the two who were down.

Whoever was driving shifted the gears and took off. The tires squealed. The doors swung shut as the car pulled away.

I watched it disappear through and out of the parking lot. I saw the bodies. They weren't moving. I looked toward Leslie. She was flat on the ground. She had her palms pressed against her head. She was sobbing and yelling the baby's name, over and over again.

I spun around to find my mother. I squinted. I couldn't believe what I saw.

Eight

OCTOBER 20, 1975

JOHN MORRIS

MY EYES WIDENED. Smoke rose from the barrel of the gun my mother was holding. She threw it onto the ground and made the sign of the cross, twice.

"What did you do?" I said.

"I did what I had to do. I did what I had to do."

Leslie was still on the ground, still calling the baby's name. I yelled that he's fine. I couldn't tell whether she heard me. She finally stopped.

Right about then she realized she'd been shot. Blood gushed from the tip of her finger. I told her to put it against her jeans and press down hard.

"It'll ruin them," she said.

"You have more," I said.

I looked back at my mother. She held her hands in the air, like she was waiting to be arrested.

"I did what I had to do," she kept saying.

I walked closer to her. "Where did you get that?"

Her eyes were closed. "I did what I had to do."

"I know you did, but where did you get the gun?"

"I did what I had to do."

"Mom, where did the gun come from?"

"Your father gave it to me," she said, still not opening her eyes.

Hearing that made my knees wobble. Two years later, he was still saving my ass. "Where did you learn to shoot it?"

"You just pull the trigger. Everybody knows that."

I stood over her with the baby. She opened her eyes and snatched him.

"Is he OK?"

"He's fine. He's still hot."

"We need to get him to the hospital. We should go."

Leslie had walked over to us, finger jammed into her thigh. A dark stain grew around it. "I should get this fixed while we're there," she said.

"The cops will be here soon," I said. "If we don't wait, they might assume the worst. They'll probably let us go to the hospital. They can take our statements there, or whatever they do. It was self-defense. We need to be sure they know that."

"Who were those guys?" Leslie said.

"I've never seen them before in my life," I said.

"Did someone drive away?" she said. "It was a blur."

"I think there were three," I said. "Two are over there. The other one took off in the car."

"Assassins," my mother said, spitting the word. "Hit men. I know the look. They were here to kill you, J.J."

"We don't know that," I said.

"I don't need nobody to tell me," she said. "I know professionals."

"They sure didn't act like it," I said.

"They freaked out when they saw the baby," my mother said. "If you'd just been going to work on your own, that would have been it."

"How do you know that?" I said.

"Did you bring a gun?" she said.

"I used to carry one."

"Used to and a quarter will buy you a candy bar," she said. "You're alive right now because I was here."

"It figures," I said. "Two years ago today, my dad saved me. Today, my mother did."

"So what do we do now?" Leslie said.

"We should wait for the police to show up," I said.

"You're already late," my mother said.

"I think they'll understand," I said.

"We should just go," my mother said. "The baby needs to get looked at."

I listened for sirens. "If they're not here soon," I said, "we will."

"What do we tell them about who those guys were?" Leslie said.

"The truth," I said. "We don't know."

"We got an idea, though," my mother said.

"We don't need to tell them that," I said.

"If we don't put a stop to it, they'll keep coming," Leslie said.

"Telling the cops won't put a stop to it," I said. "There's only one way to do it."

"I don't like the sound of that," my mother said.

"I don't either. But I have a feeling it's my only move."

Nine

OCTOBER 20, 1975

JOHN MORRIS

WE WAITED FOR the police. My mother held the baby close. The fever was making her hair wet. Strands clung to both sides of her face. She didn't bother to push them away.

Four squad cars squealed their tires into the parking lot. They jerked to a stop nearby. Eight officers swarmed, guns drawn and going through the motions of whatever training they received for situations like this. I got the sense most of them never had to actually do it before. I stretched out my hands and raised them to ear level.

An officer with gray hair lining the sides of the bottom of his hat cocked his head in my direction. He was taller than me, thick around the midsection. "What the hell happened here?" he said.

My mother started before I could. "We were ambushed," she said. "Three of them. They shot my daughter-in-law's finger off. They almost killed my son and my grandson."

The man in charge watched four others move toward the two bodies on the ground. He squeezed his gun tighter but pointed it at none of us. "What happened to those two?" he said.

"I shot them," my mother said.

"Ma'am, please. Don't insult me."

"I shot them! My gun's on the ground. My fingerprints are all over it. Not his, not anyone else's. They shot my daughter-in-law. Then they shot at my son and grandson. I shot both of them."

He walked over to confirm the bodies weren't moving. He came back and saw the gun. He told one of the others to bag it.

"We need to take this baby to the hospital," my mother said. "He's burning up. That's why we were out here. That's where we were going before they attacked us."

I could tell he was getting more confused. I also could tell he couldn't think of any other explanation. "We're going to need to get your statements," he said. "It's not every day we have two people shot dead in a parking lot."

"I just told you what happened," she said. "They shot my daughter-in-law. They shot at my son and grandson. I shot them both. Another one drove away."

"There was another one?" he said.

"He drove off in the car they came out of," she said.

"What kind of car was it?"

"It was American," I said. "It was blue."

"That's pretty broad. Ford, Dodge, Chevy?"

"Chevy," I said. "I saw the logo on the grill."

"Did any of you see the plate?" the officer said.

I shook my head. Leslie didn't say anything. She was too focused on keeping what was left of her finger pressed against her jeans.

"It wasn't Arizona," my mother said. "It might have been California."

The officer flicked an index finger to one of the others, who hurried into one of the patrol cars. I could hear him talking about an APB on all blue Chevys with California plates.

"I only said it might have been California," my mother said.

"That's what we have to work with," he said. "Unless somebody else remembers something more than might have been."

"We need to get this baby looked at," my mother said.

"Take the baby to the hospital," he said. "We'll secure the scene.

We'll get your statements tomorrow. We'll have to take your fingerprints to make sure they match the gun."

It all seemed too easy. I wasn't about to question it. I told him the apartment number. I led Leslie and my mother to the Oldsmobile. I tried to move in a way that made it seem like I wasn't holding back. The story that was working so far was technically true. The whole truth was better left unsaid, for now if not forever.

I got them into the car. I couldn't think of what else to do or say, so I gave the cops an awkward salute. I eased myself down and drove away. I wondered whether our official statements would be the end or the beginning. It was easy not to worry about it, because I had bigger concerns.

As to the problem I'd been dealing with for two years exactly, I knew it was officially the beginning of the end.

Ten

OCTOBER 20, 1975

MARCO

I THOUGHT IT was over.

I spent a few months worrying about somebody else figuring out Billy was right about the guy with nine fingers. Then we got word they called it off, after the boss got blown up or something. That was a load off my mind.

I forgot all about it. And then Frankie C was visiting his mother in the hospital. He gave the nurse a hundred bucks to let him stay after hours. He went looking for a drink of water in the middle of the night. He waited at the fountain because a worker was there with a thumb on the button. He pulled his hand away and Frankie saw he was missing the last finger.

Frankie C brought that back to Sally Balls. Sally Balls called the guys back east. They told us to sit tight. A few months later they wanted to know more about him. What name he's using, where he's living, who he's with. That wasn't hard to find out.

They said they'll get back to us. Another month went by. Out of the blue the call came. Take him out. Just like that. After all that time.

Sally Balls wanted to send me. I remembered what happened to Billy. I told them I didn't wanna do it. It still felt cursed. I couldn't say that, of course. They didn't know what Billy told me before Billy ended up dead.

Sally Balls grumbled. My dad probably made a side deal with Otto. Whatever it took. I wasn't going.

Frankie C and Ronnie the Schnoz got the order. They sent Joey Turtle to watch and learn. Eyes open, mouth shut. My dad told him three times.

They gave him a gun, in case something happened to the other two. He asked what he should do with it. Sally Balls said if he don't know when the time comes, he should just shoot himself.

Joey Turtle looked at the gun, not realizing his balls was getting busted. I didn't know why they thought that punk had potential. He showed up and said he was in a crew in Chicago and they just took his word for it. I tried to tell my dad. He gave me the brushoff.

They sent them over to Scottsdale. The guy was going to work at eleven. By the time they brought the car to the lot and walked over here, they should have been back by midnight.

I looked at the clock in the front room of the Dry Dock, the one over the cash register. It was closing in on half past twelve.

"Where are they?" my dad said.

"Maybe they stopped to get a bite to eat," I said.

"They should have called."

"Maybe they ain't got dimes."

"Who don't carry dimes? You never know when you need to make a call."

I threw my hands up and made a face. Sally Balls and Otto was in the back room, waiting for them to come back. We sent everybody else home after the football game ended.

"Should I go look for them?" I said. Not that I wanted to. I just wanted to hear what my dad would say.

"We don't send backup unless we know backup is needed. There's three of them and one of him. If they can't handle it, they're in the wrong line of work."

"One of them is, I can tell you that."

"I can tell you we've been over that. There ain't nothing I can do about Johnny Turtle."

"It's Joey Turtle," I said. And right after I said his name, the door opened and there he was.

My dad's eyes bugged out. "Now say Raquel Welch," he said, laughing at himself. He didn't notice Joey Turtle didn't look right. It also didn't register for him that Joey Turtle was alone.

"Where's the others?" I said.

Joey Turtle shook his head. "There was a problem."

My dad sprang from his stool and ran at Joey. "Where's the others?"

When Joey Turtle didn't answer, my dad grabbed him by the arm and started for the back room. I didn't wanna follow them, because I already had a pretty good idea where this was going.

Sally Balls and Otto was smoking cigarettes and playing cards. They stopped when my dad shoved Joey Turtle through the door.

"What the fuck?" Sally Balls said.

"Tell them," my dad said.

"Tell us what?" Sally Balls said.

"There was a problem," Joey Turtle said.

Sally Balls got up fast and closed in on Joey Turtle. "What problem?"

"We went to the place. We waited. He showed up. He had people with him, but they wasn't with him. They was like behind him. They was catching up to him."

"Who?"

"It was two women, Mr. Balastrero. One had a baby."

Sally Balls turned to my dad. They stood next to each other, crowding Joey Turtle. "Did anybody tell you there would be a baby?"

"Nobody said shit to me about no baby. Nobody said shit to me about two women."

Sally Balls jerked his head back to Joey Turtle. "Well?"

"Well what?"

"I'm gonna go out on a limb and assume something happened next."

"Frankie got out of the car. He took a shot. I think he hit one of the women, because she started screaming. He shot again, but he didn't hit nobody."

"Did they use the silencers?" my dad said.

"Yeah, but I heard a normal gunshot."

Sally Balls put a finger in Joey's face. "You just said they had silencers."

"The other woman had a gun. She shot Frank."

My dad shouted something in Italian. "They shot my fucking nephew? You're just telling me this now?"

"I figured you knew when I came back alone."

"I just thought they got pinched. Oh, Jesus, Mary, and Joseph. What the fuck am I gonna tell his mother?"

Sally Balls stayed calm. "Then what happened?"

"Ronnie got out of the car. Before he could get his gun up the woman shot him, too."

"The same broad?" my dad said, hollering in Joey's face. "You're telling me Wonder Woman popped two of our best guys?"

"I don't know her name," Joey said. "All I know is she shot both of them."

"Where was you?" Sally Balls said.

"In the back seat. It happened real fast."

My dad got nose to nose with Joey Turtle. "I hope this is the part where you tell me you got out and shot them."

Joey's mouth opened. His jaw was going up and down. Nothing came out.

"There's my fucking answer," my dad said. "What did you do? Run away?"

"No. I drove."

"That's the same fucking thing," my dad shouted.

Sally Balls pulled my dad away a little bit. I grabbed his other arm.

"You left them behind?" my dad screamed, trying to get free from us. "You fucking left them behind?"

"They was dead," Joey said.

"How do you know?"

"They was dead."

"What if they wasn't? What if you left two guys who was shot but still alive?"

Sally Balls tried to calm my dad down. I noticed Otto was still sitting at the table, holding his cards and watching.

"We got twenty large for this job," my dad said to Sally Balls. "The guy we was supposed to hit is still alive. And two of our guys got left behind."

"They was dead," Joey Turtle said.

My dad had worked a hand free and slapped Joey with it, hard. "Shut the fuck up!"

Sally Balls grabbed my dad's arm again and pulled him away from Joey Turtle. I thought about telling the kid he should get the fuck out for his own good. I didn't, because I already knew how it was gonna end for him.

That's when Otto started talking.

"Twenty large," he said. "We got paid up front. We didn't do the job."

"We lost two guys," Sally Balls said.

"They didn't pay us to lose two guys. They paid us to do the job. Either we go back and finish it or we give back the money."

"We can't go now," Sally Balls said. "Cops will be all over the place."

"We go back tomorrow," Otto said. "Marco and this one. Get rid of the car they used. Give them a new one. Send them back to do it."

"Let's just give back the money," my dad said.

Otto turned his eyes back to his cards. "Sally, are we gonna finish this hand, or what?"

Eleven

OCTOBER 21, 1975

LIZ MORRIS

THE BABY HAD some kind of infection. A doctor who looked younger than J.J. gave him a shot. The fever broke a little bit later. We got back to the apartment just after three. The cops and the bodies were gone.

My finger was pretty bad. They said it could have been worse. The bone wasn't hit. Just flesh was gone, but plenty of it. I'd have a big scar and the nail might not be normal again, but I'd have most of the finger. The bandage was so thick at the end that it looked like I had a lollipop stuck to my hand.

J.J. found his boss after we got to the hospital. It didn't take much for him to give J.J. the night off, with pay. I don't know what J.J. told him. I hoped he didn't tell him too much.

When we got home, J.J. went straight to the bathroom and threw up in the toilet. His mother got almost as worried about him as we were about the baby.

"I'm fine," he said from behind the door. Maria wasn't ready to let it go. I asked her to help with the baby. That got her attention.

J.J. stayed in the bathroom for a long time. I heard the water run. I heard the toilet flush. For the second time in his life, someone tried to kill him. For the second time in his life, they almost did.

I kept Maria focused on the baby. She shifted back to J.J. once he came out of the bathroom. She hurried over, touching both sides of his face and trying to press his hair into place. "Are you OK? Do you need anything?"

"I'm fine."

"You didn't sound fine."

"I'm better now. Do you think I'm starting to look like Dad?"

"You look like me."

"I think I'm starting to look like Dad."

"You could look a lot worse. Your father was a handsome man."

"That's what I see in the mirror now. A man."

"You're getting old," I said.

"Not as old as you," he said, smirking.

His mother kept pawing at him. "You've been through a lot. You need a good night's sleep. Tomorrow, this will be behind us."

"Do you think the cops believe what we told them?" he said. "Or do you think they'll keep trying to figure out why three guys showed up out of the blue and started shooting at us?"

Maria worked her way to the kitchen table and got a cigarette. "That part's over," she said. "We told them what happened, and we told them we don't know why it happened."

"You make it sound easier than it is," he said.

"Do you think they know why we came here?" she said. "Do you think they know someone in West Virginia put a contract out on you? They have two bodies in the morgue to worry about. Sure, another guy got away. They'd love to catch him. They won't, and they know it. Whoever it was will never show his face here again."

"How do you know that?" J.J. said. "What if they send him back to finish the job?"

Maria sucked on the cigarette and shrugged. "Then I guess I'll have to finish the job on him."

J.J. started laughing.

"What? You think I can't? Were you not paying attention out there?"

"I know you can. I just can't believe any of this. Maybe you're the one who should have been in Paul's crew."

"Fuck him," she said. "Yeah, I'll say it. It's too bad those morons who tried to kill him didn't pull it off."

J.J. looked at his mother and then he looked at me. "If I'd gone back there when I wanted to, this wouldn't have happened."

"Here we go again with the Clint Eastwood talk," she said.

"Am I wrong? If he was dead, who would have sent someone to kill me?"

It got quiet after that. I didn't know what to say, and I didn't want to say anything that would make things worse.

J.J. looked at his mother. He looked at me. He looked at the baby.

"I've got to end this once and for all," he said to her. "You know it. I know it. She knows it. If I don't do it now, we'll never have peace."

He was right. I didn't dare say it, not in front of Maria. I carried the baby into our bedroom and shut the door.

Twelve

OCTOBER 21, 1975

MARCO

WE STAYED ALL night at the Dry Dock. I tried to curl up in a corner and sleep but it wasn't gonna happen. Joey Turtle sat in a chair the whole time, shaking from nerves. He should have been.

Part of me wanted to feel bad for him. The rest of me was pissed at him for not finishing the job, even though I knew he couldn't. I didn't wanna take him with me. I thought about making him stay in the car while I did it by myself. But orders is orders and I had to take him in.

It was over for him. He probably wasn't smart enough to know it. He was like a mouse that got inside somebody's house. That mouse was already dead. It was just a question of when and how.

I cussed the whole way to the lot. Joey Turtle stayed behind me. I cussed him, too. I cussed everything. He knew not to say a word to me. He knew excuses didn't matter.

I stopped cussing close to the lot and turned around. "You sure they're dead?"

"I didn't check their pulse or whatever. But I saw them get shot and I saw them go down."

"What happened when you drove away?"

"I might have run over one of them."

"You don't know if you did?"

"It happened fast. That's what I was trying to tell them. I'm sitting in the backseat like they told me and the next thing I know she's shooting them."

I started walking again. "It won't be as easy for her this time around."

"Won't they think we're coming back? Won't they be ready?"

"They won't expect it so quick. We're going right to that apartment. Sally Balls gave me the number. We're gonna kick the door open, and we're gonna take them all out."

"Even the baby?"

"I'm not gonna aim for the baby," I said. "But I'm also not gonna not aim for the baby. We work fast and get out."

"Do I have to shoot?" he said.

"I'm not giving you a gun, Joey. I figure if you start pulling the trigger you might accidentally take me out, too."

"Then why am I going?"

I spun back at him again. "Because they told me to take you. I don't wanna go. You don't wanna go. We both get to do something we don't wanna do. You picked this life. I ain't sure why you did. But you got to see how it can go. You're gonna see it go a different way now."

The lot was close. Jimmy Rigatoni was by the shack near the front, waiting.

"You got a car for us?" I said.

"Where's the one they took last night?"

"Didn't you bring it back?" I said to Joey Turtle.

"I didn't know I was supposed to."

"Where the fuck is it?" Jimmy Rigatoni said.

"I parked it on the street at the place. I took off the California plates and put the Arizona one back on it."

"That was smart, but you still got a lot to learn," Jimmy Rigatoni said. "Give me the fucking keys."

Joey Turtle fished in his pocket for them. His hand was shaking.

"You got this guy scared shitless," Jimmy Rigatoni said to me.

"I'm not the one who made him that way."

"I know the whole story," Jimmy Rigatoni said. "I'm glad I'm too old to clean up this fucking mess."

He walked inside. The shack wasn't much bigger than an outhouse. He came back and threw a ring of keys toward my head.

"You'll like this one."

I looked at the keys. "Which one?"

"Over there," he said, pointing a wrinkled finger with a swollen knuckle at an orange Volkswagen Beetle.

"That thing?"

"That's the one they told me to give you."

I looked at the keys. I looked at the car. I looked at Jimmy Rigatoni. I looked at the shack.

"Lucky I got enough other shit to deal with," I said.

"Who's lucky? Me or you?"

I took a step toward Jimmy Rigatoni. I'd had enough of his attitude. It ain't my fault they was training me to run the dice game. Just as I was getting ready to tell him off, up came a sawed-off shotgun. He jammed both barrels under my chin.

"Down here it don't matter who your daddy is," he said.

"You won't do it."

"You don't wanna find out. Your friend the *Tartaruga* will back me up."

"It's Turtle. I'm Joey Turtle."

Jimmy Rigatoni kept the gun under my chin. His eyes slid over to Joey. "Jesus Christ, ain't you Italian?"

"Of course I am," Joey said.

"If you don't know Italian, you ain't a real Italian." His eyeballs came back my way. "If you get in that car right now and get the fuck out of here, I won't tell Sally Balls about none of this. That's the best deal you're getting."

I looked at the car and wrapped my fingers around the keys. “This ain’t over,” I said.

Jimmy stepped back. He pulled the gun down. “You better hope it is,” he said. “And you both better hope things turn out better than they did for Frankie C and Ronnie.”

Thirteen

OCTOBER 21, 1975

JOHN MORRIS

AFTER I TOLD them what I had to do, I went to the closet. I got the green suitcase. I carried it toward our bedroom. My mother started fussing when she saw me with it.

"Oh no, you don't!" she said. "Don't you even think about it!"

"My mind's made up."

"Leslie! Get out here and see what your husband's about to do."

Leslie opened the door. She was holding the baby. He seemed better but he was still squirming. Gnocchi was curled up in a corner. He lifted his head at the noise, but didn't move.

"What the hell are you doing?" Leslie said.

"What does it look like I'm doing?"

"Did you plan on sharing any of this with me?"

"Since I was carrying it into our bedroom so that I could pack some clothes and since you were already in the bedroom, there's a good chance it would have come up."

"He can't go," my mother said. "Leslie, tell him he can't go."

"How can I keep him from going?"

"I don't know," she said, "I don't know." I watched her. It looked like she was thinking hard. "Tell him you won't have sex with him for a year."

"Mom! What is wrong with you?"

"That always worked on your father," she said.

"Thanks for letting me know that. But this situation is a little more important than getting him to cut the grass or take out the trash."

"Well, that's why I said a year and not a month."

"Just stop," I said. "This needs to happen. I need to take care of this. Otherwise, they'll just keep coming back."

"What do we say when the police show up?" Leslie said. "They'll wonder why you're not here."

"Whatever they need, they don't need it from me. I didn't get shot, and I didn't do any shooting."

"They'll be suspicious if you're not here," my mother said.

"Not if you handle yourself the way you did in the parking lot," I said.

"Tell him he can't go," she said to Leslie.

Leslie sighed. "You can't go," she said in a flat voice. "I order you not to go."

"How can you be fine with this?" my mother said to her.

"I'm not," Leslie said. "Again, I ask you, other than refusing to have sex with him for a year, what should I do?"

I wasn't in the mood for any more games. I went to the bedroom with the suitcase and slammed the door behind me.

"I'm packing this bag," I said from the other side, "and then I'm going."

"Well, you're not taking the Oldsmobile," my mother said. "You can drive the other piece of shit."

"I'll hitchhike if I have to. I'll walk if I have to."

I could still hear them over the sounds of zippers moving and drawers opening and closing.

"How can you let this happen?" my mother said.

"How can I not let it happen?" Leslie said. "In case you haven't noticed, your son is stubborn. I have a feeling he gets it honestly."

"This is insanity," my mother said. "He'll get himself killed back there, and then it'll be you and me raising this boy by ourselves."

"He almost got himself killed right here a few hours ago," Leslie said. "At least if he's not here, we're safe. And the baby is safe. Have you thought about that?"

"The baby is already safe," my mother said.

"The baby isn't safe. He almost got shot tonight. I did. And you shot two men dead. We had two years. There was always a chance this would happen. We knew it was possible the minute I climbed into that car and rode out of Wheeling with you. I'm amazed it took this long."

I opened the door, holding the suitcase by the handle.

"What are you gonna do?" my mother said.

"What should have been done a long time ago. I'm going to end this."

"Why don't you sleep on it?" my mother said. "You've got to be exhausted. It's the middle of the night, for Christ's sake."

I put the suitcase on the floor. I walked over to Leslie. I hugged her tight. I met my mouth with hers, without lingering. I went to my mother and kissed her on the cheek. I pressed my face against the baby's forehead and breathed in his scent.

"He still feels a little warm," I said. I picked up the suitcase, opened the door to the apartment, walked into the hall, and closed it.

The moment the door was shut, the baby vomited all over my mother. I didn't find out about that until later. Sometimes I wonder what I would have done if I'd known. Would I have gone back in? Would that have kept me from leaving?

If I hadn't gone, how different would the next day have been?

Fourteen

OCTOBER 21, 1975

MARCO

I DROVE THAT orange shitmobile over to the apartment building. The only good thing about having Joey Turtle with me was he knew where it was.

I still didn't want him with me. I kept asking myself how did we ever end up with a guy that useless? And why would they send him to do a job like this, twice?

I asked him to tell me the story again. I didn't know how it might help me once we got inside the place. I wanted to pick up anything I could.

It still didn't make sense. A woman got the drop on Frankie C and Ronnie the Schnoz? She took them out? And Joey Turtle, the most worthless of the three by far, lives to tell about it?

It was early, just about eight, when we got to the parking lot.

"A lot of people will be leaving for work," I said. "Somebody is gonna see us."

"Should we wear disguises?" Joey Turtle said.

"Did you bring one?"

"We could find something somewhere."

"We're just gonna do this. We'll do it like Michael Corleone in that restaurant."

"What restaurant?" he said.

"The restaurant in *The Godfather*."

"Never seen it."

"Jimmy Rigatoni was right. You don't speak the language, and you ain't seen *The Godfather*. You ain't no Italian."

"I'm more Italian than you," he said, and technically he was right; both of his parents supposedly came straight from the old country. "So what did the guy do?"

"Who?"

"Michael whoever."

"Corleone. He comes out of a bathroom and shoots two guys in a restaurant and just walks away. He don't look at nobody. He just goes."

"So we're gonna go to the apartment, we're gonna kick the door in, we're gonna shoot everybody, and we're just gonna walk away?"

"We'll have to walk fast," I said.

"With all those people in that place, we'll have to run fast."

"Regardless, that's what we're doing. It's what we gotta do. If you handled it earlier, we wouldn't be going back."

"You act like I wanna go back."

"I didn't wanna fucking go at all. But here we are."

I parked near a door to one of the buildings. I left the car running.

"You're leaving the engine on?" Joey Turtle said.

"You worried somebody's gonna steal it?"

I turned to the back seat and picked up the pistol. I stuck it inside my jacket. It had extra big pockets sewn inside, big enough for a gun with a silencer on it. "We ain't gonna be in there long. After it's done, every second counts."

I led the way. Joey Turtle followed. A woman was walking toward us. I tried to act natural. I was hoping Joey did the same. He said hello to her in a dopey voice. I turned back and made a face at him.

We found some stairs. We followed the signs and the arrows to the apartment.

I could tell we was getting close. The numbers was moving closer to 360. I turned back to Joey with a finger over my mouth.

We got to the door. I took gloves from the other pocket in my jacket and put them on. I grabbed the knob with my right hand and twisted.

"It's locked," I said.

"So what's next?"

"Fasten your seatbelts."

I pulled out the gun and kicked the door. It flew open hard. The hinges was all bent. A runt of a dog started barking but didn't come at us.

I walked inside. Joey Turtle was behind me. We checked all the bedrooms and the bathroom.

"Nobody's here," I said.

"Should we go?"

"We should."

Joey turned to leave. When I saw the back of his head, I made the decision. I raised the gun. I didn't think much about it. I never do. This one was easy. After what he did, they would have given the order to get rid of him by the end of the day. I squeezed off a round into the back of his skull.

I wiped the gun down with my gloves, just in case. I unscrewed the silencer and put it in my coat. Then I put the gun on the floor next to Joey's hand.

I looked out into the hall. Nobody was there. I pulled the door shut best I could, and then I went back down to the car and drove away.

Fifteen

OCTOBER 21, 1975

J.J MESAGNE

I WAS DONE with John Morris. I never liked it anyway. I was who I was. If they can find me with a fake name, I might as well use my real one. From that point on, I would.

I drove the Gremlin as far as I could without falling asleep behind the wheel. I spotted a rest area just as my eyelids started to drop.

I parked as far away as I could from other cars and trucks. I cracked the windows on each side, locked the doors. I slipped into the back seat and passed out before I got comfortable. I used the jacket I'd need for colder weather as a pillow.

The sun woke me up, both the light and the heat. I was sweaty and sore. My bladder wanted to burst. I climbed into the front seat, stiff and creaky and hungry.

I unlocked the door and got out. Stretching my arms high over my head, I looked around the lot. For as early as it was, plenty of other people were coming and going.

Most of the cars crowded around a small building. I started for the bathroom that surely was inside. Along the way, I noticed a large sign: *Painted Cliffs Rest Stop.* Next to it was a smaller one: *Poisonous snakes and insects inhabit the area.*

Off in the distance, I saw a large wall of rock. It looked like it had been dropped from the sky. Faded pink and light brown layers and lines covered its face. There were dots of green bushes along the curved plateau on top. Scattered, like someone had thrown a handful of seeds.

I took it all in. I'd been in this place for two years. I never bothered to pay attention to how different it was from home. Now, I was. Just as I was leaving. Probably for good.

When I got inside, I tried not to make eye contact with anyone. I had no idea who might be looking for me. I kept my hand that was missing a finger deep in my pocket.

"Poisonous snakes and insects definitely inhabit the area," I said as I walked into the bathroom.

I found an empty stall and took a seat, just in case I needed to do more than what I had to do. That dull smell of used urinal cakes filled the air.

After I finished, I went to wash up. An old man came out of one of the other stalls. His hair was gray. His body looked brittle. I wondered how old he was. I wondered if I'd ever get to be that old.

On my way back to the car, I spotted a vending machine. For a dime, I bought a pack of crackers stuffed with chalky peanut butter. I popped one into my mouth.

I saw a payphone on the way out. I went over and dropped another dime in the slot. I dialed the number to our apartment. An operator came on and said it would cost another seventy-five cents. I pulled out all the change I had. Two quarters and three dimes. Close enough. I fed them one at a time and waited.

There was a click. Another. Then a hum. Next came a ringing that sounded more like a rumbling. I heard someone answer.

"Hello."

"Leslie?"

"J.J., is that you?" She didn't sound like herself.

"What's wrong?"

"Where are you?"

"Almost in New Mexico."

"You need to come back here. Now."

"I'm like four hours away."

"You need to come back here," she said in a louder voice. "Right now."

She hung up. I looked at the receiver. I thought about calling back. I didn't have enough change.

I wanted to keep going. It was over. It was decided. I'd driven that far. I wasn't going to waste eight more hours going back there and then back here and being no closer to Wheeling than I already was.

I slammed the receiver onto the phone. The old man who was in the bathroom stood there, looking at me. I thought he noticed my missing pinkie.

I went back to the car. I looked at the highway that would take me into New Mexico and beyond. I stood there for a while.

I got in. I drove back onto Interstate 40. Heading east. Away from Arizona.

At the first exit in Gallup, I pulled off. I turned left at the end of the ramp. I drove a little ways and took another left, back onto the highway.

Heading west. Back to Scottsdale.

Sixteen

OCTOBER 21, 1975

MARCO

I PULLED THE hair dryer on wheels into the lot. Jimmy Rigatoni wasn't there. I was disappointed but mainly glad, because once you flip that switch sometimes it don't wanna unflip.

I kicked the keys under the door to the shed and walked back to the Dry Dock. My dad was waiting for me. I told him what I told him. He sounded a little relieved about Joey Turtle. Of course he was, because that would have been our next project.

I didn't care that I lied. I needed to be done with this shit. The people who ordered the hit won't know we didn't do it. We tell them we did, end of story. What are they gonna do about it?

I hoped my dad would handle it from there. Instead, he took me to the back room.

Sally Balls was asleep, head back and mouth wide open. Otto Lollo was smoking a cigarette and reading the morning paper. Otto started clapping. That woke up Sally Balls.

"I knew you could do it," Otto said.

"You can tell them he's gone," my dad said. "All of them is gone."

"Even the baby?" Sally Balls said through a long yawn.

"Not the baby," I said. "Just the man and the two women. Like I told my dad, one of the women clipped Joey Turtle."

"Joey Turtle left two men behind," my dad said. "That's unforgivable. We should've taken care of him last night."

I felt a smile coming when I heard that. It went away when Sally Balls got up and walked toward me.

"Did you get hit?" he said.

I raised my arms. "Clean as a whistle. They went for Joey first and that gave me cover."

"So what's next?" Sally Balls said.

"We tell them we got him," my dad said. "We pocket twenty large. We bump up a few guys to replace the ones we lost."

"What are we gonna tell the people in Virginia?" I said.

"Whatever we need to tell them," Sally Balls said. "And it's West Virginia, I think. Shit, I don't know. Regardless, it's done."

"What'll we say about the other two?" I said.

"One of them killed three of our guys," my dad said. "All bets were off."

"Maybe we shouldn't tell them about the two women," I said.

Sally Balls gave me a weird look. It went away just as I started to notice.

"He's right," my dad said. He turned to Otto. "They'll only know what we tell them. Maybe we just tell them we did what they paid us to do."

Otto pulled out a new cigarette and stuck it in his mouth. "I got no problem with that. They hired us to make the guy gone. He's gone. That's all they need to know."

Sally Balls walked toward the phone. "We might as well let them know it's done."

"What if they ask you about the women?" my dad said.

"It won't be the first time we lied to somebody about who did and didn't get whacked."

That time, the smile came before I could stop it. Sally Balls gave me another weird look.

Seventeen

OCTOBER 21, 1975

LIZ MORRIS

AFTER THE BABY threw up again, we took him back to the hospital. Maria didn't fight me over it.

The doctors checked him. They gave him another shot and sent us home. They told us if he wasn't better in twelve hours we should bring him in again.

When we got to the apartment, Maria was holding the baby. I noticed something was wrong with the door. It was closed, but it wasn't straight. It also wasn't locked. I was more confused than suspicious. I twisted the knob and pushed it open. I looked at the hinges. They were bent and twisted.

Maria froze. She didn't scream. The look on her face said she wanted to. She was smart enough to not make a lot of noise, since there were so many other apartments nearby.

When I saw the body on the ground, I thought it was J.J.

Everything got fuzzy, fast. Maria handed the baby to me. Having him in my arms kept me from fainting. Maria walked inside and looked at what we'd found.

There was a large red stain on a wall that used to be white, with bits of something else. I knew what it was. I tried not to think about it. A deep pool of blood had formed near the body, on the wooden floor.

"It's not him," Maria said. "I don't know who it is. It's not him."

The dog had tracked blood all over the place. It was on his face. I felt myself starting to get sick.

"Hold yourself together," she said. "It's not him."

"Well, it's somebody."

Maria bent over to look closer. "It's probably the guy who drove off last night. He came back to finish the job."

"It sure looks like somebody finished the job."

"We shouldn't move him. Not that we could."

"What happens if the police come back?"

"We don't answer the door," she said.

"What if they break it down?"

"They'd need a warrant. They only need to get our statements. If we're not home, we're not home."

"We're not safe here. We need to go."

She ignored me while she kept looking at the body and everything around it.

"I'd say two of them came back," she said. "They broke in. When they saw no one was here, one must have shot the other."

"Why would one shoot the other?"

"Somebody shot him."

I saw a gun on the floor. I pointed at it. "We might need that."

"I already have one, as you know."

"Maybe I need one. All of a sudden it's the O.K. Corral around here."

"We just need to figure out what to do," she said.

"What can we do?"

"We can call the cops. But I have no idea how we'd explain this one."

"Your son would say to tell the truth," I said.

"The truth won't help us at this point, not with what we're up against. They sent a hit squad, twice. They ain't gonna stop. And we can't trust the cops. Too many of them are on the take. They know when to look the other way."

"What other choices do we have?"

"We pack up and leave," she said, "or we get rid of the body."

"How in the world would we get rid of the body?"

"I'm just telling you our options."

I carried the baby as far from the mess as I could. "I wish J.J. was here."

"You didn't try too hard to keep him from leaving."

"He was leaving no matter what I said. I'm surprised it took two years for him to go. Remember when he flew to Indianapolis to get the Oldsmobile? I thought for sure he'd drive to Wheeling then."

"We'll figure it out," she said. "I just need some time. I wish we could get in touch with J.J. If he knew what was going on, he'd come back."

Before I could say anything, the phone rang. It was him. I couldn't believe it. I told him to come back. I made it clear he needed to.

I spent the next few hours praying he listened.

Eighteen

OCTOBER 21, 1975

J.J. MESAGNE

I GOT BACK to the apartment that afternoon. I wasn't happy. It was a feeling I'd have to get used to. Happy felt like something I wouldn't be for a long time.

The door looked off. I noticed right away. The lock still worked. I used the key to open it.

I called out for Leslie once I was inside. The dog ran over to me. I picked him up. My mother waved her arms from the other side of the room and told me to be careful.

I looked at her. I looked down. I dropped the dog.

"I see why you told me to come back," I said.

Leslie came out of the bedroom. She wanted to come to me. The body kept her away.

"Did you shoot him?" I said to my mother.

"He was like that when we got back," Leslie said.

"Got back from where?"

"The baby threw up all over the place right when you left," my mother said. "We took him to the hospital again. When we got back, this is what we found."

"If you didn't shoot him, who did?"

"I think there were two of them," my mother said. "They came back. And when the place was empty, one killed the other and left."

I looked down at the body. None of it added up. "How could there have been someone else?"

"If there wasn't somebody else, how did that one end up getting shot?" my mother said.

"Maybe he shot himself. There's his gun."

"Why would he come back here just to do that?" Leslie said.

"I don't know what's going on," I said.

"I do," my mother said. "It's happening. Paul knows where we are. He knows who we are. They won't stop."

"Is the baby OK?" I said.

"He's fine," Leslie said. "They gave him another shot. He's been fine since we got home. He's the only thing that's fine."

"What do we do about him?" my mother said, gesturing to the corpse.

"Did you call the police?" I said.

"We decided to wait for you," Leslie said.

"What should we do?" my mother said.

"All we can do is pack up and get the hell out of here," I said.

"And go where?" Leslie said. "Where can we ever go? It's just a matter of time before they find us."

I turned to my mother. "We bought two years. We can't get any more."

"I don't wanna go back there," she said.

"It's the only way we'll be safe," I said.

"We have to protect the baby," Leslie said. "That's the most important thing."

"There's one way to protect him," I said. "I have to end this. I have to go."

"We have to stay together," my mother said. "We'll only be safe if we're together."

"Then there's your answer," I said. "Get together what we need.

We'll drive back. We'll find a hotel in Ohio. I'll go to Wheeling by myself and end this."

"Do you really think you can?" Leslie said.

"If this son of mine is ever going to have a chance, I have to try. If I don't make it, at least he'll be safe."

"I don't like the idea of the four of us going back there," my mother said. "But we can't live like this. We'll never rest."

"I have to end things with Paul," I said. "One way or the other."

I noticed Leslie crying. "I never should have left. This is all my fault."

"We knew it could go like this," my mother said. "I only wish they'd done more than blow his fucking legs off when they had the chance."

"I'm the only one who'll ever have a chance to do more than that now," I said. "I've carried this long enough. It's put all of you in danger. This is the only way."

While Leslie kept crying, I could see my mother's face harden.

"I hate to say this," she said. "I agree with you. We have to go back. We have to make sure he leaves us alone. It's us or it's him."

"No, it's me or it's him," I said. "That's the only way the rest of you can be safe. It's the only way the baby can be safe."

Nineteen

OCTOBER 23, 1975

MARCO

I CHECKED THE paper. There was nothing about Joseph George Tortelli getting shot dead in an apartment, or anywhere. Maybe it helped that he came to town just nine months ago.

He didn't even have his own place, sleeping wherever he could find a spot to lay down and shut his eyes. As far as anybody knew, Joey Turtle still lived in Chicago. Maybe there would be something about him in their newspapers.

I wasn't too worried about it. He came out here to get in a crew. He tried Vegas first, but I figure he got the impression he couldn't hang with that class of wiseguy. So he ended up here.

Frankie C and Ronnie the Schnoz made headlines the day before. They took them to the morgue, in the basement of the hospital where our guy works. We'll have the funerals. We'll bury them. We'll show up and say what we're supposed to say and do what we're supposed to do. It'll be hard to see my aunt go through losing her kid, especially since she's been sick. Still, we know it can happen to any of us. It ain't no different than being in the army.

The newspaper didn't have many details about what happened. They called it a confrontation or some shit like that. They said it was self-defense. I didn't see nothing about somebody else driving away in the car they showed up in.

I didn't tell nobody the truth about what happened when we went back. Like I said, it was over for Joey the minute he left. It was cleaner this way. They probably would thank me if they knew the truth. At least they should.

It was also cleaner to say I killed the kid they was supposed to take care of in the first place. Them guys in Whatever-The-Fuck Virginia was never gonna know. So what if we technically stole their money? We steal all the time.

You could say we earned that money. We lost three guys. And we probably scared the kid enough to get him to leave for good, to Canada or Russia or the moon. He had to think we'll keep coming back until we get him. I'd have a problem only if the kid went back to wherever he came from in the first place, and there was no way he'd do something that dumb.

I was worried some about Sally Balls. He knows how to read people. He gave me weird looks when I got back, twice. He might be thinking I wasn't straight with them.

But so what if he is? What's Sally Balls gonna do about it? He works with my dad. If the shit ever hit the fan, I'd get a talking to. I'd explain why I did what I done. Worst thing they'd do is make me go back and take care of the kid, if he's still in town. There's no way he'll be.

I know how it works. Things will die down. We'll find other ways to keep making money. We'll move on.

That's the most important part for me. Moving on. I can stop worrying about shit I don't need to worry about no more.

I decided I'll start doing that, now. No more worrying about shit that will eventually blow over.

It worked. I felt good. It lasted like an hour. Right up until I got a call that Sally Balls wanted to see me.

Twenty

OCTOBER 21, 1975

J.J. MESAGNE

IT WAS LIKE Randy Wilson and I had never even met. Whenever I saw him coming, I walked away. He would do the same if he noticed me moving his way.

It helped that he'd gotten a job on day shift. It also put him in the hospital's morgue. That's how I got my idea in the first place.

I waited for him in the parking lot, same as I had the last time I'd talked to him, almost two years earlier. I saw him coming as his shift ended. I was sitting in the same Gremlin. He was heading for a different Japanese car than the one he used to have.

I got out and approached him, just like before.

"Randy," I said. "Hey, Randy."

He seemed annoyed, but he decided to mock me. "John Morris? Is that you, John? What are you doing here, John? I thought you still worked nights, John."

I ignored his sarcasm. "I need to talk to you."

"We have something to talk about? After all this time? Let me guess, another one of my friends is about to end up dead in the desert?"

"It's sort of related to that."

He went fast for the door to his car. "I'm not getting in the middle of this shit again. Not after what happened last time."

"You won't be. I swear. And the best news is I'm finally leaving town."

That got his attention, even if he didn't buy it. "Bullshit," he said.

"Whether you help me or not, I'm leaving. I just have one thing to take care of before I go."

"I can't imagine how I can help you at this point."

"Let's talk about it," I said.

"In that same shitty diner?"

"Your car's fine. It won't take much time, because I don't have much."

"I'm gonna regret this. I'm only doing it because you're leaving. If you really are."

"I am. I promise."

He got in, like the last time we did this. I walked around to the passenger side. I opened the door and sat. Once I pulled it shut, I told him what I needed.

VINNY

I HEARD FROM the people in Phoenix. I went to a payphone and called them back. They didn't get why I was being so careful. I didn't get why they weren't being more careful.

The news was good. The shit was over. I couldn't believe it. I felt a two-year weight lift.

When I got back and told Paul, he lit a victory cigar. Like he needed a reason to have one. The difference was I decided to have one, too. We both had glasses full of ice cubes and Lord Calvert.

Why not? That fucking kid was finally gone.

"Tell me again what they told you," Paul said.

"They sent a crew down to his place in Scottsdale to do it."

"Should we go out there? To make sure?"

"Why would you wanna fly all the way to Arizona? They got him. I knew they would. Even though it's not like he was ever coming back here."

"He might have."

"Well, he ain't now." I took a puff of that nasty cigar. It made me wonder how the hell he smokes those things all the time.

"Remember when he had Bobby freaked out?" Paul said. "When he called and said he was coming back to kill everybody?"

"Nobody who plans to show up and kill everybody tells you before he does it," I said.

"I wonder what his mother and the other one will do. They still got that kid."

"Everybody finds a way to figure things out."

"You think they'll ever come back this way?" Paul said.

"What would you do if they did?"

Paul took a long draw of his cigar. He titled his head back and blew a thick cloud high into the space above him. "It would depend on how I felt that day. But it won't be an issue. The last thing they'll ever do is come back here, especially after that kid got what he deserved."

"They ain't coming back," I said. "We can focus on other shit."

Paul lifted his glass. He waited for me to do the same. He struck his against mine.

"Here's to other shit," he said.

He took a long drink and belched.

Twenty-one

OCTOBER 21, 1975

J.J. MESAGNE

"I NEED TO die."

It sounded strange, like the words were coming from someone else.

Randy didn't respond. He just looked at me, like he hadn't heard what I'd said.

"That's my only chance to get away from this," I added.

"In my new job, I deal with dead bodies. I don't deal with making bodies dead."

"I'm not asking you to kill me."

"What do you want then?"

"What's the most important ingredient in making someone dead?"

"They have to die?"

"What happens when they die?"

"When they die, they're dead. That's what happens."

"And what do you have? You just said it."

"Said what?

"What do you deal with now?"

"Dead bodies?"

"Bingo."

He sat there, still staring at me and trying to figure out what I was saying. It registered after maybe ten seconds.

"You want me to pretend one of the bodies in the morgue is you?"

"It's not what I want you to do. It's what I need you to do."

"The dead bodies in the morgue are already spoken for. I can't just make one of them you."

"What happens if someone dies and no one claims the body?"

"It gets sent away for cremation."

"What happens to the ashes?"

"I guess they scoop them out and throw them away. But so what? I don't have any extra bodies laying around."

"What if I do?"

"What if you what?"

"What if I have an extra body?"

Randy's eyes popped wide. "You're gonna kill somebody and say it was you?"

"No, no, no. Remember the people who were looking for me a couple of years ago?"

"How could I forget?"

"They sent some guys to try to kill me last night. We shot two of them."

Randy's jaw fell against the top of his chest. "That was you?"

"That was my mom. After it happened, I packed up and headed back to West Virginia."

"Why were you going there?"

I looked at him but didn't answer. I think he got the point.

"So right after I left, my wife and mom had to bring the baby here because he's got the flu or something. Whoever it was came back to our apartment while we were gone. There must have been two of them. One killed the other and left him there, right on the floor."

"Did you call the cops?"

"It's too complicated for that. We just need to go. And I need to make it look like the guy who got killed in my apartment is me."

"Where is he now?"

"Still in my apartment."

Randy sighed and shook his head. "You know, this ain't like helping you change a tire. I can get in a shitload of trouble."

"I'm in a bigger shitload of trouble."

"I ain't. At least not yet."

I didn't want to say it. I had no choice. "You know, you still owe me. All that stuff from two years ago happened because you brought a mobster around."

"I don't remember much about two years ago. I do remember saying it was your own fault for not keeping a lower profile."

"Forget I asked," I said. "I'll leave him where he is. After he gets good and ripe, you can deal with him."

"You think I haven't dealt with a few that got good and ripe?"

"You probably would prefer not to deal with another one."

"How did they kill him?"

"Bullet to the back of the head. Clean on the way in. Messy on the way out."

I stopped talking and waited to see whether he would come around. After about twenty seconds, he started shaking his head. "I can't believe I'm gonna do this. The only reason I'm saying yes to it is because the boss is on vacation this week. I'm basically running the place. I'll get a little creative with the dates on the paperwork and get rid of him."

I felt relieved. I stayed that way until Randy pointed out the one thing I hadn't thought about.

"How were you planning to get him here?"

Twenty-two

OCTOBER 21, 1975

J.J. MESAGNE

RANDY KEPT THE two red domes of the ambulance spinning when he pulled up to the apartment building. He said it would look more suspicious if the lights weren't on. I said it would be pretty hard for an orange Cadillac hearse with a white roof to not look suspicious.

The dark green shirt made me itch. It was tucked into pants that were a shade or two lighter. I tugged at the collar that was buttoned to the top. "This feels tight."

"I had two minutes to grab it," Randy said.

"Yours fits fine."

"This is what I always wear for a pickup."

He turned off the vehicle. The red lights kept turning around and around.

"What's next?" I said.

"We take up the stretcher. We go inside your apartment. We put the guy on it. We wrap a bandage around his head, we act like he's still alive, we bring him back down, and we put him in here."

"Then what?"

"We'll drive to the hospital. We'll take him around back. We'll get him inside. We'll put him in a drawer. I'll get the paperwork together with your real name on it, and then I'll send him off to the furnace in the morning."

"It sounds pretty easy."

"It probably sounds a lot easier than it'll be."

"There's only one way to find out," I said.

I wore a hat, pulled down as far as it would go. We took the stretcher and wheeled it into the elevator and up to the second floor. We didn't see anyone in the hallway.

The wheels were squeaking and squealing. It seemed loud enough to get someone to open the door and find out what was making all that noise. I was surprised no one did.

We got to the apartment. I hoped like hell Leslie and my mother would remember what I told them to do.

I started knocking, harder than I needed to. Randy grabbed my wrist. "We ain't the cops," he said. "Just do it normal."

The door opened before I could hit it again. I noticed the broken hinges. I turned to Leslie and nodded.

"Mrs. Morris?" I said. My words felt stiff and wooden.

"Yes," she said, sounding sort of like a robot. "I am. Please. Come in."

"Thank you very much," I said.

We pushed the stretcher inside. Randy closed the door. "I don't know where you're going next," he said, "but I wouldn't suggest Hollywood." He smiled at what he said before he caught sight of the mess on the floor, and on the wall.

"Have you touched him at all?" he said.

"This is exactly the way they found him."

Randy stepped on a pedal that dropped the stretcher as low as it would go. "She should go to the bedroom or somewhere," he said. "This could get a little uncomfortable."

Leslie threw her palms in the air. "You don't need to tell me twice." She turned and walked away.

Randy watched her leave. After she was gone, he gave me a wink. "Now I know why you took off."

I looked down at the body on the floor. "Weird time to be getting a compliment."

"I've been around enough stiffs to not think twice about it," he said. "We pick him up and put him on the stretcher. We're lucky he's laying straight. If he'd been curled up, we might have had to break some bones."

I felt my stomach flop and bulge. I stepped back to gather myself.

"Easy," he said. "We won't have to do that. At least I think we won't. Let's just get him on the stretcher."

Randy lifted him by the shoulders and I picked up the legs. It reminded me of when we moved Tony and Rico in Ohio. "Thank God his eyes are closed," I said, "or I'd be puking all over the place."

After the body was on the stretcher, Randy pulled a ring of gauze from a bag he'd brought with him. "Now we wrap the head," he said, "and nobody knows he got shot."

I watched him unroll it, going around and around until there was no sign he'd had his brains blown out, all over the wall. Randy tore it off and flattened the end. He used a metal clip to hold it all in place. He stepped back and put his hands on his hips.

"I think it works. What do you think?"

"I think I've seen enough dead bodies for one lifetime."

"If you don't wanna be one, let's get him to the ambulance."

"What if someone asks about him while we're going?" I said.

"If we move fast enough, they won't."

No one saw us. I felt myself getting excited as we got closer to the ambulance.

Randy noticed the look on my face. "Just keep going," he said. "Don't blow it now."

He pulled the back open. We lowered the stretcher to the ground before lifting it up and putting it inside. I slammed the door shut. We got inside and drove away, red lights still spinning.

"That was easy," I said.

"It almost felt too easy," Randy said.

We'd soon find out Randy was right.

Twenty-three

OCTOBER 21, 1975

J.J. MESAGNE

RANDY PULLED THE ambulance into the concrete bay behind the hospital. He told me to act normal. I wasn't sure how else to act, even if none of this was normal. We got out of the hearse. I followed his lead. It was late enough for no one else to be hanging around.

We went to the back, ready to take out the stretcher. Right on cue, a security guard who was making his rounds pushed a door open and came outside. He stopped and looked at us.

"Hello," the guard said.

"Evening," Randy said right away. Which was good, because I wouldn't have gotten a single word out.

"What's in the back?"

"What's usually in the back," Randy said. "We bring them in after they die."

"So you've got a body in there?"

"Ever seen a fresh one?" Randy said.

"I'm not sure I want to."

"If you hang around much longer, you will."

I felt the guard looking my way. I kept my head down. I was glad I'd kept the hat pulled low. I recognized him as soon as he showed up. If he got a good look at me, he'd wonder what I was doing there.

"Isn't it a little late to be bringing in a body?" he said to Randy.

"The grim reaper don't work nine to five," Randy said. "Whenever somebody goes, somebody has to go get them."

I could feel him staring right at me. I kept my face pointed straight to the ground.

"What's with him?" the guard said to Randy.

"He's showing respect for the dead."

It got quiet for a little bit. I tried not to shake.

"I'll let you do whatever you have to do," the guard said.

"You're welcome to hang around and watch," Randy said.

"I just ate dinner. Maybe next time."

We waited for him to leave. It felt like he never would. Once he was gone, I let out a deep breath.

"You OK?" Randy said.

"I'm fine," I said, "other than I know him and he knows me and we would have had a hell of time explaining why I'm down here in this getup instead of where I usually am when I'm working."

"Then let's get moving before he changes his mind about seeing a dead body."

We took out the stretcher and wheeled it inside. Randy got the form. It was long with pink and yellow pages under a white sheet on top. He pressed hard with a pen as he wrote my old name and my address from Wheeling. John Joseph Jenkins was officially dead. I was officially loaded into a drawer. The man with the hole blown in his head and gauze covering it up was officially me.

Me. I was dead.

Hooray.

As he wrote, Randy told me he was making it look like the body showed up two weeks before. Long enough to call the body unclaimed and send it off for cremation the next morning. He dropped the pen when he was finished. "There. Done."

"It's that simple?"

"Since we know nobody will be coming in to get you, it is. That guy is you. And he was found dead two weeks ago. An effort to find next of kin started when he showed up. By the time you're eating breakfast, he'll be gone for good. Of course, I'll still be here getting it all done."

"It still seems way too easy," I said.

"I guess it ain't all that hard to make somebody dead, as long as you got the extra body."

"The rest of it won't be easy for me. I still need to go back and deal with this."

"Why go back?" Randy said, tapping on the paperwork he'd just completed. "Why not keep going? You're dead. Why would they keep coming after you if you're dead?"

"Maybe they won't. Maybe they'll never figure out that's not me. But maybe that's what gives me my best chance to take care of them."

"So you're going back there to kill them before they can kill you, even though you're already dead?"

"I don't have another choice."

"What if you go to Hawaii? At some point, they can't find you."

"They'll only stop trying to make me dead if they're dead."

"Sorry, but you don't seem like the type to kill somebody."

The way he said it made me feel defensive. "I am when I have no other choice."

"Have you ever had no other choice?"

"You should know."

"I should?"

"What do you think really happened to your friend?"

"It was a rattlesnake."

"I did what I had to do," I said, fudging the truth since he'd never know the difference. "I'll do it again, when I have to. Hopefully, I'll only have to do it one more time."

I turned around and walked out of the hospital. I knew I'd never be back there again.

I also knew he was right. Which made me realize I'd better be ready to change my ways, unless I planned on bringing a rattlesnake to Wheeling.

Twenty-four

OCTOBER 21, 1975

J.J. MESAGNE

I OPENED THE door to the apartment. I saw a pink smear where the blood and brains had been. At least they'd cleaned the floor.

"I tried to get it off the wall," my mother called out. "It's soaked in the plaster. Maybe we can paint it before we go."

I looked at the stain. "I'll get some paint from the hardware store over by the market."

"You know how to paint a wall?"

"How hard can it be? Dip the brush in the paint, put the paint on the wall."

"You'll need drop cloths or it'll get on the floor," she said.

"I've always said we have more towels than we need. Use some of them. There's no way we'll be packing them all."

Leslie walked out of the bedroom. Gnocchi followed her.

"How's the baby?" I said.

"He's been asleep since you left. Can you take the dog out, please? He's been freaked out all day."

I gave a quick whistle and he ran to me. His stubby tail flopped left and right, like a windshield wiper without the blade. It made me feel better seeing it. Not much, but a little.

"Let's leave by noon tomorrow. That'll give me time to paint the wall. We'll pack tonight. And we all need to get some sleep. The dog's not the only one that's been freaked out all day."

"We should go before noon," my mother said. "Those cops might come back. They came earlier and we didn't answer the door."

"We'll go as early as we can. But I can't get the paint until the store opens."

I lifted Gnocchi and took the stairs. I carried him to the strip of grass where he always did his business. When I put him down, he ran to a shrub, lifted a back leg, and watered it for a solid twenty seconds. Then he shuffled around before squatting and dropping a pile.

I didn't bring a bag. I thought about going back upstairs and getting one. I looked around the parking lot. I thought better of coming back out.

I whistled for him and he ran to me. I picked him up. "Well, my friend, we're about to break the rules. They can go ahead and evict us."

VINNY

After we finished the first round of victory cigars, we had another. We drank too much Lord Calvert. I skipped doing the stuff I needed to do. Paul was happy. I didn't want him to be happy all by himself. Especially since I was happy, too.

He said he had to piss. He rolled past me in the wheelchair, down to the bathroom we had to remodel so he could lift himself onto the commode. I don't know how everything works down there, and I don't wanna know. I can't imagine he had both legs blown clean off without his gear getting fucked up. I don't even like thinking about it.

Paul rolled back after a little bit. I knew he'd get mad if I tried to help. He wanted to show he can take care of himself, even if he really can't.

When he pulled on the tops of the wheels to get back under the desk, I thought again about how easy it would be. That would have been a perfect time for it. He wouldn't have seen it coming. He was in a good mood, as good a mood as anybody with no legs could ever be in.

"You know," he said, "we should have a party."

"A party?"

"You say it like you don't know what a party is."

"I know what a party is. Christmas is coming. Let's have one then."

"We was gonna have a Christmas party right before the thing happened," he said. "Remember?"

"I remember somebody saying parties is bad luck after the thing happened."

Paul struck a match and lit his cigar. "Now that we got the job done, maybe our luck changed."

"So now you wanna have a Christmas party?" I said.

He pulled on the cigar and blew out a white cloud. "I'm thinking we don't wait that long. Thanksgiving is coming in a couple weeks."

"You wanna have a party on Thanksgiving?"

"How about the night before?"

"Where?"

"Out front. The whole crew."

"Wives or girlfriends?"

He paused to think. "Wives," he said. "Especially since I currently ain't got a girlfriend. Unless the last one plans on showing up for it."

I was surprised he was joking about that. With that fucking kid gone, maybe he was changing back to more like the guy he used to be.

"We'll get some good food," he said. "Not cheap stuff. We'll show everybody a nice time. Maybe we hire the guy we heard sing at the racetrack that time. He reminds me of Dean Martin."

"If that's what you want."

He looked at me and wagged the cigar in his hand. "It would be nice to hear a little more excitement from you on this."

"All due respect, does that matter?"

"It's a happy time for me. It should be a happy time for you. This was a long road. After all this time, it's over."

"I just wonder if it's something to celebrate. Plenty of bad things happened because of Mesagne and his kid."

Paul's good mood was gone. He shoved the desk with both hands and pushed his wheelchair away from it, turning it so his stumps pointed right at me. "You think I don't know that? You think I don't deal with those bad things that happened, every fucking minute of every fucking hour of every fucking day?"

I thought again about how easy it would be. Part of me wanted to do it. Maybe that's why I didn't pipe down. "You're proving my point. Why celebrate?"

"Because it's finally over. Because we finally won. I knew we would, and we did. Was it easy? No. Was there a price to pay? You're looking at it. We need to turn the page. That's what this party is. Turning the page to a new beginning."

I didn't like it, but it wasn't my call. I don't know why I didn't like it. Maybe it was because I knew I'd be doing most of the work to get it ready.

"I'll start making the plans," I said. "And I'll get the word out to the crew."

"I want them all here. No excuses, no rain checks, no sick kids."

"I can guarantee you one thing," I said. "Everybody will show up for this one."

Twenty-five

OCTOBER 22, 1975

J.J. MESAGNE

I GOT UP earlier than I wanted. I needed to get supplies to paint the wall. I got both cars filled with gas. I went to the same place for the Oldsmobile and the Gremlin. The guy who stuck the nozzle in the tanks gave me a weird look the second time. I thought about giving him an extra twenty, but I didn't want him remembering me any more than he would.

The white paint didn't match the rest of the room. It was still better than what had been there. They finished packing while I painted. The baby made plenty of noise and filled his diaper twice. Better now than after we were on the road. Gnocchi stayed close to me the whole time. He liked the smell. He was licking it out of the air.

They'd take the Oldsmobile. I'd drive the Gremlin, with Gnocchi keeping me company. Just like when I drove to Arizona the first time.

I filled the cars with our luggage and boxes. I bagged up the other stuff and threw it in the dumpster. I should have been paying more attention, but I needed to move fast so we could get the hell out of there.

I was nervous and sweaty the whole time. Even though nothing happened, I didn't know it wouldn't. I knew that feeling was going to stay with me.

I told them we should bring only what we absolutely needed. I gave up fighting over some of the stuff. I just wanted to go.

While Leslie and my mother were getting settled in the Olds, I took the keys to the main office. I told the old man behind the counter we were leaving. He started going through a filing cabinet to find our lease. He said we might be breaking it. I knew we were. I just walked out while he complained. The last thing I cared about was the security deposit.

When I got back to the car, Leslie was behind the wheel, window down and green eyes glowing just enough to make me almost not regret everything I'd put her through. "You lead the way," she said. "Just don't drive too fast."

"You've driven that thing. It can't do too fast."

I climbed inside the Gremlin. I looked at my watch. It was five minutes after ten.

Gnocchi barked when I finished. It startled me, made me think someone was coming. I looked all around to be sure they weren't making one last run at me before I ran away, again.

MARCO

I GOT TO the back room ten minutes early. Sally Balls sat on one of the couches, smoking a cigarette and drinking something brown with ice in it.

"On time for a change," he said.

"Early for a change, too. I guess I'm growing up."

"That definitely didn't happen early."

After what I pulled off, I could deal with an insult or two. Besides, it ain't like he was wrong.

"Who else is coming?" I said.

"Just me and you."

I wanted to gulp. I fought it off.

"Get yourself a drink. Have a seat."

I grabbed the closest bottle and poured some of it into the closest glass. I took a sip. It burned my mouth. I tried not to show it. I sat down across from him.

"I talked to Jimmy Rigatoni yesterday," he said.

"I don't get the impression he likes me."

"He don't like too many people."

"It feels different with me."

Sally Balls took a big drag on his cigarette. He held the smoke in for a long time and then blew it out. "Why do you think that is?"

"He probably don't like that my dad's one of the bosses. He probably thinks I should kiss his ass more."

"You should kiss his ass some more. It's called showing respect to your elders. You'll be an elder yourself one of these days, if you're lucky."

I was getting a weird feeling. "Did I do something wrong?"

"You tell me."

I needed to act cool. It felt like Sally Balls was setting a trap and hoping I'd step in it.

"Not that I know of," I said.

"I don't think I buy your story."

I had that urge to gulp again. "What's not to buy?"

"Any of it. Some of it. All of it." He sat back in the couch. "Tell me again."

"We did the job. One of the women hit Joey Turtle. There wasn't nothing I could do about that. I took out the guy and the two women."

"When the woman shot Joey, what did you do?"

"I shot her back. And the other woman."

"How do you know Joey Turtle was dead?"

"She got him in the head."

"Plenty of people get shot in the head and live," Sally Balls said. He tapped against the metal plate in the side of his skull.

"He was dead."

"Did you check?"

"I ain't no doctor."

"It don't take no doctor to check if somebody's dead."

"He was dead. That's all I can tell you."

Sally Balls took another drag and another drink. He didn't say nothing for at least a minute. He was trying to make me even more nervous. It was working.

"I ain't the only one who don't buy your story," he said.

"My dad never said nothing about it."

"You can't do no wrong in his eyes, but he might be coming around."

"Otto?"

"Not him. Not yet."

Sally went back to his cigarette and his drink. He sat there for a while again before he said anything else. "Jimmy Rigatoni called me after you got back. He told me something didn't seem right when you got the car."

I couldn't fight off the gulp this time. I hoped he didn't notice. "What did he say?"

"What did I just say? He told me something didn't seem right."

"Did he say anything else?"

Sally Balls shook his head. "What else could he say? So I thought about it last night. This morning, I took a ride over to Scottsdale."

"What's in Scottsdale?"

"The morgue. You know, the place where they would have taken the bodies." He stopped again to take another drag. He spun his glass. The ice clinked around in it. "Do you wanna know what I found out?"

I've lied enough times to know that, once you're in, all you can do is stick with it. "There's nothing to find out other than what I told you."

"They had the paperwork for a stiff named John Jenkins."

"Who's John Jenkins?"

"That's one of the names they gave us two years ago."

"So it was him."

"I asked to see the body. The guy working there seemed nervous.

But he also didn't seem too surprised somebody like me would show up with questions."

"Why did you wanna see the body?"

"I wanted to see if it had nine fingers."

"Did it?"

"He said it was gone."

"Where would it go?"

"He said any bodies that don't get claimed after two weeks get sent out for cremation. The way you tell it, he would have shown up yesterday. Ain't that odd?"

"I guess it is."

"You know what else is odd? They didn't have two dead women in there. And there ain't nothing in the paper about four people getting shot dead in an apartment, a day after two got guys got shot dead out in the parking lot of the same place."

"That is odd," I said, because I couldn't say nothing else.

Sally Balls sat there, looking at me. He took a slow drink. "John Jenkins. This time, they said the kid was going by John Morris. So when he shows up dead, why ain't it John Morris?"

"I don't know," I said. "But if he's dead, he's dead."

"You're right about that, Marco. If he's dead, he's dead. And if he ain't, he ain't."

"You saw it for yourself. He's dead."

"But it didn't happen two weeks ago. It happened yesterday."

"Maybe it was a mistake. What do they call that? A clerkical error?"

"Clerical error. And maybe you're right. Still, there was one more thing. I asked about our friend, Joey Turtle."

"What about him?"

"I wanted to see the paperwork."

I was less nervous about this one, since that was the one guy who I knew would be there.

"They said they didn't have no stiff with Joey Turtle's name," Sally Balls said.

Twenty-six

OCTOBER 25, 1975

J.J. MESAGNE

WITH TWO CARS and three adults and one baby and one dog, we stopped at pretty much every rest area. It didn't help that the Oldsmobile guzzled gas. I made up my mind to get rid of that thing, once this ended. If I was able to do anything once this ended.

Leslie got sick of hearing me say how fast I'd made the trip on my own. So I shut up about it. I still didn't like how long it was taking.

It took more than eleven hours to get to Albuquerque, only four hundred miles away. I wouldn't let myself do the math. Once we were done for the day, I started singing *I'll Be Home For Christmas.* Leslie gave me a look. I stopped.

We stayed in one motel room. It was cheaper and safer that way. It wasn't more comfortable. My mother and Leslie slept in one bed. I slept with the baby in the other. Gnocchi kept finding new spots to piss on the carpet.

The next day, we made it to Amarillo. I didn't do any complaining. I did do plenty of moping. At one point, my mother told me off for being in such a hurry to jab a stick into a hornet's nest. She also asked about my plan for doing whatever I planned to do once we get back to Wheeling. I told her I was working on it.

That would work for now. It won't work for long.

Leslie was trying to get me to think about going to Canada. She would throw out names of cities she must have heard while watching the Olympics on TV. I couldn't tell whether she was serious, or whether she was just nervous about what would happen in Wheeling. At one point, I grabbed her hand and held it up, showing her where her finger had been blown off.

"This is the only solution," I said. I needed to convince them of that. I still needed to convince myself of it, too, if I was going to do what had to be done when it was time to do it.

On the third day, we made it to Oklahoma City. I stopped thinking about how long it was taking. I spent more time thinking about what I'd do when we got there.

They both knew asking me about it would only make me upset. So they stopped. I figured it was all they talked about while they drove. I liked that. It let them get it out of their system before we crammed ourselves into another shitty motel room.

We made it all the way to St. Louis the next day. Five hundred miles. I was happy about that, even if I kept getting more nervous the closer we got. We had dinner at a McDonald's near the motel. When I finished my Big Mac, I sucked the rest of the Coke down to the ice and put the cup on the table.

"I think I have a plan," I said.

"Good," my mother said.

"You don't know what it is yet."

"It's good that you have one. It'll be even better whenever you decide to share it."

"Nice try, but I need to work it through some more. I think we need to find a place where we can hide out until the time is right to make a move."

"I'll find us a place," my mother said.

"You make that sound easy," I said.

"It won't be," she said. "None of this is easy. But like you like to say, this is the only way."

Leslie looked at the bandage on her finger after my mother said that. I did, too.

Twenty-seven

OCTOBER 22, 1975

MARCO

HE HAD ME dead to rights. Which was better than being dead, but not by much.

I didn't have any reason to keep lying. I told Sally Balls I shot Joey Turtle. Sally Balls didn't get too upset about that.

I told Sally Balls I didn't shoot the kid from Virginia or wherever. He got real upset about that. He calmed himself down before he talked to me.

"Why didn't you just tell the truth?" he said.

"I didn't wanna go back there again."

"That ain't your call."

"I guess I made it my call."

"You got some balls. Maybe they'll call you Marco Balls. Unless I cut them off first."

Part of me wanted to laugh at that. Most of me wanted to get the fuck out of there.

"Do you know what you're gonna do next?" he said.

"I got a feeling I do."

I could tell that made him wonder. "What do you think it is?"

"I think I'm going back to Scottsdale and staying there until the guy is dead."

He shook his head. "Too late for that."

My body twitched when he said it. If they weren't gonna let me go back and end it, it meant they was gonna end me.

"You're taking the money back to West Virginia and telling them you didn't do the job."

That time, I couldn't stop myself from laughing out loud. "You're making me fly back there with a sack of cash?"

"You ain't flying."

I was too pissed by then to watch my words. "This keeps getting better and better."

"It gets even better." He had a big smile on his face, one that showed most of his teeth, and the two spots where teeth used to be. "You're paying the money yourself."

I jumped up without thinking. "I was afraid you was gonna whack me. This is worse."

"You might wanna check with your cousin about that," he said.

"So you're telling me I'm driving all the way to Virginia—"

"West Virginia."

"Whatever. I'm driving there and I'm paying them twenty grand of my own money?"

"I always thought you was smarter than you look. You're finally smarter than you act."

"I shouldn't have to pay it all myself. Those other guys fucked up first."

"You fucked up last. And it ain't like the other guys can come up with the money. Besides, you lied about it. That's your punishment."

"What's my punishment?"

"The whole thing. We make the refund. You take the money to West Virginia by car. You pay for it out of your own pocket."

I did my best to stay calm. "This seems a little harsh."

"Not as harsh as it would have been if your old man wasn't a boss."

"What if I don't wanna go?"

"You'll get the punishment you would have gotten if your old man wasn't a boss."

By then, I was as mad as I'd been in as long as I could remember. I managed to not say anything. I didn't manage to keep a hateful expression from my face.

Sally Balls grinned. "*Se gli sguardi potessero uccidere.*"

I didn't understand what he was saying. I didn't give a shit. "When am I going?"

"That depends," Sally Balls said.

"Depends on what."

"How long it will take you to get twenty grand together. Do you have it?"

"Not really."

"How long do you need?"

"How long can I have?"

"Not as long as you're gonna want, that's for sure."

"How's about January first?"

"How's about thirty days."

"That ain't enough."

"It wasn't a question."

I decided not to push it. "Does my dad know about this?"

Sally Balls drained his glass and got up. "I got a feeling he does," he said as he opened the door. "It was his idea."

Twenty-eight

OCTOBER 29, 1975

J.J. MESAGNE

THE END OF the line, for now, was Cambridge, Ohio. Rico, Tony, and I had stopped there on the way back from Canton, after I saw someone get killed for the first time.

It would take about an hour to get to Wheeling. I told my mother we'd stay until it was time for me to go there and finish it. Or finish myself in the process. I didn't say that part.

We found a diner. I didn't worry about anyone recognizing me. I still wanted to sit in the back of the room facing the door. I watched everyone who came in. I wanted to see if they looked familiar to me or, more importantly, if I looked familiar to them.

I had the baby on my lap. After we ordered, I decided to share my plan. I didn't mean to do it. It just happened.

I told them about the time we stole the beer truck, the night Paul had a bunch of people in his place. I wanted to make the move on a night like that. I wanted to wait for the crowd to thin out. I wanted to hit them after they'd gotten drunk. It was the only way to get an edge.

I whispered when I got to the part about the weapons. I told them I'd walk in with a shotgun and start blasting. I told them I'd have two handguns to use when the shotgun was empty. I told them I'd keep shooting until I took out Vinny. I told them that, once Vinny was out of the way, Paul would be easy pickings.

They stared at me while I talked, like they were hearing it from someone else. I stopped when I was finished and waited for them to say whatever they were going to say.

"Well," my mother said, "there's only one thing left to figure out."

"What's that?"

"Whether your casket will be open or closed."

Leslie laughed until I shot her a look. "Sorry," she said. "It's not funny. I mean, it's funny. But it's not funny."

I looked back at my mother. "Do you have anything better?"

"With all those hours you've had to think this through, I'd like to think you'd have something better."

"There's nothing better," I said. "I need to get them when they don't expect it. I need to get them when their guard is down."

"Their guard is never down," my mother said.

"This is the best chance to get their guard down."

"Moose Jaw, Saskatchewan is a better idea," Leslie said, "and I had that idea before we even left Arizona."

"We can't keep running. You know that. We'll never have a real life. The only way to end this is to end it. The only way to end it is this way. I need to do something they'll never expect."

"I definitely don't expect you to do it," my mother said.

"What does that mean?"

"You don't exactly have a track record of, you know, pulling the trigger."

"If I can get in a room with Vinny and Paul, I will."

"I'll believe it when it happens," my mother said. "Even then, it's too much for you to do it by yourself."

"I'm not in position to recruit help, and the last thing I'm doing is bringing the two of you with me."

"Why not?" my mother said.

"We can give the baby a gun, too. Maybe we can strap a hand grenade to the dog."

"Leslie will stay with the baby," my mother said. "If things don't work out, she can take him and the dog and go wherever."

"You talk about this like I'm not here," Leslie said. "I'd like to think I have some say."

"Neither of you has a say," I said. "This is my thing to clean up. I'm not bringing my mommy with me to do it, that's for damn sure."

"So what are you gonna do?" my mother said. "Stake out his place every night until it looks like enough of them are inside, drinking enough booze so you'll have a chance to get lucky against whoever is still there?"

"That's all I can really do."

"I can't believe we came all this way for a suicide mission," my mother said. "That's what it is, and you know it. You're not cut out for this."

"If it's my only chance to get them, I'll be cut out for it. I have no other choice."

"This isn't you," Leslie said. "You've told me that over and over again."

I handed the baby over to her. "I don't get it. You both know why we came back. You both know this is something I have to do. Now, all of a sudden, you don't think I can do what I came back here to do?"

"Maybe we needed to get close enough to it to realize how stupid it is," my mother said. "Maybe Leslie has been right all along. Maybe we should go to one of those places in Canada she's been talking about. We can drive to Detroit, cross the border into Ontario, and disappear."

"What do we do after we disappear? Live happily ever after? While I worry every hour of every day that someone, somewhere will realize I'm the guy with nine fingers that Paul Verbania wants dead? I thought it was over. It's obviously not. It won't be until I'm dead or he's dead."

"I don't like it," my mother said.

"I don't like it, either," Leslie added.

"Well, that's something we can all agree on. Because I don't like it. Not one bit. This is my only chance. This is my only choice. And this is what I'm going to do. You can take the baby and the dog and the Oldsmobile and go to Canada or wherever. I'm staying. I'm going to end this. If it ends me, so be it. I'd rather die now than wonder when and where it'll happen later."

The waitress brought the food just as I finished. I ordered meatloaf. I ate it like it was the last piece of meatloaf I'd ever eat.

For all I knew, it was.

Twenty-nine

NOVEMBER 22, 1975

MARCO

THIRTY DAYS WENT fast. Too fast. I still got the money together. I didn't wanna find out what would happen if I didn't.

At least they weren't making me drive my own car all the way across the country and back. It still counted as an official job. It was important to use one of the cars we kept for that.

I didn't live more than a mile or two from the lot. I decided to walk over, get the car, pack up the cash, and then hit the road for my trip to see a bunch of goombah rednecks.

I wondered if they'll whack me once I told them what happened. Maybe that'll be better than driving all the way back.

I tried to get them to send somebody with me. Sally Balls said I had to clean this mess up by myself. I didn't talk to my dad about any of it, and he didn't say anything about it to me. I didn't believe Sally Balls when he said it was my dad's idea for me to pay the money myself and drive it there. I didn't ask my dad, because I was afraid I was wrong.

I asked them to have Jimmy Rigatoni's backup give me the car. Sally Balls agreed to that a little too fast, like maybe Jimmy Rigatoni already said he didn't wanna mess with me. Ricky the Wrench didn't seem to hate me as much as Jimmy did. Ricky still didn't like me too much. Not that I gave a fat shit if he did.

Ricky the Wrench. It's weird how guys get their nicknames. Somebody sees him holding a wrench one fucking time, calls him Ricky the Wrench, and it sticks. Most people thought they called him that because he was so big you could hit him with a wrench and he wouldn't feel it.

I saw him standing out there, wiping down one of the boss's cars as I got closer to the lot. That bastard wouldn't feel getting hit by two or three wrenches.

He stood up straight when he saw me. "You ready for your road trip?"

"I'm ready for it to be over."

"Sooner it starts, sooner it's over." He threw a mostly-smoked cigarette to the ground and stepped on it.

"That's poetry. Or philosophy. Or some shit like that."

"I call it fact."

"You got any other facts for me?"

"I don't keep track of my facts, so I don't know."

"How about a fact like what car I'll be driving?"

Ricky smiled. Some of his teeth was bent and some of them was broken. "I know what car you'll be driving. Jimmy picked it out for you, special."

The keys were already in the air. I didn't need to see them to know.

"Fuck me," I said.

"No thanks," Ricky said.

"This ain't the car. This can't be the car."

Ricky pointed toward the orange Beetle. "It's got a fresh plate and registration from when you used it last month. Michigan. Drive safe."

"It's like two thousand miles. Each way. That fucking thing won't make it."

"That's why we got triple-A."

I threw the keys at him. They hit him in the chest and landed on the ground.

"Pick those up," he said.

"Give me a different car."

"That's the car." He pointed with his oversized left arm tight and stiff at the Volkswagen. "Straight from up top. If I give you a different car, it's my ass."

"You can tell them that one didn't start."

"When it does, it's my ass twice for lying."

"We can do something to it so it won't start."

Ricky stepped closer. He really was a big fucker. "That's the car. You're getting in it. One way or the other. You can choose to do it the normal way. Or you can choose to let me do it the not normal way. You won't like it that way."

"Do you know who I am?" I said it without really thinking it through.

"I know exactly who you are. You're the guy who fucked up a hit worth twenty grand and you're paying the money back out of your own pocket. And you're taking that car to deliver the money to the people who ordered it. Did I miss anything?"

"Fuck you, Ricky."

"Again, no thanks. Now, if you don't mind, pick up those keys, get in that car, and get the fuck out of here."

I walked over to the spot where the keys landed. I kept my eyes on him when I bent down for them. For all I knew, he was gonna knock me down just to prove a point.

"I'll remember this," I said after I picked them up. "You better watch your back."

"You better watch your front."

I gave him the finger before getting inside the car. I had to turn the key a couple times to get the engine to start. It was chugging. I pulled toward Ricky and rolled down the window.

"The engine's out of tune," I said.

"The engine's as fine as an engine like that's ever gonna be."

"Make sure you tell Sally Balls I said thanks a lot."

"You can tell him when you get back."

I gave Ricky the finger again, and he gave it back to me with both hands.

"Don't drop the keys around them hillbillies," he yelled as I pulled away. "They might make you squeal like a pig."

Thirty

NOVEMBER 12, 1975

LESLIE

THE MORE I tried to make sense of what he was doing, the less sense I could make of any of it. We'd been camped out in that motel for two weeks. Waiting. For what, I didn't know. He'd driven to Columbus. I didn't ask why. I already knew. He needed to buy guns.

Now, out of nowhere, he told me he wants to rent a car. I asked him why in the world he needed to do that while we were on our way to get it.

"I can't take this car," he said. "It's my dad's. Someone might recognize it."

"What about the other one?"

"They know that one, too. They stole it from someone, for the day they were going to kill me. I don't know if they'll remember it. It's hard to forget. Plus, it's always had bad energy."

"Then why did we keep it for two years?"

"Last time I checked, cars aren't cheap."

"Renting them isn't, either."

"It's a lot cheaper than buying one. I can't do what I need to do without it."

He parked the Oldsmobile on a long stretch of curb across from

Cambridge Rent-A-Car. "This will be over soon," he said. "We've got a better chance of getting the outcome we need if no one says, 'Hey, I know that car. Isn't that J.J. Jenkins driving that car?'"

"When this is over, we're selling that Gremlin."

"We'll probably have to pay someone to take it."

VINNY

I PULLED THE Cadillac away from Paul's house. I heard him peel the plastic from a cigar.

"How's everything looking for the party?"

"It's coming along good," I said. "Got plenty of extra booze ordered. The guy from up in Follansbee will bring down a bunch of pasta."

"His sauce is too fucking sweet."

"You want I should find someone else?"

"People like it. I'll just eat some sausage. Make sure he sends some without no sauce."

"That guy from the track, we got him to sing for a few hours. I figure eight until eleven."

"Why so early?"

"The next day's Thanksgiving. People ain't gonna wanna stay all night."

"I ain't cooking the next day, so I'll be there as late as I want," Paul said. "Sally, if she even comes, can go home and baste the bird early. You bringing anybody?"

"I'm working that night. Making sure it all works. Eyes and ears."

"Bullshit. You're gonna enjoy yourself. If you got a gal, bring her. Either way, you're shutting it down for a night."

"You know I can't shut it down," I said.

"I'll settle for taking the foot off the gas and enjoying a drink or two with me. We've been through a lot. I've been through a lot. We need to smell the roses, before it's too late."

LESLIE

HE LET ME pick out the car, like it would make me feel better about everything. I went with a brown Dodge Dart. It cost nine dollars and ninety-five cents per day, plus five cents per mile. I could tell he wanted something a little flashier. I told him this one would blend in with the scenery. The clerk made a face when I said it. I told J.J. it was just a joke. I hoped the clerk agreed, even if it wasn't funny.

He drove the rental back to the motel. I followed in the Oldsmobile. We went in. I played with the baby a little bit. He was getting to that age where he was into everything. I felt bad that all he can explore is a tiny little room, for God knows how long.

Next thing I knew, J.J. was standing there with a baseball cap and sunglasses.

"You look ridiculous," I said. "You never wear hats."

"I'm trying to not look like me."

Then it hit me. He was driving to Wheeling.

"You're going right now?" I said.

"Where are you going?" Maria said.

"We rented a car so I can go to Wheeling and get the lay of the land. It costs like ten bucks a day."

Maria walked up to him and yanked the sunglasses from his face. "You better promise me you ain't gonna do nothing."

"I'm just going to see what there is to see. It's been two years. I need to get acquainted with town again."

"I can guarantee you it ain't changed. It never changed in all the years we lived there."

"Regardless, this is part of the plan."

She crammed the sunglasses back into his hands. "The plan stinks."

"It's the best one I got." He turned to me for support, but I kept playing with the baby.

J.J. MESAGNE

I PUT THE sunglasses back on and got in the rental car.

I bought my disguise, if it really was much of one, the day before when I went to get more diapers. I saw a sporting goods store. The idea came to me, and I acted on it.

The first stop was the house on Poplar Avenue, where they shot him. I knew there wouldn't be any sign of it. I still needed to see the place.

I went past his bar. I tried not to drive too slow or too fast. I saw someone walking in who looked familiar. I kept going.

I went past the apartment building where I lived for all of a week. Up the road was Bobby's place, the dog shop where plenty of things happened. Things I didn't realize were quite so important as they were happening. I wondered if Bobby missed Gnocchi. For a second, I sort of felt guilty for taking him.

I went by Paul's place last. I was nervous the whole time. I was glad I didn't have a gun. I might have been tempted to go in and take my chances. I sped up without thinking when I saw a Cadillac parked out front. If nothing else, that told me I wouldn't have gone in there, even if I had a tank.

I started to leave town. I thought of something I should have thought about before I even got there. I went to the cemetery. I drove around until I found it. I parked the car and got out.

The tombstone had capital letters etched into the granite. JOHN J. MESAGNE. Under his name, I saw the first date: April 18, 1933. I fell to my knees when I saw the second one: October 20, 1973.

I stayed there for a long time, wishing I felt better about my plan or that, when I got up, I'd have a better one.

Thirty-one

NOVEMBER 13, 1975

J.J. MESAGNE

AFTER I GOT back from Wheeling, I paid for a second room. Maybe after seeing my dad's grave I decided life's too short to be stuck in a sardine can with three other people and a dog. Either way, we needed more space. If my plan didn't work, it's not like I'd need the money.

We moved to adjoining rooms, the only two the place had. Leslie and I slept on one side, and my mother and the baby stayed on the other. The dog had the freedom to piss or shit wherever.

The first morning after we got the second room, I walked through the door connecting them. My mother was sitting at a small table near the window, playing solitaire.

"How many games do you think you've played over the years?" I said.

"I could have put those hours to much better use, I know."

"So why do you do it?"

"What else am I gonna do?"

"Watch TV?"

"I watch plenty. At least when I do this, I'm involved. I'm not some vegetable staring at a box. Besides, I can never really focus on the show. I end up thinking about other things."

"Like what?"

"Regrets, mainly. Things I've done wrong."

"You haven't done much wrong," I said.

She stopped flipping cards onto piles and looked at me. "You mean other than gun down those two guys in that parking lot?"

"You had to do it. They were going to kill me. And maybe Leslie and you. Maybe the baby."

"I still did it. I still carry that around. Along with the rest of my guilt. More than forty years of it."

"I've only been around for half. I haven't seen much for you to feel guilty about."

"There are things you don't remember. Things you can't remember that I can't forget."

"You're being dramatic."

"Look at your finger."

"Which one?"

"The one that ain't a finger no more. Do you know how that happened?"

"Some kind of accident."

"What kind of accident?"

"I don't know. I just thought it was an accident."

"It wasn't no accident," she said.

"How was it not an accident?" I said. "Who deliberately cuts off the pinkie of a toddler?"

My mother looked at me. She reached for my left hand and rubbed the spot where the finger was. Her eyes got wet.

"Tell me," I said. "How was it not an accident?"

She wouldn't say anything. She made her mouth tight, like she was forcing herself to stay quiet. Tears started to roll down her face. She gripped my hand.

I was getting mad. Her crying didn't change that. I pulled my hand away and stood.

"How was it not an accident?"

Thirty-two

NOVEMBER 24, 1975

MARCO

THE ROOM HAD two beds. I was on the one that was still made, watching TV. The bucktoothed cowgirl that picked me up at the bar down the street was in the other one, naked and under the covers. She was asleep or passed out.

I lit a cigar and started smoking. I didn't care if it bothered her. First, she'd have to wake up. If she did, maybe the smoke would run her off. I wanted to sleep and I didn't wanna worry about her robbing me after I was out.

Once the cigar was gone, she hadn't moved. She was sort of snoring but not really. The sound was annoying. Plus, I was getting tired.

I reached my leg across and kicked at the other bed. "Hey," I said. "Canteen."

She stirred some but didn't wake up. I kept nudging the mattress with my foot.

"Canteen. Canteen. It's late."

"My name ain't Canteen. It's Carlene."

"I like Canteen better."

"You woke me up to tell me that?"

"How long have you lived here?"

"I moved to Amarillo a few months back. Came from San Antonio. That's where I was raised." She propped herself up on an elbow. A bare boob tumbled out from under the sheet. "These sure seem like questions that can wait 'til morning."

"I might need a new place to live. Do you like Texas?"

"Don't matter if I like it. It's all I know. I only moved up here because my ma left my pa and she wanted me up here with her."

"How old are you again?"

"I done told you I's old enough."

"But how old are you?"

"Nineteen. I'll be twenty right after Christmas. Why? How old are you?"

"Too old for this shit. Too old for this life."

"Mister, I ain't done nothing to you."

I swung both feet around and put them on the ground. "I never said you did. I just wanted to know what you think about Texas. And I wanted to be sure I won't end up living in a prison here if you ain't eighteen."

"You wouldn't like it here. You sort of stand out. Not in a bad way. But you don't look like nothing we got around here. I guess that's why I bought you a drink."

"You did more than buy me a drink."

"Well," she said, "everything's gotta start with something."

As much as I wanted her to go, I climbed back into bed with her.

"Canteen," I said, "I like how you think."

I DIDN'T DO nothing stupid like stay in Texas. I also didn't do nothing even stupider like ask Canteen to come with me. But my night with that skanky tumbleweed gave me an idea.

When I got behind the wheel of my orange windup toy, I became a man with a plan.

That plan didn't involve going to West Virginia, handing over twenty-thousand dollars of my own money, and driving back to Arizona.

I could tell Canteen noticed a change. She seemed impressed. She seemed drawn to me. I rolled the crank on the window as she came over to the car. She leaned her face inside.

"Ain't you gonna kiss me goodbye?"

"Sorry," I said, "but your breath smells like shit."

She spit on the window after I rolled it up and started to drive off.

Thirty-three

NOVEMBER 13, 1975

J.J. MESAGNE

My mother told me what happened. She cried through most of it. She had to stop twice. I kept looking at the door between the rooms to see if the noise woke Leslie up.

She had ignored it all for years. Pushed it inside, she said. Deep enough that she'd never be reminded of it when seeing the spot where my finger had been. In time, it became normal. Nine instead of ten.

She said my father had stopped at a gas station to get a pack of cigarettes from a machine inside the lobby. Someone had snatched me from the car.

He told her it had to be random. She knew otherwise from the start. She told him that's not the type of thing that happens to someone in a small town who isn't involved in the stuff my father was involved in.

She thought it had something to do with a big score they'd just made. They robbed a truck that had dresses and suits. My dad found a box of diamonds in a trap door under the front seat that he opened by accident when his heel landed in the right spot.

She said he thought about keeping it and not saying anything to anyone. He decided that wouldn't be right. He told the others who were with him. They sold the diamonds, gave ten percent to Paul, and shared the rest.

"How much did he get?" I said.

"Thirty-six thousand dollars."

Two days after the money was split up, someone grabbed me. She wanted to go to the police right away. He said they should wait, just in case she was right.

"So what happened?" I said.

"We got a ransom note two days later."

"How much did they want?"

"Thirty-five thousand dollars."

"So he had the money? He had enough? That should have ended it."

"I thought it would," she said. "But there was some kind of mix-up. Someone screwed up the address for the exchange. I saw the note. Your dad went to the right place. Whoever wrote the note used the wrong address."

"So he was there with the money, but whoever took me was somewhere else?"

"That's what happened." She started crying some more as she said it. I thought about going over to console her. I didn't.

"I saw the note. I wanted to blame your dad. But I saw the note. He was in the right place. They screwed it up."

"What did they do?"

"Your dad tried to get in touch with whoever it was, to let them know he had the money and he was ready to hand it over. And then we got another note."

"What did it say?"

"I'll never forget it," she said. "It had two words written on the page. All capital letters. *STRIKE ONE.*"

"So you got another chance?"

"The note had a box with it."

I looked at my left hand, down at the spot where the rest of the last finger had been. My mother started crying harder.

"So that was it? You get a warning, I lose a finger. Then the exchange happens and you get me back?"

"Yes and no. We got another note with instructions on where to go, and your dad went there with the money. He put it where he was supposed to put it, in the back seat of a car that had been parked in a specific spot. He waited until someone came in a ski mask to drive the car away. Then he waited for someone to give you back to him, but they never showed up.

"How did you get me back?"

"Paul got you back."

"How the hell did he do that?"

"After we made the payment and didn't get you, your dad went off the deep end a little. So did I. We thought we'd never see you again. Then, all of a sudden, Paul calls and says he has you. He said one of his guys stumbled across a group of drug addicts who had a baby, and that he thought something wasn't right, so he took the baby and it ended up being you."

I shook my head at her. "You believed that?"

"Your father did. He called Paul a hero. I never talked about it. I was just glad to have you back. How it happened didn't matter. But, yes, I've always thought that son of a bitch was behind it. Of the three guys who found the diamonds, your dad was the only one who had a kid or even a wife at the time. Your dad was the most vulnerable."

"Why are you telling me this now, after all these years?"

"There was never a reason to. There was never a time to. With whatever it is you're planning to do, consider this a little extra motivation to finally give that mutherfucker what he deserves for what he's done to this family."

Thirty-four

NOVEMBER 24, 1975

LESLIE

HE MADE FIVE more trips to Wheeling. I didn't know what he was looking for. He probably didn't, either. He only said he needed to feel comfortable when the time came to do what he had to do.

I wasn't thrilled about the cost of two rooms and day after day of a rented Dodge Dart. He said if this works it would be money well spent and, if it doesn't, money would rank fairly low on his list of things to worry about. I didn't know what to say to that, so I told him it would be nice not to have Thanksgiving dinner in this crappy motel. He just raised his eyebrows when I said it.

Maria stayed out of it. I think she liked that it was taking some time. She didn't say it, but I knew. If her son would be walking into something he might not walk out of, there was no reason for him to run.

Maria was up to something, too. I wasn't sure what. There was a payphone by the office at the motel. She was talking to people in Wheeling. She didn't say much about who it was and what they were telling her. She promised me nobody knew where we were staying.

She asked me not to tell J.J. about her phone calls. After I agreed, she started telling me a little bit more.

He went to Wheeling again today. After he left, Maria made more calls. I held the baby and watched from the room while she stood in the phone booth, filling it with cigarette smoke. After a while, I saw her shove it open and start walking as fast as she could in her shoes that had low heels and bad grip.

I opened the door as she got closer. She rushed past me and grabbed a cigarette.

"What's going on?"

She didn't answer until a fresh one was lit and she'd taken a long drag. She held in the smoke and blew it out.

"I think I have good news."

J.J. GOT BACK a few hours later. The dog ran over to him when he walked in. The baby tried to chase the dog.

He looked at Maria and me. We were smiling.

"What's going on here?" he said after he picked up the baby.

"I got some information for you," Maria said.

"I haven't changed my mind. We're still not going to Canada."

"We know the next time they'll all be at Paul's," she said.

"You what?"

"We know when they'll be there."

He looked at both of us, back and forth. "How do you know?"

"You were never going to find anything out without blowing your cover. I had to see what I could dig up."

He put the baby down. The baby followed the dog toward the door connecting the rooms. "So what exactly did you dig up?"

"Wednesday night," she said. "Night before Thanksgiving. He's having some kind of party for his people. They're celebrating."

"What are they celebrating?"

Maria shrugged and smiled. "Apparently, Paul thinks they got you."

J.J. smiled, too. Then he stopped. "That's only two days away," he said.

Maria and I stopped smiling, too.

Thirty-five

NOVEMBER 25, 1975

MARCO

I GOT A flat tire just outside of Indianapolis. I managed to pull the Beetle off the highway. I rolled in lopsided to a service station near the bottom of the ramp. It had two bays and no cars on the lifts.

A guy who looked to be about my age walked over. He was drying his hands on a shirt that had a patch over the chest. Wayne. He seemed as happy as a mechanic could ever be.

I gestured to the car that was tilted toward the wheel with no air in the tire.

"Let me guess," Wayne said. "Dead battery."

"Let me guess, this ain't the first time you ever used that joke."

He stopped seeming so happy. "I ain't the one who needs a tire fixed. You want my help, maybe you should pretend my joke is funny."

"Look, I've been driving a long time. I need to get to where I'm going."

"See," he said as he went over to look at the tire, "this is better. Now we're making conversation. Where is it you're trying to get to?"

"Wheeling," I said. "West Virginia. Ever been?"

"I've never even heard of it."

"They tell me this highway will take me there. That it's right on the other side of Ohio."

"You ain't getting there without a fresh tire," he said. "This one's fucked. We'll get it on a jack. I'll see if you bent the rim."

I didn't think about the rim. That's all I'd need. Twenty grand plus the cost of a new rim for this soap bubble on wheels they made me drive.

Wayne opened the door to one of the bays. "Where you coming from?"

"Phoenix. Ever heard of that one?"

"You afraid to fly or something?"

"The reason for the long drive is a long story. One you ain't got time to hear."

He opened the front end of the car. "Well, if that rim is bent, you might have plenty of time to tell it. You ain't got no spare in here."

"What do you mean, no spare?"

"I don't know what else no spare means. What did you do with it?"

"Those fucking bastards," I said.

Wayne tried not to smile. "Since you said more than one, I can only assume you ain't talking about me."

He pulled the car onto the rack. He got out and hit the button to lift it. Part of me wished I had a job that simple.

The wheel came off fast. He peeled the tire away. He rolled the rim on the floor of the shop. "Looks fine to me. I'll check to see if we got a tire in the back that'll fit."

"How long will it take?"

"That's the easy part. If you want a spare, I need to make a couple of phone calls."

"Fuck the spare. I got this far without it. How long until I can get going?"

"Well," he said as he picked up the wheel. "It's two days to Thanksgiving. I can guarantee you'll get to where you're going without missing out on the pumpkin pie. Unless you get another flat."

Thirty-six

NOVEMBER 26, 1975

LESLIE

HE WAS WEARING a vest I'd never seen before. I asked him what it was. He said it'll keep him warm. I said it looked like it had bullets or something in it. He told me not to worry about that. I knew when to stop.

He told us to stay at the motel. He didn't want any goodbyes. He said he'd be back later that night. He seemed confident when he said it. I was glad one of us was.

Maria and I held it together until he left. After the door closed, we hugged each other and cried. The baby looked at us. The dog looked at the baby and then pissed on the floor again.

We heard a trunk slam. We waited for the sound of a door closing and an engine starting. After it happened, Maria pulled the curtain back just enough to look outside.

She let it go and turned toward me. Her mascara was running down her face, under both eyes.

"He's gone," she said. "Let's go."

MARCO

IT WAS GETTING dark when the Volkswagen crossed the big concrete bridge into town. There was a giant neon sign that said *Marsh Wheeling Stogies* on the other side, sitting on top of a brick building that must have been five or six stories high. I got off right there, onto Main Street.

Every town got a Main Street, I thought. Even a shit town like this.

It was time to deliver the twenty large, or whatever else I'd be giving them. The bag with the cash was in the back seat. A .38 with six in the cylinder was next to me. I had a box with fifteen or twenty more bullets in the glove compartment.

I found a map of Wheeling in this armpit of a state when I stopped near Columbus for the last splash of gas. I studied it until I knew where I was going. I didn't wanna have it open once I got here, or I'd look like some schnook who don't know where he is or where he's going.

For a minute or so I wished I wouldn't find the place. That wouldn't go over too good with Sally Balls. I could picture that phone call.

Hey, Sally, I came all this way and I can't find it. I'm heading home.

So I kept going to where I needed to go. I wasn't happy about giving them my money. They might not be happy about the way they might be getting it.

VINNY

PAUL WAS RIGHT. The guy sounded like Dean Martin. He sure as shit didn't look like him, not up close. He must have been pushing fifty. He had pock marks on his cheeks and his hair was dyed blacker than lumps of coal. I had to hand it to him. He showed real confidence in front of that three-piece band. Plus, he wore a tux that looked like it cost more than a few bucks.

The alcohol helped. It helped the performer, and it helped the audience. Most of the people in the joint was a drink or two away from thinking the guy really was Dean Martin.

The smoke helped, too. A few steps back from the front and, yeah, maybe he could pass for the real thing.

Everybody was smoking cigarettes or cigars, all night. I saw Bobby with one of each. Everybody had been drinking plenty, too, and they kept going.

The food was pretty good. It got better the more we drank. Meat, cheese, crackers, pasta, sausage. Paul wanted a party after we got that fucking kid, and he got one.

He kept saying I should cut loose. I kept saying I was working. He said he ordered me to do it. I had a hard time arguing with that. So I had a few drinks. I tried to have some fun.

Paul sat near the back of the room in his chair. He had a box of Cubans he opened for the party. He was on his second or third. Not everybody got one. Most of the guys was smoking cheap ones that came in plastic wrappers.

I walked back toward Paul. Bobby was sitting on the other side of his table.

"How about a refill?" Paul said to him. He didn't say what he wanted. He didn't need to. We knew he only drank Lord Calvert and ice.

The seat next to Paul was empty. I sat down and leaned his way. "How many is that for you?" I said.

"Tonight, I ain't counting."

"I am. So how many?"

"How many for you?" Paul said.

I took a drink from my glass. "You just said you ain't counting."

"Well, get over there and count yourself another. I told you, this is a fucking party. This is a night to be happy."

I finished what was in my glass. I think I smiled. I got up and walked back to the bar. I caught myself humming along to Dean's long-lost *cugino*.

J.J. MESAGNE

I FOUND A spot close enough to see who was coming and going. At that point, they were mostly going. They straggled out in pairs, man and woman together. Every time the door opened, I could hear music from a band.

I'd been sitting in the Dodge for more than two hours. In the trunk, there was a Mossburg magazine-fed shotgun and two AMT Automag III semi-automatic pistols. I didn't know what that meant when I bought them, but it sounded good. I kept running my hands over the ammo I stuffed into the vest. Six clips for the handguns. Nine shells for the shotgun. That would be more than enough, if I could get them all loaded and fired.

If I managed to fire at least once.

I kept looking at the spot where my pinkie had been.

I checked the time. It would be eleven soon.

MARCO

I FOLLOWED THE directions I'd memorized. I parked down the block from the place. I started to get out but noticed a bunch of people going in. I could hear music when the door swung.

It looked like they were having some kind of party. That probably wouldn't be the best time to show up with bad news. Or maybe it was the perfect time.

Most of the people came from a parking lot on the other side of the street. I was back far enough so nobody could see me. I kept sitting in the car, watching and waiting and getting the lay of the land.

At one point, I saw somebody sitting in another car, like I was doing. Sitting there, doing nothing.

I took the box of bullets out of the glove compartment. I counted them. I put half in the left front pocket of my pants. I put the other half in the right pocket.

LESLIE

I DROVE THE Oldsmobile to Wheeling. We got close to Paul's place. We saw the rental car. We parked far enough behind J.J. so he couldn't see us.

"I still don't understand what you're going to do," I said.

"I'm gonna do whatever I have to do. You'd do the same for your son."

"I can't believe we just left him with someone I've never even met."

"Didn't I introduce you when we got there?"

"Sure."

"Then you've met her."

"You know what I mean. What if something happens to us?"

"Nothing will happen to you. Whatever happens down there, you're driving away and picking up the baby."

I turned around to look at the dog. He was curled up on the back seat. "I still don't understand why we didn't leave him with your cousin, too."

"She didn't seem too happy about the dog. Then again, she never seems too happy about anything since her nephew died."

"Then why did we leave the baby with her?"

"We had no other choice. We agreed a long time ago we can't let J.J. do this by himself. I trust her. I wouldn't have left my grandson with her if I didn't. Do you remember where she lives?"

"I know exactly where it is."

"If this ends up going to shit, you get him and you take him and the dog to wherever else you feel safe."

"That damn dog."

He raised his head. He whimpered when he saw the look on my face.

"He's not so bad," Maria said. "Maybe one of these days he'll actually be housebroken."

"So how long is this going to take?"

"As long as it takes. I'll move when J.J. does."

I sighed and shook my head. "Well, there's at least one good thing that came out of this."

"What's that?"

"I got to see my old car again. You see it parked over there, right? The orange Volkswagen."

"I've seen it since we got here," she said. "I saw something you didn't."

"What's that?"

"Somebody is sitting inside."

Thirty-seven

NOVEMBER 26, 1975

VINNY

I WATCHED THE band pack up their instruments. They started taking stuff out to the van, one load at a time. Music was coming from the jukebox. Paul threw quarters at whoever was close to it, telling them to play songs he liked.

Most of the people had left. Paul's wife didn't come. Bobby and a couple of others came back after they took their dates home.

Paul called for Bobby to get him another drink. Bobby glanced over at me.

"Don't look at him," Paul said. "Don't ever look at him." Paul threw his glass toward Bobby. It missed and busted on the floor. Paul shoved forward on his wheels, pushing the chair so close that his stumps almost pressed into Bobby's legs. "You hear me? You don't fucking look at him. I'm in charge here."

I hurried over and got a fresh glass for Paul. "It's OK," I said. "Bobby didn't mean nothing by it."

"Clean that shit up," Paul said to Bobby. "And Vinny, gimme my fucking drink and you better pour yourself another."

"I had enough. I still gotta drive you home."

"We can sleep wherever. It ain't like Sally's waiting up for No-Legs to come home tonight."

Bobby's head jerked in Paul's direction. Mine did, too.

"What? I know what they call me. I figure you guys call me that, too. No-Legs. It's fine. It's accurate."

I carried the drink to Paul. "We don't call you that," I said.

"I don't give a shit. It's true. I ain't got no legs. At least they can't call me No-Dick."

J.J. MESAGNE

I PERKED UP when I saw people I didn't recognize carrying boxes out of Paul's place. Someone pulled up in a van. They started filling it, one at a time.

I didn't know what it was at first. When I spotted a bass drum, I figured it out. The band was leaving. I hoped that meant the party was over.

I waited until the last ones walked out and didn't go back. I watched the van pull away.

Once it was gone, I opened the door and stood.

I went to the trunk. I could feel the clips and the shells shifting inside the vest. I started to put the key in the lock. I looked around. I stopped when I saw something on the other side of the street, over my right shoulder. I couldn't believe my eyes.

Leslie's car. The orange Beetle. The one I left in the alley by my apartment the night I escaped. I walked toward it, without considering whether it was a good idea.

As I got closer, I noticed someone sitting inside. I started to turn around when the window came down.

"Can I help you, pal?" The voice was rough and choppy. I saw a profile that looked less like it was chiseled from granite and more like it was carved from a tree trunk.

"Sorry. I didn't see you in here."

"Now you do. So get the fuck out of here."

I raised my hands. "I didn't mean anything. I recognized the car. I wanted to see if it was the same one."

I turned to walk away. I heard that voice again.

"Wait, are you missing a finger?"

LESLIE

"He's getting out," Maria said. "I think he's getting out."

We saw J.J. stand up. He moved to the back of the rental car. We saw him look behind it.

"Does he see us?" Maria said.

"I think he's coming this way. What should we do?"

"He's going over to that Volkswagen."

"Why's he doing that?"

"I have no idea," Maria said.

We watched him. He was talking to whoever was in the car. He put his hands up. He started to walk away. Then he turned back.

"Now what's he doing?" I said.

J.J. got closer to the window. He was talking to the driver. He stayed there, for a while. He stepped back. He walked around to the front of the car. He opened the passenger door and disappeared.

"What's going on?" I said.

"He got in that car. Why would he get in that car?"

MARCO

After I saw he was missing a finger, I made it clear right away I wasn't looking to finish the job we tried to do in Arizona. He thanked me. It sounded sarcastic. I guess I can't blame him.

I told him they made me drive all the way from Phoenix to give back the money. I left out the part about going to his apartment with Joey Turtle, and the part about leaving without him.

He said he needed to tell me something. He asked if he could get in the car. I shrugged.

After he closed the door, he told me there's a good chance I can keep my money. That got my attention. It also got me thinking I can keep my money if I changed my mind about not taking care of him then and there.

But how would that work? I kill him and then what? Put the body in the back seat and drive away? I can't get the local crew to help me. They'd never believe I tracked him all the way back to West Virginia, not after we already told them he got killed in Arizona. His idea made more sense, even if it was gonna take some real balls.

"What are you gonna do?" I said. "Go in there guns blazing?"

He looked down the street. He looked back at me. "Basically."

"You ain't ever killed nobody. You don't have the look."

"There's a look?"

"You ain't got it, at least not that I can see."

"Do you have it?"

"You tell me."

"So what are you suggesting?"

"How many guns you got?"

"A shotgun and two pistols. You?"

I held up the .38.

"Have you had that in your hand the whole time?"

"I was holding it so you wouldn't notice. That's one of the things you learn when you actually done this before."

"It sounds like you want to do this again," he said.

"I want to keep my twenty grand. So, yeah, if you're already planning to bum rush those assholes, it's worth my time to help you. I might have been thinking about doing it anyway."

"I've got my stuff in the trunk." He pointed a finger from the hand that didn't have all of them. "Over there."

We checked the front door. The coast looked clear. We got out of the car and walked across the street.

Thirty-eight

NOVEMBER 26, 1975

LESLIE

"IT'S HAPPENING," MARIA said.

"What's happening?"

"They're getting ready to go in. J.J. and that other guy. Did you know he was working with somebody else?"

"How is there someone else?"

"You see there's two of them, right? Whoever was in the car that looks like your old car is going with J.J. back to the other car. He didn't tell me there was anybody else."

"In case you haven't noticed, he hasn't told me much of anything," I said.

We watched J.J. open the trunk. The other man lifted a shotgun with one hand, and he held out the other while J.J. reached into his vest and handed things to him. I could see their breath, coming together in a cloud that disappeared before the next one started.

"He's giving him shells for that shotgun," Maria said.

"How do you know that?"

"What else would he be giving him?"

I saw J.J. reach back into the trunk. He pulled out two guns, one in each hand. He pushed the lid shut with his elbow.

"Yep, it's happening." Maria said.

They went toward the door to Paul's place. Maria pulled her purse from the floor of the Oldsmobile. She zipped it open and took out her gun.

"Not again," I said.

"Who saved the day back in Arizona? I don't want a medal, but I'd like to think you realize I'll do whatever has to be done. If I was willing to do it then, I'm definitely willing to do it now."

"What did I marry into?"

Her eyes flashed. "Don't start with that shit. Not here. Not now. You knew damn well what you were getting into the first time you climbed into bed with Paul. I don't care how young you were. That's the moment you signed your name for everything that came after that."

Maria swung the door open and started to get out. She held the gun in her left hand.

"Wait," I said.

"What now?"

"I just didn't want that to be the last thing my mother-in-law ever said to me."

She looked at the gun. "You're not getting away from me that easy."

VINNY

PAUL KEPT THROWING quarters at Bobby. He kept barking out the names of songs he wanted to hear. I had enough booze by then to laugh at what was happening. I took another drink. I liked the feeling of being in a good mood, probably because it didn't happen too much.

Everybody else laughed, too. Even Bobby. It helped that he was drunk. I mean, Paul was out of line a little bit. It felt more like he was just having fun. Like we was a bunch of kids, fucking around and having a good time.

There was six of us in the room, now that the band was gone. It was like old times. Like it was back when we was coming up and didn't have a care in the world. I tried to think about how long it'd been since I felt that way.

That's when the door flew open and the flashes and the booms started.

J.J. MESAGNE

"I'LL TAKE THE shotgun," he said. "How many shells you got?"

"There's two in the magazine. I got more in my vest."

"They ain't gonna do me no good in there."

I started digging into the vest and handing over the other shells I'd packed.

"I'll go in first and start blasting," he said. "You cover me."

"What does that mean?"

"Are you fucking serious?"

I just looked at him.

"Look," he said, "you shoot at them if they start shooting at me. That'll draw their attention away. Got it?"

"So that means they'll start shooting at me?"

"They're gonna be shooting at somebody. At some point, they'll be shooting at both of us. The idea is to get them before they get us."

I had the urge to throw up.

"You sure you can do this?"

I thought about what he said. If I was alone, I probably couldn't have done it. It helped to have someone else who would fire the first shots. I looked at my hand with the missing finger. I thought about my father. I thought about my son.

"I'm sure I can do it."

"Then let's get this shit show on the road."

He started walking. I followed. We crossed the street and moved down the block. He didn't stop. If anything, he started moving faster.

He went right to the door and kicked it open. I flinched at the sound of the shotgun. He fired twice and reloaded. He yelled something at me before he fired again.

Thirty-nine

NOVEMBER 26, 1975

J.J. MESAGNE

I FOLLOWED HIM inside. He kept shooting. I hadn't fired yet. I held both guns up and looked for someone to aim at. I heard a bullet whizz by my ear. I thought that would get me to pull the trigger. It didn't.

The other guy kept shooting twice before reloading. I wondered whether he knew I hadn't gotten off a single shot.

VINNY

AT THE FIRST sound, Barbasol Larry had his chest blasted open. I threw my drink down and went for my piece.

I seen Hardhead's arm get blown off, under the elbow. Another shot put a huge hole in the wall.

I tried to shoot back. My brain and my eyes didn't wanna focus. The guns going off helped snap me out of the booze some. Not enough.

Paul had blood all over his chest. "Am I hit? Am I hit?" I put my hand all over him and didn't feel no holes. "What the fuck is happening?"

"I'll protect you," I said.

I had my gun out. At first I forgot there was another one on my leg. I started shooting. I shot without trying to see what I was shooting at. It made me think of what those schmucks who go off to war have to deal with. Just shooting at anything, shooting at nothing.

I kept doing that. Shooting at anything. Shooting at nothing.

J.J. MESAGNE

EVEN THOUGH I wasn't shooting, I wasn't afraid to get shot. I wasn't even thinking about that. I just assumed it would happen. The only question was whether it would kill me.

Not many shots came back at us. When they stopped, the other guy quit shooting. The song *Rhinestone Cowboy* was playing. I saw the other guy put fresh shells in the shotgun. I could see smoke coming from its barrel.

He looked at me. He looked at my guns. I wondered if he noticed there was no smoke coming from either one.

I saw the jukebox. Someone was on the ground. His combover was pulled away, showing his bald head.

"It's him!" Bobby shouted. "It's the guy that stole my fucking dog!"

Before I could say anything back, the other guy hit Bobby with a shotgun blast, right in the neck. The record skipped but kept playing.

That's when I saw Vinny, standing there with a gun pointed at me. "You're supposed to be dead," he said. "We paid twenty large."

"Twenty large don't buy what it used to," I said.

I thought the other guy might shoot him, the same way he shot Bobby. He didn't. It made me wonder if he was out of shells.

He yelled at Vinny to drop the gun. Vinny said it was empty anyway. He threw it on the floor.

I heard another voice, from behind Vinny.

"Who's that? Who's here?"

Vinny stepped away. I saw Paul. Paul saw me. The look on his face was disgust and surprise and resignation, all in one. I liked it.

"You picked one hell of a way to come home," he said to me.

"You picked one hell of a way to come kill me in my home," I said.

"I don't know what you heard. Look at me." He pointed toward the stumps in his wheelchair. "I got no legs. What can a guy with no legs do?"

I heard someone start screaming from behind me, loud and piercing. Then the words started coming. I heard them, plain as day.

"A guy with no legs can crawl straight to fucking hell!"

It was my mother. She ran through the room. She had her gun up. She fired twice. The first one hit him in the sternum. It pushed his wheelchair back into a wall. The next one got him right above the eye.

Vinny made a move for his leg. He pulled out a gun he had strapped to it. He pointed it at my mother.

She pointed her gun at Vinny. Neither one fired.

I remembered I was holding two guns. I remembered I hadn't been able to pull the trigger, in Arizona or here. I forgot whatever it was that kept me from doing it when I saw it was my mother who was about to get shot.

That's when the switch finally flipped, down inside me.

I started firing at Vinny. I closed my eyes after the first one. I stepped forward with each shot. I must have pulled the trigger seven or eight times.

I opened my eyes. He was slumped over Paul in his chair.

"It's about time you used them fucking guns," the other guy said.

"Is that it?" I said.

"What else did you expect?"

"I guess I just thought it would be harder."

My mother stepped over to hug me. "If you don't think it was hard," she said, "you ain't been thinking too much since you came home from college."

Forty

NOVEMBER 26, 1975

J.J. MESAGNE

WE RAN OUT of Paul's place. The other guy went to the Volkswagen. Before he got in, I shook his hand and asked his name.

"Marco," he said. "Marco Morelli."

I should have known it was him. "We've met before," I said.

"We have?"

"Sort of."

He made a face but didn't say anything else. He got in the Beetle and left. I went for the rental car. I told my mother we'd meet at the motel. She hugged me and told me to be careful driving, that there are a lot of crazy people on the highway.

"If I was going to die tonight, it would have happened down there," I said.

"You still could," she said.

At that point, I figured I'd take my chances.

LESLIE

After J.J. drove away, I went down to pick up Maria. Before we pulled out, we heard the sound of sirens.

"Just act normal," she said. "Don't go too fast."

That was easier said than done. I wanted to get away from there. I worried someone might be chasing us. I tried to focus on getting back to Locust Avenue.

"What happened?" I said. I could see police cars flying by us the other way.

"It's over."

"What do you mean?"

"It's done. It's over. Over over."

"So that's it?"

"That's the same thing your husband said."

"I just thought it would feel different."

"Give it time. For now, we pick up the baby and go back to the motel. We should stay there for a few days. If we show up in Wheeling tomorrow, somebody might start connecting dots."

"I can't believe it's really over."

"Almost. I'll feel better once we get the baby from Aunt Carol and we're back in Cambridge."

"I thought you said she was your cousin?"

"She's my grandmother's brother's daughter's sister-in-law. First cousin, once removed. By marriage."

"Why do you call her Aunt Carol?"

"She's older than me. It's a sign of respect. I've known her all my life."

"Including the last two years?" I said.

Maria smiled. "Especially the last two years."

ACKNOWLEDGEMENTS

IF YOU MADE it this far, thank you for reading. I hope you enjoyed it.

Thanks to Clair Lamb, who provided excellent advice as to the structure of the novel. She helped me streamline the story and improve it, significantly.

Thanks to my nephew, Anthony Zych, for designing another excellent cover.

Thanks to my wife, Jill, for tolerating this hobby that takes up many of the hours when I'm not working at the job that, 24 years ago, was the hobby. (And for putting up with me for 30 years now, and counting.)

And thanks to my late dad, Butch, who lived certain aspects of the life described in *Father of Mine* and *Son of Mine*, and to my late mother, Marge, who worked hard to keep life at all times normal when I was growing up. I know Butch would probably hate these books. I think Marge would probably love them.

Made in the USA
Middletown, DE
06 September 2024